Moonlight in Vermont

The Official Biography of Johnny Smith

By Lin Flanagan

www.johnnysmith.org

ISBN: 978-1-57424-322-2
SAN 683-8022

Cover by James Creative Group

Published by CENTERSTREAM Publishing, LLC
P.O. Box 17878 - Anaheim Hills, CA 92817

www.centerstream-usa.com

Dedication

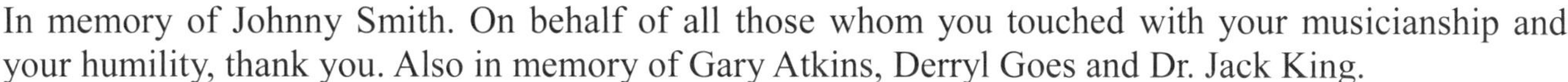

In memory of Johnny Smith. On behalf of all those whom you touched with your musicianship and your humility, thank you. Also in memory of Gary Atkins, Derryl Goes and Dr. Jack King.

This biography is a great tribute to our father, Johnny Smith. It encompasses not only his life, his contribution to music, his achievements and his guitar skills, but it also reveals a great deal about the man himself. We are grateful for Lin Flanagan's integrity and the sensitivity which he extended toward each of us, particularly our father, who was in failing health during the final stages of writing the manuscript.

Kim Stewart, David Smith and John Smith III

CONTENTS

Acknowledgments

Sincere thanks are due to all those who contributed so much to the research for this biography. Many interviewees leaped at the opportunity to take part and added that this tribute should have been carried out years ago. These included former members of Johnny Smith's combos, former students, audience members, longtime close friends, several distinguished figures within the jazz guitar alumni and members of his family.

While everybody's generous time and efforts were priceless, there are a few individuals who should be identified for their specific contributions. Without the invaluable enthusiasm of Dave Kintzele, this biography would quite simply never have left the ground. The late and sorely missed Gary Atkins was a precious source of guidance and provided so much of his unique inside knowledge. Without his encouragement this research would have undoubtedly been much shorter and less worthy of its subject. Jude Hibler's support was also crucial in keeping the momentum going when the task in hand seemed far beyond reach. Towards the end, Bob Yelin generously stepped in to help see the project completed when it would otherwise have been beyond reach. Rick Gustafson kindly provided invaluable archaeological artifacts that did far more than just enhance the research process. Michael Randolph is deserving of my sincerest gratitude for his noble contribution of photographs from the collection of his father, William "*PoPsie*" Randolph. The librarians at the Library of Congress, the Institute of Jazz Studies, and Joanne Goble at the Colorado Symphony Orchestra were patient beyond belief in permitting me to take up residence in their libraries for extended periods. I am indebted to Ron Middlebrook for his faith and guidance in ensuring that this project saw the light of day.

Johnny Smith and his family are due my utmost gratitude. It must be an unnerving experience to have somebody research one's own life, or that of one's father. The trust that Johnny, John, David and Kim bestowed upon me was nothing short of humbling. Their kindness and generosity in contributing to this research were also wholly unexpected. David Smith deserves special recognition. For two years, he worked tirelessly in arranging numerous telephone conversations and personal visits with his father, as well as handling a significant amount of written correspondence. He also kept his dad's dog, Peanut, quiet during the many interviews. Further thanks go to Johnny Smith, himself. His music was the inspiration for this whole adventure.

Foreword

By Robert Yelin

To those of us who know the name of Johnny Smith, he will forever be considered as the undisputed Master of the plectrum-style jazz guitar. Some of us were fortunate to hear him play live, while many more have marveled at his recordings. Those readers who are yet to discover his music have a great treat ahead of them.

Johnny had no peers. He was revered by the top jazz guitarists, including Barney Kessel and Wes Montgomery. Many of us bought every Johnny Smith album that we could find. His playing was instantly recognizable from as little as a single note, or a solitary chord, not to mention his breathtaking three-octave lines. Aside from his superior virtuoso technique and his beautiful tone, his repertoire was different to that of everybody else, and he took the concept of chord-melody playing to a whole new level of sophistication. His parallel work in the classical field, including atonal music, was far beyond the abilities of any other jazz or plectrum-style guitarist. His single-line playing was beautiful and his chords were so lush. Many of them had long, difficult-to-reach stretches. I once asked him why he played those long-stretch chords. He simply replied, "That's the way I've always played chords." I then asked him to put his palm and his fingers against mine. I was stunned to see that his fingers were of a normal length. In fact, my own fingers were a little longer than his. We all wanted to recreate his sound. When I had my own teaching practice in New York during the 1970s, I discovered just how far Johnny's music had traveled. I had students from across the United States, Canada, Australia and even India who wanted to play like the Master.

During the late 1940s and the early 1950s, Johnny was well known among Manhattan's musicians for his prolific studio work, particularly at NBC. At one time, he arranged, performed or conducted thirty-seven shows per week. He later told me, "Never write to me. I'm allergic to pencils." In 1952, his version of 'Moonlight in Vermont' with Stan Getz was released on Roost Records. It was a huge hit and brought him out of the studio shadows and into the smokey lights of New York's jazz scene. While still working for the networks, he began to play the city's major jazz venues, such as the plush Embers and the larger and more raucous Birdland. At the latter of these clubs, he regularly shared the bill with the Count Basie Orchestra, Cannonball Adderley, Dizzy Gillespie, and the father of Bebop, Charlie 'Bird' Parker. Johnny told me, "Parker would come with his girlfriend and sit right in front of me. We were good friends but when he was using drugs he was a frightening force."

Johnny played throughout the United States, Canada and Europe during his career, but he will forever be remembered by those of us who have heard of him as the foremost guitarist on the demanding East Coast jazz scene during a golden era. Whenever he played in Manhattan, there was always a contingent of guitarists in the audience. Mundell Lowe, John Pisano, Lou Mecca, Joe Cinderella, Dale Bruning, Les Paul, Chet Atkins and so many others frequently came to listen, learn and admire. He was unique. His music appealed to listeners beyond the boundaries of jazz.

Johnny suffered an unfair share of tragedy in his younger days. Somehow, these events did not lessen his gratitude and appreciation for life. In 1958, he turned his back on New York to begin a more conducive family life in Colorado Springs. As a consequence, he was forgotten by the jazz media. Today, his name is known to relatively few outside of those who take their jazz guitar seriously, and yet his musicianship is still cited by the jazz guitar greats as the benchmark to which they all aspire. Johnny was revered by guitarists, celebrated by jazz musicians, respected by classical musicians, admired by audiences, and adored by his friends. Remarkably, at no point in his life did his superior virtuosity diminish his humility.

The jazz guitar giant Barney Kessel famously said that while Johnny Smith was not the greatest jazz guitarist, he was undoubtedly the greatest player of the guitar. In 2011, Johnny and his family were asked to donate his personal Gibson guitar to the Smithsonian Institution in Washington D.C., where it will in due course be displayed alongside other precious artifacts of American culture, such as Dizzy Gillespie's trumpet. These two acknowledgments are testaments of Johnny's stature within the jazz community.

The author of this fascinating biography, Lin Flanagan, lives in Britain, where he is a recognized performer, educator, writer, scholar and academic. For twenty-five years he has studied Johnny Smith's music. He was so captivated by Johnny's musicianship that he set out to write the complete story of the Master. Having already conducted a considerable amount of ground research, in 2011 he contacted Johnny to ask for his approval of this biography. Johnny was more than pleased. After several telephone conversations, Lin flew from Britain to Colorado Springs in order to conduct an extensive interview with him. They had a very fruitful time together, and in the ensuing period Johnny and his son, David, greatly helped with Lin's continuing research. Lin also interviewed several of Johnny's close personal friends, former band members and students, and many jazz guitar legends during his research. He trawled through thousands of newspapers and magazines, and spent countless hours in various archive centers in the USA, including the Library of Congress in Washington, D.C., and the Institute of Jazz Studies at Rutgers University in Newark. From all of these sources, he has uncovered an outstanding amount of information about Johnny's professional life, and he has left no stone unturned in his investigation. I refer to Lin as 'Scotland Yard'. The result of his meticulous research is this highly informative, readable and definitive biography, in which Lin has presented a detailed account of Johnny Smith's multifaceted career in music. Many readers will be surprised by the true magnitude of his stature and his impact upon the jazz guitar world. Lin has also provided a comprehensive account of Johnny's musical equipment and an analysis of his musicianship. This book has been long overdue. Thankfully, we can now all read about the life, the achievements, the importance and the legacy of the man whom jazz guitarists still call the Master.

Robert Yelin

(A loving and loved friend of Johnny Smith for thirty-two years)

Preface

Johnny Smith is revered by many of the world's elite jazz guitarists as the benchmark by which all others are measured. His name is synonymous with the height of technical virtuosity, musical sophistication, impeccable taste and meticulous attention to detail. Many of those who have heard his music consider him to have been the ultimate plectrum jazz guitarist. However, while he is celebrated by serious jazz guitar players, many students and amateur players remain unaware of his name and his music. In fact, relatively few guitarists are fully cognizant of the magnitude of his stature during the 1950s and his important contribution to the development of the jazz guitar. It is not an exaggeration to say that he was as significant as Django Reinhardt, Charlie Christian and Wes Montgomery. His influence in raising the standards of technical virtuosity in the instrument justifies his position as one of the most important figures in the development of the jazz guitar.

Smith was not a typical jazz guitarist. His work extended far beyond the regular boundaries of the musical genre. Between 1946 and 1958, he worked as a versatile network studio musician and arranger in New York, taking the city's guitar community by storm upon his arrival with the broad range of his abilities as well as his virtuosity. His technical command of the plectrum guitar and his reading skills were unrivaled. Aside from his radio and television work, most notably at NBC, he also found himself performing challenging atonal art music with the country's top classical musicians and swing jazz as a member of Benny Goodman's sextet.

In 1951, he began to focus more of his attention upon playing jazz. A year later, he redefined the boundaries of the plectrum jazz guitar with his first record 'Moonlight in Vermont'. His pianistic approach to harmony, his virtuosity, his immaculately clean execution and his beautifully warm tone had a profound impact upon players around the world. He was the first plectrum guitar virtuoso to truly possess a classical guitarist's sense of technique. His command of the instrument was unique outside the realm of the classical field where performers are noted for striving over many years to perfect their technical abilities. These superior skills, combined with his creative musical imagination, enabled him to exploit the full range of the electric plectrum guitar. In doing so, he revealed the previously unrealized potential of the instrument to other guitarists and paved new roads that other plectrum jazz guitarists have since followed. His superior technique, precise execution, pureness of tone, sense of good taste and romantic interpretation of his solo guitar arrangements led a reviewer in the *Billboard* to describe him has the Segovia of the electric guitar.

The jazz guitar community considered Smith to be without an equal. He was by far the most celebrated and prolific guitarist on the New York jazz scene between 1954 and 1958, sharing the bill at the Birdland club and major venues across the USA with musicians of legendary status, such as Charlie Parker, Dizzy Gillespie, Miles Davis, Lester Young, Count Basie, Art Tatum, Cannonball Adderley, Gerry Mulligan, Oscar Peterson, George Shearing, Teddy Wilson, Lee Konitz, the Modern Jazz

Quartet, Billie Holiday, Ella Fitzgerald, Sarah Vaughan, and Dinah Washington. However, he was far from being a mere second-tier support act. Instead, his musicianship earned him a high profile that was on a par with these legends who acknowledged and respected him as their peer. Nevertheless, Smith always maintained a modest opinion of his own musicianship. His humble self-assessment was both legendary and entirely genuine, and he never enjoyed listening to his own recordings. His perfectionism caused him to feel that there was always room for improvement. Interviewing him towards the end of his life, it was felt that he had a more comfortable sense of personal pride in the acquisition of his airline pilot's license than he had for his achievements with the guitar.

Aside from guitarists and other musicians across the jazz scene, Smith was also celebrated by jazz audiences. He won several reader's polls in magazines including *Down Beat* and *Metronome*. His popularity during this period was remarkable when it is considered that as a network studio musician he had to suffer the prejudices of some of the powerful critics, who believed that certain criteria of authenticity should be met by jazz musicians, such as race and a singular devotion to the genre. Furthermore, the guitar was an instrument that was still not afforded serious consideration by many of the jazz journalists at the time.

Smith's importance to the development of the jazz guitar extended much further than purely as a performer. He had a pivotal impact upon the construction of the archtop instrument. His design features, which were ultimately incorporated into the Gibson model that carried his name, have since been frequently employed by luthiers and manufacturers of high-end archtop guitars. Once again, he raised the standards. He was also a significant figure in the development of dedicated guitar amplifiers.

In yet another dimension, he was heavily involved in the education of advanced jazz guitarists with his pioneering seminars across the USA. Through these clinics, as well as his own private teaching practice and the publication of his method book, he influenced new generations during the 1960s and 1970s. He also had an indirect but highly significant influence upon the education of jazz guitarists as a result of his impact upon Bill Leavitt at the Berklee College of Music, whose own method books would become essential study material for serious plectrum guitarists around the world.

Despite Smith's stature in serious jazz guitar circles as a performer, he modestly refused to accept that he was a true jazz guitarist, citing that he had too many musical interests to devote himself sufficiently to, and therefore excel in, a single genre. The overwhelming majority of renowned jazz guitarists disagree with him, citing his recording catalog and live performances as irrefutable evidence. Perhaps the most celebrated aspect of his wide-ranging work was his pioneering chord-melody arrangements. In these innovative masterpieces, he brought the intricacies of self-accompanied, classical guitar-type arrangements to the plectrum instrument. Although this side of his musical output was more in line with the predetermined classical approach to music rather than the improvised jazz approach, it merely served to increase the reverence in which he continues to be held by dedicated jazz guitarists.

In 1958, when Smith was the most admired guitarist on the New York jazz scene, he left the city to begin a more conducive family life in Colorado Springs. There, he opened a music store and continued to enjoy an active career as a performer on the local jazz scene, while also making occasional journeys back to the East Coast for recording dates and appearances in New York's jazz clubs. Gradually, he reduced the frequency of these excursions, preferring to work closer to home around the Colorado area. Consequently, he began to be neglected by journalists in the national jazz media, who chose to maintain the focus of their attention upon the traditional centers of New York and Los Angeles. Meanwhile, his recordings, most of which had been released on the small Roost Records label, were not reissued for several decades. This further contributed to the diminishing public awareness as new generations of jazz guitarists were increasingly unable to gain access to his music. Consequently, while some amateur jazz guitarists merely associate Smith's name with his recording of 'Moonlight in Vermont', to the rock music fraternity he is known solely for his 1954 composition 'Walk, Don't Run', which became an instrumental pop hit for the Ventures in 1960.

In 2002, Mosaic Records issued all of Johnny Smith's small group instrumental recordings from his Roost Records catalog on a limited-edition, eight-CD box set. Finally, guitarists were once again able to access his musical output. However, the availability of Smith's music is a separate challenge from the creation of an awareness of it. The boom in simpler pop music since the late 1950s has continued to the present day at the expense of other musical genres, such as jazz. In the early years of the twenty-first century, jazz guitar and jazz music in general are no longer of interest to the mass media. The observations of guitarist Pete Kennedy are echoed by many in the guitar community who contributed to this research:

> I'm gratified to hear that someone is doing a full-on study of Johnny Smith and his contribution to the art of the guitar. It's tragic that his name is practically unknown, and when I see the published "100 Best Guitarists" lists, his name is always omitted, as well as Lenny Breau, Ted Greene, Gene Bertoncini, Mundell Lowe, Tal Farlow, et al, leading me to the sad conclusion that my own 'baby boomer' generation missed the boat when it came to guitar, by focusing only on blues-rock players and running the pentatonic scale up and down without ever actually learning to be musicians. The reason I so readily launch into a rant on the subject is that I easily recall the sense that I felt when I studied with Johnny that he was opening up the portal to a whole world of music and a treasure chest of potential on the guitar that I never would have discovered on my own had I only listened to rock stars.

Many of the contributors to this biography expressed their gratitude that it was finally being conducted, adding that recognition of Smith's importance, stature and legacy as a performer, educator and guitar designer were long overdue. While much has been written about more popular but lesser musicians, this is the first dedicated and detailed research into one of the most significant and overlooked figures in the history of jazz guitar.

Several distinct areas of importance became apparent during the research process. Consequently, this biography is structured into chapters which address Smith's formative years; his arrival in New York and the impact that he had upon the guitar community, including with his atonal classical performances; his work at the network broadcasters, in particular NBC; his prolific work on the jazz scene while he was living in New York; his activities as a performer after he left New York in 1958, most notably in Colorado; his music store; his crucial role in the education of advanced jazz guitarists; his musical equipment and his significance in the development of archtop guitar design and amplification; a look at the personality of the man; and a closing epilogue. An appendix features a catalog of his recordings.

Numerous sources were employed during the course of this investigation. Existing literature on the subject of Johnny Smith was extremely limited. The handful of published articles and interviews with him were useful as a starting point, but they were often repetitive and not always reliable. It quickly became apparent that there was a considerable amount of misinformation and mythology in the public domain which needed to be corrected. Some of these errors may appear to be minor. For example, contrary to popular belief his tours with Stan Kenton and Count Basie did not run concurrently in 1955. Other errors were more profound, however. For example, Smith did not effortlessly sightread his way through a live performance of Arnold Schönberg's *Serenade*. The truth is, in fact, even more impressive. Perhaps the most erroneous piece of misinformation, however, is that on moving to Colorado Springs in 1958 he stopped playing the guitar and became a recluse. This could not be further from the truth.

References in contemporaneous literature, such as the *Billboard*, the *New Yorker*, *Down Beat* and *Metronome* magazines, local newspapers and tour program notes, provided invaluable evidence regarding his live performances and recordings. Although much of the investigation was conducted from Britain, information that was unobtainable from a distance was gathered during visits in person to essential contributors and archive collections in the USA. In particular, the *NBC Collection* in the Library of Congress yielded a substantial amount of information regarding Smith's work at the broadcaster. A sizable amount of highly informative interviews was conducted by email, telephone, postal correspondence and in person. Interviewees included musicians who performed with Smith between the 1950s and 1970s; guitarists who were on New York's jazz scene at the same time as Smith; current members of the jazz guitar alumni; former guitar students from his private practice as well as his guitar seminars; close friends; and members of his family. Almost all of the interviews were conducted in the two years prior to his death, hence the testimonies are in the present tense. Music legends are invariably shadowed by mythology regarding their exceptional standards of musicianship. Therefore, anecdotal evidence has been avoided in favor of verifiable first-hand accounts from reliable sources. Crucially, Johnny Smith was also very generous in helping with the research process by correcting, clarifying and elaborating upon discoveries.

While he truly could not understand why anybody would want to make him the subject of a research project, the jazz guitar community embraced the concept. Regardless of his genuinely modest opinion towards his own musicianship, the tributes on the following pages are telling. It is clear that in the ears of serious jazz guitarists he remains the pinnacle of musicianship and the Master of the plectrum guitar.

Tributes

An extraordinary virtuoso. As far as I'm concerned, no one in the world plays the guitar better than he. They might play it differently, but nobody plays better. Johnny could easily overplay because he's got chops unlimited, but his musical taste would not allow him to make an overstatement. As a result, he makes beautiful music. **- Barney Kessel**

Man, I can never be that perfect. No one plays like Johnny Smith. **- Wes Montgomery**

Johnny became for me, at a very early age, one of three individuals who held my attention to the most important specifics within an on-going evolution as a serious artist on my own. The first was Les Paul (for an incredibly inventive imagination). The second was Johnny Smith (for accuracy and precision beyond question). The third was Wes Montgomery (for heart, and an intuitive soul, encased within each creative moment). After exposure to such artists, my personal absorption moved to many other priorities in the study of life itself, but to this very day when the word 'Master' appears, so too does the name Johnny Smith, as one of the most effective sages met on the path. **- Pat Martino**

He used to get the most gorgeous sound out of the guitar, whether it was electric or acoustic. He just understood how to capture that sound. Bill Finnegan always referred to Johnny Smith as the point of the guitar, which I think fits very nicely. We love talking about Johnny Smith. He's a hero. He's a wonderful man. He's an original. **- Mundell Lowe**

Words are useless – Johnny Smith was the greatest musician I ever worked with. **- George Roumanis**

He's so modest. You know, one day I was swooning over something that he had done. And he looked at me and said, "Gary, bullshit! It's just music." I thought to myself, 'Well, that's really how he thinks of it.' He doesn't realize how extraordinarily gifted he is. He really doesn't. **- Gary Atkins (Nephew of Chet Atkins)**

I'm not in Johnny Smith's League. Johnny has an incredible range of musicianship. You need only hear a bar or two of Johnny Smith playing, and you know instantly without the slightest doubt who it is. He's a giant. The first truly major jazz guitarist since Charlie Christian. **- Tony Mottola**

Johnny was flawless in his musicianship. The only way that you can play that fast and that accurate is by practicing very slowly. The foundation is very important. So, he always insisted that I never practiced these things fast. It's not important. He never practiced for speed. He practiced for accuracy.

You get it really clean and flawless from the beginning. You build up from that. **- John Pisano**

His perfectness was just ridiculous. **- Tim May**

Smith set the standard for excellence in guitar playing. Johnny remains the standard we all aspire to, and there's no-one, even among today's leading innovators, who has approached his levels of virtuosity and musicality. **- Jimmy Bruno**

He has such an awesome command of the instrument. Johnny was really committed to breaking down all of the limitations of the guitar. He was among the first people I ever heard to pursue a pianistic approach to the guitar, and he really expanded the orchestral possibilities of the instrument with his elevated levels of technical clarity, tone, touch, harmonic richness... everything! **- Bill Frisell**

What most people don't realize is that the modern legato style of chord-melody playing – the harmonies, the phrasing, the voice-leading – all derive from Johnny Smith's innovations. [...] *Johnny codified everything that came before him, and took it to another, much higher level.* [...] *He's the man.*
- Jack Wilkins

First there was Django Reinhardt, then came Charlie Christian, and then there was Johnny Smith. He was really a giant. **- Gene Bertoncini**

He was one of the first. When he first went to New York, he took it by storm. Guys were amazed at how well he played and how he played through chord changes so beautifully. His control... He had amazing technique. People look at him as a ballad player. But let me tell you, man, he can really put the tempos up there, too. **- Jack Petersen**

Johnny Smith represents, to me, the epitome of perfect pick technique. His accuracy, economy, fluency and sonorous full tone make his playing immediately recognizable. He is a guitarist's guitarist; a legitimate and schooled player to whom others look as a model of playing correctness. Reading back through years of guitar and jazz guitar-related literature, this reverence for Smith's guitar playing has been a constant. I have personally championed his music since I first heard it in my early teens. I have regularly mentioned his name in magazine articles, various guitar-related publications and have also set his music for the Guildhall, Oxford 'A' Levels and the guitar syllabi at Leeds College of Music. Johnny Smith is definitely one of the greats, his pure crystalline tone and perfect execution produced a clean, sparkling tone unlike anyone else before or since. One Christmas wind-down (end of term) at Leeds College of Music (c. 1984), I played my students a Johnny Smith recording. One of them asked after hearing the first tune, "Is that a guitar?" Unfortunately, processed guitar sounds are now so much the norm that Smith sounds fashionably anachronistic. Hopefully, Lin Flanagan's biography will set the record straight! **- Adrian Ingram**

Oh my! He was sensational. He has been one of my heroes since I was twelve years of age. I got that 'Moonlight in Vermont' record. You know, the one with Stan Getz. Oh man, I'm still amazed by his playing on it. **- Louis Stewart**

He was one of the most graceful players I've ever seen. His hands were so fluid and his technique was just about perfect. It looked effortless to me, though I know it wasn't. **- George Hess**

Oh my God. We're getting letters of religious-awakening proportions as players discover this guy.
- Michael Cuscuna (Founder of Mosaic Records)

Johnny was the finest jazz guitarist in the country, as far as I'm concerned. - **Ted McCarty (Former President of the Gibson Guitar Corporation)**

When I became aware of his international fame, it struck me that a lot of people categorized him or characterized him as a rather 'commercial' chord-melody great, but not a bona fide burning jazz player. I so disagree. I don't think the albums truly represent what I heard live. He was smokin'!
- Fred Hamilton

So many others like me still think his recording of 'What's New' is the definitive statement for that tune. Around age sixteen, I learned that solo right off the record. It gave me a first step into understanding jazz vocabulary. **- Larry Coryell**

Johnny Smith is the ultimate pick-style guitarist. His approach to playing is immediately recognizable and it has to be placed with the playing and technique of Andrés Segovia. He is one of the most important artists of the instrument. I am so humbled and thankful I studied those four years with Johnny. **- Tom Bruner**

There are a lot of really good guitarists who came through Berklee, like Mike Stern, and they all had to do that. Playing classical pieces with a pick. And I think that's all because of Johnny Smith and the impact that he had upon William Leavitt. **- Jim Fox**

Johnny Smith is an absolute genius in my opinion. An absolute genius. **- Trefor Owen**

In my early years of making guitars, Johnny was a tremendous influence. His ideas of what an archtop guitar should be brought our beloved jazz guitar to a level of refinement yet to be surpassed.
- Bob Benedetto

I was truly fortunate to spend a week there, learning from a man whom I consider to be one of the most consummate musicians who ever played the guitar. **- Pete Kennedy**

He said, "You have a really good sense of time, and you depend upon that. But what you don't know is that you have a really beautiful natural vibrato, and you should really not be afraid to sing ballads." He was the one that persuaded me that I could. I still remember that conversation. **- Ruth Price**

It was a happy time. Not only was I getting to play with someone of his stature musically, but that someone was a master musician who was never condescending to band mates not at his level of proficiency. **- Bobby Greene**

Oh, Jeeez, every now and then, I tell my present wife about those days, and she always says that she's sorry that she missed it. They were great times. **- Neil Bridge**

If someone were to ask me to describe Johnny Smith, not musically, but as a person, I would describe him as a perfect gentleman. That's how he was with me. Totally. Everything from a business standpoint was done so professionally. His regard, not only for other musicians but other people was... Just the perfect gentleman. **- Dale Bruning**

In 40+ yrs in the 'biz', he is one of the few grown ups I've known. **- Kenny Vaughan**

Most people think of John as one of the world's finest musicians who also happens to be a very good man. I think of John as a very good man who also happens to be one of the world's finest musicians. He deserves all the good that could ever come to him. He has brought so much joy to so many people through his work. **- Dr. Ron Uscinski**

I want to say how gracious, generous and kind he was to me when I was a twenty-two-year-old kid.
- Barry Zweig

He's a man with a wonderful heart. He's so caring and very modest, as you know. He changed my life and helped me with my career. Things that I never expected to happen happened, and a lot of it I give the credit to Johnny for the time he took with me in learning my instrument. **- Dick Eliot**

Johnny Smith was the best thing that ever happened to me. **- Jock Bartley**

Johnny is well received and well respected by everyone he touches. People are very much into supporting and affectionately talking about him. **- Gordon Close**

Johnny is an old school gentleman. From my conversations with him (twenty years ago), I truly believe he does not understand what the big fuss is about. Why so many people want to know about him.
- Al Owens

The greatest thing about Johnny is the size of his heart. **- Bob Yelin**

The man has had a great life and will leave a lasting impact on music. From a very humble beginning to a world class musician with limited schooling, he has had an amazing run. **- David Smith**

I've listened to Johnny Smith my whole life and have loved every note he's played. His willingness, and ability, to play with pure unabashed beauty and expression tops all the reasons I have considered him to be so musically important. His music lives deep inside me." **– Jody Fisher**

Chapter One: The Formative Years

John Henry Smith Jr. was born into a musical environment on 25 June 1922 in Birmingham, Alabama, to foundry worker John Henry Smith Sr. (1885-1957) and his wife Katie Louise Smith, née Clopton (1890-1974). The couple had six sons; George Carlton, Herman Godkin, Thomas Merrwell, John Henry Jr., Benjamin Lloyd and Emmett Eugene. In a thankfully bygone age, the mortality rate was high among children. Herman died of diphtheria when he was only six years old in 1925.

The Smith family lived in a close-knit community. Neighbors regularly gathered at their house for musical evenings, often leaving their instruments behind at the end of the night. When he was five years old, the young Johnny began to take advantage of the opportunity to experiment with the numerous instruments that were available to him. Of these, it was the guitar which captivated him the most. Ben Smith recalls his memories of his brother's first encounters with the guitar:

> I remember that Dad had got hold of an old metal guitar from somewhere. John couldn't pick it up, but he dragged it all over the house. He couldn't reach around the neck, but believe it or not, he played fairly well over the top. With that guitar sitting on his lap, on the floor, he would play over the top of that thing with his left hand.

A decade into the twenty-first century, the perception of Alabama during the 1920s and 1930s is of an area where racism was at its most extreme and vicious. There were pockets of humanity, however. Interviewed in 2012, Johnny Smith recalled that his upbringing was untypically balanced:

> Well, it has changed a lot. It used to be that way. But my folks, my mother and father, they were never prejudiced at all. As a matter of fact, we had a black lady help raise us kids. We really loved her.

When asked if the aforementioned helper was a neighbor, Smith's response was both instant and insightful:

> Hell, no! It was all segregated back then. We weren't allowed to live in the same neighborhood. Terrible. There were black areas and white areas. She used to come in and help my mom to clean the house. She was great.

Ben Smith retains similar memories:

> My mom told me that she was almost part of the family. You can imagine that down

> there, during those times. We used to walk along the sidewalk, and the black people had to get off and walk in the gutter around us. It was terrible. But my dad, who was originally from West Virginia, told me many times that he would much rather work with a good black man than white trash.

The community into which Johnny Smith had been born was shattered by the consequences of the Wall Street Crash of 1929. Birmingham's whole economy had been founded upon the uniquely abundant deposits of coal, iron ore and limestone that were present in the Jones Valley, as these raw materials were essential in the manufacture of iron. Beginning in the 1870s, the iron and steel production industries had gradually expanded, drawing in investment from across the USA. By the 1920s there were four main companies in operation in Birmingham – The Tennessee Coal, Iron, and Railroad Company (TCI); the Republic Iron and Steel Company; Sloss-Sheffield; and the Woodward Iron Company. The last two of these four companies had become the biggest producers of pig iron in the USA. However, the Great Depression, which followed the Wall Street Crash, reduced the production of pig iron and steel to their lowest levels since 1896. Birmingham's economy was devastated as output at the big four manufacturers was drastically reduced. The foundries were by far the chief employers in the area, and John Smith Sr. became just one of many who found themselves out of work without any alternative form of employment. Johnny Smith later recounted the family's migration across the Southern States in the search for work, before eventually arriving in Maine:

> It was an iron foundry. I don't remember which one. When the Depression came, he lost his job, and we started moving around wherever he could find work. We lived in New Orleans, Chattanooga, Tennessee... We were sharecroppers. We farmed with an old broken down horse on a hundred and twenty-five acres. So, it was pretty mean times. When we were in Chattanooga, Tennessee, a friend of my father got him a job at the foundry in Portland, Maine. And so we migrated to Portland, Maine. That's where I kind of grew up.

Ben Smith shares his additional memories of the family's movements during this period:

> When the Depression came along, Dad lost his job at the iron foundry. Like everyone else, he took any work that he could get. Then, we moved to a place around ten or twelve miles out of Harpersville in Alabama. John and I... We helped as much as we could, but being youngsters it all fell on Dad. We stayed there through a harvest. Then, we moved to Tarrant, which is a little satellite city just north of Birmingham. Then, we went to a farm where Dad was sharecropping. We came back to Birmingham, then we moved to just outside Chattanooga, Tennessee. We rented a house... There was a piano in there. Oh, we had been there just a couple of weeks, and John was playing beautifully on that piano. He had never had a lesson.

The impact of the financial destitution of Johnny Smith's childhood should not be underestimated. As is often the case with those who have endured severe hardships in early life, his later ethos towards his employment as a musician in New York was nothing short of that of a workaholic. John Henry Smith III poignantly explains the significance of the circumstances of his father's early life upon shaping his attitude towards work and life in general:

> My dad saw his dad lose his house during the Great Depression. He had to come home and tell his wife that he had lost his job and therefore the house. My dad vowed that he would never be put in that position. He's like a bulldog. When he decides that he's going to do something, you had better get out of the way because it's going to happen. He's very determined when he puts his mind to something.

Ben Smith's memories of the Smith brothers' childhood portray images which are reminiscent of the literature of Mark Twain and John Steinbeck:

> Mom stayed at home as a housewife and mother. We were just a good, happy family. No dissent or anything like that. I'll never lose those memories. As kids, we didn't know how bad the bad times were. It was a hard time for parents during the Depression, but it was like that for everybody all over the world. Down in Harpersville, Mom and Dad both smoked then. We lived in what we called a shotgun house. You know, you could shoot a shotgun right through the middle of it from front to back. The rooms were on each side. The floorboards were around half an inch apart. When the grass grew too long it would come up through the floorboards. Mom would get a pair of scissors and cut the grass from inside. Mom or Dad would send us under the floorboards every now and again to look for cigarette butts. We would pull out quite a few, and give them back to Mom or Dad. They would roll them again.
>
> John, Emmett and I would often find hornets in our room. They didn't bother us, and we didn't bother them. They were called dirt dobbers. My mom used to make what were called Dutch girls. It was so hot and humid that she would take a big towel and roll it up. We would sleep with that. It would take up the perspiration. It was just as hot and humid at night as it was in the daytime. It was so hot down there. Our mother found some material and made each of us a poke bonnet. And she made us wear them. It's a good thing that we didn't have any close friends, because we would have been so embarrassed. Down there, you left off your shoes in the spring and you didn't put them on again until the fall. Your feet were tougher than leather. But you stayed away from the sugar cane, because they cut that at an angle with a machete type of thing. When it dried, it was as sharp as a razor. It would go right through your foot.
>
> We used to go down to the creek, near the house, and fish for catfish. We would watch the water moccasins. Deadly poisonous snakes. They used to come swimming down the creek and pass right over our fishing lines.
>
> I remember, John and I were picking cotton one day... My dad raised some sugar cane, and he was going several miles up the road to get the sugar cane pressed. There was this thing that was like two great rollers on a washing machine. The juice would run down into this big black pot which had a fire under it. The old mule would go round and round all day long. So, my dad took his sugar cane up there. My brothers and I... We weren't too happy. They left us to pick cotton. So... We had some corn. Now, when the corn silk is dry, you can smoke it. Well, we got hold of the cream and we made cigarettes with it. I tell you, we laid down between those rows of cotton and we were as sick as hell.

Our dad knew, but he didn't say a word. He didn't have to! It took a few days to get rid of that. I couldn't get out of the hammock for three days.

I remember my dad had this old horse, and he got an old buggy for it from somewhere. He would go across the creek to town with this horse, but they would always come back well after dark. Every time they came back, that old horse would get right in the middle of the creek and lie down. Dad had a terrible time trying to get him back on his feet. We kids used to ride him, but he was smart. He would find a tree, and if it had low enough limbs, he would rake us right off. All three of us.

Despite Johnny Smith's early interest in the guitar, his father wanted him to play the violin in order to augment the family's hillbilly group line-up, which already consisted of John Sr. on five-string banjo, George on tenor banjo, and Tommy on guitar. With John Jr. adding the fiddle and occasionally an additional guitar, the ensemble played domestically for themselves and for visiting neighbors, rather than at any professional engagements. John Jr. clearly had an aptitude for the fiddle. His father even put him forward for contests, which he often won. Johnny was a fiddle champion at the Alabama State Fair Hoe Down as a youngster. His fiddle-playing childhood sometimes brought precious rewards. He later recalled, "My dad insisted upon me playing the fiddle. The violin. I must have been pretty good, because I used to win all of the fiddle contests. Once, first prize was a five-pound bag of sugar. That was back in the Depression." Ben Smith also fondly remembers the joyous rewards of his brother's fiddle competition successes:

THE SMITH FAMILY WITH YOUNG JOHNNY ON FIDDLE

> When we were in Tarrant city, our dad played the five-string banjo. He played it beautifully. My brother, Tom, played the guitar. John played anything. The picture [above] shows him with the violin. He would go to these places, along the lines of the Grand Ole Opry, and play. They didn't pay money then, but sometimes we were allowed to stay up and they would come home with three or four bags of groceries. Oh boy! That was a celebration when they did that. You know, when John was around ten or eleven years old, he won several things like that. The third or fourth time that he went to one particular place, they wouldn't let him play because they said that he was too young. They just wouldn't let him play anymore.

When Johnny Smith was eight years old he won a competition at the Municipal Auditorium in Birmingham before he was disqualified for being underage, but regardless of his success and obvious ability he did not enjoy playing the violin. His heart was in the guitar and he much preferred to accompany his father on that instrument instead. Smith later commented that he would have walked fifty miles for a guitar lesson if he could have found a teacher when he was a youngster, but in the absence of any available tutor or instruction book he was driven into teaching himself. It would be wrong, though, to assume that music was the sole focus of his attentions during this early stage of his life. He was also an exceptional marbles player, and even won the Alabama State Marbles Championship.

When the Smith family eventually arrived in Maine during this era of financial desperation, they found that their Southern accents did not help their cause. Ben Smith remembers that life did not improve greatly:

> Around the middle of the 1930s, our dad got a job up in Portland, Maine, at a foundry. He saved and saved until he could afford to bring the family up there. Forty-five cents per hour doing foundry work was not much, but he saved enough to get us up there on the train. When we moved to Portland, our apartment was smothered with cockroaches. Dad gave us each a dime and sent us to the movies. He and Mom got sulfur and something else, blocked up all the gaps in the doors and left it in there for three or four hours. It didn't get rid of all of them, because they were in the walls.

As with the overwhelming majority of Americans throughout the Depression years, the Smith family remained far from wealthy. Johnny began working in pawn shops, tuning the guitars in return for being allowed to hang around and play before he even had a guitar of his own. Although he was entirely self-taught, he developed a good ear for working out music quickly.

Initially, his parents had significant reservations about his aspirations to become a professional musician. The playing of a musical instrument as a hobby was deemed to be more than acceptable, but it was quite a different matter to make a career from it. Undeterred by his parents' opposition, by the time that Smith was thirteen years old he had progressed to the point that he was teaching adults. In 1937, during his sophomore year, one of these adult students, Bill Glovsky, bought himself a new Gibson L-7 guitar, and gave his old Gibson Kalamazoo to his young tutor. This was the first guitar that Smith could actually call his own.

The Hillbilly Days

Smith was soon proficient enough to join a dance band in Maine, the Fenton Brothers' Orchestra, for a short period before moving on to play in local hillbilly groups around Portland, most notably Uncle Lem and His Mountain Boys. He also played, briefly, with the Katahdin Mountaineers and even tried an East Coast interpretation of Hawaiian music with the Kiana Hawaiians.

Despite the continuing poverty of the Great Depression era, country music offered a relatively lucrative profession, particularly in the eyes of a teenager, for those musicians who were prepared to work hard. Smith had not long begun high school when Uncle Lem asked him to join his group. The outfit appeared on radio broadcasts for both the WGAN and WCSH stations in Portland, but these were only a part of an extremely hectic apprenticeship. Smith was soon earning a sizable four dollars per night playing predominantly across Maine, which was as much as his father was earning for a full day's work in the Portland foundry. He was able to eat two substantial meals each day for a single dollar, while giving the remaining three dollars to his parents. His regular weekday schedule throughout this period consisted of a local radio broadcast at six o'clock in the morning, followed by high school from eight o'clock until one o'clock, after which Uncle Lem and the rest of the group would collect him and drive typically anywhere between twenty and fifty miles for a live show. One of Smith's endearing memories of these times as a teenager on the road was the habitual stop for an Italian sandwich and a bottle of beer on the way to the gigs. The group's repertoire consisted of popular songs, folk songs and polkas, which they played at country dances, square dances, schools and fairs. More importantly, they also played swing. Occasionally, Smith was called upon to sing. He later described his voice as "like a slow leak in Frank Sinatra's navel."

THE KIANA HAWAIIANS: BILL, PHIL, MARGIE, JOHNNY SMITH AND EARL FLAG

It was quite usual for the group not to return to Portland after their shows until the early hours of the morning. As the young Smith was often the only member to remain awake, he frequently found himself driving. With only a few hours sleep, the routine would be repeated on the next day. Some bookings were further afield, such as Lac-Mégantic, Quebec, which, at a distance of one hundred and eighty-five miles from Portland, and with consideration of the road infrastructure in the 1930s, was an unforgiving journey.

Ben Smith recalls that any reservations that his parents may have had about his brother's choice of career were dispelled when he was able to earn a living during this time of desperate global poverty:

> Oh, they didn't mind at all. Mom used to play the piano, and Dad was a fine five-string banjo player. All of my brothers, except my younger brother and myself, played an instrument. They didn't mind at all. They were proud of him. We all were. I think he left school when he was around thirteen or fourteen and started playing regularly.
>
> I remember when we were young, during the Depression, my mom would have my brothers and I wash the dishes after dinner. John had the perfect alibi. He said, "I can't get my hands wet." He didn't want to soften his fingers. Mom agreed with him. So, he never had to do a dish [laughs]. Well, that didn't sit too well! Yeah, right! You can imagine how well that went down! Oh, yeah!

Later in life, Johnny Smith retained some vivid memories of his hillbilly days:

When I was fourteen or fifteen years old, I was playing with this hillbilly band up in Maine. Our bass player was Tom Robbins. He was shell-shocked from World War One. He had this bass... You couldn't believe it. It was all held together with adhesive tape. Band Aids. Anyway, we were playing on the fourth of July. Driving up [to the gig], people were throwing firecrackers. So, he was kind of upset. We were playing at a dance with no air conditioning. Tom, when he played, he smoked a pipe, and he was always looking up. He never looked down at the people. So, we were playing away, and this guy and this lady were dancing around. They kept looking at Tom. Finally, the guy lit this big cherry bomb firecracker and walked over, and slipped it in the *f*-hole of the bass. This thing went off and the bass disintegrated. Tom went running out the door with just the neck and a few strings. We had a hell of a time finding him. We finally located him in an old abandoned outhouse. Oh man! We got him settled down, we thought. When we went to drive home, which was a long drive, he had ripped out all of the ignition wires in the car. The guy who had dropped the firecracker... He felt really bad. He ended up buying Tom a new bass. Tom Robbins was almost a genius. This guy taught me how to grind telescope mirrors. He taught me how to play chess. We lived just one block from where he lived. He had about nine cats, and in the winter time... The only heat was from a meter. You had to drop a quarter into the meter to get the thing to work. We used to drop quarters in for him. It was not really a pleasant place to be in, because the cats never went outdoors.

JOHNNY SMITH (ON GUITAR) WITH UNCLE LEM AND HIS MOUNTAIN BOYS,WITH TOM ROBBINS ON DOUBLE BASS

Traveling country musicians during the Depression years had a definite modus operandi. Firstly, it was typical for the performers themselves to hire community halls for a percentage of the gate money rather than for a flat rate. The musicians were responsible for the preparation of the venues as well as the clearing up at the end of each night. In a practice that was reflective of the community spirit, it was also traditional for a local family to invite the musicians to dinner in their home before a show. In return, the touring group would give a small and private performance. This interaction with the patrons in a personal environment brought the performers closer to the local communities by shaping the musicians' respect for their audiences, which would in turn impact upon the music that was performed at the show. Conscientious musicians gave consideration to their audience's tastes, and accordingly played music that they wanted to hear. This ethos undoubtedly stayed with Smith throughout his career.

As a consequence of working such a demanding schedule up to six days per week, Smith soon dropped out of high school. The US National Archives and Records Administration's Enlistment Records state that he attended three years of high school. He later recalled how his brother used to help him to prepare for each arduous day:

> Oh, I never slept through high school. I would get to bed at four or five o'clock in the morning. We would have a broadcast to do at six o'clock, which we would do to advertise where we were going to play. I told my brother [Ben] to wake me up with a cold wash cloth. Well, one time I knocked him down. So, after that he stood across the room and [threw it] 'splat' right in my face. Needless to say, I never graduated from high school.

Ben Smith also remembers the daily routine:

> John went to school and then started playing with this little country band. I think it was Uncle Lem and His Mountain Boys. He would play with them each day after school. He was probably around thirteen years old at the time. He would go and play until two or three o'clock in the morning and then have to get up around six or seven o'clock to go to school. He paid my brother and I a nickel each to wake him up. Sometimes, we could hardly wake him. So, we developed a system with a cold washcloth. For a few days, we went over and put it on his face, but we learned not to do that! So, we got pretty good at sailing that thing across the room and landing it on his head.

JOHNNY SMITH (SECOND FROM LEFT) WITH UNCLE LEM AND HIS MOUNTAIN BOYS

With the extra time available after he left high school, and the money in his pocket that he was earning from his work with Uncle Lem, Smith was able to indulge in an interest in aviation by spending time at Portland airport and taking flying lessons. His passion for being airborne would become a significant part of his life for many years. A similar enthusiasm for fishing had also been established by this time.

Significant Early Influences

Smith was far from a narrow-minded country boy in his musical tastes. He passed a great deal of time during these formative years playing along with jazz bands on the radio and on records. The guitar was always the main focus of his attention. He frequently fell asleep at night while thinking of chords, which he would then try out as soon as he awoke in the morning. By his own admission, not all of his ideas were successful.

Django Reinhardt during a visit to the US in 1946

During this period, his early influences included the gypsy jazz guitarist Django Reinhardt. He bought as many 78rpm recordings by Reinhardt as were available and affordable. These records were, in effect, the principal part of his schooling in jazz, as he tried to copy the solos by ear. The technology at the time was so poor that the records soon deteriorated beyond use, but Reinhardt's playing, more than that of any other musician, showed Smith the potential of the guitar as a musical instrument.

He soon came to also idolize Les Paul, and later Charlie Christian. He regularly listened to Paul with Jimmy Atkins when they appeared with Ernie 'Darius' Newton as the Les Paul Trio on Fred Waring's *Chesterfield Pleasure Time Radio Show*. Reinhardt, however, remained Smith's favorite of his early jazz influences, citing that his own style lent more towards the gypsy's flare for technique than the styles of either Christian or Paul. The other hugely significant influence upon Smith during his formative years was the great classical guitarist Andrés Segovia. Although this acknowledgment has often been mentioned in guitar literature, it has rarely been afforded the pivotal importance that it deserves. Smith would become the first plectrum jazz guitarist to develop a classical guitarist's sense of technique. Meanwhile, the romantic use of rubato that he employed in his classical-type, self-accompanied, chord-melody arrangements owed much to the Segovian style of interpretation.

The Les Paul Trio: Les Paul, Darius Newton and Jimmy Atkins

By 1940, Smith had left Uncle Lem and His Mountain Boys to play with another hillbilly group, Bud Bailey and his Downeasters. The personnel of Bailey's band at this time included Rusty Rogers on rhythm guitar and yodeling; Vinny 'Jimmy Cal' Calderone on accordion; Ray Young on guitar and vocals; Little Rose Rio of Dover on vocals; and Johnny Smith on lead guitar. The band played twice per day, six days per week, on the local WHEB radio station in Portsmouth, New Hampshire, and they used the opportunity to advertise their live shows which they also performed six nights per week. The venues were usually town halls within a range of two hundred miles from Portsmouth, in areas such as Dover, Rochester and Newmarket. Once again, Smith was playing a varied range of musical styles. The group's nightly shows typically consisted of four hours' worth of ballads, comedy routines, novelty and yodeling songs, and square dance music, which they performed to audiences of between two and three hundred people.

In January 1940, the Benny Goodman Sextet arrived in Portland for a week-long engagement at the Strand Theater. Goodman's guitarist at the time was the aforementioned Charlie Christian. As a result of both his musicianship and his membership of Goodman's high profile group, Christian was a hugely influential figure in the history of the electric jazz guitar, and he came to have a profound impact upon Smith's own musical direction as well as those of many other renowned jazz guitarists. Smith heard and met Christian while he was playing after hours in a small club in Portland. As a consequence of this encounter, he was moved to focus his attention primarily upon the electric guitar. As with his study of Reinhardt's recordings, he now also began to copy Christian's recorded solos.

The Airport Boys

Shortly afterward, Smith moved to Boston and joined another group, the Airport Boys. Contrary to popular belief, he did not found the group. Furthermore, it was neither a dedicated jazz trio nor a country and western outfit. The threesome played a variety of music. Before Smith joined, the group had consisted of Ed Kemmer on rhythm guitar and vocals, his half-brother Lloyd 'Slim' West on double bass and vocals, and Frank 'Buck' Nation on additional guitar and vocals. On 30 September 1940, they recorded one of the first versions of 'You Are My Sunshine'. Nation left sometime afterward and was replaced by Smith. On 13 August 1941, the Airport Boys entered a studio in New York and recorded 'Worried Mind', 'It Ain't Gonna Rain No Mo', 'You Can Depend on Me', 'Pay Me No Mind', 'You're My Inspiration' and 'You Belong to Me'. Of these cuts, only 'It Ain't Gonna Rain No Mo' and 'You Belong to Me' were released on disc. Asked about these recording sessions seventy years later, Smith was unable to recall them, but he felt sure that they were completed before he joined the group. This would consequently put his membership of the Airport boys as commencing sometime after 13 August 1941, a year later than has often been cited.

With Smith on board, the trio continued the lineup of two guitars and a double bass, playing a broad range of musical genres with Smith providing some simple arrangements in the styles of his idols Charlie Christian, Django Reinhardt and Les Paul. They played at county fairs, nightclubs and theaters, and performed on the inaugural broadcast of the new WEIM radio station in Fitchburg, Massachusetts, on 23 October 1941.

ON THE STAGE TONIGHT!
Inaugural Broadcast
Radio Station WEIM
with
LONNY STARR, Your Favorite Radio Announcer
RADIO and STAGE STARS
Featuring the Airport Boys
Clayton Eaton's Concert Orchestra
Most Novel Event In The History of Fitchburg Theatricals

The trio also toured the Vaudeville chain of venues on the Radio-Keith-Orpheum (RKO) Corporation's circuit. By the early 1940s, Vaudeville had been superseded by talking motion pictures and was in its last days as a prominent form of entertainment. For a while, RKO attempted to combine stage and screen by presenting live stage acts during the intermissions of films. On 24 and 25 October 1941, Smith and the Airport Boys were featured at Boston's Colonial Theater as one of the intermission acts for a showing of Tim Whelan's film *International Lady*. In true Vaudevillian tradition, the other performers were a magician, the Great Huber, and a slack-wire artist, Bert Sloan.

FRIDAY and SATURDAY • ON OUR STAGE
The Internationally Famous Magician
THE GREAT HUBER
The Sensational Slack-Wire Artist
BERT SLOAN
THE VICTOR RECORDING AND NBC RADIO STARS
"THE AIRPORT BOYS"
HEADING A TERRIFIC R. K. O. STAGE SHOW
On Our Screen!
George Brent • Ilona Massey
"INTERNATIONAL LADY"

Aside from their live work, the Airport Boys had their own thrice-weekly radio show during late 1941 on NBC's affiliated station WBZ. Of his brief time in the group, Smith recalled, "We worked out of Boston. We worked in several states, mostly in New England. Eventually, we worked south of New York... Pennsylvania... Chester, Pennsylvania." Gertrude Parker was present during Smith's time with the Airport Boys and was soon to become his first wife. Her son, Chris Parker, recalls, "Mom tells me that they were really popular with the female following. The girls used to scream for them when they were on stage. It was like the Beatles."

Although the Airport Boys worked in a relatively small area, some of their engagements were mentioned in the national press. On 14 March and 4 April 1942, the *Billboard* publicized the trio's engagement at the El Rancho nightclub in Chester, Pennsylvania, and on 25 April 1942 it noted a move to Irvin Wolf's Rendezvous club in Philadelphia. The group was a short-lived venture for Smith. World War Two interrupted the lives of all but a few. After the war, Lloyd West reassembled the group with two new members in place of Kemmer and Smith. Meanwhile, Ed Kemmer went on to play the role of Commander Buzz Corry in the 1950s science-fiction television series *Space Patrol*.

THE AIRPORT BOYS:
ED KEMMER, LLOYD WEST AND JOHNNY SMITH

WORLD WAR TWO AND THE ARMY AIR CORPS BAND

In 1942, with the USA at war, Smith returned to Portland and took a job for a short period of time as a machinist in a shipyard. This was the first employment that he had taken outside of the world of music:

> I served an apprenticeship in the machine shop. My father didn't trust the music business.

So, I did that to please him. I made twenty-five cents an hour. I was in charge of what they called hull plating. There was a big pre-cut piece of steel that went into the side of these Liberty ships.

The Liberty Ships were built for cargo transportation purposes in two emergency shipyards in South Portland. The East Yard was operated by the Todd-Bath Iron Shipbuilding Corporation, while the West Yard was run by the South Portland Shipbuilding Corporation. Smith worked in the latter. In 1943, the two yards would become amalgamated into the New England Shipbuilding Corporation. Between them, they employed up to thirty thousand workers, and were by far the biggest employers in the area.

By the end of 1942, Smith had attempted to enlist as a pilot in the Army Air Corps with the hope of furthering his passion for flying. According to the US National Archives and Records Administration's Enlistment Records, Private John Henry Smith Jr., Serial Number 11122108, enlisted on 10 November 1942 in Portland, Maine. His civilian occupation, based upon his recent work in the shipyard, was listed as a machinist. However, his hopes of being taken on as a pilot were soon dashed:

> They took me into the Service and sent me down to Macon, Georgia. The first stop that I did was at the flight surgeon. He examined me, and my left eye was not one hundred percent. So, he couldn't approve me for the pilot training. They gave me a choice. One was to go to Biloxi, Mississippi, to mechanic's school, or... [laughs] being a guitar player, he said that he might be able to get me in the local marching band. I went over... The old band director wasn't very impressed. Not much room for a guitar player in the marching band. He gave me an Arban's book and a cornet, and told me to get in the latrine. I had two weeks to learn how to play it. Well, motivation is a wonderful thing. I made the band. I guess they figured that I would do more damage playing the trumpet. Had they let me fly, and had I survived, which some of my friends did not, I would have been a career pilot rather than a guitar player.

While he was stationed in Macon, Georgia, he married Mary Gertrude Larrivee on 1 March 1943.

Although Smith was a competent musician when he joined the Service, he had been raised in the aural tradition. At this time, he could not read music notation, but he taught himself sufficiently well and quickly on the cornet that he soon took the first chair in the 364th Air Corps Band, which was based outside of Macon.

In the Service, he also played both the violin and the viola in a concert group, where part of his duties included performing at recruitment drives. Aside

JOHNNY SMITH (CIRCLED) PLAYING CORNET WITH THE ARMY AIR CORPS BAND

from the musical literacy that he acquired during his military years, he also learned the art of music arranging. Both of these skills would later become invaluable in his employment as a network studio musician in New York City, where he and Tony Mottola were among the few guitarists who could read standard music notation.

Smith's placement in a military band during the war years did not completely halt his guitar playing. Guitarist Steve Silverman remembers his former teacher, and friend and colleague of Smith, Billy Bauer, recounting a story about Smith's time in the Service:

> When the other guys were sleeping, Johnny would practice quietly. He was so well liked and played so well that no one wanted to say anything, but many were losing sleep. The sergeant caught on and told Johnny, reluctantly, that he would have to stop. That's when he began working things out without the instrument, and he told Billy he could just pick up the guitar and play them. He was offering instruction, not boasting.

In fact, as has already been mentioned, Smith had begun practicing without a guitar at hand when he was a youngster. It is possible that by the time he was in the Air Corps Band he was aware that these visualization techniques had long been used by classical musicians, most notably the pianist Arthur Rubinstein. It is highly unlikely, however, that he was aware of the concept when he began implementing it as a youngster in Portland. Outside of the classical music genre, the technique was unknown. Gary Atkins recalled a conversation which occurred during the 1950s regarding Smith's practice technique:

> Johnny and my dad [Jimmy Atkins] got into a big argument [laughs] about practicing. Johnny said, "Well, I practice in my head." And Dad said, "You what?" He said, "Yeah, I practice in my head all the time." Well, that's a big deal now with the sports training psychology and all that, you know. But not then.

Smith's daughter, Kim Stewart, remembers that her father continued to use the technique throughout his life:

> When I was a child, I would sometimes talk to my dad, but his mind was miles away. He was thinking of something else and his fingers were moving. I didn't realize at the time, but he was practicing without having the guitar in his hands.

During his time in the Service, Smith continued to study jazz guitar from records. Hearing Charlie Christian's recording with Benny Goodman of 'Airmail Special' on a jukebox during this period was a particularly significant moment. His skill with the guitar did not pass unnoticed by the higher authorities within the Services. He was assigned to the 8th Air Corps in Montgomery, Alabama, where he was instructed to assemble a small jazz group for tours in the south east of the USA. For this purpose, he created a quartet of two guitars, a mandolin and a double bass. As Smith recalled, the celebrated band-leader Glenn Miller was present at one of his group's performances at Maxwell Field during December 1942 and subsequently tried to requisition him for his own orchestra:

> One night, we were requisitioned to play at the officers' club at Maxwell Field. I played

> with my little group, and... I didn't know it, but Glenn Miller was in the audience. When I got to Macon, Georgia, he had requisitioned me to go with his Glenn Miller band. The commander of the base where I was stationed wouldn't release me, because he had a little symphonette and I was the only viola player. He wouldn't release me, and I was really heartbroken. But for some reason, somebody upstairs must have been looking out for me, because when Glenn Miller disappeared over the English Channel... [in December 1944] the band members, who weren't liked by other G.I.s because they were really treated like royalty... They sent these band members over to Belgium. They were living in mud and tents, and they were used as pallbearers. From what I understand, all but one of them fell chronically ill.

Although the opportunity to work with Miller's orchestra was scuppered, Smith found himself playing the guitar with another large ensemble of prominent musicians during his years in the Air Corps, in the form of the Philadelphia Orchestra, who were under the baton of the Hungarian-born conductor Eugene Ormandy.

Smith's reputation as a talented guitarist spread beyond the confines of military circles. In an article in *Just Jazz Guitar* in May 1995, guitarist Lou Mecca recounted meeting him at the barracks of Valley Forge General Hospital in Phoenixville, Pennsylvania. At the time, Smith was one of four trumpet players in the marching band who were performing for wounded soldiers. His position at these barracks had a lasting impression upon him, as the horrific injuries to servicemen that he witnessed there gave him a profound sense of gratitude throughout his life for his own well being, despite some appalling tragedies. A mutual friend, a drummer by the name of Billy Phillips, had told Mecca about Smith and took him to meet the guitar-playing trumpeter. After lowering the sixth string down from its standard E tuning to an unconventional D, Smith performed his own solo guitar arrangements of Nikolai Rimsky-Korsakov's 'Flight of the Bumble Bee', Grigoraş Dinicu's violin showpiece *Hora Staccato*, 'The Lord's Prayer', 'Danny Boy', and George Gershwin's *Rhapsody in Blue*. His virtuosity and humility left Mecca astounded.

JOHNNY SMITH (CENTER FRONT) AS A VIOLINIST WITH THE PUBLIC RELATIONS OFFICE LITTLE SYMPHONY ORCHESTRA ON 14 DECEMBER 1944

Unfortunately, it is not possible to uncover further documented details of Smith's movements as a member of the Army Air Corps Band during World War Two. His military records were destroyed, along with millions of others, in the fire at the National Personnel Records Center in 1973.

Chapter Two:
Early Days in New York, NBC, Jazz and the Atonal Classical Works

In 1946, with the war over, Smith was discharged and returned to Portland, Maine, where he worked in nightclubs, played the trumpet in the orchestra pit at a local Vaudeville theater, and played guitar and wrote arrangements for WCSH, a National Broadcasting Company (NBC) affiliated local radio station. His work at WCSH, where he was a staff musician, included playing in Wally Harwood's orchestra.

Johnny Smith with Wally Harwood's orchestra

Despite the broad range of his work in Portland, he struggled to earn a hundred dollars per week. He resumed his hobby of flying and became a flight instructor. He went on to teach on single and multi-engine aircraft for the next forty years.

Meanwhile, Arthur Owens, the station program director at WCSH, sent some tapes of Smith's work to Roy Shield, the music director at NBC headquarters in New York City. As a result, Smith received an invitation to join the network broadcaster in 1946, which he did as a staff guitarist and arranger.

NATIONAL BROADCASTING COMPANY, INC.
A SERVICE OF RADIO CORPORATION OF AMERICA
RCA BUILDING · RADIO CITY
NEW YORK 20, N. Y.
CIRCLE 7-8300

May 6 1946

Mr John Smith
25 Montreal Street
Portland
Maine

Dear Johnny:

I am interested in having you come to New York, and I am sure we will be able to work out some kind of a deal for you so that you won't starve to death while you are waiting out your time. I would suggest you get a transfer and come in and see me at your convenience so that we can talk over plans.

I looked at your arrangement and it looks O.K., except for a few minor things.

I would like to have you make an arrangement for a small combination, featuring yourself — a combination such as drums, piano, bass and three or four other instruments, which might be three woodwinds and trumpet, or four woodwinds - possibly flute, oboe, and two clarinets, one interchangeable with bass clarinet. The arrangement should be stylish.

Yours sincerely,

Roy Shield

Roy Shield

INVITATION FROM ROY SHIELD AT NBC TO JOHNNY SMITH
ON 6 MAY 1946

At NBC, his wages leaped to $278 per week. However, there were bureaucratic formalities which had to be completed before he could take up his post. Although casual work was permitted, the regulations prevented him from working on a full-time basis until he had joined the local musician's union. While he waited to receive his union card, he lived in Clifton, New Jersey. It took six months for Smith to receive his union card, although he was permitted to write arrangements for NBC's radio and television shows as a freelancer during the interim period. When his application was eventually completed, he was listed in the 1947 edition of the Local 802 American Federation of Musicians' Union Directory as member CI 6-7550, residing at 318 West 51st Street, New York.

ART TATUM

Smith invested much of his spare time wisely. He continued his education in jazz by frequenting the venues around 52nd Street, such as Eddie Condon's. Some of the clubs had no cover charge. These were consequently packed with less-affluent customers, including Smith. He could regularly be found at one particular club listening to Art Tatum, where he regularly sat as close to the piano as possible, so that he could listen attentively. He came to know Tatum on a personal level through talking backstage between sets. Tatum was a notoriously heavy drinker, and Smith later recalled that the pianist drank straight whiskey with beer chasers. One of his most vivid memories of Tatum at the club was of watching him play an upright piano, the top of which was covered with beer bottles and shots of whiskey that the audience had sent up for him. Mid-piece, Tatum, who had only very limited vision in one eye and none at all in the other, reached up with his left hand and took a shot, followed by a bottle of beer, replacing each of them on the piano without either knocking over the other drinks or missing a note with his right hand.

DJANGO REINHARDT

Having briefly met one of his guitar-playing idols, Charlie Christian, in Portland before the war, Smith was delighted to spend considerably more time with another in New York. When the legendary guitarist Django Reinhardt came to the city in 1946, Harry Volpe asked Smith to chaperone him for a period of time, partly because he owned a car, although he could not speak French and Reinhardt could not speak English.

Reinhardt had been performing across the USA with Duke Ellington and his orchestra. After the tour, he stayed in New York to play a month-long engagement at the classy and interracial Café Society Uptown at 128 East 58th Street from December 1946 until January 1947, where he appeared opposite clarinetist Edmond Hall and pianist Pete Johnson. Smith regularly met

Reinhardt in his room at the Hudson Hotel in Manhattan, where they sometimes jammed together. In an insightful interview with the British guitarists Trefor Owen and Ike Isaacs for *Guitar* magazine in 1976, Smith modestly insisted that he was very much a spectator during those jam sessions and did little more than listen. At other times, the two guitarists went out drinking together. In one of his favorite reveries, Smith recalled his time with the gypsy:

> Harry Volpe asked me if I would meet Django and take him down to the Paramount Theater where Les Paul was playing. So, I went up to 58th Street, picked him up, and went down to the Paramount Theater. We spent the afternoon talking with Les and playing. Les worshiped Django. When we left... Django was playing at the Café Society Uptown. He asked me to take him there, and I did. We were not properly dressed and I didn't even have on a neck tie. He insisted on me coming in with him and having dinner. Well, I didn't want to, but he insisted. We went in, and they sat us at a table in the corner. It was pretty full of people. All of a sudden, Django picked up a knife and started thumping it on the table. The waiters, who came over, all spoke French. They couldn't console him, but finally they brought over a flower, because our vase didn't have one. And that's what had triggered him off.

NBC

Even while Smith's union membership was being processed, his name was becoming increasingly well known around New York, and the city's guitar community recognized that they had a phenomenal talent amongst them. The guitarist and educator Jack Petersen recalls, "He was one of the first. When he first went to New York, he took it by storm. He was one of the biggest! He was the top guitar player in New York. He was the number one guy." Bob Yelin remembers, "Sal Salvador told me that he thought he was a pretty good jazz guitarist, but when he saw Johnny play he wanted to hide in a closet and forget about playing guitar for a living."

Smith had arrived in New York without a guitar. His Gibson L-5 had been stolen shortly before his departure from Portland. Harry Volpe took him to the Gretsch company to obtain a new instrument soon after his arrival. A resultant press advertisement showed Smith with a bespoke version of the 400F Synchromatic model. Volpe, who was more proficient as a publicist than he was as a guitarist, almost certainly had a hand in the text, which proclaimed:

> A New Star on the Horizon... Johnny Smith from Portland, Maine, and his Gretsch "400"... Be it classical, jive or rhythm... he's terrific! NBC's outstanding guitar soloist and gifted arranger, heard from coast to coast on many of the best radio programs, chooses the Gretsch "400" Synchromatic for tone, volume and all 'round flexibility. Watch for and listen to this young man who is destined to become the nation's outstanding guitarist of his generation. (Reproduced from *Metronome*, February 1947)

An almost identical advertisement for the instrument, declaring "It's terrific" rather than "He's terrific" was also placed in the press.

At the time that Smith began working at NBC as a full staff member in 1947, the union's rules restricted the studio musicians not only to working a maximum of five days per week, but also to a limited amount of hours that they could work per day. This enforced a considerable degree of planning upon the networks in order to ensure that their live broadcasts ran smoothly. At the start of each week, the musicians were assigned their work quotas. Often, they had no knowledge of their designated shows, with whom they would be performing, or the repertoire, until they sat down to play on the live broadcasts themselves. Only the very best musicians could cope with such traumatic working practices. Smith admitted to having habitually suffered from bouts of anxiety before performances, particularly in the studio where there was pressure not to make any mistakes. A small shot of whiskey went a long way towards helping him to gather himself if he was overly uptight before a live show.

In his work at NBC, he refined his multifaceted musicianship to a high level. He became revered for his superior sight-reading skills and his ability to improvise over any chord progression that was placed in front of him. His musical literacy was all the more remarkable when it is remembered that at this time the guitar was not yet accepted as a serious instrument. Many arrangers were still unfamiliar not only with its limitations and its potential, but also with the established convention of notating an octave away from concert pitch. This issue did not pose any problems for Smith, however, who had taught himself to read the grand staff system of simultaneous treble and bass clefs. Studio arrangers frequently presented him with either piano parts or conductors' scores from which to work. He found this to be preferable as he could then create parts which avoided clashes with the designated bass notes. Late in life, Smith reflected upon the environment in which he had found himself upon his arrival at NBC:

> When I first got to New York City, Tony Mottola and myself were the only guitar players who knew how to read music. So, we did a lot of the recordings for different people because we could read music. When I was at NBC... Of course, everything was reading music. The guitar parts were all misnamed. So, I told them that it would be better if they gave me the piano parts to work from. If they didn't have the piano parts, then give me the bass part. And if they didn't have the bass part, then give me the drum part. Anything but the guitar part.

The extreme working conditions at NBC created the sense of a fraternal community among the contracted musicians. After working hard together all day, many of them regularly drank hard together until late at night. Inside of this brotherhood, New York's guitarists built themselves an inner circle. Tal Farlow, Jimmy Raney and Sal Salvador, for example, all lived under the same roof for a while, and Smith often stopped by with John Collins. Bobby Greene, who was Smith's pianist from 1963 to 1964, remembers the guitarist telling him about the social life during his days in New York City:

> Johnny told us a story from his younger, wilder days. It seems that he and three buddies in NYC would periodically assemble in one of their apartments to boil peyote buds in water for the requisite time and then drink the pot liquor. From previous experience it had been determined that one eight-ounce tumbler was the proper dose for a manageable high. Well, on one occasion, one of the guys decided to up the dose to two glasses, causing great concern among the three who kept to the standard one glass. They vowed to keep an eye on him, but since they were all stoned, they discovered at some point that he had disappeared. They frantically searched the neighborhood for him in the ensuing

twenty-four hours, unsuccessfully, worried sick, until he suddenly reappeared. When he determined that they weren't going to inflict serious bodily injury 'cause he had scared the shit out of them, he recounted his experience. It seems that after he had wandered off, he found himself down at Grand Central Station, standing in front of that out-sized grandfather clock listening to it tick. As stoned as he was, he nevertheless retained the presence of mind to move on when he noticed the beat cop in GCS eyeing him suspiciously. When the cop's attention was elsewhere, he returned to the clock and resumed his monitoring. When asked how he got so hung up on a clock, albeit a large one, he replied, "It was cosmic, man!"

Despite the hard recreational lifestyle that was prevalent on the New York music scene, there was a line of professionalism that Smith was not prepared to cross. In reminiscing about his NBC days, he lamented the fate which befell the pianist Sanford Gold during a recording session with Meredith Willson and Marlene Dietrich in the 1950s:

> We got a call to do this record date with Marlene Dietrich. The call was for nine o'clock in the morning. His [Sanford Gold's] apartment was within walking distance of Decca Records where we were going to record this. On the way... Sanford Gold was a heavy pot smoker. Sure enough, walking to this date, he had to light up a joint and get high before we got to the studio. We got there and he was stoned. Meredith Willson, the conductor with this big orchestra, gave this down beat for the piano player to hit an octave. We call it the 'bell tone'. You know, to give out the pitch... Sanford couldn't even hit an octave. Finally, Meredith said, "I think we'll have the harp give the octave." So, he did. I was so embarrassed. Anyway, it took us all day to get this side with Marlene Dietrich. She was singing 'See What the Boys in the Back Room will Have'. It took us all day to get enough to splice together for one song. After the date was over, I walked back to NBC to put my guitar away in the musicians' lounge. I overheard Meredith talking to the music contractor at NBC. He was telling this contractor, "I never want to see that piano player again."

Guitar Interludes

On an unidentified date around 1947, Smith recorded a collection of solo guitar arrangements for Lang-Worth Feature Programs titled *Guitar Interludes for Low Level Background.* These recordings were intended for use by disc jockeys as background music while they promoted sponsors' products. Although the arrangements, which consisted of 'Song of India', 'Rhythm', 'Oh Bury Me Not', 'Oh Susanna', 'The Little Shanty', 'Home Sweet Home', 'Carry Me Back to Old Virginny', and 'Auld Lang Syne', were primitive in style by his standards of just a few years later, his virtuosity was already undeniable. After listening to these recordings several years later, Smith was somewhat embarrassed by their lack of sophistication, but despite his own reservations it is clear from these recordings why the guitar community in New York was in awe of him.

Mary Lou Williams

Mary Lou Williams

Smith's dedication to his education in jazz soon began to reap rewards. In 1947, he recorded two bop sides, 'Mary Lou' and 'Kool', as part of a trio with Kenny Dorham on trumpet and Grachan Moncur on bass, accompanying the innovative jazz pianist Mary Lou Williams. This was an isolated recording session, and Smith was not a regular member of Williams' combo. These two sides are hugely significant in that they mark his first jazz recordings in New York. They also illustrate that he already had an excellent grasp of bop phraseology.

Mary Lou Williams was a rare jazz talent in that her musical style continually evolved with the times. She was greatly respected for her support and encouragement of young, burgeoning jazz musicians during the bebop era, such as Dizzy Gillespie, Charlie Parker and Thelonious Monk. Her brief work with Smith, Dorham and Moncur was a continuation of her dedication to young jazz performers.

Schönberg, Ibert and Berg

Throughout his life, Johnny Smith was revered for his versatility as much as for his virtuosity. The astounding range of his musical abilities during the late 1940s extended much further than the already impressive demands that were placed upon him as a studio musician at NBC. He also found himself performing near-contemporary classical music.

One of the most frequently referenced pieces of mythology regarding Smith concerns his legendary part in the performance of Arnold Schönberg's atonal *Serenade for Septet and Baritone Voice*, Op.24, at the Museum of Modern Art on 23 November 1949. The recital was arranged by the United States Section of the International Society for Contemporary Music as a celebration of the composer for his seventy-fifth birthday. Various dignitaries from the world of classical music were invited to hear Dimitri Mitropoulos conduct on the prestigious occasion.

An unnamed classical guitarist had initially been engaged to play the guitar part in the *Serenade*. However, Schönberg's music is notoriously difficult to read, interpret and perform. In the original score, the guitar part is written at concert pitch using the grand staff system, which is an alien practice for most guitarists. Despite the organizers' redrafting of the part into conventional guitar clef and pitch notation, it was still beyond the ability of the classical guitarist whom had been hired for the concert. It should be noted that despite their technical virtuosity, most classical guitarists are far more familiar with presenting solo recitals than they are with performing within orchestral ensembles under the direction of a conductor. Smith was of the generous opinion that this particular aspect may have been the main factor in the original candidate's inability to play the music satisfactorily within the septet.

In the apparent absence of a capable guitarist, Mitropoulos had resigned himself to canceling the concert, but he was persuaded by the violinist Louis Krasner to delay his decision for a little longer while further inquiries were made. Krasner possessed a greater network of musicians than Mitropoulos.

He contacted his brother-in-law, Felix Galimir, who was a violinist with the NBC Symphony Orchestra under Arturo Toscanini. Even as early as 1949, Smith's reputation for his extraordinary musicianship was widespread around the NBC studios, reaching far beyond merely New York's guitar community. Galimir recommended Smith, passing comment that although he was NBC's staff guitarist and was considered to be primarily a jazz musician, he was sure that he would be able to play the part.

While Smith was waiting for an elevator at the NBC studios on the night of Friday 18 November, about to head home for the weekend, he was approached by both Krasner and Galimir, the latter of whom had been asked to act as a translator between the classical purist Krasner and the jazz guitarist. Krasner's concerns were unnecessary. It quickly became apparent to him that Smith was much more than just a jazz guitarist and that he was also an admirer of the atonal music of both Schönberg and Berg. Krasner presented Smith with his dilemma and inquired if he would be willing to attempt the part. Smith's response was to ask if he could view the notation in Schönberg's original grand staff version as this was his preferred system of musical text. After briefly scanning the score, he was reluctant to accept their offer. However, as an admirer of Schönberg, Smith did not wish to see the concert canceled. The first rehearsal had been arranged for the Monday morning, two days before the recital. Believing that he had the weekend to prepare, he agreed to take on the part.

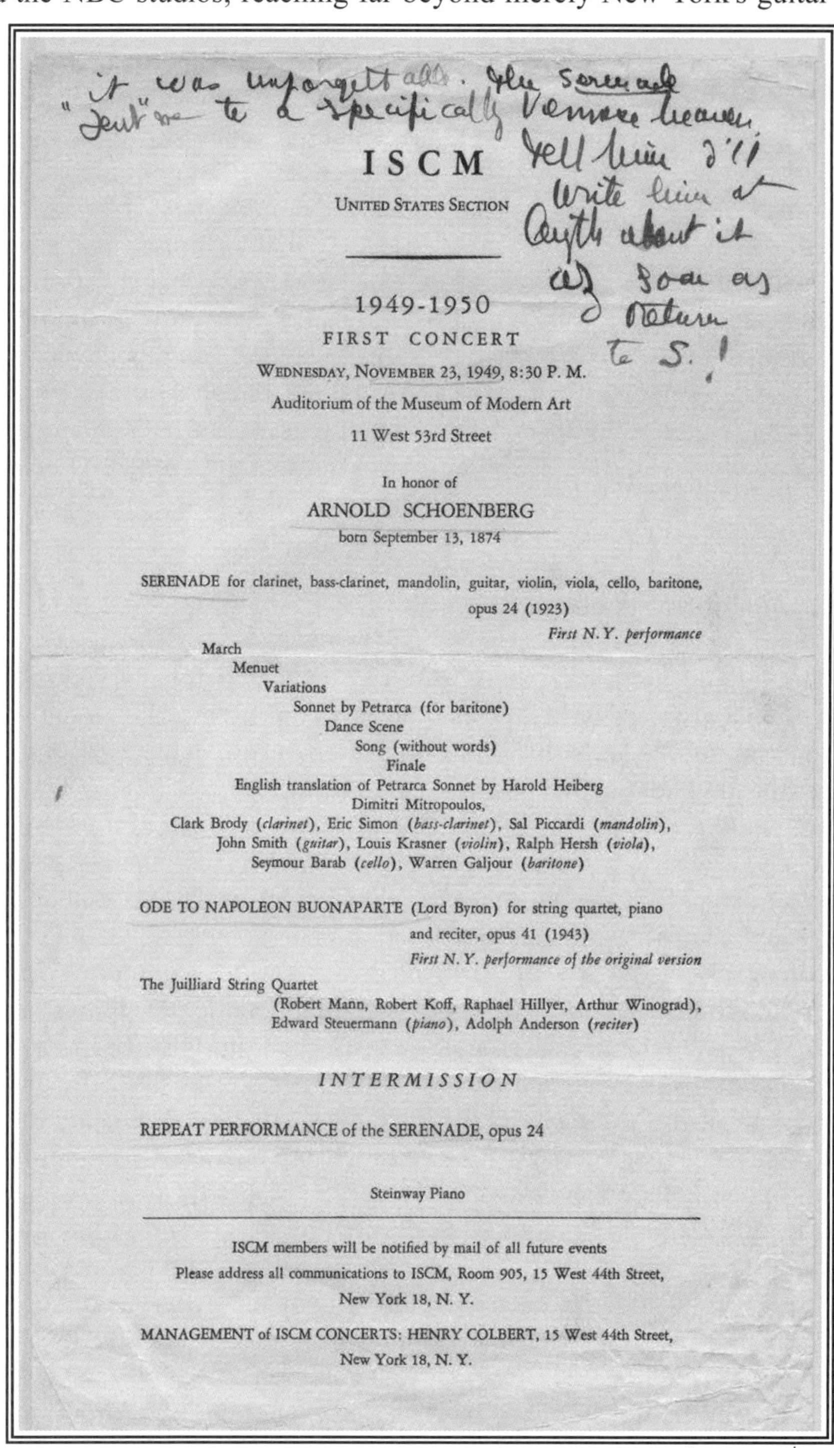

"It was unforgettable. The Serenade "sent" me to a specifically Viennese heaven. Tell him I'll write him at length about it as soon as I return to S.!

ISCM

UNITED STATES SECTION

1949-1950

FIRST CONCERT

WEDNESDAY, NOVEMBER 23, 1949, 8:30 P. M.

Auditorium of the Museum of Modern Art

11 West 53rd Street

In honor of

ARNOLD SCHOENBERG

born September 13, 1874

SERENADE for clarinet, bass-clarinet, mandolin, guitar, violin, viola, cello, baritone, opus 24 (1923)

First N.Y. performance

March
Menuet
Variations
Sonnet by Petrarca (for baritone)
Dance Scene
Song (without words)
Finale

English translation of Petrarca Sonnet by Harold Heiberg

Dimitri Mitropoulos,
Clark Brody (*clarinet*), Eric Simon (*bass-clarinet*), Sal Piccardi (*mandolin*),
John Smith (*guitar*), Louis Krasner (*violin*), Ralph Hersh (*viola*),
Seymour Barab (*cello*), Warren Galjour (*baritone*)

ODE TO NAPOLEON BUONAPARTE (Lord Byron) for string quartet, piano and reciter, opus 41 (1943)

First N. Y. performance of the original version

The Juilliard String Quartet
(Robert Mann, Robert Koff, Raphael Hillyer, Arthur Winograd),
Edward Steuermann (*piano*), Adolph Anderson (*reciter*)

INTERMISSION

REPEAT PERFORMANCE of the SERENADE, opus 24

Steinway Piano

ISCM members will be notified by mail of all future events

Please address all communications to ISCM, Room 905, 15 West 44th Street, New York 18, N. Y.

MANAGEMENT of ISCM CONCERTS: HENRY COLBERT, 15 West 44th Street, New York 18, N. Y.

THE PROGRAM FOR THE PERFORMANCE OF SCHÖNBERG'S SERENADE FOR SEPTET AND BARITONE VOICE

Saturdays were non-working days for Smith at this time. Consequently, he continued his intention to spend his Friday night by unwinding and did not return to his home at 221 East 8th Street, Clifton, New Jersey, until five o'clock in the morning. An hour after falling into bed, he received a telephone call informing him that an emergency rehearsal had been arranged for seven o'clock. Still the worse for alcohol, he made his way to Mitropoulos' suite in the Great Northern Hotel on 57th Street, New York. Contrary to widespread mythology, he did not then effortlessly sightread his way through his part. By his own admission, he clung on for dear life during the fairly shambolic rehearsal. He did well enough, though, to satisfy the conductor that he could follow direction, and it was therefore decided that the recital would proceed as scheduled.

Smith spent the remainder of the weekend studying his guitar part with the help of his friend Irwin Kostal, with whom he had worked in a combo at NBC. Kostal was an extremely accomplished musician and went on to arrange music for Sid Caesar and substantially contribute to the scoring of Leonard Bernstein's music for *West Side Story* in both the Broadway production and the screen version, as well as several other films including *The Sound of Music*. Smith and Kostal worked together on the guitar part throughout the weekend at the latter's house in Long Island. By the time the septet had reconvened and rehearsed the *Serenade* on the Monday and Tuesday mornings, followed by a dress rehearsal on the Wednesday evening, it was ready for the recital. The performance was received enthusiastically by the full house and was repeated in its entirety after the intermission.

Mitropoulos remained eternally grateful to Smith for his critical part in enabling both the live performance and the subsequent recording of the *Serenade* to go ahead. In the late 1950s, Smith unexpectedly encountered him on 57th Street in New York. Although he had noticed the conductor approaching him from the opposite direction, and it was the conductor who approached the guitarist to thank him for one of the great personal thrills of his career.

For both the recital and the ensuing recording, which took place in December, Smith used his unamplified Epiphone Emperor archtop guitar, which was later stolen during a break at NBC studios. His choice to play unamplified remained a minor regret about the recording of the *Serenade*, as his guitar is not always easy to hear, and he would have preferred to have amplified the instrument in order to increase its presence. The septet was seated in a semi-circle around a solitary microphone for the recording, which was not ideal.

For both the recital and the ensuing recording, which took place in December, Smith used his unamplified Epiphone Emperor archtop guitar, which was later stolen during a break at NBC studios. His choice to play unamplified remained a minor regret about the recording of the *Serenade*, as his guitar is not always easy to hear, and he would have preferred to have amplified the instrument in order to increase its presence. The septet was seated in a semi-circle around a solitary microphone for the recording, which was not ideal.

Smith's participation in the performance and recording of Schönberg's *Serenade* was not the only occasion upon which he was called in by classical musicians to play their repertoire. On an unidentified date around 1950, he took part in a recording of Jacques Ibert's *Entr'acte* with the celebrated flute virtuoso Julius Baker. As a plectrum guitarist, he had reservations about his suitability when Baker asked him to play the fingerstyle classical guitar part in the duet. For the recording, which Baker issued on his own Oxford Recording Company label, Smith resorted to muffling the steel strings on his Epiphone Emperor archtop guitar with rubber bands in order to reduce the metallic tone. He remembered the occasion vividly and with great pride:

> We recorded that in some guy's apartment. Uptown New York. We had a hell of a time, because the traffic noise was so bad. I felt really privileged to work with Julius Baker. I worked with him in certain settings after that, including with the New York Philharmonic. It took us all day to record that.

Although it is not possible to pinpoint an exact date for this recording, according to Smith his aforementioned Epiphone Emperor guitar was stolen in 1950. It must be inferred, therefore, that his recording with Baker was recorded by then at the latest. Furthermore, Baker relocated to Chicago in 1951 to become a principal flautist with the Chicago Symphony Orchestra.

In 1951, Dimitri Mitropoulos called upon Smith once again and asked him to take part in a concert presentation of Alban Berg's atonal opera *Wozzeck*. He performed in the three recitals at Carnegie Hall on 12, 13 and 15 April 1951. The first of these challenging presentations was recorded and issued on vinyl. Over sixty years later, it is still considered by many aficionados in classical music circles to be a landmark recording and Mitropoulos' masterpiece of a performance. Guitarist and friend Mundell Lowe recalls witnessing Smith's superior musicianship in action during one of the rehearsals:

> John was one of the most fantastic readers that I've ever seen. I went along to one of the rehearsals for those *Wozzeck* dates. It was written very strangely, like a bar of 3/4 then a bar of 2/8 and so forth. The conductor was going out of his mind trying to hold everything together. John went through the whole thing without missing a cue. Amazing.

Toscanini

Aside from Smith's classical performances with Dimitri Mitropoulos and Julius Baker, there is a more frequently cited reference in the guitar literature to his work with the tyrannical conductor Arturo Toscanini and the NBC Symphony Orchestra. Towards the end of his life, Smith admirably took the opportunity to put the record straight:

> Well, you know... The word got around that I worked with Toscanini. I never did anything with Toscanini. I was supposed to, but I got back from California where I was working on some shows, and they had hired another guitar player to do whatever it was. An opera or... Anyway, the word got out that I worked with Toscanini, but the truth was that I never did anything with Toscanini.

Chapter Three: Radio and Television Shows

While Smith's musicianship made him the only candidate for the demands of the atonal classical repertoire, these engagements were merely a part of the broad range of music that he was called upon to play in New York, most notably in his hectic work schedule at NBC, between 1946 and 1958. His versatility, virtuosity and musical literacy caused him to be the first choice of the guitarists on the broadcaster's books. Most of his work was in the medium of radio rather than television as this was at a time when the former and not yet yielded to the latter. He worked on television for CBS, ABC and NBC, and at one time appeared on the *Tonight* show, presented by Steve Allen. He also worked on the *Fireside Theater* television program for a year, as well as the *Ed Sullivan Show.*

Johnny Smith in the television studio

The majority of radio shows in the late 1940s and early 1950s were of fifteen or thirty minutes in duration. Many programs had a short life span with some lasting no longer than a few weeks. In researching through the NBC radio archives in the Library of Congress and the library of the Wisconsin Historical Society, it became apparent that it was not possible to identify each and every broadcast on which Smith appeared. The *NBC Index Cards* and *NBC Master Books* often make no reference to the staff musicians unless it had been deemed that an unusual and noteworthy event had occurred. Undoubtedly, Smith's work at NBC placed him in an environment with some of New York City's finest musicians during a golden era. It is lamentable that while the broadcaster went to significant efforts to document the existence of their radio shows during the 1940s and 1950s, they did not see fit to acknowledge the individual orchestral musicians who contributed so much to each transmission. Where staff orchestras or groups were performing, there was usually no identification of the full personnel. The featured soloists were only occasionally cited. However, it has been possible through these collections and other sources to identify a substantial number of the NBC shows on which Smith performed.

As a staff member until 1951, and a freelance musician thereafter, Smith worked in numerous settings at NBC. These ranged from solo appearances, through those with small combos, to full-scale orchestras. The most frequently documented of these within the NBC archives was a trio called the Playboys, which usually consisted of Smith with organist Arlo Hults and pianist Mort Lippman. Leadership of the group revolved between the three members for different radio shows. Sometimes, this was denoted by a change of name to, for example, Arlo's Trio. After Smith left his post on NBC's full-time staff and the Playboys dissolved, Arlo Hults went on to provide the music for several of the broadcaster's television shows as the medium began to supplant radio in the homes of America. Meanwhile, Mort Lippman enjoyed a successful and prominent career after changing his name to Mort Lindsey. Among his many achievements as a bandleader, he conducted the orchestra for Judy Garland's comeback concert at Carnegie Hall on 23 April 1961 and was the musical director for the *Merv Griffin Show* for over twenty years.

CHAUNCEY MOREHOUSE AND JOHNNY SMITH AT NBC

LINGER AWHILE WITH LYNN COLLYER

One of the first radio programs at NBC to which Smith contributed was the short-lived *Linger Awhile with Lynn Collyer.* On this show he provided guitar accompaniments for the vocalist while she performed popular songs. He appeared on the opening show on Saturday, 14 September 1946, and again a week later on 21 September. On the two Tuesday night broadcasts, music was provided by pianist Joe Kahn and his quintet. The brief series of four programs then ended, but returned on 7 December 1946 as the retitled *Lynn Collyer Sings*, with Kahn and his quintet providing all of the music thereafter. An article in the Australian *Barrier Miner* newspaper earlier in the year described Lynn Collyer as a "husky-voiced blues singer" who had been been establishing herself in New York's nightclubs and hotel cabaret venues.

CITIES SERVICE HIGHWAYS IN MELODY

Cities Service Petroleum, Inc. sponsored one of NBC's longest running and most popular radio programs. *Highways in Melody* began on 27 October 1944, and was renamed *Cities Service Highways in Melody* on 20 September 1945 when the oil company's sponsorship took effect. The show underwent another name change, becoming *Cities Service Band of America*, on 4 June 1948.

It has not been possible to ascertain the exact date on which Smith joined the show, but he was already a regular member of Paul Lavalle's Cities Service Orchestra when he was featured as a soloist on 6 June 1947, and then again on 1 August 1947 when he played a swing version of 'Minstrel Man of Richmond, VA' and an interpretation of 'Ida'.

The series often celebrated and commemorated significant anniversaries and dates, including those overseas such as St. Patrick's Day, St. David's Day and Bastille Day, which required the musicians to perform a broad range of musical styles and repertoire.

PAUL LAVALLE

When *Highways in Melody* was broadcast for the last time on 28 May 1948, special credits were announced in acknowledgment of a few select musicians who had contributed greatly towards making the season such a success. These included vocalist Mac Morgan, concertmaster Jules Schachter, violinist Nathan Gordon, pianist Mario Janero, and guitarist Johnny Smith. With good reason, Smith maintained vivid memories of working on *Highways in Melody*:

> We started off with a big orchestra. All the string players from the NBC Symphony worked on that show. Then, he [Lavalle] changed over to *Band of America*. I didn't do... There were a couple of things where I played guitar.
>
> On that show [*Highways in Melody*], I used to have a microphone in front of me. If I wanted the sound of the electric guitar, I had the microphone in front of the amplifier. If I wanted an acoustic sound, I pulled the microphone in front of the guitar. Once, I pulled the microphone across... I had my other hand on the guitar strings. About four hundred volts went straight through me. It blew me right off the stool. I landed on the floor and there was this huge 'ca-ching' from the guitar strings. This was live on air. I picked myself up and got back onto the stool. I was shaking and I had this big cadenza to do with the strings. I managed to get through it, still shaking. Paul Lavalle just looked at me at the end and said, "Are you through?" Yeah, that electric shock sure sobered me up. After that, Lavalle always made sure that he accompanied me to Hurley's bar.

Campana Sales Solitair Time

As well as performing as a guitarist at NBC, Smith also conducted the orchestras for some of the shows on which he worked, such as *Campana Sales Solitair Time*. The show's sponsor, Campana Sales, was a producer of cosmetics, of which Solitair was a particular line. Dick Dudley was the show's regular announcer from 29 August 1948 when he replaced Tex Antoine. The program's singing star, Bob Houston, who had replaced Warde Donovan on 22 June 1947, performed popular songs with orchestral accompaniment conducted by the trumpeter Henry 'Hot Lips' Levine. Smith deputized for Levine on 16, 23 and 30 January 1949 when the regular leader was unable to attend due to illness. On these occasions, the orchestra was referred to as "Henry Levine's orchestra conducted by Johnny Smith." On 7 August 1949, Smith once again stood in for Levine who was away on vacation. Occasionally, he also played trumpet.

Slight changes were made to the show's format from 19 November 1950, with each fifteen-minute broadcast now including a performance of a hymn. Furthermore, while Smith performed guitar bridges for the program, he also featured with a newly assembled group called Johnny Smith and his Little Symphony. He continued on the show as a regular musician until it ended on 21 January 1951.

The Betty Harris Show

Smith headed his own group when providing the music for the *Betty Harris Show*. His combo usually took the form of a trio, but it was sometimes augmented into a quartet. In both guises, the outfit accompanied the singer and also played instrumental pieces. NBC considered this fifteen-minute lunchtime radio program as Pop Operetta, with Harris singing popular songs and "occasional selections from operetta in the informal style." The first broadcast was aired on 21 August 1947. Several cancellations were enforced by more important programs, such as Holy Week Services and the Inauguration; topical broadcasts such as *What's Right with the UN?*, and *Thanksgiving in Paris*; as well as religious programs by the American Council of Christian Churches, the United Council of Church Women, the Convention of the Federal Council of Churches of Christ in America, and the National Association of Evangelicals, all of which took precedence over NBC's sustaining show.

The *NBC Master Books* have yielded detailed information about one particular broadcast of the *Betty Harris Show* on which Smith and his trio of guitar, organ and piano appeared. The entry for the broadcast on 7 January 1948 provides the show's full script and play-list, and even extends to include the keys of the pieces of music. Between each song, Betty Harris and announcer Wayne Howell advertised products and engaged in the type of banter that was typical of the radio programs of the period. The running order for this broadcast consisted of the opening theme song 'Pack Up Your Troubles'; Betty Harris singing 'It's Only a Paper Moon' in B flat, and 'Don't Mention Love to Me' in A flat; The Johnny Smith Trio performing an instrumental arrangement of 'Nagasaki'; Betty Harris returning to sing 'For Heaven's Sake' in B flat, and 'Put On Your Old Grey Bonnet' with the verses in C and the choruses in F; before closing with a reprise of the theme song. The trio's personnel consisted of Smith on guitar, Arlo Hults on organ, and Mort Lippman on piano. From 28 July 1949 until the close of the show on 11 August 1949 they appeared under their usual title of the Playboys.

The Dave Garroway Show

Smith was dispatched to Chicago by NBC in order to accompanying the singer Ray Heatherton who was appearing as a guest on the radio program the *Dave Garroway Show* on 6 June 1948. This unusual assignment away from New York testifies to the reputation that Smith had at NBC for his musicianship. Although there undoubtedly must have been capable guitarists on their books in the Windy City, the broadcaster was obviously keen to display his talent. Smith would later appear regularly with Dave Garroway when the presenter was brought to New York.

Here's Jack Kilty

The Playboys were a regular outfit in NBC's radio schedule. They began a relatively long tenure on 13 September 1948 on the radio show *Here's Jack Kilty*. The fifteen-minute program ran at lunchtime for five days per week until its end eight months later on 13 May 1949 when Kilty moved to Britain in order to appear as Curly in a stage production of *Oklahoma!* in London's West End.

Smith, Hults and Lippman provided music to accompany the stories that Kilty narrated during the programs. Once again, they were called upon to perform a diverse range of repertoire, including songs by Arlo Guthrie, Cole Porter, Burl Ives, and Rodgers and Hart, as well as American and British folk music.

The Rey Rodel Program

The eponymous host of the *Rey Rodel Program* was a Yugoslavian-born baritone singer who was making his American radio debut. His five-minute show, which was broadcast at 6:30 p.m. each weekday night, ran for three months from 22 November 1948 until 18 February 1949, and featured performances of ballads, popular pieces and folk songs. Smith, Lippman and Hults worked throughout the series as the Playboys, providing accompaniments for Rodel. The guitarist picked up a valuable tip from Rodel on a cold and rainy day, that he would later use to keep Bing Crosby warm during an outdoor concert. In 2012, he recalled, "Oh, Rey Rodel. He's the guy that I saw stuff newspapers... I was doing this show with him. He came in, and he had his shirt all stuffed with newspapers. That's where I got the idea to do it for Bing."

The Playboys

Smith, Hults and Lippman earned their own fifteen-minute NBC radio program at 12:15 p.m. on Wednesday 23 February 1949. Simply titled *The Playboys*, the show featured a typically broad range of music genres. With Mel Brandt as the announcer, the trio opened with the signature tune of Duke Ellington and Irving Mills' 'Sophisticated Lady', before following with Sullivan and Ruskin's 'I May Be Wrong', Johannes Brahms' 'Hungarian Dance No.5', the Gershwin brothers' 'Someone to Watch over Me', Morton Gould's 'Pavanne', and Fats Waller and Andy Razaf's 'Honeysuckle Rose'.

The Eddie Albert Show

The Playboys were also the house-band on the *Eddie Albert Show* from 10 October 1949 until 7 April 1950. The *NBC Index Cards* describe the Monday-through-Friday thirty-minute broadcasts as "a morning variety program starring Eddie Albert, star of stage, screen, and television and radio as emcee and vocalist in informal entertainment featuring songs, anecdotes, and chatter."

Aside from Smith, Hults and Lippman, the other regularly featured contributors were Beryl Richards and Jack Arthur. Meanwhile, the visiting guests included singer Nick Lucas; Eddie Albert's wife, Margo; writer Les Lieber; Maid of Cotton pageant winner Elizabeth McGee; and Albert's dresser

Bill Gadsden. From its start until 17 February 1950, the program was broadcast from New York. The show on 13 February 1950 was written as a spoof of hillbilly radio programs and significantly drew upon Smith's musical roots. This was followed by a show on the following day that featured a quiz between the guests and the regular cast members. The Quiz Kids team were pitted against Arthur, Richards, Hults, Lippman and Smith, with Albert taking the role of the quiz master. The program then moved to Hollywood from 20 February 1950 until its end on 7 April 1950 in order to accommodate the big screen commitments of Albert, who was filming Lloyd Bacon's *The Fuller Brush Girl* with Lucille Ball at the time. Mort Lippman stayed in New York and was replaced at the piano by Sanford Gold. Announcer Jack Arthur and vocalist Beryl Richards also remained in New York, to be replaced by Eddie King and Brookes Randall respectively. Meanwhile Smith, Hults and the new recruit Gold continued under the name of the Playboys until the series ended. Smith recalled enjoying a well-earned rest during his dispatch to the West Coast:

> I was doing a show with Eddie Albert. He got called to go to California to do that film with Lucille Ball called *The Fuller Brush Girl*. I was working with that trio. You know, Arlo and... So, we went out to the West Coast. We taped all of the shows for the week in two to three hours, and then I had the rest of the time off. So, it was great.

Sammy Kaye's Disc Jockey Discoveries

On 12 May 1950, Smith took part in a new NBC evening radio show titled *Sammy Kaye's Disc Jockey Discoveries*. The network's archives describe the concept of the show:

> NBC presents a special program, a new type of amateur program in which outstanding disc jockeys from NBC affiliate stations select local talent to be auditioned over the network. The winner in the competition and the disc jockey who discovered him are presented with RCA television sets, and all participants and disc jockeys receive Benrus wrist watches.

As one of the contestants, Smith was presented by Norman Brokenshire of WNBC in New York. Also in the competition were singer Marjorie Shearer, who was supported by Al Ross of WBAL in Baltimore; baritone Dick Estes, who was championed by Dick Tucker of WBZ in Boston; and, perhaps bizarrely, elocutionist Irving Goldstein, who was presented by Bob Steele of WTIC in Hartford, Connecticut.

In receiving more audience applause than any of the other contestants, the show and the RCA television sets were won by Smith and Brokenshire. It should be noted, however, that this was an 'amateur' talent contest and that the guitarist had been a staff musician at NBC for three years by 1950. Sixty years later, he coyly recalled his memories of the show:

> Oh, I wasn't supposed to win. They had three acts booked for the show, and they asked me to make up the numbers and be the fourth act. I got the most audience applause, but I wasn't supposed to win [laughs]. I think I played *Hora Staccato*.

Star Time, the Kreisler Bandstand, the Ken Murray Show, and Benny Goodman

Smith made several appearances with the clarinetist and bandleader Benny Goodman in a slot called 'Club Goodman' on the DuMont Television Network's hour-long variety show *Star Time*, which starred Frances Langford. Sponsored by the Food Store Programs Corporation, the live series was broadcast on Tuesday nights at 11 p.m. between 5 September 1950 and 27 February 1951. Goodman's thirteen-week commitment ran from the show's start until 28 November 1950.

Benny Goodman

Unfortunately, although the programs were recorded onto kinescopes only a limited number appear to have survived. In 1958, much of DuMont's library was destroyed in order to recover its valuable silver content. Most of those which had escaped recycling are reputed to have been deposited in the Upper New York Bay during the 1970s. Two complete shows featuring Goodman are known to have survived, and are currently held in the *Film and Television Archive* at the University of California, Los Angeles. These were originally broadcast on 21 and 28 November 1950.

By 1950, Goodman had decided to take a break from his full orchestra and return to his earlier sextet format. Rather than attempt to regroup the survivors of his original lineup, he recruited new and younger musicians who would also provide the outfit with new arrangements. In joining the group, Smith found himself taking the chair of one of his early idols, the late Charlie Christian. As a guitarist and an arranger, he not only played in Goodman's new sextet, but also in his subsequently revived orchestra from 1950 until 1951. With a personnel of Johnny Smith; Teddy Wilson; Terry Gibbs; Bob Carter; and Terry Snyder, who was replaced by Charlie Smith for the November programs, the Benny Goodman Sextet's pre-recorded performances for *Star Time* during 1950 were as follows:

'Slipped Disc' and 'Come Rain or Come Shine' (5 September)
'Three Little Words' (12 September)
'Get Happy', 'Body and Soul' and 'Somebody Loves Me' (19 September)
'Just One of Those Things', 'Maybe My Baby Loves Me' and 'Temptation Rag' (26 September)
'Lullaby of the Leaves', 'Blues in the Night' and 'After You've Gone' (3 October)
'Memories of You', 'Blue Skies', 'The Jazz Me Blues' and 'The World Is Waiting for Sunrise' (10 October)
'It's Only a Paper Moon', 'Limehouse Blues' and 'Jamboree Jones' (17 October)
'Oh Babe' and 'Airmail Special' (24 October)
'Rose Room' and 'Temptation Rag' (31 October)
'On the Sunny Side of the Street' and 'Rachel's Dream' (7 November)
'Avalon', 'Just One of Those Things' and 'China Boy' (14 November)
'These Foolish Things', and 'Honeysuckle Rose' (21 November)
'Stompin' at the Savoy' and 'I Want to Be Happy' (28 November)

Smith also recorded seven 78rpm discs with Goodman's sextet during the year, including 'Oh Babe', 'You're Gonna Lose Your Gal' and 'Walkin' with the Blues' in a session on 10 October 1950. This was followed by 'Lullaby of the Leaves', 'Then You've Never Been Blue', 'Walkin'' and 'Temptation Rag' in another session on 24 November 1950.

In an interview for Massachusetts' *Springfield Sunday Republican* newspaper, which was published on 19 November 1950, Goodman praised the line-up of his new sextet. He unsympathetically criticized the many former members of his sixteen-piece orchestra who had moved on to lead their own groups. He added that the sextet format caused him less aggravation when it was necessary to find musicians to deputize for absentees.

After a winter break, Goodman reassembled his sextet in March 1951. The personnel now consisted of Johnny Smith, Teddy Wilson, Terry Gibbs, Eddie Safranski and Jo Jones. On 21 March, the sextet appeared on the ABC Television Network's *Kreisler Bandstand*. Aside from playing 'After You've Gone' as a unit, part of the group's duties included providing accompaniment for singers Mel Tormé and Peggy Lee.

On 1 April 1951, just eleven days before appearing on the concert stage at Carnegie Hall to perform Alban Berg's *Wozzeck* under the baton of Dimitri Mitropoulos, the versatile Smith was playing swing jazz with Goodman at the famous concert for the Fletcher Henderson Fund. An article in the *Billboard* on 14 April 1951 brought the recording of the concert to the wide attention of the public. Although the event had been broadcast to the people of New York on the WNEW radio station, only a specially invited audience consisting of friends and representatives from the press had been physically present at the performance. According to the *Billboard* article, twelve-inch discs were available solely through the disc jockey Martin Block, who had instigated the event to raise money for the arranger Fletcher Henderson after he had suffered a paralytic stroke. Block was a vibrant campaigner for a revival of swing music. The limited pressing of 2,500 records, which were supplied by Columbia at cost price, were sold for a nominal fee of $7 each, although purchasers were offered the opportunity to donate more if they so wished.

On the eve of the concert for the Fletcher Henderson Fund, tragedy struck when Smith's house in Long Island burned down while he was out dining with the guitarist Mary Osborne and her husband. As well as his home, he also lost his beloved dog and his first D'Angelico guitar in the fire. For a while, he stayed with his pianist friend and NBC colleague Sanford Gold until he was able to find somewhere to live.

Smith made several more recordings with Goodman in 1951. As a member of the clarinetist's full orchestra, he recorded 'Down South Camp Meetin'', 'Mean to Me', 'South of the Border' and 'Muskrat Ramble' on 26 April, followed by 'Lulu's Back in Town', 'Stardust', 'Wrappin' It Up' and 'King Porter Stomp' on 29 April. In May and early June, he took time off from his NBC schedule to join Goodman's sextet on tour. The group recorded 'Farewell Blues' and 'Toodle-Lee-Yoo-Doo' on 13 June. Later in the year, on 22 September, the sextet appeared on the *Ken Murray Show* on the CBS Television Network. The personnel on this occasion consisted of Johnny Smith, Terry Gibbs, Bernie Leighton, Eddie Safranski and Terry Snyder. With Smith remaining on board, the full orchestra reconvened to record 'When Buddha Smiles' and 'Sunrise Serenade' on 26 September. Despite the implication of the significant number of television shows, live appearances and recordings, Smith's work within Goodman's sextet did not constitute membership on a full-time basis. He was primarily still a staff member at NBC.

Goodman had a notorious reputation as a leader who was difficult for many band members to tolerate. In reminiscing about his time with the clarinetist, Smith recalled that he wrote the arrangements of 'Lullaby of the Leaves' and 'Temptation Rag' for Goodman, which they recorded in a converted church in New York City. He also recalled a typical example of the clarinetist's behavior:

> I remember that I did a couple of arrangements for a recording date. The first thing that we did was 'Lullaby of the Leaves'. I did that arrangement. Then, I gave him a bill for the arrangement. Then, for the rest of the sessions [laughs], he didn't give me any solos.

Mundell Lowe, who took over from Smith as Goodman's guitarist in the sextet, elaborates upon the behavior that he, Smith and many other members of the clarinetist's group had to endure:

> I worked with Benny Goodman five times. He fired me twice and I quit three times. He just got to an impossible stage. You know, you might do something or say something that he didn't like and he would give you the stare. Intimidate you. This went on until one night I went up to him and said, “Benny, I love your playing, but as a man you're full of shit. I'm leaving you.”
>
> I have a wonderful story from Red Norvo, who played with him for quite a time. He used to do the same thing to Red. Well, Red told me that on one occasion when he [Goodman] started this, Red went over and put his arm around Benny's shoulder and said, “Benny, you're absolutely correct. I don't deserve to be in your band. I'm not good enough.” Well, Benny Goodman did a reversal and put his arm around Red's shoulder. He said, “My boy, I want you to be in this band! You're most important to this orchestra!” He did a complete flip-flop, which gives you an insight into Benny Goodman.
>
> He would try to squeeze you for the last dollar, talk you down. Here's an example. Years ago, they were doing *The Benny Goodman Story*. I was living in Connecticut at the time, and he was living nearby. One Saturday morning, he called me and said, “Pops, we're going to do *The Benny Goodman Story* and I want you and [George] Duvivier to go out to the coast and be the main part of the band. Next Friday, come into the office on Madison Avenue and pick up your ticket. I'll see you out on the coast.” Well, I went in to the office. Miriam, who was running the office, handed me the ticket and said, “That'll be $350.” I said, “No, no, it doesn't work like that. Either the studio pays the cost or the leader pays the cost.” All hell broke loose. Benny came in, chewing his tongue like he did and said, “Errm, no, you have to pay that.” So, I took Benny into his office and I told him, “Benny, I should take that clarinet and shove it up your ass. You know, and I know, that what you're doing is against union rules and it's wrong.” He wouldn't have it. So, I said, “I don't want to do your damn show. I've already taken leave of absence from NBC for two weeks. So, get somebody else.” I knew who he was going to call. The guitarist. So, I went straight home, called him, and explained what had happened. I said, “You must do me a favor. We've been friends for a while. When Benny calls to ask you, you must double the figure.” So, he did this, and Benny hit the ceiling, but he had to pay him.
>
> We enjoyed playing the music. If you could get past his personality, then everything was fine. Once we got off the bandstand, we would just run away from him. I didn't want any kind of social scene with him. I just wanted to be one of the musicians. When it's over I don't know you until the next time. He was like that with a lot of guys.

Mundell Lowe's testimony that the attraction of playing with Goodman lay in the quality of the music was the underlying reason why Smith later agreed to accompany the clarinetist for a show in 1974 at the Red Rocks Amphitheater in Colorado. As he discovered, Goodman's financial practices had not changed during the two decades since they had previously worked together. John Pisano, who also took the guitar-chair in Goodman's group, remembers that there was another side to the clarinetist, however:

> Benny was good with me. I know a lot of people had problems with him, though. George Van Eps played with Benny Goodman for a while. George told me that one of the guys in the orchestra had serious health issues. Benny went and paid the whole hospital bill without telling anybody. George had heard all the stories about Benny, but he said there was another side to him.

The Chamber Music Society of Lower Basin Street

The *Chamber Music Society of Lower Basin Street* was a radio series which combined a serious approach to jazz music with the authoritative but humorous outlook that was usually associated with classical music programs. The description on the *NBC Index Cards* of this Moe Gale package, which began on 8 July 1950, continues:

> While the program spoofs and satirizes the "long-haired musicians," albeit good-naturedly, most of the cast members have serious musical backgrounds. The selections performed are varied and the musicians get a brief rest while the "Intermission Commentary" feature is presented in each broadcast. The series is dedicated to "The Three B's – Barrelhouse, Boogie Woogie, and Blues."

The show's resident orchestra was the Dixieland Octet, which was sometimes referred to as the Barefoot Philharmonic, and was conducted by Henry 'Hot Lips' Levine. Jane 'Dixiecup' Pickens and the Escourtiers performed most of the vocal work. Significantly, there were two frequently featured instrumentalists. One of these was trombonist Fletch Philburn. The other was Johnny Smith, who was also a member of Levine's orchestra.

Broadcast for thirty minutes on Saturday nights, the guests included Arthur Fiedler, conductor of the Boston Pops Orchestra; Dr Martin Hellman, musicologist; Alec Templeton, pianist and composer; Dr Erich Leinsdorf, conductor of the Rochester Symphony; W.C. Handy; George Simon, co-editor of *Metronome* magazine; comedian Jackie Gleason; and pianist Skitch Henderson. The show on 2 September 1950 featured Smith with his trio of Eddie Safranski on bass and Sanford Gold on piano. Safranski and Gold were also members of the show's orchestra.

The series ran until 30 September 1950. After a lengthy break, it returned on 12 April 1952, half an hour later in the schedule, and continued until 19 July 1952. The guests in this season included Bob Hope, Joan Crawford, Phil Harris and Alice Faye.

The Big Show

MEREDITH WILLSON

TALLULAH BANKHEAD

Smith was a member of Meredith Willson's orchestra on NBC'S aptly titled radio series the *Big Show*, which was a huge, ninety-minute, variety program. Aired on Sunday evenings against CBS' *Jack Benny Program* and hosted by Tallulah Bankhead, it was broadcast from NBC's Center Theater in front of a live audience of three thousand people. Willson had forty-four musicians under his baton for the show, as well as a sixteen-voice choir.

The first series of twenty-seven shows ran from 5 November 1950 until 6 May 1951. A second series of thirty shows began on 30 September 1951 with a program that had been recorded in London and continued until 20 April 1952. The list of guests who appeared on the *Big Show* represented a roll call of show business at the time and included Louis Armstrong, Ella Fitzgerald, Frank Sinatra, Dean Martin, Jerry Lewis, Frankie Laine, Perry Como, Danny Kaye, Rosemary Clooney, Josephine Baker, Carmen Miranda, Marlene Dietrich, Benny Goodman, Peggy Lee, Tony Bennett, Sarah Vaughan, Joe Bushkin, Ethel Merman, Hoagy Carmichael, Victor Borge, Jimmy Durante, Groucho Marx, Bob Hope, José Ferrer, George Sanders, Laurence Olivier, Vivien Leigh, Yul Brynner, Claude Rains, Olivia de Havilland, Rex Harrison, Eddie Fisher, Gary Cooper, Vincent Price, Edward G. Robinson and Patrice Munsel.

The star of the show, however, was its hostess Tallulah Bankhead, who engaged in scripted, acerbic exchanges with her guests, in accordance with her reputation. Smith remembered, "She was a firebrand. I was playing at a restaurant in New York. She came in, and something happened that she didn't like with the Maitre D'. She picked up a chair a flung it right through the restaurant. Oh yeah!"

At a cost of $30,000 per episode, the *Big Show* was extravagant in every sense. It required a vast production team and a huge array of sponsors to contribute to the funding during its two seasons.

Roy Shield and Company

There was one particular NBC radio show which was to have a pivotal effect on Smith's career. *Roy Shield and Company* was a weekly radio series that began on 3 June 1951, in which the NBC Orchestra, conducted by Shield, performed popular tunes, ballads and symphonic jazz. Each week, two rising singers, one male and one female, were featured with accompaniment by members of the orchestra. These vocalists included Jeannie McKeon, George Sawtelle, Jane Morgan, Bob Carroll, Eve

Young, Kitty Crawford, Bob Manners, Ginnie Powell, Don Cherry and Russ Emery. The show was initially broadcast on Saturday evenings before it was moved to late on Friday nights, and then finally to Sunday evenings. The series ran, with two missed weeks, until 23 September 1951.

Smith was both a member of the show's orchestra and a featured soloist, performing regularly from the second broadcast and throughout the remaining twelve shows with his own small instrumental group. Crucially, the genesis of his move into the New York jazz scene is to be found in this radio program. Shield, had assembled a large orchestra and asked Smith to form a small combo within it, providing one arrangement per week. The personnel continually revolved depending upon which of Smith's NBC colleagues were available. He already knew the pianist Sanford Gold and was able to persuade NBC to hire him for his combo. The group was usually announced as the Johnny Smith Quintet, although at times it was called Johnny Smith and his Pilgrims, which Smith attributed to Shield's reference to his background in Maine. Gold would return the favor by being a crucial element in Smith's successful launch onto the jazz scene. The guitarist appreciatively remembered both the show and Roy Shield:

Roy Shield

> He was a contractor for NBC. He was the man who hired me for NBC originally. Roy Shield. He was from Chicago. He did all of the hiring and firing of the musicians at NBC. They called him the contractor. We did a big show... He had a big orchestra and he asked me to form a small group. I got him to hire Stan Getz. Stan wanted to get off the road and everything. That's where the original quartet started.

Bob and Ray

The popular comedians Bob Elliott and Ray Goulding began their own daytime radio series *Bob and Ray* on 2 July 1951. The music for the fifteen-minute, Monday-through-Friday, tea-time program was provided by the Paul Taubman Trio, which consisted of Taubman on organ, Sanford Gold on piano, and Johnny Smith on guitar. The *NBC Index Cards* indicate that the leader's tenure ended on 20 July 1951 and that Mort Lippman conducted the trio on 23 July 1951. From the following day's broadcast until 10 August 1951, the Arlo Hults Trio took over. This group was therefore the Playboys performing under an alternative name. Lippman conducted when Hults was absent, such as on 6 August 1951. Paul Taubman returned to lead the trio on 13 August 1951 until the show's end as a sustaining program on 29 February 1952.

Elliott and Goulding were awarded an additional program on 7 July 1951. This was an hour-long variety show on Saturday nights. The guest on the first broadcast was the jazz vocalist Peggy Lee, followed a week later by Kitty Crawford. The music for these two shows was provided by Paul Taubman's Quintet. For the third show on 21 July 1951, which saw Peggy Lee making a return appearance, the music was performed by Arlo and the Playboys. The group continued as the show's house-band until 11 August 1951. Taubman then returned to lead his quintet on 18 August 1951. From 25 August 1951, the music was provided by the eight-piece Alvy West Orchestra.

> Smith retained fond memories of working with the two comedians and impersonators: Bob and Ray. Yeah, I worked with them. They were very funny! I fell off the stool laughing at them once. They had an audience for them on their show, with a microphone pointing out at the audience. They kept hearing this funny sound and couldn't figure out what was causing it. The engineers came down. They checked the control room and everything. Finally... There was this old boy who used to come down. They called him 'Gates Ajar'. He used to sit in the front row. It was his hearing aid that was causing the problems [laughs].

Hollywood Love Story

Sometimes, Smith was called upon to make isolated contributions to some of NBC's programs. For example, on 25 August 1951 he was required to play the guitar on a single episode of the radio drama series *Hollywood Love Story*, which ran from June 1951 until January 1953.

Armour and Co Dial Dave Garroway

In December 1951, Smith found himself working again with presenter Dave Garroway. This time, it was on the *Armour and Co Dial Dave Garroway* program. The eponymous host had previously broadcast for NBC from Chicago where the Art Van Damme Quintet had been his regular house-band from 4 September 1950 until 7 December 1951. The program then moved to New York, where the Red Norvo Orchestra provided the music for a week before Smith and a small combo took over from 19 December 1951 until 4 January 1952. The guitarist was the conductor and musical director for the show.

Saturday Night Review

Smith and his quintet were regularly featured on NBC's short-lived *Saturday Night Review* radio program from its premiere on 2 February 1952 until its close on 22 March 1952. The original cast was headed by the singer and former British Forces' wartime favorite Vera Lynn. She left the show after her appearance on 16 February 1952 and returned to England. The rest of the cast, which included vocalists Kay Armen and Bob Carroll, Roy Shield and his Orchestra, Johnny Smith and His Quintet, and announcer Dick Dudley, remained on board. Interviewed in 2011 about her time on this show, Dame Vera Lynn recalled that it was one of the most treasured memories of her long career.

Luncheon with Buster Crabbe

NBC's Saturday radio series *Luncheon with Buster Crabbe* heavily featured the Johnny Smith Trio throughout its weekly run from 20 December 1952 until 7 February 1953. The program, which was broadcast from the Hotel Shelton in New York City, was a mix of variety show, amateur talent contest and promoter of good citizenship among children. This last aspect was conducted through general knowledge competitions and inspirational interviews with children who had carried out acts of heroism. While the show was hosted by the former swimmer and actor Buster Crabbe, the special guests included basketball player Walter Dukes; the Executive Director of the Boys Clubs of New York, Peter Copra; singer Johnny Johnston; Cub Master Mel Hammer; actor Gabby Hayes; and baseball player Jackie Robinson. Meanwhile, the Johnny Smith Trio provided all of the music, including the accompaniments and bridges.

Best Plays

The aforementioned *Hollywood Love Story* was not an isolated example of Smith's occasional contributions to radio dramas. On 6 September 1953, he provided a brief guitar accompaniment for a single program in the NBC series of *Best Plays*. The particular play in question, *Kiss the Boys Goodbye*, required a simple guitar performance while the female lead, Helen Claire, feigned playing along with her own vocal rendition of a Southern folk song.

CHAPTER FOUR:
THE NEW YORK JAZZ SCENE

Smith's schedule at NBC was hectic, to say the least. At one time, he was involved in as many as thirty-seven radio and television shows per week playing guitar, trumpet, violin and viola with orchestras and small combos, as well as composing, conducting and arranging. Although he thoroughly enjoyed the variety of musical styles that he was called upon to perform as a studio musician, he began to develop the desire to focus much more of his attention upon his primary passion of jazz and started to play in New York's nightclubs. He left his position as a full-time staff musician at NBC in 1951, although he remained a union member and continued to accept work from the broadcaster on a freelance basis. He later explained the circumstances of his departure from the full-time staff at NBC:

> The union had 25,000 musicians, so called, but only 5,000 worked. So, anytime that anything came up to vote, the 5,000 didn't amount to anything. All of the rest of the 25,000 voted against the working musicians. We weren't allowed to work on two days per week. I began to get calls to do other shows. They offered a lot of money. I had to quit the staff at NBC, so that I would be allowed to work seven days per week.

Guitarist Steve Silverman remembers a story that his former guitar teacher, Billy Bauer, imparted to him regarding the aftermath of Smith's departure from his post at NBC:

> He [Billy Bauer] took over from Johnny when he left NBC, and he was very quick to say he wasn't hired to replace him. John left, Sanford Gold put in a good word, and Billy was hired. Anyway, they were doing close to forty live broadcasts a week. There was an awful lot of written music involved, over which all had scribbled the agreed-upon changes, intros, endings, modulations and such. Billy was handed Johnny's pile and after stopping a couple of times because Billy wasn't keeping up, they realized Johnny hadn't made a single mark on any of the many pages. All of it had been in his head! He could envision/hear a solo in his mind, pick up a guitar and play it.

One of the first steps in Smith's move into the jazz scene came in a series of engagements that he undertook at the Albert club at 139 East 56th Street in New York City. Following a performance of the Johnny Smith Trio opposite the pianist Cy Walter at the club's gala opening on 25 October 1951, a succession of advertisements for both acts appeared in the New York press between November 1951 and January 1952.

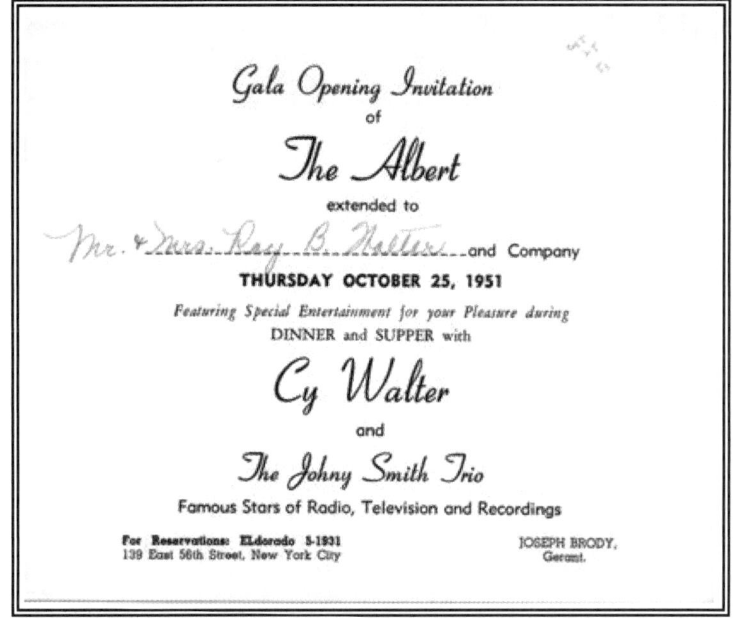

Gala Opening Invitation
of
The Albert
extended to
Mr. & Mrs. Ray B. Walter and Company
THURSDAY OCTOBER 25, 1951
Featuring Special Entertainment for your Pleasure during
DINNER and SUPPER with
Cy Walter
and
The Johny Smith Trio
Famous Stars of Radio, Television and Recordings

For Reservations: ELdorado 5-1931
139 East 56th Street, New York City

JOSEPH BRODY,
Gerant.

AN INVITATION TO THE OPENING OF THE ALBERT CLUB

CY WALTER

Although the Albert club was regularly listed in the 'Goings on about Town' entertainment guide of the *New Yorker*, it was not one of New York's major jazz venues. Smith's residency should not be exaggerated into anything more than the traditional paying-of-dues in a small, fringe establishment along the road to more celebrated clubs.

Remarkably, Smith came fourteenth in *Metronome* magazine's reader's poll for favorite guitarist of 1951 despite having yet to release a record in his own name or make any appearances at New York's major jazz venues. In stepping out from the shadows as a largely anonymous studio musician, he gradually began to establish himself much further with the public.

'Moonlight in Vermont' and Teddy Reig

On 11 March 1952, Smith entered the recording studio with tenor saxophonist Stan Getz, pianist Sanford Gold, bassist Eddie Safranski and drummer Don Lamond to record four pieces – 'Moonlight in Vermont', 'Tabu', 'Where or When' and 'Jaguar'. In the following month, his quintet returned to the recording studio with Zoot Sims in place of Stan Getz, to record 'A Ghost of a Chance', 'Vilia', 'My Funny Valentine' and another version of the self-composed 'Jaguar'. Of these titles, 'Moonlight in Vermont' and 'Tabu' were chosen for alternate sides of the first publicly released disc to be issued in Smith's own name.

ZOOT SIMS

Although he was already a revered figure within New York's guitar community, 'Moonlight in Vermont' now brought him to the attention of wider jazz audiences. Reminiscing sixty years later, he had understandably forgotten that his appearances at the Albert Club slightly preceded the recording of his first release, but despite this confusion, he vividly recalled the genesis of the record that he often referred to as 'Moonlight in Vermouth':

> I was strictly a staff musician at that time [at NBC], but I worked for the other networks as long as I didn't work on my days off. I did a program [*Roy Shield and Company*] and I formed a little group within a large orchestra. I would do an arrangement of a song, and we would feature every week on the show. Stan Getz wanted to get off the road, and I got him a job with NBC. So, I formed this group with Stan, Sanford Gold on piano, Eddie Safranski on bass, Don Lamond on drums, and myself. We were featured with a song each week on the program.
>
> My piano player [Sanford Gold] was a friend of Teddy Reig [the owner of Roost Records]. He took an aircheck over to Teddy, and Teddy agreed to record me with Stan Getz and the group that I had at NBC. I did two sides – 'Moonlight in Vermont' and 'Tabu'. Teddy figured that 'Tabu' might make some noise, because it was flashy and up tempo. I went on vacation in Florida, the first one... I went on vacation for two weeks. When I got back to New York, the guys started saying, "Man, your record of 'Moonlight in Vermont' is getting a lot of plays." I couldn't believe it. What happened was that the disc jockeys were using it as background music to talk over. And that was the start of 'Moonlight in Vermont'. It was because of that, that I finally started working in nightclubs. So, 'Moonlight in Vermont' came first.

SANFORD GOLD

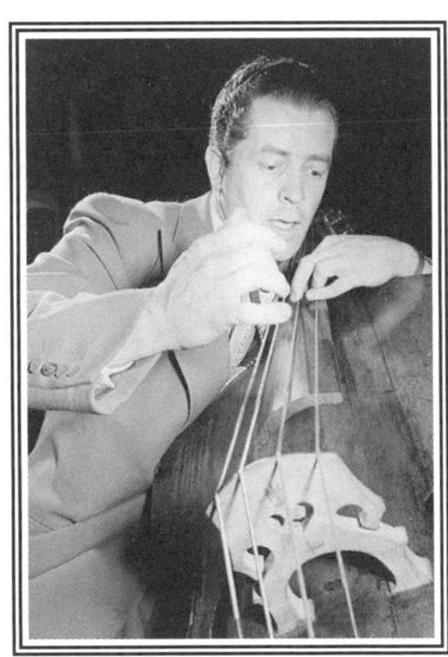
EDDIE SAFRANSKI

DON LAMOND

Smith and Teddy Reig subsequently entered into nothing more than a verbal agreement and a handshake, which they trustingly went on to maintain throughout almost two decades of working together. From 1952, Reig was Smith's de facto manager and acted on the guitarist's behalf in negotiations for bookings at jazz clubs, as well as tours across the USA. It should be noted, however, that although Reig was credited as the producer on many of Smith's albums, he had no input whatsoever.

Reig was a formidable businessman and, by his own admission, something of a hustler. Mundell Lowe endured his own encounter with Reig. Lowe had been booked to play at a party with bassist George Duvivier and singer Sarah Vaughan. On his arrival, he was surprised to find that Reig had set up recording equipment, although he was assured that this was merely for private purposes. The recording was subsequently released by Reig in Sarah Vaughan's name as *After Hours*.

STAN GETZ WITH MILES DAVIS

Despite some underhanded tactics, Reig was extremely protective of his musicians, although it must be acknowledged that he had a vested interest. Smith remembered a particular occasion on which he saved Stan Getz's life:

> When Stan Getz was, you know, on narcotics... Teddy once stood in front of him, because the pushers were going to kill Stan Getz. Yeah, he hadn't made payment. Teddy stood in front of him and kept him from being shot. He was a legend. He never divulged his weight, but it was somewhere around four hundred pounds. But he was like a butterfly on his feet. Oh yeah, you didn't want to mess with him.

The story of Reig's heroic actions at Charlie Parker's funeral is infamous in jazz circles. While carrying the huge casket down the steps outside the Abyssinian Baptist Church on 138th Street in Harlem, one of the pallbearers lost his footing, catching the others off-guard. The Herculean Teddy Reig took most of the casket's weight until the others had regained their positions.

Smith and Reig did not have any great expectations of achieving a hit record, not least of all at their first attempt. While Smith was a behind-the-scenes studio musician who was largely unknown to the jazz public, Royal Roost was a relatively small label without the financial power to promote its artists to the level that they would have been able to enjoy with the main record companies. In fact, there was no promotion of 'Moonlight in Vermont' by Reig at all. It therefore came as a surprise that the response to this first release in Smith's own name was hugely favorable. The record became far more than just a jazz hit. It was also popular with those listeners who did not usually listen to the genre. The jazz pianist Herbie Hancock cited Smith's recording of 'Moonlight in Vermont' has having introduced him to jazz when he was in high school listening to a rhythm 'n' blues radio station. In an interview in *Down Beat* magazine in 1965, he stated that although he did not understand what was going on, he knew that he liked it. Bob Yelin was one of many guitarists who were also initially drawn to the jazz genre by Smith's interpretation of 'Moonlight in Vermont'. As a teenager in 1958, Yelin took guitar lessons from Gus DeGazzio in New York with the typical teenage desire to play the contemporary rock 'n' roll music of Chuck Berry and Bo Diddley. In his second lesson, DeGazzio played him Smith's recording. Yelin still remembers that he had never heard anything so beautiful. He was hooked from that moment onwards and consequently began to listen to other jazz guitarists. The recording also reached Europe where it became a favorite with jazz guitarists there, too. It has even been cited as a favorite of the rock 'n' roll performer Eddie Cochran. Its broad appeal was matched by its longevity. In an article for the *Boston Daily Record* nine years after its release, Bill Buchanan wrote that whenever local disc jockey Norm Nathan invited telephone requests for his radio show on WHDH, someone always called for Smith's 'Moonlight in Vermont'.

Aside from being both a jazz and pop hit, not to mention *Down Beat* magazine's number two jazz record of the year in 1952, 'Moonlight in Vermont' was a landmark recording in the history and development of the electric jazz guitar. Since Charlie Christian's influential recordings with Benny Goodman between 1939 and 1941, jazz guitarists had followed his linear approach to the instrument. The potential of the guitar as a harmonic instrument, capable of pianistic textures and sophisticated counter-melodies, had been neglected. Smith's perfectly smooth and harmonized guitar playing was a totally new sound, and this undoubtedly contributed to its popularity. Meanwhile, the contrasting 'Tabu' demonstrated his startling virtuosity and impeccably clean execution at high speed. In comparison to his recording of *Guitar Interludes for Low Level Background* for Lang-Worth Feature Programs five years earlier, Smith had by now clearly formed a level of sophistication in his musicianship which matched his virtuosity. He had also formed his own distinct musical style. For many jazz guitarists, including Louis Stewart, Smith's recording of 'Moonlight in Vermont' is still as spellbinding now as it was when it was released over sixty years ago. Stewart declares, "Oh my! He was sensational. He has been one of my heroes since I was twelve years of age. I got that 'Moonlight in Vermont' record. You know, the one with Stan Getz. Oh man, I'm still amazed by his playing on it."

TEDDY REIG

FURTHER RECORDINGS

In 1952, 'Where or When' was also released as a single, with 'A Ghost of a Chance' on the opposite side. Before the year ended, Smith's first four sides were united for issue as EP 303, titled *Johnny Smith Quintet: Jazz at NBC*.

MOREY FELD

Despite his increasing success, he continued to work as a freelance musician at NBC while he was scoring jazz hits. With Stan Getz back on board in November 1952, he returned to the recording studio. Sanford Gold once again took his place at the piano while Bob Carter (née Kahakalau) and Morey Feld replaced Safranski and Lamond, respectively. The session produced recordings of 'Sometimes I'm Happy', 'Stars Fell on Alabama', 'Nice Work If You Can Get It' and 'Tenderly'. More singles were issued and these were soon followed by a second EP. 'Tenderly', 'Jaguar', 'My Funny Valentine' and 'Vilia' were released as EP 305, which was somewhat confusingly also titled *Johnny Smith Quintet: Jazz at NBC*. An enthusiastic review of the single 'Jaguar'/'Tenderly' appeared in *Metronome* magazine in June 1953:

> Johnny's associates (Stan Getz, Eddie Safranski, Sanford Gold, Don Lamond) are a help in the well-named 'Jaguar', which Johnny has outfitted with a figure almost as sleek as the elegant British auto of the same name. Johnny's guitar is better displayed in the solo overleaf, however, where he does soft and moving things with the tune, single-string and chords, and Stan contributes a fittingly restrained few measures. Quite a boy, John. (Reproduced from *Metronome*, June 1953)

Smith's uniquely broad taste in his repertoire was already beginning to manifest itself. 'Vilia' was an interpretation of the classical composer Franz Lehár's song '*Vilja*' from his 1905 operetta *Die Lustige Witwe* (*The Merry Widow*).

JAZZ ARTS CONCERT

Smith was not instantly propelled by the success of 'Moonlight in Vermont' and the ensuing record releases into the New York's top jazz venues. Engagements on New York jazz scene only began to open up for him gradually as he continued to pay his dues. He climbed from fourteenth to eighth in the *Metronome* magazine reader's poll for 1952.

On 4 October 1952, NBC transmitted the first program from the Theatre De Lys of a brief, late-night, three-part series called *Jazz Arts Concert*. The theater was certainly not a dedicated jazz venue. The network described the show in its *NBC Index Cards* as:

> A modern music program series which brings together the best in modern music of drama, dance, concert, opera and jazz. Presented direct from the Theatre De Lys, itself a stage innovation, in New York's Greenwich Village, the concerts are staged on a dais which is constructed as a physical composite of the Greek, Coedia and the Elizabethan stage. Different stars of the modern music field are heard each week. The concerts are

conducted by Eddie Safranski, bass player now with the NBC music staff, formerly with the Stan Kenton aggregation.

The guests on the first show, which hit the airwaves at 12:30 a.m., were the Johnny Smith Trio and vocalist Thelma Carpenter. The second show featured Jimmy Rushing and his All-Star Orchestra, pianist Marian McPartland, and vocalist Betty McLaurin. The Johnny Smith Trio returned for the third program on 18 October 1952 when they appeared on the bill opposite the Ink Spots vocal group. The series was then canceled before it had time to feature the broad range of music that had been promised.

Jazz at NBC

In 1953, Smith's first two EPs were amalgamated into his debut album, which to add further confusion was yet again titled *Johnny Smith Quintet: Jazz at NBC*. His technical superiority was acknowledged in a review of the album in the August 1953 issue of *Metronome*:

> Technically, Johnny Smith stands all by himself among present-day guitarists. His skills extend from radio studio salon music to Schönberg to fluent jazz improvisation. Needless to say, the first two categories are not represented here, but the ease and taste which make the rest of his varied career possible do show all over this LP. (Reproduced from *Metronome*, August 1953)

It was a common practice during the 1950s for record companies to encourage the musicians on their books to include their own compositions on their recordings in order to limit royalty payments to other publishers. This was a case in point with Smith's own composition 'Jaguar', which he had previously performed with his combo on NBC's *Roy Shield and Company* radio program. When composing new pieces, it was typical for jazz musicians at the time to use chord changes from existing songs over which they would lay new melodies. Guitarist Larry Coryell remembers a conversation that he had with Smith in which the latter recounted that he was occasionally called upon to compose new pieces at extremely short notice:

> I had asked him about a particular original composition of his (which I believe was based on the changes to 'Cherokee') and he told me that that piece was basically conceived, rehearsed and recorded that same day in the studio. Plus, all this time I for some reason assumed the piece (I can't remember the title) was something he would have played on gigs. Not so. Johnny told me that the recording date was the only time it was played!

Recordings as a Sideman

Although Smith had long since been revered within guitar circles for his studio work, neither the increasing public recognition of his obvious virtuosity, or the huge popularity of 'Moonlight in Vermont', affected his humble opinion of his own worth. While continuing to work as a network studio musician and performing in some of New York's jazz clubs, he also found the time to record as a sideman. By the end of 1952 he had performed as a member of Gene Krupa's orchestra on the unreleased 'Bolero, Part One' and 'Bolero, Part Two'. He also appeared as a member of Sanford Gold's orchestra in accompanying the singer Bob Houston on 'It's Christmas Everyday (When You're in Love)' and 'This Is the Real Thing Now'.

Tom Talbert

Smith's unparalleled versatility was demonstrated on 23 April 1953 when he was featured in a program of music by the contemporary composer Tom Talbert at the Carnegie Recital Hall. With accompaniment provided by strings and woodwinds, Smith performed a four-minute piece titled 'The Wharf'. The concert also included music for a twenty-one-piece orchestra conducted by the composer. A favorable review in the *New York Times* the following day described Talbert's music as a mixture of jazz, Debussy and Stravinsky. Talbert was so impressed by Smith's musicianship that he determined to work with him again as soon as possible.

The Embers

By this time, Smith was beginning to play at New York's more prestigious jazz venues. On 27 April 1953, just four days after his appearance with Tom Talbert at the Carnegie Recital Hall, his Johnny Smith Trio took over from Red Norvo's threesome at the Embers club at 161 East 54th Street for a run that continued until 16 May. One of the combo's performances during this residency was broadcast by NBC radio. The 'Goings on about Town' entertainment guide of the *New Yorker* magazine described the Embers jazz club a year later as "a well-appointed finishing school for warm but subdued jazz musicians." Guitarist Mundell Lowe recalls the then newly established Embers:

> Ralph Watkins opened the Embers. That was his club. He broke away from the Levy brothers, because he didn't like some of the things that they were doing [at Birdland]. Mine was the second group in there. Erroll Garner's trio were first. When he closed, we came in and stayed there for something like a week. The great part about that is that Ralph hired Art Tatum to come in and play at the bar during the intermission. So, the band used to finish for a break, and then rush to the bar for a drink just to hear Art play [laughs].

Divorce and Remarriage

While Smith's career on the jazz scene was on the rise, his domestic life was not running so smoothly. His marriage to his first wife, Gertrude, ended in divorce on 22 May 1953. By the end of the year, he had married Ann Westerstrom, who gave birth to their daughter, Kim, in August 1954.

Ann Westerstrom and Johnny Smith on their wedding day

Johnny Smith with his wife, Ann, and their daughter, Kim

Joe Mooney

Back on the music scene, Smith, Safranski and Lamond were reunited and joined by the blind singer, organist and accordionist Joe Mooney at the organ for the recording of 'Terry's Theme from Limelight' and 'Ramona' on 5 June 1953. These two distinctly non-jazz recordings were initially released as the two sides of a single, but the former would later be also included on the album *Johnny Smith Quintet Featuring Stan Getz*.

Joe Mooney

Mundell Lowe retains fond memories of Joe Mooney and his work at Frank Dailey's Meadowbrook club:

> Well, all the bands used to play there. Now, Frank Dailey originally had a band. Of all people, the arrangements were written by Joe Mooney. He was married to a gal... and he would sit there and dictate, note by note, what she should write on the score. Then, they would have copyists put it together and the band would play it. Joe was always around in those days.

Paul Quinichette

Paul Quinichette

With the personnel of Smith's jazz combo continually revolving according to availability, Stan Getz discovered the desire to tour again. Teddy Reig suggested Paul Quinichette as a replacement. Smith, Quinichette, Gold and Lamond were joined by bassist Arnold Fishkin for a studio session in August 1953 at which they recorded 'Yesterdays', 'I'll Be Around', 'Cherokee' and another Smith composition 'Cavu'. According to the composer Tom Talbert, he wrote the arrangements for this session in his aforementioned determination to work with the guitarist again after their appearance together at the Carnegie Recital Hall.

At the end of the month, Smith received critical recognition for his jazz work when *Down Beat* magazine's critics voted him as their top new star of the guitar.

Hank Jones

Hank Jones

On 4 September 1953, Smith joined bassist Ray Brown in accompanying the pianist Hank Jones for the recording of four pieces at New York's Fine Sound studio. 'Thad's Pad', 'Things Are So Pretty in the Spring', 'Little Girl Blue' and 'Odd Number' were committed to tape, but at only thirteen minutes in duration there was insufficient material for an entire album. Consequently, these recordings were held back and eventually released as one side of Jones' *Urbanity* album in 1956. In his liner notes for the CD re-issue in 1997, Steve Kuhn observed that this session was the first time that Smith and Jones had played together. He also provided a succinct assessment of Smith's musicianship in his approach to accompanying a soloist in adding that "Johnny's style is understated, as he does a lot of close listening in order to underpin the music."

The Joe Bushkin Quartet

Three days after the recording session with Jones, Smith was playing opposite him at the Embers club, as a member of pianist Joe Bushkin's quartet alongside drummer Ed Shaughnessy and bassist George Duvivier. Hank Jones was joined in his own trio by Jo Jones and Tommy Potter. The Bushkin quartet's four-week residency continued until 4 October 1953.

Jazz Studio 1

At the time that Smith had recorded with Paul Quinichette in August 1953, the tenor saxophonist had been under contract to Decca Records, who would only allow him to record for Teddy Reig's Royal Roost label if the guitarist returned the favor by contributing to one of their recordings. Reig had negotiated a deal which allowed him to cite Quinichette's name on the records that he made with Smith on the Roost label, while Decca had to use a pseudonym for the guitarist. Thus, on 10 October 1953, Smith joined Hank Jones, Paul Quinichette, Benny Green, Frank Foster, Joseph Newman, Kenny Clarke and Edward Jones in the recording of the *Jazz Studio 1* album, under the name of 'Sir Jonathan Gasser'. The obvious imbalance of the agreement between the small Roost and the larger Decca may have resulted from Reig's sometimes dubious business activities. Nevertheless, Smith's unique style betrayed his hidden identity from the very first notes of his extended introduction of the opening 'Tenderly'.

Johnny Smith Quintet Featuring Stan Getz

More singles were released by Smith with his own combo. These were again drawn upon to form the core body of two new EPs, both of which were titled *Johnny Smith Quintet Featuring Stan Getz*. EP 310 was comprised of 'Yesterdays', 'Sometimes I'm Happy', 'I'll Be Around' and 'Nice Work If You Can Get It'. Meanwhile, 'Stars Fell on Alabama', 'Cherokee', 'Terry's Theme from Limelight' and 'Cavu' formed EP 311. In 1954, these two EPs were amalgamated for the album which was also titled *Johnny Smith Quintet Featuring Stan Getz*. Although some of the pieces on these discs feature Quinichette rather than Getz, it is clear from the repeated title that Reig was keen to capitalize upon the latter's higher profile.

The Return to the Embers with Bushkin

On 7 December 1953, Smith and Joe Bushkin's combo, which now featured Cozy Cole and Clyde Lombardi in place of Shaughnessy and Duvivier, returned to the Embers, replacing Artie Shaw's Gramercy Five, which had included Hank Jones. In total, Smith spent fifteen weeks performing at the Embers in 1953. His residency with Bushkin's quartet at the club on this particular occasion lasted for over two months, and finally ended on 20 February 1954, after which Artie Shaw returned with his Gramercy Five.

Smith began to receive increasing and positive attention in the music press. A favorable review in the *New Yorker* noted the effect of his presence in mentioning some of the distinctive features of the Joe Bushkin Quartet's sets which were already characteristics of the guitarist's work with his own group and with Hank Jones:

Cozy Cole

CLYDE LOMBARDI

The guitarist, Johnny Smith, is especially brilliant, and because he is allowed plenty of latitude, he gives the quartet an extra dimension. It may be his presence that has persuaded Bushkin to occasionally interweave the two sets of strings – his piano and Smith's guitar – which produces the effect of a musical arrangement. (Reproduced from the *New Yorker*, 6 February 1954)

On an unidentified date in either late 1953 or early 1954, Smith went into the studio on his own to record 'My One and Only Love' and 'Lullaby of Birdland', which were subsequently released together as the two sides of a single. Both recordings featured Smith playing overdubbed guitar duets. His arrangement of George Shearing's tribute to the famous Birdland jazz club was highly original with counter-melodies that evoked a sense of the baroque style. Furthermore, the precision of his timing in the overdubbed track was immaculate.

REACHING THE TOP: BIRDLAND

By now, Smith was well and truly beginning to establish himself on the jazz scene. In February 1954, he won the *Metronome* magazine reader's poll for favorite guitarist of 1953. On 25 March 1954, just over a month after finishing his lengthy engagement with Joe Bushkin at the Embers, and two years after recording 'Moonlight in Vermont', he took up his first billed residency with his quartet at the Birdland club at 1678 Broadway, New York, opposite Sarah Vaughan, and Benny Green and His Orchestra. All three acts closed on 14 April before Dinah Washington, Earl Hines' Orchestra, and Miles Davis and His All-Stars took over.

The significance of this landmark occasion should not be underestimated. Birdland was the apex of New York's jazz scene. The *New Yorker* described the club as “the meeting place of an extremely feverish free-thinking, freewheeling society. The mood is anything-goes progressive.”

Already the biggest selling artist on Reig's small Roost label, Smith soon became a regular feature at Birdland, appearing far more often than any other guitarist. He was popular with both the audiences and his fellow musicians.

THE ENTRANCE TO BIRDLAND

In recognizing the true height of his stature on the New York jazz scene between 1954 and 1958, it is important to catalog the names of the musicians who performed at the same venues around the time of Smith's residencies and who are still celebrated sixty years later. He shared and alternated the bill with legends such as Charlie Parker, Dizzy Gillespie, Bud Powell, Thelonious Monk, Charlie Mingus and Erroll Garner. Parker, who was a good friend of Smith and one of his biggest admirers, frequently made a point of sitting in the front row while the guitarist was playing, in order to listen to him attentively.

FROM QUINTET TO QUARTET

On 9 May 1954, Smith went back into the studio to record four new sides. There were two distinguishing features of his combo at this session. Firstly, he had dispensed with the need for a saxophone and was now fronting a quartet rather than a quintet. In truth, on some of his earlier recordings, such as 'A Ghost of a Chance', the saxophone was under-employed. Secondly, with pianist Sanford Gold no longer available, Perry Lopez stepped in to provide harmonic accompaniment on an additional guitar. Throughout the continual changes to the personnel of the combo, Lopez was the only guitarist to ever play within the group alongside Smith. Later, after leaving the quartet, Lopez would front his own combo in jazz clubs across New York. In what must have been a daunting task, Lopez's presence in Smith's outfit was well justified and his performances were entirely sympathetic to Smith's own guitar work. With Arnold Fishkin on bass and Don Lamond on drums, the quartet recorded 'What's New', 'I'll Remember April', 'Easy to Love' and 'Sophisticated Lady', which were subsequently released as the four sides of two singles.

In an unpublished article for *Down Beat* in 1954, which is currently housed in the library of the Institute of Jazz Studies, the jazz critic George Hoefer observed that the quartet was not inferior in the absence of a pianist. He also revealed that although Smith was the major guitarist on the New York jazz scene by this time, his recordings were still being employed by disc jockeys as mere background music:

> The new sounds emanating from guitarist Johnny Smith's Quartet are being used as background music for disc jockey programs on 56 stations across the country. Smith's transcriptions have found favor as introductory themes and as a pleasant accompaniment

to the chatter between records.

Here in New York City, the avant garde's favorite man with the platters, Al "Moonbo" Collins has been introducing his nightly Collins On The Moon stint over WNEW with a Smith "tranc" entitled 'One and Only Love'. Al avers Johnny's music and has stirred up so much interest that the 'Love' will now be released commercially by Teddy Reig's Royal Roost label.

Both Johnny and Teddy are very enthusiastic about the relaxed things that are happening on the transcriptions. The Smith Quartet has Johnny and Perry Lopez on guitars, Arnold Fishkin, bass, and Don Lamond is on drums. The unusual combination does not miss the piano.

Eddie Condon after listening to one of Johnny's records on Leonard Feather's blindfold test complimented him with the statement, "He doesn't make the electric guitar too offensive."

Within three days of the recording session, Smith and his quartet were appearing at George Wein's Storyville club in Boston, Massachusetts, on 12, 13 and 15 May. By now, his profile on the New York jazz scene was well established. On 14 July 1954, he was featured as a guest on the ABC radio series the *Whiteman Varieties*, which was a vehicle for the legendary Paul Whiteman and his orchestra with singer Shirley Harmer.

The 1954 Newport Jazz Festival

Further evidence of Smith's stature in the jazz community at this time can be found in his next major engagement, which was at Rhode Island's inaugural *Newport Jazz Festival* over the weekend of 17 and 18 July 1954 at the Newport Casino Clubhouse. The festival's official title for that year was the *First American Jazz Festival*, although the media preferred to use the shorter title which would be adopted by the promoters in the following year. The event was sponsored by Elaine and Louis Lorillard, who employed the knowledgeable and well-connected jazz impresario George Wein as its organizer.

There were no minor figures on the bill. Those present were the cream of the jazz scene during a golden era. The *Billboard* reported on 31 July that the Saturday night show had consisted of performances by the Eddie Condon Combo; the Modern Jazz Quartet; Dizzy Gillespie; the Lee Konitz Quartet; the Oscar Peterson Trio; the Gerry Mulligan Quartet; Ella Fitzgerald; the John Lewis Trio; and a jam session led by Stan Kenton at the piano. Thirty minutes of the Saturday concert was broadcast by ABC radio. The running order on the Sunday night featured a tribute to Count Basie by his sidemen; the Oscar Peterson Trio; Johnny Smith with the Oscar Peterson Trio; Dizzy Gillespie; the George Shearing Quintet; the Gil Mellé Quartet; the Teddy Wilson Group; Lennie Tristano and Lee Konitz; Billie Holiday with Buck Clayton, Lester Young, Gerry Mulligan, Vic Dickenson, Teddy Wilson, Milt Hinton and Jo Jones; and the Gene Krupa Trio. Smith's presence alongside so many celebrated names of the jazz world not only testifies to the high profile that he had with the public during the 1950s, but it also highlights his stature among his fellow musicians as a jazz guitarist. Clearly, he had earned his place at the festival alongside contemporaries of the highest regard.

The mere thought of the performance by Smith with the Oscar Peterson Trio, which reunited him with bassist Ray Brown, alongside guitarist Herb Ellis and the pianist Peterson, is mouthwatering for any jazz guitarist. Gene Bertoncini explains the excitement of such a collaboration:

> Wow! Now, I remember, he did do some work with Oscar. That must have been phenomenal, because he had the same chops that Oscar had. I mean, the other guys had chops... like Barney [Kessel] and Herb [Ellis], but Johnny's chops flowed more like Oscar's did.

The script with which Stan Kenton introduced Smith to the audience acknowledged the guitarist's position as the unrivaled master of his instrument:

> It is an axiom in jazz that if a musician wants to be a major jazzman, he must know his instrument, its range and its possibilities even better than he knows himself. The reason, of course, is that the better you know your instrument, the more extensively and intensively you can improvise on it. The fact that jazzmen today can do literally astonishing things on their instruments comes from that knowledge. A good example is our next soloist. Like many young jazz musicians, his training has been both the classical and jazz disciplines. In the classical field, he has performed during his staff duties at NBC with a number of symphonic groups. He has recorded the Schönberg *Serenade for Septet and Baritone* under the direction of Dimitri Mitropoulos, and has performed under other prominent conductors.
>
> As a jazz musician, his performances at Birdland and Storyville and on Royal Roost records have introduced jazz followers to an artist of unusual control over shades of tone color and rhythmic dynamics... His is a subtle art and often a very tender one... A man who is a thorough master of all the possibilities of his instrument.... JOHNNY SMITH.

Understandably, Smith's set featured a version of his hit record 'Moonlight in Vermont'. The four pieces from Peterson's own set were eventually released on his album *Canadian Keys*. Unfortunately, the recordings of Smith's performances with the trio remain unreleased, and ABC did not return for another broadcast on the second night of the festival. Sadly, this was the only occasion upon which Smith worked with Peterson, and it was cruelly sabotaged by the weather which very nearly cost him his life:

OSCAR PETERSON

> Oh boy. Yes... Well... They just hired me in, and they signed Oscar Peterson to back me up with his trio. It was raining and the weather was terrible. Every time I went to play... Every time I touched the strings, I got shocked. There was water on the stage and evidently it shorted something out. That's how I tried to play – being shocked. It was terrible. I didn't enjoy that one bit! I was embarrassed.

The journalist Howard Taubman initially gave an extremely favorable review of the groundbreaking festival in the *New York Times* on 19 July 1954, writing that the organizers' optimistic hopes of an audience of 5,000 were exceeded by figures which were closer to 7,000. However, by 25 July he had taken more time to reflect upon the events of the previous weekend. He sympathized with the musicians who merely wanted to play, but he felt that by including panel discussions the well-intended organizers had been guilty of pontificating too much about jazz music, its meaning and its history. Furthermore, he felt that they had fallen short by not putting an infrastructure in place that could cope with the underestimated audience numbers for what was a highly publicized event. The jazz critic Marshall Stearns, who contributed significantly to the organization of the festival, wrote a private letter to George Wein on 3 August 1954 in which he addressed Taubman's comments:

> Did you see Howard Taubman's review in the *Sunday Times*? He heard Saturday night only and wrote as if he preferred the *JATP* [*Jazz at the Philharmonic*] “Go-Go-Go” type of performance. I don't think he knows or cares what it's all about, and since he is the music editor I don't see how we could have a reply printed. I would write it, too, since he missed the whole point AND the panel. But Wilder Hobson's piece in *Newsweek* was fine. And Lillian Ross' piece comes out next week in the *New Yorker*.... keep your fingers crossed.

Correspondents from *Esquire*, *Life*, *Time* and even France's *Le Figaro*, were also present at the festival. Despite the shortcomings that were highlighted by Taubman, and the torrential Sunday night rain, the festival was a huge commercial and artistic success. In a letter to George Wein on 8 May 1954, Louis Lorillard had estimated that the cost for “talent” would be $10,000. The final statement of accounts, which was issued on 28 September 1954, shows that the actual cost was $14,750. Nevertheless, the festival returned a profit of over $4,000.

Radio, Live from Birdland

On 5 August 1954, Smith's quartet returned to Birdland for a run which saw them playing opposite the Count Basie Orchestra, the Modern Jazz Quartet and the Billy Taylor Trio. The residency was completed by the end of the month, at which time Dinah Washington, Charlie Parker and Dizzy Gillespie took over. One of Smith's performances during his tenure was broadcast by NBC. On 25 June 1954, the network had begun a new radio series called *Hear America Swingin'*, which it described in its *NBC Index Cards* as:

> A new popular music program series designed to give listeners “ringside tables” at the nation's top nite spots where dinner and dance music is being presented by the country's name orchestras, star vocalists and popular recording artists as they are playing regular engagements at these entertainment spots.

The first show, which was subtitled *Stars in Jazz*, was twenty-five minutes long and was broadcast at 8 p.m., but in the ensuing weeks the program extended to two hours in duration with two news-breaks and also half-hourly regular station breaks. Each act was awarded between fifteen and thirty minutes of live airtime, although some performances were recorded prior to broadcast. Venues included the Starlight Roof at the Waldorf-Astoria Hotel, Basin Street, the Embers club and the Birdland club. Notable artists who were featured on the radio show included the George Shearing Quintet at the Embers club; Sarah Vaughan at Birdland; Rosemary Clooney; Percy Faith and his Orchestra; the Harry James Orchestra; the Billy May Orchestra; the Stan Kenton Orchestra; the Modern Jazz Quartet; Count Basie and His Orchestra; Perez Prado and His Orchestra; Les Paul and Mary Ford; Louis Armstrong and His All-Stars; the Woody Herman Orchestra; Charlie Parker and His Strings; Jimmy and Tommy Dorsey; and on 20 August 1954, the Johnny Smith Quartet from Birdland.

It was a common occurrence for Smith's gigs at Birdland to be broadcast over the radio. Disc jockey Bob Garrity broadcast the *Birdland Show* on the WABC 770 radio station from midnight to 6 a.m., seven nights per week, with live sections from the club. The guitarist and educator Jack Petersen remembers how, as a youngster, he first heard Smith on the radio:

> Oh, I guess it was back in high school in the late '40s or early '50s. Out of New York... I think it was on Tuesday nights, maybe, after all the news was done on the radio from ten to ten-thirty, you could turn the knob and catch bands from all over the country. Chicago, New York, L.A., New Orleans, everywhere. And they would have a shot from Birdland. I remember, the first time I ever heard Johnny was with his quartet playing at Birdland on the radio.

In a Mellow Mood

On 10 September 1954, Smith, Lopez, Fishkin and Lamond went back into the recording studio. Some of the material that was recorded during this session was amalgamated with the four sides from their previous visit to the studio earlier in the year and was issued as the album *In a Mellow Mood*. Five titles from the September recording session were held back for later release. The *Billboard* was quick to acknowledge Smith's virtuosity in its review of the album:

> Most welcome is this collection of eight standard tunes as delicately handled by guitarist Johnny Smith – a most remarkable man for a modern-day "progressive" musician. He's got all the technical ability plus warmth and sincerity. Backed by Don Lamond on drums, Arnie Fishkin on bass, and, at times, Perry Lopez on rhythm guitar, Smith turns in a wonderful session of expressive musical interpretations. Recording is excellent and when the fans hear it, they'll have to buy. (Reproduced from the *Billboard*, 8 January 1955)

Stan Kenton and the Festival of Modern American Jazz

Smith continued to enjoy the freedom to accept bookings which had not been available to him when he was a full-time staff musician at NBC. It is impossible, however, to perceive any lightening in his workload after he left the network's full-time employment. Aside from his increasingly prolific appearances in New York's jazz clubs, and recording his own albums, he continued to work for all of the major networks. Meanwhile, Teddy Reig had been conducting negotiations which resulted in Smith joining Stan Kenton's second *Festival of Modern American Jazz* tour in the autumn of 1954.

Kenton's first outing under this banner had included jazz luminaries such as Charlie Parker and Dizzy Gillespie and had returned well financially. He began preparations for the second tour during the summer of 1954. In an article for the *Billboard* on 5 June 1954, he declared his intention to showcase young jazz talent this time around. Kenton was a passionate campaigner for jazz education and later became a crucial figure through his Kenton Clinics. However, the reality of commercial pressures enforced a change of mind with regard to this particular tour and it soon became apparent to him that he would once again have to feature established jazz figures in order to maximize the ticket sales' revenue, if only to break even. Smith was thirty-two years old at the time and he was flying high on the New York jazz scene. Meanwhile, the legendary pianist Art Tatum, who was also on the tour, was forty-four years old and experiencing a resurgent interest in his music from new audiences. The other featured soloists were Charlie Ventura, Mary Ann McCall, Shorty Rogers and his Giants, Shelly Manne, and Candido.

Kenton's tour began on 16 September at San Diego's Balboa Park Ballroom, followed by a concert at the Shrine Auditorium in Los Angeles on 17 September, and then further appearances at major venues across North America. These included the Golden Gate Theater in Oakland, California, on 18 September; the Arena Auditorium in Oakland, California, on 19 September; the Public Auditorium in Portland, Oregon, on 21 September; the Civic Auditorium in Seattle, Washington, on 23 September; the Municipal Auditorium in Kansas City, Kansas, on 27 September; Paramount Theater in Omaha, Nebraska, on 28 and 29 September; the Public Music Hall in Cleveland, Ohio, on 7 October; the Syria Mosque in Uniontown, Pennsylvania, on 8 October; Carnegie Hall in New York on 9 October; Boston's Symphony Hall on 10 October; a return to the Syria Mosque in Uniontown, Pennsylvania, on 11 October; the Bushnell Memorial Stage in Hartford, Connecticut, on 13 October; two performances at the Lincoln Theater in Trenton, New Jersey, on 15 October; two shows at the Opera House in Chicago, Illinois, on 23 October; the Bowling Green High School in Park City, Kentucky, on 25 October; the Forum in Montreal, Canada, on 2 November; the War Memorial in Syracuse, New York, on 3 November; two shows at the Paramount Theater in Brooklyn, New York, on 6 November; the Mosque in Richmond, Virginia, on 10 November; the Raleigh Memorial Auditorium, Raleigh, North Carolina, on 11 November; the Bell Auditorium in Augusta, Georgia, on 13 November; an unidentified venue in Mobile, Alabama, on 19 November; and the New Loyola Field House in New Orleans on 20 November. The tour ended on 21 November 1954. The package, which was handled by the Gale Agency, covered a grueling seventy consecutive nights, coast-to-coast, across America. As well as the advertised performers, the entourage also featured Kenton's own twenty-piece orchestra, which included Lee Konitz, Frank Rosolino, Conte Candoli, Milt Bernhart and Maynard Ferguson, with the bandleader doubling as the Master of Ceremonies. The accompaniment for Smith's sets was by provided by Kenton's rhythm section of Max Bennett on bass and Mel Lewis on drums. They were joined by tenor saxophonist Jack Montrose for the performances of the evergreen

STAN KENTON

'Moonlight in Vermont' and 'Tabu'. Some of the concert at Portland, Oregon, on 21 September was recorded onto a reel-to-reel tape which is currently housed in the *Stan Kenton Collection* at the California State University, Los Angeles. Smith's performances included 'I Remember April' and 'S' Wonderful'.

A review in the *San Diego Union* on 17 September reported the previous night's show at the Balboa Park Ballroom. Smith's performance was singled out for high praise. Under the subheading of "Guitarist Lauded", the reviewer wrote:

> In his introduction to coast audiences, guitarist Johnny Smith showed an astonishing virtuosity in a set highlighted by 'Moonlight in Vermont'. (Reproduced from the *San Diego Union*, 17 September 1954)

Smith and Tatum, who had met in a jazz club shortly after the guitarist had arrived in New York in 1946, took residence opposite each other on Kenton's tour bus. The piano virtuoso was so taken by Smith's musicianship that he asked him to teach him to play the guitar. Smith lightheartedly refused, adding that he had enough problems already without Art Tatum playing the guitar. After repeatedly being pressured by Tatum, who was absolutely serious about his intentions, Smith explained that the pianist would have to cut his fingernails. As Tatum considered his unusually long nails to be an integral part of his piano technique, he allowed the matter to rest.

Some of the venues at which they played were in southern, redneck territory where black people were excluded from some of the roadside dining establishments. For his own safety, Tatum stayed on board the bus while Kenton brought his food out to him. An advertisement which appeared in Louisiana's *Times-Picayune* newspaper announced the tour's show in New Orleans. In a shameful reflection of the times, it proclaimed, "West Side reserved for colored."

Smith remembered that life on the road during this tour was arduous. Typical nights began around 9 p.m., and those with a second show at midnight often did not finish until 4 a.m., by which time the tour bus would be reloaded and ready to hit the road again, traveling throughout the morning, and sometimes the whole day, to the next show.

Although the second *Festival of Modern American Jazz* tour did not gross as much as its forerunner, the *Billboard* attributed this to the presence of several other major tours on the road at the same time as Kenton's troupe, including Norman Granz's fourteenth *Jazz at the Philharmonic* tour, and a Duke Ellington – Dave Brubeck – Gerry Mulligan – Stan Getz package. However, Kenton's tour fared better financially than the others. The concert at Carnegie Hall on 9 October was particularly noted for receiving high accolades in the music press.

The text from Smith's biography page in the tour program once again highlighted both his versatility and virtuosity:

> Johnny Smith's enviable position as a jazz guitarist has now been well established. It has only been in the last few years that he has risen to prominence in the field of jazz and his career has been as varied and interesting as his musical talents.
>
> Born in Alabama and raised in Portland, Maine, Johnny, a completely self taught musician, began his professional career playing hillbilly music. During four years in the Army with various Army bands he learned to play the trumpet, violin and viola, but found the guitar the best instrument with which he could express himself and his deep

feelings for jazz. It was on the guitar that he played with conductor Eugene Ormandy and after the Army he established himself at New York, leading his own group at NBC, as well as conducting the music for the *Fireside Theatre*, the *Dave Garroway Show*, and many other radio and television programs. He has been a leader of many impressive modern groups and has played in the City Center Opera. He has arranged and played for Benny Goodman, and recorded with Gene Krupa and Dimitri Mitropoulos – he has indeed had a varied musical career.

Johnny, an unusual type of musician, who is completely at home in any of the musical forms – as leader, composer, arranger and performer – brings to all of them the essential elements of beauty, simplicity and a sincere desire to communicate to the listener, as well as to his fellow musicians. In Johnny's case, this amazing skill of clearly portraying thoughts while maintaining a polished and melodic sense, makes listening to his jazz guitar an inspiring experience.

The New York Jazz Scene

Little more than a week after the Kenton tour finished, Smith was back at Birdland with his quartet for a two-week run, taking over from Lester Young and Bonnemere's Mambo Sextet, and playing opposite Sarah Vaughan and Eddie Davis from 2 December through until 15 December. The *New Yorker* reported that he was to move into the Embers from 20 December, taking over from the Modern Jazz Quartet. On Christmas Day, the magazine provided a description of the contemporaneous events at the club:

> Serious thinking is being replaced, over the holidays, by musicianship of a cheerier bent. Weekdays, around nine, the trio of Erroll Garner (who, laughing fit to kill, lets his unique chords fall where they may on the keyboard) and the hustling, bustling Johnny Smith Quartet report for duty. (Reproduced from the *New Yorker*, 25 December 1954)

Two weeks later, after reviewing Garner's contributions, the *New Yorker* gave a slightly more informative account of the performances of Smith's combo at the Embers:

> The rest of the music is a masterpiece of understatement – the beguiling guitar duets of Johnny Smith and Perry Lopez overlaying the sound of bass and drums. (Reproduced from the *New Yorker*, 8 January 1955)

Both Garner and Smith's lengthy tenures at the Embers came to an end on 29 January 1955.

While 'Moonlight in Vermont' in 1952 had been the start of Smith's move from revered studio musician to celebrated jazz guitarist, 1954 was without doubt the year in which he reached a position on the top tier of New York's jazz scene alongside the great horn players and pianists whose names are still celebrated over sixty years later. He had become a regular feature at Birdland and was the most prominent jazz guitarist in the city. At the end of 1954, he won both the *Metronome* and *Down Beat* readers' polls for the most popular guitarist of the year. His profile on the New York jazz scene could not have been higher. In 1954, he spent nine weeks working at the Embers, another nine weeks at

Birdland, and ten weeks on the road with Stan Kenton's tour package.

At Birdland, Smith and his combo played between four and six sets per night as they and the other acts on the bill continually rotated. George Roumanis, who was Smith's bass player during the mid-1950s and on many occasions at the Birdland club, remembers how the guitarist was admired by the other performers on the New York jazz scene. He recalls, "Most of the musicians who were around, they had the utmost respect for him, because he was not just a damn good player. He could play anything! And he could read anything!"

The Birdland club was very much home for the top jazz musicians who wanted to hear or play with each other. Monday nights, when the billed acts were off duty, were the officially designated times for jam sessions, but it was also common for performers to join other musicians' sets on regular nights. George Roumanis has memories of some of the jazz glitterati who used to sit in during Smith's sets:

> There were so many of them. Pretty much everybody, you know. Chico Hamilton, Count Basie, Dizzy Gillespie a lot. Most of them would sit in with us. Some of the guys in Basie's band... There were a lot of musicians who wanted to play with us. If they wanted to play and they were good, John just said, "Play." There were a lot of guys who wanted to get up and play... Gerry Mulligan, Charlie Parker. Cannonball Adderley used to sit in all the time! George Shearing used to play with us a lot. Teddy Wilson...

Smith, however, was quick to correct his bass player's memories of their Birdland days:

> Charlie Parker and Dizzy Gillespie never sat in with myself at any sessions. Only one time in Denver did myself and Dizzy get together in the early 1970s. I did not sit in on other people's sets. I did not particularly like jam sessions.

Undoubtedly, no other guitarist commanded the degree of respect from across the jazz community that Smith was awarded. Having already established himself as New York's leading studio guitarist at NBC, his performances in the city's jazz clubs merely heightened the reverence in which he was held by the jazz guitar community. Guitarist Joe Cinderella played opposite him at Birdland and commented that he never heard him miss as much as a single note. Cinderella was astounded by Smith's technical virtuosity, in particular his huge two and three-octave arpeggios, which were always perfectly balanced and smooth. He was unreservedly of the opinion that Smith was the greatest plectrum guitarist who ever lived, observing that nobody could play smoother or cleaner. Guitarist John Pisano played with Chico Hamilton's group later in the 1950s when they too appeared opposite Smith at Birdland. He also remembers Smith's immaculate playing and his ability to execute his huge and challenging arpeggio flourishes without a fault:

> I joined Chico Hamilton's band, and one of the engagements was at Birdland in New York. That had to be around 1958 or 1959. Birdland had several different acts each night. You would be there from nine o'clock until four in the morning. You would alternate sets. I think it was Count Basie's band, Johnny Smith, and our group. So, you would hang out together all night, and I had a lot of time to hang out with Johnny. He was just amazing. I was so impressed with his playing and his ability. The stamina that he had... playing those long extended arpeggios without ever missing a note! Johnny always liked... I think

> it was Scotch in those days. By the end of the night, he was never... but you could see that he was a little... One night, I asked him, "Johnny, how do you manage that?" He looked at me and said, "Son, it's a matter of pacing yourself," [laughs].

Many guitarists, including Mundell Lowe, made a point of seeing Smith in the New York jazz venues whenever possible. John Pisano remembers Les Paul frequently spending entire nights in the city's jazz clubs solely to listen to Smith play. Many guitarists admired him so much that they went to John D'Angelico's store at 40 Kenmare Street in New York City to have the master luthier build them the exact same instrument that Smith was using. D'Angelico began to list it in his ledger as the Johnny Smith model.

Aside from Smith's superior technical ability, impeccable taste and meticulous attention to detail, there was another feature of his sets that had a huge impact upon those who saw and heard him perform. Just as his solo guitar arrangements had also astounded listeners before he came to New York, and would do so again when he later relocated to Colorado, they were also a captivating part of his sets during the 1950s in the New York jazz clubs and venues across the USA. Guitarist and educator Dale Bruning, who later became Smith's bass player for two years in the late 1960s, often saw Smith on the New York jazz circuit. He was just one of many who were taken aback by these chord-melody arrangements. Although the concept of self-accompaniment was not new to the plectrum guitar, Smith elevated it to a higher level of sophistication. It was not only musicians who were spellbound by his musicianship with these innovative masterpieces. George Roumanis fondly recollects that the guitarist frequently silenced rowdy audiences with the beauty of his chord-melody arrangements:

> Several times, we had to go to places like Philadelphia. There would be Count Basie's band. Now, all we had was a trio. Bass, guitar and drums. Basie's band was so loud and the audience so excited, that you couldn't hear yourself with the noise. Now, the three of us get up there. Strange as it may seem, we were the only white guys there. This was a very heavily black club, which was great, and that's who I'd rather play to. So, we would get up there, and we would play 'Cherokee' or something, and we can't even hear. We would play another song and still can't hear anything. So, what does John do? He says, "Sit down, and I'll play a solo." He starts playing 'Wait 'Til You See Her' or 'The Boy Next Door', one of those things... By the time he got to the end, you could hear a pin drop. They all shut up, listened to him, and then clapped like hell! And from then on they listened to us. But it took the solo to do it. And he didn't care. He just looked straight at the people and played. He was not intimidated by anybody. He knew what he could do, and he did it. Nobody intimidated him. Wherever we went, he just got up there and played. He didn't talk much in front of the microphone. Sure, he would announce 'Cherokee' or whatever, but he let the music do the speaking. When you can play like that, you don't have to talk. When he was playing a solo... Nobody was doing what he was doing. Nobody. Not like that. Perhaps later on, but it was different. He had that low D and those chords and things.

The personnel of Smith's jazz combos continued to revolve during the 1950s. This was the norm on the New York jazz scene where every first-class musician accepted whatever work became available. There are some notable musicians, such as drummer Joe Morello, whose membership of

Smith's combo has not been well documented due to the absence of any recordings, and while the entertainment guide in the *New Yorker* regularly listed Smith's jazz club appearances across New York, it did not identify the members of his group. An article in the Massachusetts *Springfield Union* newspaper in May 1958 reported that Morello had become a member of Smith's combo shortly after arriving in New York, and had played at Birdland, the Embers and the Blue Note clubs with him before he went on to join Dave Brubeck's quartet.

Although jazz musicians often had a near addiction to playing their music, financial circumstances also had a part in their apparent workaholic lifestyle. Morris Levy, who was the co-owner of Birdland and who was renowned for his extremely shady business dealings, was far from generous in paying the performers who appeared at his fashionable club. At this time, legendary jazz musicians played at Birdland more for their love of the music than the financial remuneration. Some of New York's top studio musicians were sufficiently proficient as jazz players to warrant appearances in the jazz clubs, but for a mere $90 per week it was not financially viable for them to turn down the comparatively lucrative studio work in order to undertake bookings at particular venues. To put this into perspective, when Smith had been a staff musician at NBC he had been earning $278 per week from the broadcaster. An American Federation of Musicians' contract between George Wein's Storyville club in Boston and the vocalist Jeri Southern, which is housed in the *George Wein Collection* at the Institute of Jazz Studies, shows that the singer and her two accompanists earned $1,750 between them for a week-long engagement in September 1958. In contrast at Birdland, Morris Levy certainly exploited the opportunity to benefit from the musicians' love for their art. Smith experienced an insightful episode with the club owner. He recounted, "Oh yeah. He was a hood. I went up to his place once. He opened up the closet and showed me... He had cowboy boots all stuffed with hundred-dollar bills."

MORRIS LEVY

The musicians' fees at Birdland were reduced further by the notorious dwarf Master of Ceremonies, Pee Wee Marquette, who made use of his own opportunity to humiliate the performers by incorrectly announcing their names unless he received payment. Even then, he was prone to cruel errors. Smith was one of the very few who brokered a friendship with Marquette:

> Pee Wee and I were actually good friends. He never hit me up for much money. We were good friends. When my wife in New York died, Pee Wee was very kind to me. He took me to Harlem, to a nightclub where a big orchestra was playing. That was after Birdland. The place was packed, but he parted the way to the bar. People moved out of his way. It was like magic. People just parted for him. He was a dear friend.

John Pisano was well aware of Marquette's reputation and ensured that he did not cross his path. He remembers, "Oh yeah! Pee Wee would never announce your name correctly. He was a small guy. I never had any real 'encounters' with him. I was too busy trying to play the right notes."

Smith's two young sons, John and David, sometimes came down from Maine to see their father playing at Birdland during their school breaks. David affectionately recalls these occasions:

> My brother and I used to spend the summers with Pop. My father would put my brother and I on a train back up to Maine at the end of our stay. It always seemed to leave in the middle of the night. We would go down to Birdland around midnight. He always got me a bowl of ice-cream, because right outside Birdland was the subway. Those things used to just shake the hell out of everything. He would get me an ice-cream, take me across to Grand Central Station, and put me on a train straight up the East Coast. I remember Birdland. You used to go down those stairs and turn to the right...

According to eye-witness accounts, Smith's recordings provide an invaluable partial testimony of his live performances at clubs such as Birdland. Although he was certainly less reserved in a live environment, his characteristic sense of good taste, which is present on all of his recordings, was also carried through to his live work. The members of his combo, himself included, did not partake in overly extended self-indulgent solos.

A True Jazz Guitarist?

Despite his prolific and popular appearances at the most renowned of New York's jazz clubs during the ensuing years, Smith famously refused to accept that he was a true jazz guitarist. He opined that the dedication that classical musicians give to their genre of music is matched by those who dedicate themselves to jazz. In a self-assessment of his musicianship, he commented that although he was able to improvise solos, he was too diverse in his musical interests to be able to devote himself to the development of a jazz vocabulary on a par with guitarists such as Barney Kessel, Jim Hall, Wes Montgomery, Jimmy Raney, Tal Farlow or Chuck Wayne. Certainly, Smith's recordings with Mary Lou Williams in 1947, Benny Goodman in 1950 and 1951, Hank Jones' *Urbanity* in 1953, and with his own combo on 'Jaguar', 'Cavu', 'What's New' and 'Have You Met Miss Jones undoubtedly testify to his fluency in the contemporary language of jazz. However, when many jazz guitarists were imitating each other during the 1950s, he gradually set out to shape his own distinctive style.

Most of the jazz guitarists who contributed to this biography disagreed with Smith's refusal to accept that he was a jazz guitarist. Furthermore, in their ears, he was more than just one of them. He was the jazz guitarist's jazz guitarist. Whereas some of the jazz critics resented non-purists, such as Smith, jazz musicians admired him without prejudice. The broad range and high standard of his musicianship merely enhanced, rather than diminished, the respect that he was afforded. His improvised lines brought him the admiration of the elite of the New York jazz scene during the 1950s. Gene Bertoncini remembers, "They all admired his technique. He had these lines that almost seemed to be worked out, but they weren't! They were just coming out of him like machine-gun fire." The revered jazz guitarist Louis Stewart recalls the aspects which attracted him to Smith's music and shares his own assessment of Smith as a jazz guitarist:

> I was always amazed by his technique, the cleanness of his playing and his phrasing. When I was a kid in 1960, I joined this band playing on the road in Ireland. We went to

> America for three or four weeks. I came back from New York with half a dozen Johnny Smith LPs, which I still have. I used to listen, wondering how it's done. And a copy of his *Aids to Technique for Guitar*. It was actually the single-note stuff which appealed to me mostly, especially on 'Moonlight in Vermont' and also the album *Moods*. I think that contains his best work. You know, I've read some things about him not really being a jazz guitar player, and he actually says that himself, but when you hear those two records... It's as good as anything that I've heard. On that *Moods* album, particularly, two of my favorite tracks are 'Easy to Love' and 'I'll Remember April'. He's swinging for his ass on them.

Meanwhile, the respected guitarist and educator Jack Petersen also takes issue Smith's refusal to accept that he was a true jazz guitarist:

> Well, I disagree with him, because I think he was. He put out a lot of great jazz albums. Oh, he influenced everybody, man! You know, all through the 1950s there were a lot of great jazz guitar players, and Johnny was right at the top of those guys. Like Tal Farlow, Herb Ellis and Barney Kessel... The 1950s is where they really shone, you know. When Johnny came out with 'Moonlight in Vermont'... Boy, everybody just went... Because it was so different.

Jack Petersen is undoubtedly correct in drawing attention to Smith's many jazz recordings. Although his vocabulary was different to that of other jazz guitarists, he could play the typical jazz phraseology when he wanted to do so. Guitarist Larry Coryell acknowledges the importance of Smith to his own musical development as a jazz musician through his recording of 'What's New':

> All during my career in NYC I kept running into Johnny Smith freaks, even at the height of the Fusion era. So many others like me still think his recording of 'What's New' is the definitive statement for that tune. Around age sixteen, I learned that solo right off the record. It gave me a first step into understanding jazz vocabulary.

Meanwhile, guitarist John Pisano shares his own thoughts on Smith's self-assessment:

> Certainly, he had his way of improvising. Perhaps it wasn't as harmonically 'adventurous', if that's the right word, as Jimmy Raney, or Tal Farlow, or Chuck Wayne in those days. But they all admired his playing and his musicianship. His improvisation wasn't in that style, but he wasn't interested in doing that. The technique and clarity of his playing...

For many listeners, including jazz keyboard legend Herbie Hancock, Smith made jazz accessible without diluting its content or value. Studio guitarist Tim May speaks for many of the jazz guitar alumni with his own thoughts:

> I would never say that he wasn't a jazz player. In my work, I recognize that a lot of styles overlap. They're not clearly defined. I can appreciate music for what it is, rather than feel the need to categorize it. Although I play many musical styles, I would like to think of

> myself as a jazz guitarist. But if Johnny Smith isn't a jazz guitarist, then none of us are!

Mundell Lowe's evaluation of Smith's validity as a jazz guitarist shows that the term was simply too restrictive to correctly describe his musicianship:

> John was known for his studio work, rather than being an out-and-out jazz player. You know, he was a guitarist. He was not necessarily a jazz artist. He was far beyond that. He could cover a lot of fields.

Gary Atkins provided an example of the phenomenal musicianship to which Mundell Lowe referred:

> I'll tell you a Barney Kessel story. Thcy were dear friends, you know. One time, Johnny came up to visit at my father's house. I was still a teenager. This would have been in the late '50s. Dad had Barney Kessel's latest record. Now they [Johnny and Jimmy] were on their second Martini. Johnny was sitting on the piano bench, holding his guitar, and Dad put on this solo that Barney played which was quite nice. Dad played the record and said, "Well, what do you think of that?" So, Johnny says, "Mmm... Play it again." Johnny sat there and played the solo, the improvised solo, along with Barney on the record player, note-for-note with double-stops! Dad and I just... [laughs]. How did he do that?

The observations of guitarist Dale Bruning, who played double bass for two years in Smith's combo during the 1960s, offer a perspective into his approach to improvisation, as well as his chord-melody arrangements:

> During those couple of years, you know, John would often remind me of the classical musicians, perhaps as much as a jazz musician. His improvising was beautiful, but what he himself preferred was to play these arrangements that he had worked out beforehand, because there were certain melodic lines that he found desirable, and he would repeat them. So, some of his arrangements stayed the same, and some of his improvised melodic lines stayed the same, not because he didn't know where to go. It was just his preference sometimes. His approach on some of those songs was almost like variations on a theme. He would arrive at something that he liked and then decide to keep it in. So, a lot of his solos would be spontaneous, but there would be certain places where he just felt that a particular phrase was the best way to negotiate those chord changes. This might include a certain ending where he would run over an arpeggio or something. He was very comfortable and very effective with that. It was part of the charm of his performances. You felt like you had been to a concert. Particularly with those chord-melody arrangements, he would perform those things note-for-note the same each time, because he had decided that he had found the best way to do those things. Just like a good classical guitarist, memorizing the literature, and so on, except that in his case he wasn't memorizing other people's material. OK, so he didn't write 'Shenandoah' or 'The Girl with the Flaxen Hair', but what I mean is that he would arrange it in a way that suited him. Once he had locked in on what he liked, he would play it as a set piece, the way that a classical guitarist would. But by saying that, I don't mean that he wasn't a

great improviser, it's just that this was his preference for doing things.

As Dale Bruning correctly points out, Smith's premeditated chord-melody arrangements had their roots in a classical, rather than a jazz, approach to music. It would be wrong, however, to misinterpret these observations into the belief that Smith's improvised lines were all but written down. Single-line soloing in jazz music contains some degree of premeditation. Musicians work out, rehearse and refine an amount of predetermined phrases, which make regular appearances in their 'improvised' lines and are often retained for specific pieces.

While Smith's chord-melody arrangements were hugely popular with the jazz community and audiences, many guitarists feel that his improvised single-line work has been unfairly overshadowed by them. Jack Wilkins has no doubts about Smith's lead playing:

> I've been a fan of Johnny Smith since I first heard him. I was seventeen at the time. I didn't understand a lot of what he was doing, but I was so taken with the sound. It gave me goosebumps! I bought every record I could find. I have every record he has recorded. I became a bit of a Johnny Smith clone, transcribing many of his solos. I've since gotten away from playing exactly like him, but the influence is always there. It's a thrill for me to introduce my students to his music. Even some seasoned professionals aren't that familiar with his majestic single-line work. It makes me grin when someone hears his single-line playing for the first time, and they say to me that they can't believe that's Johnny Smith.

Jack Petersen places the two aspects of Smith's playing, his single-line work and chord-melody arrangements, on a par:

> I think they're about even. Harmonically, he was brilliant. And that shows up in his single-line playing, as well. How he would work against a set of chord changes... He was really fluent with that. Guys were amazed at how well he played and how he played through chord changes so beautifully. His control... He had amazing technique. People look at him as a ballad player. But let me tell you, man, he can really put the tempos up there, too.

One of the most technically impressive features of his single-line playing was his ability to immaculately execute huge flourishes, which frequently covered two or three octaves. The precision with which he performed arpeggios and scales over this range was faultless to the point that their deceptive ease does not cause the listener to be distracted from the music by the virtuosity. Smith's employment at NBC had provided him with the opportunity to work with several pianists, and he admired the long arpeggio runs that were typical in their music. Consequently, he set about recreating these on the guitar. It took him a considerable amount of effort to learn and execute these flourishes with immaculate alternate picking. Bob Yelin shares his thoughts on Smith's piano influences:

> The most important thing about how and why he plays his guitar... It all comes from the piano. He loved the long legato lines of the piano. He tried to copy them as best he could. He spent countless hours trying to play from low to high, or from high to low, on the

fingerboard. Whenever he had a moment, he practiced those lines and double-stops. He would play them on breaks, or after a gig, and have a drink or two. He could be seen at three in the morning just practicing them.

The Boston Jazz Scene

In researching Smith's engagements at jazz venues outside of New York, across the rest of the USA, it has proved to be difficult to compile a comprehensive list of clubs and dates. Unlike classical concerts that are habitually well documented in archived program booklets, or some jazz club residencies in New York that were regularly listed in the entertainment guide of the *New Yorker*, there is no database of gigs across the USA. Local newspapers merely provide occasional evidence. It has been possible to uncover some instances of Smith's work outside of the jazz capital during the 1950s. For example, on completion of his six-week residency at the Embers at the end of January 1955, the *Boston Herald* reported on 2 February that he was appearing at the Hi Hat club in Boston. The *Billboard* announced on 19 February 1955 that he and his group had recently undertaken a week-long residency at George Wein's Storyville in Boston. Stan Kenton's introductory announcement for Smith at the *Newport Jazz Festival* in July 1954 indicates that this was not his first visit. Wein's club was the premier jazz venue in Boston. Notable names, other than Johnny Smith, who frequently appeared there included Art Tatum, George Shearing, Dave Brubeck, Erroll Garner, Billie Holiday, Ella Fitzgerald, Sarah Vaughan and Sidney Bechet.

The *Billboard* also reported on 19 February 1955 that Smith had moved on from Storyville to Detroit, St Louis, and Columbus, Ohio. In Detroit, the Johnny Smith Quartet played opposite Charlie Parker at the Rouge Lounge on 15 February 1955, just four weeks before the saxophonist died.

Johnny Richards

On 22 February, Smith was back in the recording studio in New York, as a member of the orchestra for Johnny Richards' *Annotations of the Muses* album. The composer's classical-jazz, orchestral work was both contemporary and American in style, and featured Smith as a prominent soloist alongside some of New York's finest classical musicians, including his old friend Julius Baker. As with Smith's earlier recordings with Dimitri Mitropoulos, it is impossible to consider any other guitarist in New York as capable of either reading or playing Richards' part for the instrument.

Richards had already established himself as a respected arranger, particularly in his work for Stan Kenton. *Annotations of the Muses* was released on Roost Records' Legende subsidiary.

Johnny Richards

New York and Beyond

Smith returned to Birdland on 31 March 1955 when he took over from Dizzy Gillespie and Stan Getz. The *New Yorker* alluded to his quartet's role as the de facto house-band during a residency that was followed by Perez Prado and the Modern Jazz Quartet on 7 April:

> The gathering place of the jet-propulsion, Buck Rogers music-makers and music lovers. At the moment, though, Dinah Washington, a singer not as farfetched as most of them, is doing the words, and Johnny Smith's quartet, which is calm and collected, is doing the major ensemble work. (Reproduced from the *New Yorker*, 2 April 1955)

By 16 April 1955, Smith, whom the *New Yorker* were now describing as a "gentleman, scholar and virtuoso guitarist," was once again at the Embers with his quartet, playing opposite the pianist George Shearing until 23 April. He then undertook another tour outside of New York City, during which he could be found playing with his quartet at Dick's 620 Club on Clinton Avenue in Rochester from 23 until 29 May. This was followed by his first residency at the Cotton Club in Cleveland, Ohio, from 20 until 26 June. Other acts who appeared earlier in the month at what was a significant venue for touring jazz musicians included Art Tatum and the Australian Jazz Quartet.

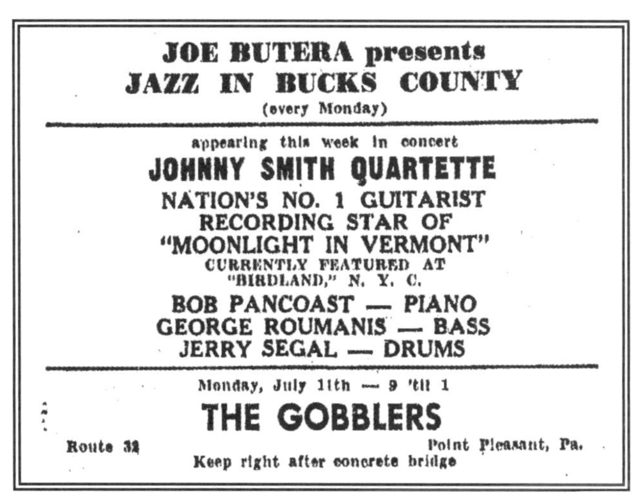

With Perry Lopez having left the fold, in early 1955 the line-up of Smith's combo consisted of pianist Bob Pancoast, bassist George Roumanis, and drummer Jerry Segal. On the night of 11 July, the quartet could be heard playing at the Gobblers in Point Pleasant, Pennsylvania.

George Roumanis recalls that he had met Smith when they were both playing at a jam session at clarinetist Billy Kretchmer's jazz club in Philadelphia not long after the guitarist had been working with Benny Goodman. Smith had been part of Goodman's sextet from 1950 until 1951. In March 1952, Smith, Bobby Hackett, Bud Freeman, Billy Butterfield and Hot Lips Page had all been booked by Kretchmer for a series of one-night stands in Philadelphia. It is likely that this was the occasion which Roumanis recalls.

JOHNNY SMITH AT A JAM SESSION

The 1955 Newport Jazz Festival

On 14 July 1955, Smith and his combo were once again in Birdland, taking over from George Handy's group. This residency, opposite Count Basie's orchestra, continued until 27 July. He took a night off from his Birdland commitment on 17 July in order to appear at the second *Newport Jazz Festival* on Rhode Island.

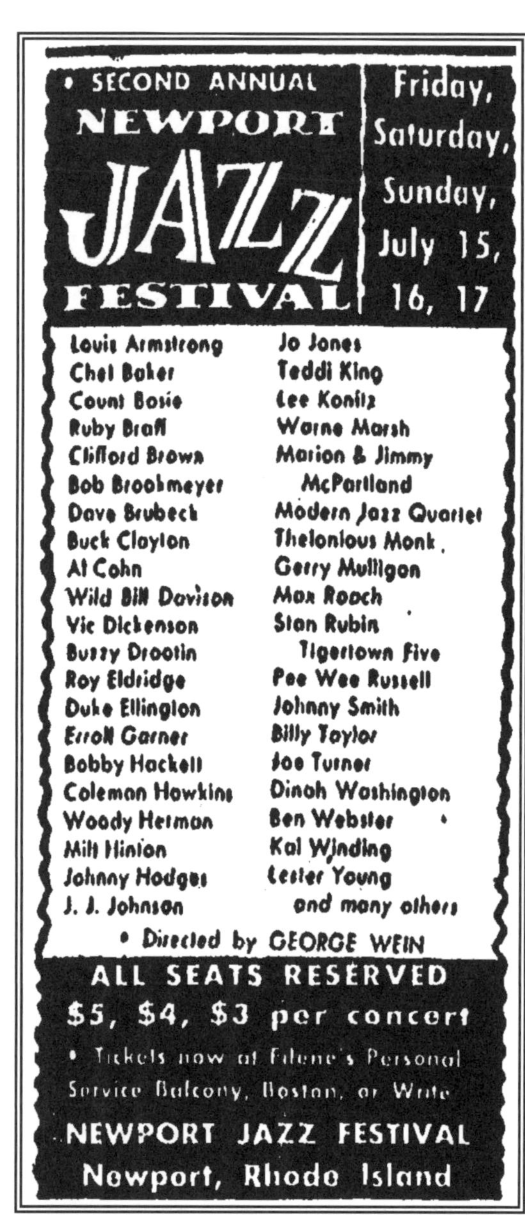

The festival's program booklet lists the headlining soloists for this year as Stan Rubin and his Tigertown Five; Erroll Garner; Teddi King; Woody Herman and His Orchestra; Roy Eldridge and Coleman Hawkins; Joe Turner; Louis Armstrong and His Orchestra; the Max Roach-Clifford Brown Quintet; the Marian McPartland Trio; Bob Brookmeyer, Al Cohn and Ruby Braff; Dinah Washington; the Chet Baker Quartet; Lee Konitz and Warne Marsh; Wild Bill Davidson, Buzzy Drootin, Vic Dickenson, Pee Wee Russell, George Wein and Milt Hinton; Dave Brubeck; Duke Ellington as narrator; the Modern Jazz Quartet; Lester Young, Jo Jones and Buck Clayton; Gerry Mulligan; and Count Basie and His Orchestra.

After the previous year's experience as a soloist when Smith found himself repeatedly electrocuted while he was accompanied by the Oscar Peterson Trio, on this occasion he was a member of an all-star group alongside Bob Bates, J.J. Johnson, Ben Webster, Billy Taylor, Percy Heath, Jo Jones, Peanuts Hucko, Bud Shank, Bobby Hackett and Kai Winding. The program booklet announced that each of the members of the group were to feature as soloists during the set.

The 1955 festival was recorded in its entirety by the Voice of America, and some of the performances were transmitted on NBC's *Bandstand USA*. The Voice of America also recorded interviews with some of the musicians, a copy of which resides in the Library of Congress' Recorded Sounded Center. A review in the *New York Times* on 18 July 1955 reported that a well-behaved crowd of 27,000 people had attended the three-day festival.

Just three weeks after their Birdland tenancy had finished, Smith and his quartet were back at the club, from 18 until 31 August 1955, playing opposite J.J. Johnson and Kai Winding's quintet, and Helen Merrill, after Dizzy Gillespie and Neal Hefti had moved out. The combo then embarked on a tour, which included two weeks at the Blue Note club in Chicago, Illinois, from 14 September. They were followed at the Windy City's top jazz venue first by Dave Brubeck and then by George Shearing.

In a Sentimental Mood and 'Walk, Don't Run'

In early 1955, Smith, Pancoast, Roumanis and Segal cut three new sides in the recording studio. These were amalgamated with the five tracks that had been held back from the previous session in September 1954. The result was the album *In a Sentimental Mood*. One of the unissued recordings from the earlier session was a self-composed piece that would go on to become a huge pop hit. The instigation for 'Walk, Don't Run' was typical of its time, in that it was composed and recorded in order to reduce Roost Record's royalty payments to outside publishers. Smith's chord progression for 'Walk, Don't Run' was based upon the harmonies of Sigmund Romberg and Oscar Hammerstein's old standard 'Softly, as in a Morning Sunrise', with some adjustments to accommodate his new melody. Unable to proffer a name for the piece himself, he simply called it 'Opus'. It was Teddy Reig who provided the title 'Walk, Don't Run'. This caused something of a problem, because trumpeter Shorty Rogers had recently recorded a piece with the same title. The recording in the *Stan Kenton Collection* at the California State University of the second *Festival of Modern American Jazz* show at Portland, Oregon, on 21 September 1954 contains a performance by Rogers of his own composition.

In 1957, the country guitarist Chet Atkins, who was a close friend of Smith, came to see him at Birdland to ask for his permission to record his own interpretation of 'Walk, Don't Run'. Smith gave his unconditional consent, but Atkins insisted that Smith should hear his version before awarding it his blessing. Smith took him to a backstage room. In an informative interview with Jim Carlton for the book *Conversations with Great Jazz and Studio Guitarists* in 2009, Smith humorously recalled Atkins' horror at witnessing several musicians shooting up drugs, which was quite the norm on the jazz scene at the time. After Atkins had overcome his shock, he played his interpretation and received consent from the composer. He subsequently released his version on his *Hi-Fi in Focus* album. It was this particular rendition, rather than Smith's original, that was picked up, reinterpreted and recorded by the Ventures and turned into an international pop hit in 1960.

At the time of Smith's original recording of 'Walk, Don't Run', his two sons from his first marriage, John and David, were living with their mother in Maine. As youngsters, they were understandably unaware of the height of their father's stature on the New York jazz scene. By the time that the Ventures' pop interpretation became a hit in the early 1960s, they were of an age to appreciate his success. John recalls that the Ventures' version was a huge hit with his own generation:

> I guess I didn't realize how big he was, or what an influence he was on jazz, until I was in high school when I was around fifteen or sixteen years old. Dave and I would go from Maine down to New York City and spend the summer there. I didn't go around telling everybody that Johnny Smith was my dad, because the first thing that they would want to know is, "Well, do you play?" In 1962, I was a senior in high school. The Ventures had broken through with 'Walk, Don't Run' a year or two before that and it had been a big hit. I was telling my friends in school that my dad had written that tune. They just looked at me and said [sarcastically], "Oh yeah, right," [laughs].

On Smith's original version of 'Walk, Don't Run', he made use of Perry Lopez's fine abilities by intertwining the counter-melodies of the two guitars, and there are straight-feel hints of a baroque style in the arrangement. In 1967, he would record a new interpretation for his second album for Verve, *Johnny Smith's Kaleidoscope*. This version contrasted notably from the original Roost recording. Not only was the tempo considerably faster and the mood much more energetic, but the straight baroque lines were replaced by a swing groove throughout. Due to his Roost catalog's somewhat dormant status over several years, the marginally more accessible Verve recording has sometimes been mistakenly referred to as the 'original' by those who are unaware of his 1955 release.

The Segovia of the Electric Guitar

Smith also found time in 1955 to record the album *Johnny Smith Plays Jimmy Van Heusen* with Bob Pancoast, George Roumanis and Jerry Segal. A review in the *Billboard* identified the appeal of Smith's music to those both within and beyond the jazz spectrum:

> Although Smith's original following has been among jazz buffs, his scintillating, tasteful guitar work has been winning over a lot of pop fans, and this collection of Van Heusen tunes is a strong pitch for more pop support. This is extremely smart "mood" music, inventive and absorbing, but thoroughly relaxing too. The tunes include such great ones as 'But Beautiful', 'Deep in a Dream', 'Darn That Dream', 'Imagination' and more of an equally familiar and satisfying ilk. What Segovia is to the classical guitar, Smith is to the electric and jazz guitar. (Reproduced from the *Billboard*, 3 September 1955)

The reviewer's comparison of Smith with Segovia was not hyperbole. Smith's classical approach to his guitar playing technique, his attention to a pureness of tone, and his romantic use of rubato in his chord-melody arrangements, certainly drew parallels with the classical guitar maestro.

Johnny Smith Plays Jimmy Van Heusen is a notable entry in Smith's catalog of recordings. Whereas many jazz instrumentalists at this time favored the reworking of old standards, or composed new tunes based upon old chord charts, Smith's repertoire regularly extended into the Great American Songbook. His choice of repertoire was a significant aspect which distinguished him from other jazz guitarists.

Johnny Smith Quartet

On 17 October 1955, Smith and his quartet returned for another residency at the Cotton Club in Cleveland, Ohio. They closed on 23 October, after which point the Australian Jazz Quartet took over.

A few days later, and with Elmer 'Mousie' Alexander on board in place of Jerry Segal, Smith and his combo recorded the album *Johnny Smith Quartet* in New York. Once again, the *Billboard* acknowledged his appeal across the musical spectrum. Smith's own compositions on this album included '0500 Blues' and 'Tired Blood'. Meanwhile, 'Wait 'Til You See Her' and 'Little Girl Blue' were featured as solo chord-melody arrangements.

In Smith's own opinion, this line-up with George Roumanis on bass, Bob Pancoast on piano and Mousie Alexander on drums was the best that he ever had while he was living in New York. He singled out Pancoast in particular for his unique style and approach. For this reason, he was later highlighted on the group's recording of 'Prelude to a Kiss'. George Roumanis remembers that the quartet assembled once per week, in order to rehearse new material, with all of the musicians contributing to the arrangements.

Mousie Alexander

Beverly Kenney

With Knobby Totah taking over bass duties from George Roumanis, Smith's combo also found time during 1955 to record an album with the rising singer Beverly Kenney, titled *Beverly Kenney Sings for Johnny Smith*. This was the first of three occasions upon which Smith and his group accompanied female singers in the recording studio, each of whom had markedly different vocal identities.

Kenney had just begun to make a name for herself through her live performances when Smith was called in to record her debut album with her. A comparison of the featured songs with her 1954 demo tapes shows that the guitarist and his combo adapted themselves to accommodate her repertoire, which Smith later recalled that she had chosen herself. Her demo recordings, on which she was solely accompanied by pianist Tony Tamburello, were eventually released on a CD album entitled *Snuggled on Your Shoulder*. Five of the twelve songs that constitute her album with Smith had previously appeared on her demo recording.

Smith's sympathetic arrangements and guitar playing on *Beverly Kenney Sings for Johnny Smith* allowed the singer's attributes to shine brightly. A review in the *Billboard* predicted a promising future for the vocalist, and described the combo's contribution as “Typically tasty backing by Johnny Smith's guitar and rhythm section.” Winthrop Sargent, in a review in the *New Yorker*, observed that Kenney's performance was somewhat lightweight for a jazz singer, but acknowledged that she was a promising talent. He recognized her undeniably disarming charm in 'The Surrey with the Fringe on Top', 'I'll Know My Love (Greensleeves)' and 'This Little Town Is Paris'. It would perhaps be more accurate to describe her voice as unconventional for a jazz singer, and girlish rather than lightweight. Regardless, Smith's arrangements and performances with his group are sublime throughout the entire album.

Kenney's work with Smith propelled her career onto a much higher level, and this was in no small way due to the guitarist's input. According to a report in the *Billboard* in January 1956, she was subsequently signed by Morris Levy for twenty weeks at Birdland. A residency which began at the club on 31 May 1956 saw her accompanied by Lester Young's quintet. This was hardly the path of a 'lightweight' singer. As her career progressed, she occasionally shared the bill with Smith's quartet on live shows. On 11 and 12 November 1955, they both could be heard opposite Dizzy Gillespie's sextet at the Basin Street club on Broadway at 51st Street. A week later, on 18 and 19 November, Kenney and Smith's combo returned, playing opposite Miles Davis' sextet and Erroll Garner's trio.

Beverly Kenney recorded another five albums in relatively short succession, the last three of which were for Decca. Sadly, she was a melancholy figure who tragically took her own life in April 1960 at the age of twenty-eight.

BOB PANCOAST, KNOBBY TOTAH, JOHNNY SMITH AND JOHNNY LEE AT BIRDLAND

After his appearance opposite Kenney and Davis at Basin Street, Smith moved to the Bandbox on State Street in Rochester from 21 until 27 November. He returned with his quartet to Basin Street on 2 and 3 December, sharing the bill with Gerry Mulligan's sextet. On 11 December, the Johnny Smith Quartet were back at the Embers for a residency which continued until 7 January 1956. The *New Yorker* described his tenancy somewhat lyrically as:

> The living is easy once more in this temple of the fine arts, mostly because of Johnny Smith's thoughtful string quartet and Eddie Heywood's extrovert trio. (Reproduced from the *New Yorker*, 31 December 1955)

During 1955, Smith spent over eight weeks at the Embers club and a further five weeks at Birdland.

THE CRITICS

At the close of 1955, Smith was voted the favorite guitarist by the readers of *Metronome* magazine for the third consecutive year. He also won *Down Beat* magazine's reader's poll for the second successive year. It must be pointed out that magazine reader's polls, and to an extent critic's polls, reflect a winning musician's popularity rather than the quality of his or her output. These acknowledgments indicate Smith's high profile and popularity with jazz audiences during the 1950s. Although he is known today primarily by serious jazz guitarists, a look at the line of winners of the *Down Beat* award through three decades provides a revealing perspective of his popularity with the public in the mid-1950s. From 1940 through to 1969 the recipients were Benny Heller, Charlie Christian, Eddie Condon, Allen Reuss, Oscar Moore, Billy Bauer, Les Paul, Johnny Smith, Barney Kessel, Wes Montgomery, Charlie Byrd, Jim Hall, and Kenny Burrell.

Although Smith won the *Down Beat* reader's poll in 1954 and 1955, it is significant that he did not win the magazine's critic's poll. The winners in these two years were Barney Kessel and Jimmy Raney respectively. Fellow guitarist Mundell Lowe maintains that jazz musicians such as himself, Smith and trumpeter Clark Terry, all of whom carried out studio work for television and radio networks, received an unfairly rough ride from the jazz critics. Lowe remembers that he and Smith also made recordings for commercials, which sent the jazz purists into a frenzy. He recounts, "Sometimes, we did record dates together, but no club performances. Some of those record dates were what we call transcription services. You know, background music to sell toothpaste to, things like that."

While the announcements of Smith's live performances in the entertainment guide of the *New Yorker* were always positive, the reviews in the *Billboard* of his jazz recordings during the 1950s were similar but often a little muted. Smith was of the opinion that most of his records were panned by those critics who considered themselves to be experts, such as Leonard Feather of *Down Beat*. It is fair to say that when he first reached the top of the *Metronome* reader's roll in 1953 and the parallel *Down Beat* poll in 1954, it was achieved in his own typically understated manner. There were very few feature articles about Smith in either of these publications prior to his success in these polls, and there was no hyperbole around him whatsoever. In contrast, the *Metronome* magazine was littered with articles about Les Paul during this period. This may have been to satisfy the Gibson guitar company who, in promoting its Les Paul model, was one of the magazine's most prolific advertisers. Smith was a high-profile figure on the New York jazz scene by 1954, and it would consequently be incorrect to excuse the jazz critics on the grounds that he had crept in under the radar to win these polls. It would be only partly correct to accuse them of musical ignorance. As Mundell Lowe recalls, the full truth was much darker:

> When I first went to work at NBC, Leonard Feather was a big friend of mine and Betty... And when I accepted the job at NBC, when Johnny was vacating and moving out to Colorado Springs to be with his mother [in 1958], I ran into Leonard. He just laced me up and down for giving in and going to the studios, as opposed to working Birdland. I said, "Leonard, I have a family to raise. I can play Birdland and also play NBC." So, I used to work Birdland quite a lot with all the bands. I worked there for quite a long time with Billy Taylor, Charlie Mingus and Charlie White, the drummer. The quartet... We were there a long time. So, that's absolutely true. The 'critics', so to speak, came down hard on us for giving in and moving into the studios so that we could make a living. But none of us are in the jazz business for money. And then they didn't know what to think when we started getting people like Clark Terry, Jimmy Nottingham, Jimmy Crawford... black musicians in there, real jazzers who came out of the bands... Well, the critics didn't know what to say. It really confused them, which I thought was wonderful. A lot of those people didn't know what the hell they were talking about. We used to go out with Leonard Feather to listen to a band, a player, whatever. And in the middle of it, he would turn to us and say, "What do you think?" He was trying to get us to say what he should write the next day. Leonard should have known better than that, but he simply did not know. He was a nice man, but like a Swiss cheese, he had holes in his knowledge. That was the case with a lot of critics and writers.

Many of the jazz critics generally commanded more professional respect from their unwitting readership than from New York's jazz musicians. Some performers referred to Feather as the 'Empty

Suit'. An article in the *Billboard* in April 1955 described Smith and Lowe as "top technicians and studio men" and acknowledged them as being "among the most popular and accomplished guitarists." It added that they, alongside Barney Kessel, Tal Farlow, Joe Puma, Chuck Wayne and Jimmy Raney, fell "easily on the untutored ear." However, with a veiled accusation which suggested that for all of their admirable qualities they were not serious jazz musicians, the article continued:

> Smith, Lowe and some of the others seem to like good tunes that embody colorful harmonic changes, and their output along those lines will appeal to mood music and cocktail music lovers. (Reproduced from the *Billboard*, 23 April 1955)

Clearly, fellow jazz musicians, such as Charlie Parker, Lester Young, Count Basie and Art Tatum, not to mention the jazz-buying public, heard something in Smith's music that the critics did not.

Although not applicable to the specific poll-winning of Kessel and Raney, there were also racial issues involved in some of the white critics' opinions of jazz musicians. In a prejudiced practice that is referred to as 'positive racism' in current terminology, some of the white critics were often condescending about white jazz musicians, whom they considered to be inauthentic. Black jazz performers were perceived as genuine and pure jazz musicians, who would never lower themselves to lesser forms of music. Mundell Lowe experienced the prejudices of some of the critics:

> That's true. That's true. They thought that the only jazz players were black. That's a problem that I had with a couple of guys who used to write for *Down Beat*. We used to lock horns over that very same thing. And I used to say, "Look, a jazz player is a jazz player. What would you call Benny Goodman? A commercial player? He was one of the great clarinet jazz players of all time. How do you face that?" No answer. They didn't know what to say.

The issue of some of the white critics' attitudes towards white jazz musicians was, at times, markedly more unpleasant. Smith's longtime friend Gary Atkins recalled a particularly vicious occasion:

> Sandy [Smith's third wife] told me that [one of the critics] had written an article accusing some of the jazz musicians of racism. Johnny wrote him a letter telling him that he was out of his mind, and that he was actually fermenting racism with his comments. After that, he flatly refused to mention Johnny in *Down Beat* magazine. He just black-balled him.

Smith reluctantly elaborated upon this particular story:

> Well... actually... Stan Kenton, due to the fact that he was working an engagement down South and everything, he didn't hire any black musicians. [The critic] got a hold of this and accused him of being racial... He did a lot of damage.

For the sake of clarity, it should be pointed out that Kenton had no racial prejudices whatsoever, and his choice of an all-white orchestra was a decision that had been forced upon him by the social climate of the particular geographical area in which he was touring. It is also important to note that

Smith's subsequent treatment by the critic in question undoubtedly contributed to the lamentable 'forgotten man' status which still surrounds him today.

In the opinions of some of the critics, the criteria for recognition as a great jazz musician extended even further than the supposed authenticity that was defined by race and a single devotion to the genre. The guitar was still not accepted as an instrument worthy of a level of respect that was comparable with the established jazz instruments, such as the alto and tenor saxophones and the trumpet. Even New York's Local 802 union of musicians listed guitarists after zither and banjo players in its annual directory during the 1950s. Furthermore, in order to stand respected by some of the journalists, a jazz musician had to be harmonically innovative with his music. To be groundbreaking with regard to a specific instrument was not sufficient, and to play beautiful jazz was simply not enough to warrant their respect. As a white jazz guitarist who also worked for the radio and television networks, and who was innovative on his instrument but not in the harmonic development of jazz music theory, it is not surprising that Smith did not truly receive the recognition from the self-professed experts that his musicianship deserved. It must be added that Wes Montgomery fared only a little better during the 1960s. Although he rightly remains revered within the jazz guitar community, the only criteria that he fulfilled in the eyes of some of the white critics was that of race. Meanwhile, his ventures into the popular music genre did nothing to enhance his standing in their ideology.

Count Basie and the Birdland Stars of '56

1956 was another hectic and high-flying year for Smith on the New York jazz scene. After closing at the Embers on 7 January, he took up a further residency at his second home, Birdland, on 19 January opposite the singer Jeri Southern and the Australian Jazz Quartet. The two-week run continued until 1 February, after which the Terry Gibbs Quartet, the Tony Aless-Seldon Powell Sextet, and Beverly Kenney took over at the club.

JOHNNY SMITH WITH THE COUNT BASIE ORCHESTRA

While Smith was working prolifically in New York's premier jazz venues, Teddy Reig was arranging for him to join Morris Levy's *Birdland Stars of '56* tour, which ran through February 1956. This outing has often been wrongly described in guitar magazines and other published literature as a Count Basie tour. In truth, although the bandleader and his orchestra were on board, it was a Birdland excursion. The featured artists consisted of some of the club's regular performers, such as Sarah Vaughan, Count Basie, Al Hibbler, Johnny Smith, Lester Young, Bud Powell, Joe Williams, and the East-West Jazz Septet, which consisted of Al Cohn, Conti Candoli, Roy Haines, Joe Benjamin, Henry Dorham, Phil Woods and Jimmy Jones. Smith opened the show each night and was accompanied by Basie's orchestra, for whom he wrote the arrangements.

The tour dates included the White Plains

Community Center in New York at 8:30 p.m., and Carnegie Hall at midnight on 3 February; the Mosque in Newark at 8:30 p.m., and Carnegie Hall at midnight on 4 February; two shows at the Symphony Hall in Boston, Massachusetts, on 5 February; the War Memorial in Syracuse, New York, on 6 February; the Auditorium in Rochester, New York, on 8 February; the Memorial Auditorium in Canton, Ohio, on 9 February; the Sports Arena in Toledo, Ohio, on 10 February; Columbus, Ohio, on 11 February; Beloit College in Wisconsin on 16 February; two shows at the Civic Opera House in Chicago, Illinois, on 18 February; Charleston, South Carolina, on 21 February; two shows at the Public Music Hall in Cleveland, Ohio, on 22 February; three shows at the National Theater in Washington D.C. on 26 February; and the Paramount Theater in Brooklyn, New York, on 28 February.

The *New York Times* printed a rather uninformative review of the midnight performance at Carnegie Hall on 3 February. Although the critic was positive in his assessment of Bud Powell, he was more reserved about the performances of Count Basie and Joe Williams. The other performers, including Smith, merely received name-checks. In contrast, local newspapers across the country heaped praise upon the tour, which was extremely well received by audiences. Ticket sales were even more profitable on this road trip than Stan Kenton's second *Festival of Modern American Jazz* tour sixteen months earlier, and at the midway point they were a third ahead of Levy's previous 1955 version of his tour.

Business as Usual

With the *Birdland Stars of '56* tour completed at the end of February, Smith was back with his quartet at the Bandbox in Rochester from 5 until 11 March, sharing the bill once again with Beverly Kenney. On 29 March, he took his quartet into Birdland for a three-week residency opposite Dinah Washington and Al Belletto's sextet until 18 April. This was followed by a series of engagements outside of New York, including the Cotton Club in Cleveland, Ohio, from 14 until 20 May opposite Carmen McRae.

In June 1956, Smith could be found playing opposite Sarah Vaughan at the Blue Note club in Chicago, with the show on 3 June broadcast live on NBC's *Monitor* program. Earlier in the year, the syndicated press across the US had announced that, in June, Smith would be flying from Chicago to be the best man at the wedding of New York disc jockey Bob Garrity to model and dancer Bonnie Collins. Smith was still able to recall Garrity's wedding nearly sixty years later. His son, David, recalls, "Bob's wedding was held in New York City. My dad was indeed the best man. He remembers it because he had to kneel on some marble steps that he says just about killed him."

Celeste Birch, Bonnie Collins, Bob Garrity and Johnny Smith on Collins and Garrity's wedding day

Smith and his quartet returned to New York and Birdland on 21 June 1956, where they shared the bill with Jeri Southern and the pianist Friedrich Gulda. When Southern and Gulda's tenures ended on 5 July, Smith and his quartet stayed on to be joined by Count Basie and his orchestra. His lengthy residency came to an end on 25 July, five weeks after he had opened at the club.

In researching through all of the Birdland listings in the entertainment guide of the *New Yorker* during the mid-1950s, it is evident that not only did no other jazz musician appear at the club as frequently as Smith, but also that his residencies were often notably longer than those of other performers. This testifies as much to his reliability as to his popularity with audiences. These characteristics were no doubt appreciated by both the club owners and patrons, particularly in a period when many jazz musicians were either mentally or physically absent due to encounters with narcotics. Smith earned himself a reputation with club owners as not only a first class musician, but also an extremely reliable one. At a time when nightclubs would underhandedly draw in audiences by booking Charlie Parker in the full knowledge that he would be too stoned to make an appearance, Smith was often called in to deputize without receiving any acknowledgment in the press.

As Birdland's most regular attraction during these years, Smith was by far the most prominent guitarist on the New York jazz scene. During a golden era of musicianship, he was the first guitarist to truly reach the top tier in the city of jazz. After a summer break, he was on the bill at Birdland yet again, along with Julian 'Cannonball' Adderley's quintet, from 13 September until 26 September 1956. He then moved across to Basin Street from 26 until 28 October, to play opposite Jutta Hipp. During 1956, Smith spent over thirteen weeks at Birdland, a single week at the Embers, and almost four weeks on tour as a Birdland star. The list of his jazz engagements for this year illustrates a continuation of his workaholic ethic of the previous two years. Ben Smith recalls the impact that the late-night Birdland gigs were having on his brother:

> Oh, I went and saw him play there quite a few times. During the 1950s, I stayed with him in New York for around a year. He would play until late. There was a restaurant close by. So, I would go and have a bite. John would come home late and really washed out. He was just so busy all the time.

Record Releases in 1956

Still content to take bookings as a sideman parallel to his prolific work fronting his combo, Smith took the guitar seat in Tito Puente's orchestra for a recording of Bertolt Brecht and Kurt Weill's 'Moritat', which is better known to American audiences as 'Mack the Knife'. The album *Beverly Kenney Sings for*

Johnny Smith, which had been recorded in the previous year, was also issued in 1956. Meanwhile, his contribution to Hank Jones' *Urbanity* album, which had been recorded in 1953, was finally released to the public. Two compilation albums – *Moonlight in Vermont* and *Moods* – of his earlier output were also issued, with the *In a Mellow Mood* and *In a Sentimental Mood* albums cherry-picked to provide the material for the latter.

On 24 October 1956, he went into the studio to record a new selection of pieces for his album *The New Johnny Smith Quartet*. The line-up of his piano-less quartet on this occasion featured George Roumanis on bass, Johnny Lee on drums, and Johnny Rae (née Pompeo) on vibraphone and bongos. The album opened with a delicate arrangement of Rodgers and Hart's 'It Never Entered My Mind', during which Smith displayed his command of the guitar with an extended section of harmonics in an exquisite juxtaposition with Rae. Meanwhile, on 'Pawn Ticket' and 'S'Wonderful', both Smith and Rae demonstrated their virtuosity at a high tempo. Two of the guitarist's own compositions were included on the album, in the form of 'Samba' and 'Montage', while the folk song 'Black Is the Color (of My True Love's Hair)' was presented as a chord-melody arrangement for solo guitar for the first time.

JOHNNY SMITH AND JOHNNY RAE DURING THE SESSIONS FOR THE NEW JOHNNY SMITH QUARTET

By November, Smith and his quartet were back on the road. They took up a two-week residency at the Modern Jazz Room in Chicago, Illinois, on 5 November 1956. At the end of the year, *Metronome* readers voted Barney Kessel as their favorite guitarist, with Smith placed third.

RUTH PRICE

During 1956, Smith, Lee and Rae, with Clyde Lombardi in the fold on bass duties, recorded an album accompanying another female singer, Ruth Price, titled *Ruth Price Sings with the Johnny Smith Quartet*. Interviewed in 2011, Ruth Price remembered how, as a child, she had first met Smith, and then inadvertently found herself working with him in New York a decade later when Teddy Reig put them together:

> Well, I actually met Johnny when I was just a kid and he played trumpet in the band at the Valley Forge General Hospital in Pennsylvania, which was a huge rehabilitation center. I wasn't a singer at the time. I was into ballet. I used to go down and listen to the band, and he had a black Cocker Spaniel. I love dogs. So, I used to sit and pet the dog. That's how I met him.
>
> But then flash forward 'til when I was about eighteen and I had a gig in New York, which was at the Blue Note. It was a fundraiser to save somebody's piano, I can't remember whose. Anyway, I was put up there to sing with Johnny Smith. Now, obviously by this time I knew about jazz and this wonderful guitar player named Johnny Smith, but

> I didn't put this together in my head with the trumpet player that I had met when I was a kid. I went up to rehearse with him, and it was my Johnny Smith! So, we then started working out in Forest Hills during that period of time, and his was the band that I sang with. I forget the name of the club, but we were there a long time. So, that's how I got together with him again.

Smith concurred with Ruth Price's memories:

> I was stationed in Phoenixville, Pennsylvania. Ruth was a young girl, and I was stationed at Valley Forge General Hospital, which was for wounded veterans. I got to know Ruth. That's where I first met her around '44 or '45, I think.

It was not necessary for Ruth Price to rehearse with Smith's group for their studio recording. Most of the repertoire had formed a part of their live sets. As was sometimes the case with Smith's recordings, a fair amount of the repertoire on this album consisted of ballads, although the pieces were selected by the singer. This demanded a particular musical ability that Ruth Price had not previously felt she was capable of meeting:

> You know, you get a lot of advice, in fact a lot of good advice, from older musicians. And it depends upon if you're open to it at the time. But I remember something that John said that has always stayed with me. He said, "You have a really good sense of time, and you depend upon that. But what you don't know is that you have a really beautiful natural vibrato, and you should really not be afraid to sing ballads." He was the one that persuaded me that I could. I still remember that conversation. Johnny actually asked for me to record with him.

Ruth Price's vocal style was distinctly untypical of a jazz singer, while also very distant from the soft style of Beverly Kenney. In the liner notes for her album with Smith, Barry Ulanov described her as "a singer who belts a song, who unashamedly and unabashedly takes on a tune and gives it a couple of lungs full of breath and a fist full of force." By the time that she was working with Smith, Ruth Price was already beginning to make a name for herself on the New York jazz scene and her star was in its ascendancy. As with Beverly Kenney before her, Price's album with Smith launched her onto a higher level. Soon after it was released in 1957, she relocated to Los Angeles where she performed and recorded with West Coast jazz musicians, such as Shelly Manne and Stan Getz. In 1992, she founded a not-for-profit jazz club, the Jazz Bakery, in Los Angeles and became hugely respected for her work as a patron and campaigner for jazz, as well as an educator at UCLA.

Club Dates and Recordings in 1957

1957 began well for Smith. Birdland continued to be his second home. As early as 24 January, he was back in the club with his quartet playing opposite Al Hibbler, and Bud Powell with his trio. Hibbler and Powell were replaced on 7 February by the ever popular Count Basie and His Orchestra with Joe Williams, but Smith and his quartet stayed on to complete a three-week tenancy on 13 February.

A fortnight later, he returned for a week-long residency from 28 February until 6 March, sharing the bill with Chris Connor and Ralph Sharon's trio. When Smith moved out, Tito Puente took over with his orchestra.

With the personnel of Smith's combo revolving once again, the quartet entered the recording studio on 18 March 1957. On this occasion, the combo consisted of pianist Bob Pancoast, Palestinian-born bassist Nabil 'Knobby' Totah, and drummer Jerry Segal. The results from the session were issued as the album *The Johnny Smith Foursome*. Four of the tracks - 'Hello Young Lovers', 'Love Letters', 'Love for Sale' and 'Good-Bye' - were also released as EP 313. In typical Teddy Reig style, it carried the same title as its corresponding album. There were no Smith compositions on this release, but Hugh Martin and Ralph Blane's 'The Boy Next Door' and Claude Debussy's 'The Girl with the Flaxen Hair' appeared as virtuoso chord-melody arrangements for solo guitar.

Three days later, on 21 March 1957, Smith and his quartet were once again in Birdland playing opposite Count Basie's orchestra and Pat Moran's quartet. Oscar Pettiford's group took over from Basie's band on 28 March. This line-up continued until 3 April, with Cannonball Adderley's quintet and Maynard Ferguson taking over on the following night. Smith then embarked upon another tour outside of the jazz capital. From 1 until 7 July 1957, he was playing at the Modern Jazz Room in Cleveland, Ohio. It is, once again, reflective of his stature at the time that he was followed at the popular club first by Toshiko Akiyoshi and then by Dizzy Gillespie. The Modern Jazz Room had been a frequent venue on his previous tours in its former guise as the Cotton Club.

After a lengthy break, Smith's ownership of the stage at Birdland resumed for a two-week run from 1 until 14 August opposite Matthew Gee's All-Stars, and Morgana King. Bud Powell and Johnny Richards' orchestra were the relief crew.

By September 1957, the personnel of Smith's combo had revolved to consist of Bob Pancoast, George Roumanis and Mousie Alexander. A recording session produced the material for another album, *The Johnny Smith Foursome Volume II*. There were no outright chord-melody solo guitar performances included on this album, although 'Laura' contained minimal involvement from the combo.

On 26 September, Smith's quartet were again at Birdland for a three-week residency, which began opposite Dizzy Gillespie. Chris Connor and Stan Free joined Smith for his second week on the bill from 3 October, and Henry Coker's sextet joined him for the third week. When Smith's tenure came to a close on 16 October, Miles Davis and Stan Getz moved in. On 21 November, Smith and his quartet took up their sixth and final residency of the year at Birdland, opposite Sarah Vaughan. Smith, Vaughan, and the Jimmy Smith Trio all ended their tenures on 4 December, with Count Basie then taking over duties.

Tragedy

In October 1957, tragedy struck Smith's life when his wife, Ann, died of complications during childbirth. In furthering his grief, the baby also died. This devastating episode left him to bring up their three-year-old daughter, Kim, with the aid of close friends Marjorie and Sam Atkinson.
The consequence of Ann's death could not have been greater, and it would soon force him to make a decision regarding his music career that would change the rest of his life.

The End of 1957 and Roost Records

Although Smith made several appearances in numerous jazz venues across New York, such as the Hickory House and others which have already been mentioned, Birdland was by far his favorite club. The standard of musicianship on display at the most famous of jazz venues was, in his opinion, continually higher than anywhere else in the city.

The long list of his identified jazz engagements in 1957 shows an obvious similarity with the previous year's workload, as he spent another thirteen weeks at Birdland. Once again, it should not be forgotten that he was also still working for the radio and television networks on programs such as the *Patrice Munsel Show*. The Metropolitan Opera star's television show was broadcast by ABC from October 1957 until June 1958, with music arranged by Smith's old friend Irwin Kostal.

Despite his undeniable position as the city's most celebrated jazz guitarist, Smith remained content to accept work as a sideman. In 1957, he again joined Tito Puente's orchestra, to record eight pieces for the percussionist's album *Mucho Puente*. He also joined fellow guitarists Mundell Lowe and Tony Mottola in contributing performances to Richard Wess' quaintly titled album *Music She Digs the Most*.

During the year, Teddy Reig discovered that he had taken his eye off the ball and that his Roost label was on the verge of bankruptcy. He sold out to Morris Levy's Roulette company. On 13 October 1958, the *Billboard* reported that Reig, who was by then handling the jazz department as a member of the A&R staff at Roulette, had noticed that the takeover had resulted in a renewed interest in his Roost catalog. Smith's *Moonlight in Vermont* compilation album, Charlie Parker's *All-Star Sextet* and Dizzy Gillespie's *Concert in Paris* had received the most curiosity. This may have been nothing more than an advertisement disguised as a news item. All three of the aforementioned albums were relatively recent releases. Nevertheless, Roulette was a sizable label with much greater distribution capabilities than Roost had previously been able to implement. Levy was able to disseminate Roost's back-catalog, including Smith's recordings, more widely. Unfortunately, his primary attention was soon to be drawn towards the more lucrative marketplace of rock 'n' roll music.

The end of Roost Records as an independent label should have fractured the relationship between Smith and Reig, but this was not the case. When Reig died on 29 September 1984, he left a small but significant amount of money to Smith in his will as repayment of a business debt. Smith was contacted by Reig's lawyers and required to provide an affidavit explaining the circumstances of this debt. His response provides an insight into the trusting relationship that he had maintained with Reig:

> The late Theodore S. Reig, to be referred to henceforth as "Teddy Reig", was a very unique individual to which anyone who knew him closely will attest. His word and his

handshake were his Bible and his friendship could be jeopardized by a request for an agreement in writing, and especially if the request came from someone he considered a friend.

I started recording for Teddy's record company, Royal Roost, in 1951 [*sic*]. At that time Teddy had a partner, Jack Hook of New York City, who later left Royal Roost to pursue the Rock and Roll market. I never had a written contract with Royal Roost or Teddy Reig as it was obvious from the very beginning that I was dealing with a man of unquestionable honesty. After Jack Hook left the company, Teddy informed me that he was making me a partner in Royal Roost. It was further agreed that I would forego royalties from the sale of records in lieu of a cash investment in Royal Roost records, these royalties being referred to in his Last Will and Testament as "debt".

In the years between 1951 and 1967 [*sic*], Royal Roost released 25 to 30 Johnny Smith albums. Finally, with the increase in sales of rock and roll records and the decrease in the sales of jazz records, Teddy discontinued releasing Royal Roost records and the Master records were sold to Roulette Records of New York City. There was no payment made to me at the time of that transaction, nor has there been since then. I was never concerned, because I knew that someday, somehow, I would be paid the money due to me.

The last time I saw Teddy was during an engagement at the Uris Theatre in New York City with the late Bing Crosby. His last words to me when I walked him to his car were, "No matter what happens to me, John, you will be paid the money I owe you." I was not aware of the amount of the debt until his Last Will and Testament was published after his death on September 29, 1984.

While Reig should be recognized for abiding by his word, and the bequest was not an insignificant figure, he undoubtedly came out of the arrangement better than the guitarist. The royalties that Smith was due for his recordings twenty to thirty years earlier amounted to a notably greater sum than he ultimately received.

Chapter Five:
The Colorado Years

From the outside, 1958 appeared to begin in the same vein as the preceding four years for Smith. His quartet were once again to be found in Birdland with a two-week engagement commencing on 30 January opposite Jeri Southern, closing on 12 February. The *New Yorker* described the residency as:

> Devoted to those who are eager to fall under the swing and sway (if any) of the new music. The spellbinders are Jeri Southern, a voice to remember; Johnny Smith's foursome, who like to put counterpoint on their cereal; and Sonny Rollins' quartet. (Reproduced from the *New Yorker*, 1 February 1958)

Another witty account followed a week later:

> The gathering of the clan for which music is the end-all, be-all, and be-bop. Jeri Southern, the singer of the evening, is relaxed about the whole thing; Johnny Smith, his electronic guitar and his quartet are intent but calm about it. As for the attitude of Sonny Rollins' foursome, keep in mind that he was tenor sax in the lamented up-in-the-clouds group run by Clifford Brown and Max Roach. (Reproduced from the *New Yorker*, 8 February 1958)

In reality, however, although he reveled in the music that he was playing in New York, he had come to dislike the lifestyle. His work schedule was grueling, to say the least. Even as a freelancer, he had been working around the clock in the radio, television and recording studios, as well as in the nightclubs of New York and across the USA. It should be noted that his workload was largely self-inflicted. Abject poverty in childhood often leaves those who are self-determined with a highly driven approach to their work. The fear of a return to desperate financial circumstances is a powerful incentive to seize every work opportunity that presents itself. Denisa Hanna remembers Smith telling her of the impact that the lifestyle and work schedule in New York had upon him:

> When I was at college, he told me that he had been on a self-destruct path in his New York days, taking stuff just to try to keep going. I think he told me that because... you know... the tendency that I was headed for higher-louder-faster guitars at the time.

Bobby Greene recalls the guitarist recounting the typical commute to his daytime studio work:

> John said that when he was working in New York at NBC, he was living at Long Island.

> In order to be in the studio by nine o'clock in the morning, he had to leave home by six. It only took him twenty minutes to get to work, but if he left any later it was questionable that he would get there on time because the traffic was so bad. I think that's one of the things that contributed to his decision to leave New York.

Relocation from New York to Colorado

By 1958, the music scene was changing. Rock 'n' roll had become the popular sound of the day, and jazz was beginning to take a modal direction with Miles Davis' new sextet, featuring John Coltrane and Cannonball Adderley, due to appear at the Village Vanguard in July. Meanwhile, the broadcasting networks had started to dissolve their orchestras. In Smith's own words:

> I didn't like New York City. I loved working there, but not living there. No. But from when I got there in '46, until '58, it was really the apex of live music. Everything was live music, right down to the commercials. When I left, it started to deteriorate. The three networks all had over a hundred musicians on their full-time staff. But when I left, it was all gone. Yeah, I was very fortunate to get out of there when I did.

The changing music scene, traffic issues and even the self-inflicted overload of work certainly contributed to Smith's decision to leave New York. However, they paled into insignificance compared to the unexpected death of his wife, Ann, in October of the previous year. The Colorado jazz impresario Dick Gibson later noted that Smith's playing had understandably lost some of its energy for a period after Ann died, but added that he had returned to his old vitality in due course. He further added, "I heard him about a year ago and he was really playing. You listened to him for a while and your butt started to twitch."

Arthur Godfrey and Johnny Smith

Realizing that he was struggling to raise his daughter responsibly, Smith consulted a pediatrician to ascertain if there was any possibility of her enjoying a healthy and balanced upbringing with the help of a nursemaid, considering his work commitments and single-parent status. The professional opinion was not positive. Thus, in February 1958, when he was thirty-five years old and the most popular and revered guitarist on the New York jazz scene, he left New York to begin a new chapter in his life. The huge network of personal friends and work colleagues that he had established in the city, including his de facto manager Teddy Reig, understood his reasoning and supported his decision to leave. Arthur Godfrey attempted to persuade him to stay, offering him any financial or personal help that he might need. Smith had been working on Godfrey's CBS radio show at the time, alongside Jack Lesberg, Bobby Hackett, Peanuts Hucko, Urbie Green, Dick Hyman and Cozy Cole.

Reig's response to Smith's departure was testament to their friendship. The guitarist had been the biggest selling act on his Roost label, and he continued to be a sizable earner for him when Roost became a subsidiary of Morris Levy's Roulette record company. David Smith recalls that Reig even provided a new home for his father's dog when he left New York:

JOHNNY SMITH WITH HIS AFGHAN HOUND, DUNCAN

> I remember big Teddy coming over to my dad's house once in a while. What a large man! When Dad left New York, Teddy took possession of his dog. It was a pure white Afghan Hound named Duncan. Dad told me that Teddy used to walk Duncan around Harlem, but, with or without the dog, Dad said nobody fucked with Teddy because the man was connected.

Reig's 'connections' were along the same lines, if perhaps not as severe, as those of Morris Levy. Mundell Lowe elaborates, "The truth of the matter is that he was kind of hung in with the mob. You know, the mobsters. I think that's the way he managed to get that record label going."

The story of Smith's departure from New York has provided one of his most famous quotations, when he commented, "The greatest view I ever had of New York City was when I emerged from the Lincoln tunnel on the New Jersey side and watched the Manhattan skyline recede in my rear-view mirror." Before vacating his address at 9-22 College Place, College Point, Long Island, he chose Colorado Springs for his new home. His parents had recently moved to the area, and just a month before his wife had died, Smith had paid a final visit to his father, who had been dying from cancer. John Smith Sr. was buried in Fairview Cemetery in Colorado Springs on 19 November 1957. Ben Smith explains the causes of his father's death:

> You know how these forges are. That's what killed our dad. We used to go and see what they called the runoff. On Friday nights, they would tip all of these big buckets over and run off all the sludge. They didn't have anything in the way of breathing protection. You couldn't see in there, because of all of the fumes. That was what got our dad in the end.

With his two younger brothers, Ben and Emmett, also living nearby, Colorado Springs was therefore a logical place to which to relocate. Aided by his family, Smith was able to provide a preferable environment for his daughter, Kim, while he was establishing himself financially in the area. Within a few weeks of his arrival, he moved into a modest house and continued to reside there until his death in June 2013. Throughout the rest of his life, he never voiced any regrets about leaving the limelight of New York. With absolute conviction, he was entirely satisfied that he had made the right decision for both his daughter and himself. With typically good humor, he often said of Colorado that it "locates you as far away from New York as you can be without getting too close to L.A.."

Contrary to popular belief, Smith did not become a recluse when he relocated from New York to Colorado Springs. Furthermore, he did not retire or even semi-retire from performing. Instead, he gradually built and maintained an extremely active musical life as a performer on the local jazz scene, particularly around Denver. There, his work was shamefully ignored by the American national music press, who lazily remained focused upon jazz in traditional centers, such as New York and Los Angeles, where musicians were more easily accessible for interviews. John Smith III, speaks for many people who were around his father at the time of his departure from New York:

> You know, he doesn't have the notoriety that many people, myself included, think that he should have. In New York, he was absolutely the attraction. He had a very loyal following. Then, he had that tragedy in 1957 when he lost Ann and his dad within a few months of each other. He was at the top of the music world - guitarist at NBC, the Birdland thing, he had won the *Down Beat* award for a few years. He was at the apex. He had two brothers, Emmett and Ben, who had already moved to Colorado. He contacted them, sold the house in Flushing, shut down everything that he had going and moved to Colorado Springs. He decided to throw it all away and go into obscurity. You know, his music continued, but just not under the spotlight of New York City.

Elsewhere in the media, syndicated journalists in local newspapers across the United States were also guilty of continually misrepresenting Smith to the public after he had relocated to Colorado. In reviewing his *Johnny Smith's Kaleidoscope* album a decade later, the *Wichita Eagle and Beacon Magazine* lamented that jazz had "lost its most lyrical and adept guitarist when Johnny Smith went into semi-retirement nine years ago." In reality, he continued to travel to New York to record and perform in clubs such as Birdland for a number of years after his relocation.

To some degree, his performances in New York over the next few years were the result of an understandable inability to draw a line under that particular chapter in his life with immediate finality. Some of his most admired recordings were completed around this time, and he was unquestionably still at the top of his game. Having resigned himself to leaving New York, the quality of the musicianship there was difficult for him to ignore. These excursions held him in the public consciousness for the period through the jazz media's limited attention, and also helped him to stay financially afloat while he was establishing himself in Denver and the surrounding area.

While he was far from living in affluence, he was also not destitute. His workaholic lifestyle had rewarded him with enough capital to purchase a modest home in Colorado Springs. Due to the tax laws, it would have been financially better for him to have paid for the property over several years, but the abject poverty and forced migration of his childhood haunted him, and he was determined that nobody was ever going to be able to remove him from his own home.

Jeri Southern

On 19 and 22 May 1958, three months after leaving New York, Smith was back in the city to record his third album with a female vocalist, when his quartet entered the studio with Jeri Southern. Unlike Beverly Kenney and Ruth Price before her, Jeri Southern was already a well-established performer by the time that she recorded with Smith. The torch singer had appeared opposite him on the bill at Birdland on numerous occasions.

Smith was requested by Teddy Reig to record with Southern, for which occasion he provided new arrangements. By his own reluctant admission, her voice was not at its best by this time:

JERI SOUTHERN

> Oh yeah. But she had a terrible problem with alcohol. She never got drunk, but she would drink like a quart of booze per day. When we did that album, she was just out of an alcoholic's recovery center. She was a lovely lady. You would never know about her drinking. She was always a perfect lady.

Despite Southern's faltering voice, her performance on *Jeri Southern Meets Johnny Smith* is still highly enjoyable. Smith, Pancoast, Roumanis and Alexander put in some of their finest performances on this album. The guitarist's arrangements of Southern's choice of repertoire are exquisite, and the tight interaction between the musicians is immaculate. Smith remembered the recording session with Southern, and the standard session rules, vividly:

> We just showed up on the date, ran through the music once and then recorded it. That was the same thing with the strings, you know. As a matter of fact, that's what I hated about recording, because we were required by union law to record four songs in three hours. So, you just had to keep from making bad mistakes. I wasn't able to relax at all like that.

Jeri Southern Meets Johnny Smith was released late in the year, with a review in the *Billboard* in December proclaiming that this was her best recording since she had moved to Roulette from Decca.

Birdland and Easy Listening

On 22 May 1958, Smith finished his recording session with Jeri Southern and went straight into Birdland on the same day to began a two-week residency with his quartet opposite Chico Hamilton's quintet and J.J. Johnson's quintet, with all three acts closing on 11 June. He was selected to feature on the front cover of a special issue of *Metronome* magazine in June which focused upon jazz guitarists.

He returned to Birdland later in the year, on 4 September, for a week-long engagement. In describing the contemporaneous events at the club, the *New Yorker* colorfully alluded to the changing times in jazz, but acknowledged that Smith was still a welcome presence on the scene:

> Devoted to those who are eager to fall under the spell of the new music. The spellbinding is now being done by Maynard Ferguson's orchestra, which frequently sounds like forty-four angry young men, and the Sonny Rollins trio, which does everything the hard (or at least the hard-bop) way. Their last night is Wednesday, Sept. 3. Next evening, Count Basie's hobbledehoys will open a jar of hot mustard, which will (among other things) be

> background music for Joe Williams, a genuine handmade blues singer of the pre-electronic era. Johnny Smith, his guitar (electronic era, but all right), and his quartet will show up, too. (Reproduced from the *New Yorker*, 30 August 1958)

On 13 November 1958, Smith began his fourth residency of the year at Birdland, totaling seven weeks of performances at the club across the year. On this occasion, his combo was reduced to a pianoless trio, once again playing opposite Chico Hamilton's quintet. Six days later, on 19 November, he recorded the album *Easy Listening* with bassist George Roumanis and drummer Charlie Mastropaola at the Penthouse Sound studio. Dick Gibson's observation of Smith's mood following the death of his wife a year earlier is supported by the performances on this album. While there are mid-tempo pieces such as 'Like Someone in Love', 'People Will Say We're in Love' and 'A Foggy Day', and there are displays of his superior technical command of harmonics in pieces such as 'I Didn't Know What Time It Was', 'It Might as Well Be Spring' and 'Scarlet Ribbons', the predominance of slow ballads results in a definite overall feeling of melancholy. 'Black Is the Color' was included again as a chord-melody arrangement for solo guitar.

Flower Drum Song

1958 also saw the release of perhaps Smith's most unexpected album. While he was recording for Roost Records, he generally had the freedom to choose the repertoire for each session and subsequent release. In his own liner notes to his earlier *The Johnny Smith Foursome* album, he took the opportunity to thank Teddy Reig for allowing him the freedom to record whatever and whenever he chose to do so. Occasionally, however, Reig asked him to record specific musical works due to financial pressures, for which Smith obliged. This was particularly true of the album *Flower Drum Song*, which was recorded with George Roumanis, Mousie Alexander, and Charles McCracken on cello at the Penthouse Sound studio in New York City in the middle of 1958. Reig had sent Smith to hear the new Rodgers and Hammerstein musical in Boston before it opened on Broadway, with the intention of assembling an album of some of the pieces and thereby benefiting from its anticipated commercial success when it arrived in New York. Smith felt that, although he had done the best that he could, the resulting album was a disaster as there was little in the material that lent itself to a jazz interpretation. In fairness, the musical itself is not generally considered to be one of Rodgers and Hammerstein's better works.

Struggling in Colorado

Back in Colorado, life for Smith was not running smoothly. As a stranger in town, he initially struggled to break into the local music scene. By his own admission, he had not seriously considered how he was going to make a living before his arrival in Colorado. Although it was ignored by the national media, the state had an extremely active jazz scene in the closing years of the 1950s and throughout the 1960s into the 1970s. The thriving economy in the area, which was founded upon the oil and banking industries, generated a demand for entertainment. Denver, in particular, was awash with venues for jazz performers, including the Senate Lounge at the Argonaut Hotel; the Top of the Park at the Park Lane Hotel; the Bandbox; and the Melody Lounge, where Smith became a regular feature.

Pianist Bobby Greene recalls how the social climate affected the music scene in Colorado at the time:

> The music business is always a case of feast or famine, you know. You either had more jobs than you could take, or you were praying for people to call. Back in the 1960s and 1970s, it was much better than it is now and has been for the last twenty-five years or so. Before they got serious about the drinking and driving. Between the lawyers and the classes that you have to attended if you get caught... It's expensive. And that affected the music business around Colorado. The drinking used to pay for the band. These days, there just aren't that many venues for musicians to play at.

Murder at Birdland

In New York, the events at Birdland were temporarily interrupted on 26 January 1959 when Morris Levy's brother, Zachariah 'Irving' Levy, was stabbed to death in the club during a set by Urbie Green. The consensus of opinion among the jazz community is that Levy was killed in a case of mistaken identity, and that his brother had been the intended target of a mafia assassination. The murderer, Lee Schlesinger, pleaded self-defense and was sentenced to twenty-two years imprisonment for second-degree murder in December. Mundell Lowe, whose quartet was booked to appear at Birdland on 29 January, recalls that the club was only closed for a short period, perhaps just a day or two, before business resumed as normal. Smith and his trio did not return to Birdland until 30 April 1959 when they took up a three-week residency opposite the Harry Edison Quintet, with Sarah Vaughan joining them on the bill a week later. All three acts finished on 20 May, vacating the premises for Count Basie and Joe Williams.

Johnny Smith Favorites and Designed for You

Smith made good use of this time in New York during May 1959. He and George Roumanis reunited with drummer Mousie Alexander for the recording of *Johnny Smith Favorites* and *Designed for You*. Remarkably, both of these albums were recorded on 20 May, the same day that the trio performed the final night of their residency at Birdland. The former of these albums included new versions of 'Moonlight in Vermont', 'My Funny Valentine' and 'Little Girl Blue'. It also included some new additions to Smith's uniquely broad-ranging repertoire, such as an arrangement of classical composer Maurice Ravel's '*Pavane de la belle au bois dormant*', which has often been mistakenly assumed by many jazz guitarists to be the same composer's more famous '*Pavane pour une infante défunte*'. Although this is the only true outright solo guitar piece on this album, many of the guitar parts fall into the chord-melody category. In the absence of a pianist with whom to share chordal duties, there is a greater musical responsibility upon the Smith's shoulders in these recordings.

The same observation is applicable to the less melancholic *Designed for You* album. Here, Smith returned to up-tempo virtuosity on 'Three Little Words', 'The Lady Is a Tramp' and 'There Will Never Be Another You'. Meanwhile, the highly original gypsy-style arrangement of 'Autumn Leaves' featured him playing on an unamplified archtop guitar for the first time on one of his own records. 'My Romance' and the introduction of 'I'll Take Romance' received the solo guitar chord-melody treatment.

Birdland and Beyond

The *Denver Post Empire* reported in July 1959 that Smith was spending time working in Miami, Florida, as well as New York City. In the Sunshine State, he was reunited with the accordionist and organist Joe Mooney for some club dates. However, these were not the only cities outside of New York and Colorado in which Smith was playing. On 21 September 1959, he performed two shows with his trio at the 90th Floor club at 2052 McKinney Avenue in Dallas, Texas.

He returned to Birdland with his trio on 22 October 1959 for a lengthy four-week residency that continued until 18 November, and which included a period playing opposite the revolutionary Miles Davis Sextet. While his mother attended to his daughter back in Colorado, Smith spent a total of seven weeks working in New York's premier jazz venue during 1959. Although this figure was a substantial reduction upon the annual statistic of bookings that he typically fulfilled at Birdland when he was a resident of New York, it was nevertheless on a par with the number of his appearances at the club in 1958, and he was undeniably still an active contributor to the city's jazz scene.

Remarriage

One aspect of Smith's life in Colorado started to fall into place. On 12 February 1960, he married Sandra Jean Harrel (née Robbins) in Colorado Springs. Sandy's importance to her husband's life cannot be overestimated. She took on the role of a mother to his young daughter, Kim, and would become the business mind behind his successful music store in Colorado Springs.

Sandy and Johnny Smith on their wedding day in 1960

Johnny Smith Plus the Trio

In early 1960, Smith was back in New York alongside George Roumanis, Mousie Alexander and Bob Pancoast for the recording of *Johnny Smith Plus the Trio*. He was clearly pleased to have Pancoast back within the fold and featured him on a version of Duke Ellington's 'Prelude to a Kiss'. The album also included Roumanis' witty composition 'Hippo, the Sentimental Hippy'. The review in the *Billboard* commented favorably:

> The impeccable artist of the jazz guitar is accompanied here by George Roumanis, bass, drummer Mousey Alexander, and pianist Bob Pancoast. The set is pleasingly paced with alternate up-tempo, swing, and mood ballad tunes. Standards like 'Over the Rainbow' and 'I Can't Get Started', 'Out of Nowhere' and 'Un Poco Loco', all out of the regular Smith repertoire, should get much deejay play and should appeal to the hip pop as well as the jazz buyer. (Reproduced from the *Billboard*, 23 January 1961)

My Dear Little Sweetheart

Also in early 1960, during the same visit to New York that resulted in the recording of *Johnny Smith Plus the Trio*, Smith recorded the first of two very unexpected albums. *My Dear Little Sweetheart* featured him with orchestral accompaniment and was decidedly non-jazz in its musical style. An anonymous reviewer for the *Billboard* acknowledged the guitarist's unanticipated musical direction, but responded favorably:

The photograph of Kim taken during a photo session for the album cover of My Dear Little Sweetheart

> This is an unusual Johnny Smith LP. The guitarist is backed by a large string ensemble, adding warmth and lushness to Smith's guitar work. The tunes include the title song and such standards as 'Indian Summer', 'Softly As In a Morning Sunrise', 'Once in a While', and 'It Never Entered My Mind'. Good wax for Smith fans and a good deejay programming set. (Reproduced from the *Billboard*, 7 March 1960)

The title of *My Dear Little Sweetheart* was a reference to Smith's daughter, Kim, and originated from his late second wife's Swedish mother, Dagmar Westerstrom, who often addressed her granddaughter with this particular term of endearment. The cover of the album featured a portrait painting of Kim which had been worked from a photograph. Smith later recalled that the photographer had not been particularly adept at encouraging his young and understandably impatient daughter to sit for the photograph. It took a considerable amount of time to achieve a satisfactory result.

Guitar and Strings

Smith's next album, *Guitar and Strings*, also featured orchestral accompaniment, and included Barry Galbraith on second guitar. It was recorded in May 1960 while Smith was in New York for another engagement at Birdland and was initially intended to be titled *The Heart of Johnny Smith*. The anonymous reviewer for the *Billboard* found Smith's new musical direction more difficult than his predecessor to accept:

> Somewhat disappointing wax by Johnny Smith. He is backed with so many strings here that at times it is difficult to hear the guitarist. When you can, his work is as faultless as ever, and he gets a chance now and then to solo. (Reproduced from the *Billboard*, 29 August 1960)

The orchestral arrangements for both *My Dear Little Sweetheart* and *Guitar and Strings* were Smith's own work and gave him a great sense of personal pride. On the latter album, he even incorporated some harmonic ideas that had been inspired by Berg's atonal opera *Wozzeck*. Always self-critical, however, he felt that his guitar parts were far from spectacular. The three afternoon recording sessions for the album passed more than satisfactorily, with the exception of Ralph Hersch sitting on his own viola. The proceedings had to be momentarily suspended while he hurriedly found a replacement instrument. Meanwhile, the musicians in his vicinity patiently crawled around the floor and were able to gather up the shattered pieces which were then successfully used to rebuild the instrument.

Goodbye to Birdland

On 12 May 1960, Smith began his only residency of the year with his trio at Birdland. The respected French jazz guitarist and singer Sacha Distel was present at the club during this tenancy. A syndicated article by Dorothy Kilgallen, which appeared in newspapers across the USA, reported that he was so overwhelmed by Smith's virtuosity that he was heard to say to a friend, "I give up for all time. I sell guitar tomorrow and learn trumpet." Smith's lengthy three-week residency ended on 1 June and inspired the reviewer for the *New Yorker* to provide another typically witty and affectionate review of the events at the club:

> The most compulsive underground movement on Broadway. The Horace Silver quintet, which must often have icy fingers up and down its spine, and the Johnny Smith trio, which quietly passes the evening analyzing itself, are on view at the moment. (Reproduced from the *New Yorker*, 14 May 1960, 8)

Not only was this Smith's only residency of the year at Birdland, but it was also his final appearance at the club. As jazz evolved into its next phase, he decided that it was time to let go of New York:

> I remember good times and good music. Count Basie, Sarah Vaughan, George Shearing, Dizzy Gillespie, Stan Getz... But then they began to get these 'radicals' in there. I would be the first guy to go on, and the place would be packed. The second guy came on, put the Altec microphone right in the bell of his saxophone... 'honk, honk, honk...', and cleared the whole place. I don't know why they did that. It ruined the good music of Birdland.

Although Smith was an admirer of Schönberg and Berg's atonal music, this was not to say that he was caught up in the 'Emperor's New Clothes' syndrome that blinded several of the free-form jazz and avant-garde practitioners. He felt that many of the lesser musicians had jumped on that particular bandwagon either in order to avoid the travails of studying jazz theory, or because they mistook novelty for quality.

His difficulty in cutting his ties with New York had been entirely understandable. The city's music scene had been a major part of his life since 1946, and he was a well-established figure. In contrast, while the opportunities in Denver and Colorado Springs for first-class musicians certainly existed, breaking into the local jazz scene was a different matter. He found work with the Sammy Colon Trio, but this was far from lucrative. In fact, his paltry income must have come as quite a shock in comparison to the figures that he had been earning in New York, even at Birdland. He later recalled, "I was invited to join a local group headed by Sammy Colon. I worked on a percentage basis, and made around $16 per week playing at Eddie's Skyroom."

Aside from Eddie's Skyroom, the quartet also worked at the Foxes Lounge in the Alamo Hotel in Colorado Springs, where the line-up alongside Smith consisted of Sammy Colon on piano, Mickey McPherson on drums, and Jim Rasmussen on bass. In September 1960, the *Colorado Springs Gazette Telegraph* reported that the Alamo Hotel was a nightly gig for the outfit, which was now being advertised in Smith's name.

With an insufficient income from local work it is not surprising that Smith had been compelled to make numerous trips back to New York. Although the fees that he had received for playing at Birdland had been far from generous, they were still significantly better than anything that was available in Colorado. It seems beyond reason that the guitarist who was revered by all of his contemporaries in New York and across the US struggled to make ends meet in Colorado. He was forced to work hard to raise his profile and appeared regularly at the delightfully named McRobert's Gut Bucket Seven fortnightly jam sessions in Colorado Springs.

The Sound of the Johnny Smith Guitar

In 1961, Smith returned to New York, where he assembled a new lineup of Hank Jones on piano, George Duvivier on bass, and Ed Shaughnessy on drums for the recording of his album *The Sound of the Johnny Smith Guitar*. Smith had worked with Hank Jones in 1953 when they had recorded the pianist's *Urbanity* album with bassist Ray Brown. He had also worked with George Duvivier and Ed Shaughnessy in 1953 when they were all members of Joe Bushkin's quartet playing opposite Jones at New York's Embers club. Of all the pianists with whom he played over the years, Hank Jones was Smith's favorite, and the musical understanding and interaction between the two of them on this album is nothing short of sublime. The *Billboard* gave a glowing review:

> Another fine set from one of the jazz world's most talented guitarists, Johnny Smith. Smith is in excellent form, running through nine tracks composed mainly of standards. But it's on the ballads that he shows special warmth and feeling. 'Come Rain or Come Shine', 'Embraceable You' and ''Round Midnight' come in for special acclaim. He is supported by a superb rhythm section of Hank Jones, piano; George Duvivier, bass; and Eddie Shaughnessy, drums. (Reproduced from the *Billboard*, 18 December 1961)

The Sound of the Johnny Smith Guitar once again demonstrated Smith's uniquely broad repertoire. Alongside the jazz standards and ballads, he included a short solo guitar chord-melody arrangement of the Russian classical composer Alexander Scriabin's piano *Prelude* Opus 16, No. 4. It is not coincidental that the piece had been recorded by one of his primary influences, Andrés Segovia, in 1956. Smith's arrangement, like that of Segovia, was written in the key of B minor, rather than Scriabin's original key of E flat minor.

Don Gibson

Anita Kerr, Don Gibson, Harold Bradley, Hank Garland and Johnny Smith in the studio

Clearly far from retired since he had relocated to Colorado Springs three years earlier, the versatile Smith flew into Nashville for three recording sessions at the RCA Victor Studio on 1 and 2 May 1961 as a sideman on singer Don Gibson's country album *Girls, Guitars and Gibson*. The sessions were produced by his friend Chet Atkins while Anita Kerr provided the exquisite arrangements. Pianist Floyd Cramer and country guitar legends Hank Garland and Harold Bradley joined Smith in the studio. This was one of the last records on which Garland appeared. In September 1961, he was seriously injured in a car accident which all but ended his professional career as a guitarist.

Smith's hillbilly-country roots were invaluable during these recording sessions. The combination of his stylistic awareness of the genre alongside his ability to read and execute Anita Kerr's arrangements was rare for a first-rate jazz guitarist. The unity of the three guitarists on this album is astounding, particularly in the sections of rapid harmonized phrases, and credit should also be afforded to Garland and Bradley.

Anita Kerr recalls her memories of the recording sessions as well as the admiration that she had already developed for Smith prior to working with him. In doing so, she provides an important example of the appeal of his jazz recordings to listeners outside of the jazz spectrum:

> I remember working with Johnny on the Gibson LP. In fact, I was honored to be able to meet him for I had several of his albums and was a fan of his. Sorry to say, I only saw him in the studio during the sessions so we didn't get to sit and talk with each other personally. I just remember that he was very quiet, polite and read through the arrangements like the pro that he was.

Small Beginnings in Colorado Springs

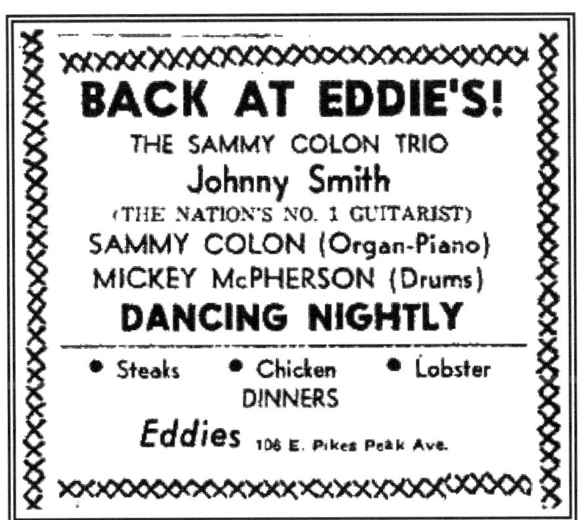

Back in Colorado, Smith completed a ten-week residency at the Alamo Hotel in March 1961 and was about to return to Eddie's Skyroom. Other venues in Colorado around this time included the lavish Broadmoor Hotel. Smith's son, David, describes the Broadmoor, which still exists today:

> The Broadmoor is a five-star resort here in Colorado Springs, and there aren't many of them in the country. If the president comes here and stays for the night, he stays at the Broadmoor. It started out as a dairy farm, and then with money from the gold rush days...

Unfortunately, as Johnny Smith recalled, the lucrative Broadmoor Hotel turned out to be a short-lived engagement:

> I call it the Brownmoor. I was playing with this little group downtown when I first came out here. It was a pretty steady job. In fact, one week I made $16 [laughs]. Anyway, this guy came to us and said, "We want you to play at the Broadmoor." So, we quit the gig that we had and went up to the Broadmoor, figuring that it would be a lasting thing because business was excellent. Packed houses every night. But after one month we got fired. I asked why, and he said, "You're making too much money." Huh?

In need of an additional local source of income, he continued to indulge in his passion for flying by working as a flight instructor. In March 1961, he opened his own music store in Colorado Springs using the commission that he had received from the Gibson guitar company for endorsing the Gibson Johnny Smith model that he had designed. After a slow start, the music store would provide him with some degree of financial stability for he next twenty-five years.

JOHNNY SMITH WITH HIS GIBSON GUITAR

A year later, Smith returned to Nashville to join Don Gibson, Harold Bradley, Floyd Cramer, vocal group the Jordanaires and producer Chet Atkins for three recording sessions on 12 and 13 March 1962. Of the twelve selections that were recorded, only three were included on the Gibson's *Some Favorites of Mine* album. The remaining material on the album was drawn from two sessions on 17 March, by which time both Smith and bassist Bob Moore had left town. Gibson's revised lineup included country guitar legend Jerry Reed.

THE MAN WITH THE BLUE GUITAR

By 1962, Smith had begun to establish himself in Colorado, although he was still far from financially comfortable. He had also come to accept the closure of the New York chapter of his life and had no wish to return unnecessarily to the hustle and bustle of the city for recording sessions. For this reason, he chose to record his solo album *The Man with the Blue Guitar* in the basement of his music store.

This album broke new ground within the genre of the plectrum guitar. Previously, Smith had regularly included one or two solo guitar pieces on each of his albums. *The Man with the Blue Guitar*, however, consisted entirely of solo chord-melody arrangements. The material was sourced from a wide range of musical styles, and included folk songs such as 'Shenandoah' and a revisited 'Black Is the Color'; classical compositions such as Claude Debussy's 'The Girl with the Flaxen Hair' and Maurice Ravel's '*Pavane de la belle au bois dormant*', both of which were new interpretations of earlier recordings; and jazz standards such as Rodgers and Hart's 'My Funny Valentine'. The significance of Smith's innovative album was not missed by the musicologist Dr Albert Seay in his liner notes, and it remains one of his most admired collections of recordings among the jazz guitar community.

Despite this album's position of reverence, Smith felt that some of the arrangements did not meet his satisfaction because they were created on the spur of the moment and therefore lacked his typical sophistication. Al Owens, who was a customer at Smith's music store several years later, remembers the owner telling him that the arrangement of 'Shenandoah' was improvised in order to meet the amount of material that was required to complete an album. Nevertheless, an anonymous reviewer in the *Billboard* described the album in a typically favorable manner:

> One of the true guitar virtuosos is heard in a program of solos which can draw plenty of pop as well as jazz interest and which figures as a natural for good mood programming. An unusually appealing selection includes 'My Romance', 'Little Girl Blue', 'Black Is the Color', 'Funny Valentine' and 'Old Folks'. Handsome stuff. (Reproduced from the *Billboard*, 1 September 1962)

The cover of *The Man with the Blue Guitar* contained a curious feature that has been overlooked by almost all of Smith's admirers. The silhouetted figure of a guitarist seated on a stool was not that of Smith. Rather, it was an image of his friend Chet Atkins in a distinctive and familiar pose. A life-size statue by Russell Faxon of Atkins in a similar position was unveiled on the corner of 5th Avenue and Union Street in Nashville, Tennessee, in 2000.

The Improving Situation in Colorado

In October 1962, Smith could once again be found playing at Eddie's Skyroom. Gradually, as he began to establish himself further in Colorado, he started to work with other local musicians. Regular venues in Denver including Sonny's Lounge and the Bandbox. Bobby Greene describes how some of these local jazz clubs were perceived by the local residents:

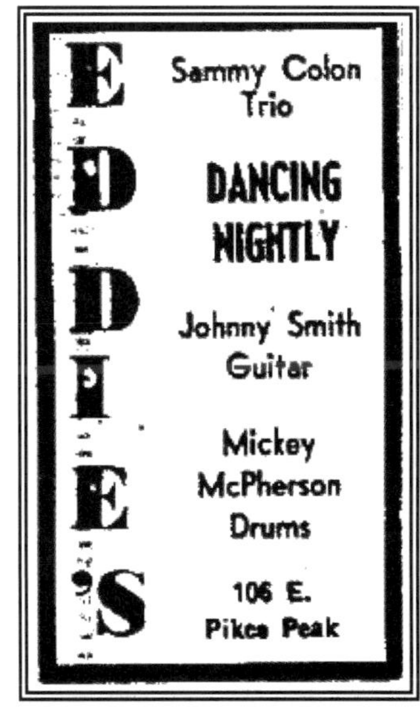

> Sonny's Lounge was just off downtown. When I was in high school, none of our dads would take us to any of these places. They were considered 'joints'. We went down there a couple of times and just stood outside the door, because we weren't old enough to get in. We could hear a little muffle of sound, and then we would get a blast of the real thing when somebody opened the door.
>
> At one time [later on], Johnny used to alternate between the Springs and Sonny's. When he was playing down in the Springs, the Al Belletto Sextet would play at Sonny's.

Smith was regularly featured with club house-bands. Over a period of time, the house-band at Sonny's Lounge became his own combo. When a new drummer was required at Sonny's, the owner of the club recommended Derryl Goes to Smith as a replacement. Goes was far from merely a local part-time musician. He taught percussion at both the Colorado State College in Greeley and the Colorado State University in Fort Collins. He had also toured with Stan Kenton. Pianist Neil Bridge, who was a local high school music teacher by day, was in turn recommended to join Smith's quartet by Goes. Although Bridge never recorded with Smith, he was his pianist for live engagements for the majority of the next thirty years. Bill Bastien joined as the new bassist. Bastien was also a school teacher by day.

The continually improving situation in Colorado gradually placed Smith in a position whereby he no longer had to depend upon long distance excursions, although he did not terminate them completely. He appeared on 17, 18 and 19 August 1962 at the outdoor Midwest Jazz Festival at the University of Indiana opposite Cannonball Adderley, Donald Byrd, the Four Freshman, Johnny

Richards, and Stan Kenton's orchestra. The proceeds from this festival were donated to a scholarship fund to enable young musicians to attend the fourth annual Kenton Clinic on the university's campus. Education in jazz music was an area in which Smith was to become increasingly more active, particularly during the 1970s.

By early 1963, Smith's work schedule had begun to improve substantially. Unfortunately, his workaholic lifestyle was taking its toll on Neil Bridge:

> Well, I began with him [Smith] in the late 1950s. Something like '59 or '60. I had to stop playing at the Bandbox after two or three years, because I was teaching during the day, and I just couldn't keep up that schedule. I had to be at school at 8:30, and a lot of thc time we were playing until two o'clock in the morning. After a few years of that, I just had to quit.

For a brief period after Bridge's departure, Smith played with the Lee Arellano Trio at the Bandbox.

An up-to-date compilation of Smith's broad ranging musical output, titled *The Guitar World of Johnny Smith*, was released in 1963. Chet Atkins also brought him back to the RCA Victor Studio in Nashville to record once again with the country singer Don Gibson on 11 and 12 February 1963. All twelve pieces were released on *I Wrote a Song*. Other members of the studio band included Harold Bradley, Joe Tanner, Floyd Cramer and the Jordanaires. The year also saw Smith receive an award from *Playboy* magazine in recognition as one of the outstanding jazz artists of the year.

Art Van Damme

In 1963, Smith recorded an album of new material with the accordion virtuoso and former NBC colleague Art Van Damme. For the aptly titled *A Perfect Match*, Smith and Van Damme were accompanied by Bob Wessberg on vibraphone, Herb Knapp on double bass, and Marty Clausen on drums. The impeccable interaction of the two leaders on this album illustrated their high level of musicianship and their reciprocal musical understanding. The fine performances of Wessberg, Knapp and Clausen should also be acknowledged. Bob Wessberg remembers that the album was recorded in two relaxed sessions on a single day. Art Van Damme's daughter, Sandra Van Damme-Mummert recalls her father's excitement at working with Smith:

> My dad said that Johnny Smith was one of the best guitarists that he had ever known. He was very honored to work with him. He liked him very much as a person and as a musician. He absolutely revered his playing, and he respected his talent very highly. I remember that he was so excited that he was going to record an album with Johnny. He was very particular about the musicians with whom he worked, especially his guitar

> players. The first guitarist in his quintet had left town when he got married. Then, he had Freddie Rundquist who was with him for years. He was great. So, Dad was very discerning about his musicians, and that tells you something about him working with Johnny. He was just so excited about it. And he had some of his favorite pieces of music on that album.

A Perfect Match included an infectious new composition by Smith, 'Satan's Doll'. The accordionist Kenny Kotwitz was studying with Van Damme at the time of the recording sessions and subsequently studied music theory with Smith during the mid-1960s. He vividly recounts Van Damme's memories of the particular session for 'Satan's Doll'. He also recalls Van Damme's admiration of Smith's meticulous musicianship:

> Yeah, he was knocked out by John's playing. He was a big fan, already. He said that there was one tune that John had written and wanted to do several takes on it. And then wanted to do another one. Art said to him, "Oh my God, John. You can't do any better than that. It's so fabulous. Just leave it alone," [laughs]. In other words, he was remarking on what a perfectionist John was. They really hit it off together. They just loved working with each other. Art said that Johnny read [notation] great, but the message that I got from him the most was how much of a perfectionist John was. And socially, I know that they really hit it off. It was very much a mutual admiration.
>
> They did the Stan Kenton Band Clinics together. I know that they did a couple, maybe three, together. They did one in Reno. I was studying with Art between '61 and '63, so it was during that period. Art came back and told me that while the other guys were doing this and that, he and Johnny just hung out together.

Meanwhile, Smith recalled one particular memory of his own from the recording session with Van Damme in Chicago:

> I remember that I arrived without my amplifier. Somebody lent me their amp, but I had to go and get it. Well, it was right at the other end of the Wrigley building, a quarter of a mile away! It was heavy. By the time I got back, my hand was numb from carrying it. Suddenly, Art called the first tune. It was a fast one and I thought, 'Oh hell!' I got through it. Just!

The virtuosity and tasteful musicianship which was displayed on *A Perfect Match* was nothing short of sublime. The aforementioned 'Satan's Doll' was a particularly fine illustration. Van Damme was in top form, and he set the bar high with his own beautifully crafted solo. Following on from a tough act, Smith's complementing response was pure genius. His well-structured solo began with a stunning and seemingly effortless ascending run across almost the full range of the guitar. This was a typical Smith concept, which he had previously employed to open his solo on 'Moonlight in Vermont'. After an eight-measure section of single-line melody, he enriched the harmonic interest and color through a further eight measures of his trademark rapid and immaculately smooth chords. Despite having left New York five years earlier, his virtuosity was still clearly high above that of any other jazz guitarist, and he remained the only jazz guitarist to possess the command of the instrument that was necessary to flawlessly execute such challenging techniques.

Career-Threatening Injury

A Perfect Match would be the last album that Smith was to record before a brutal accident very nearly ended his guitar-playing days forever. In 1963, the tip of the third finger on his left hand was torn off in an altercation with an aircraft seat. Gordon Close was one of his guitar students at the time that the incident occurred. He remembers that his tutor was remarkably phlegmatic about the situation:

> I was studying at the time with Johnny when I received a call on the day I was to go in for our session telling me in a calm voice that his airplane seat had dropped down accidentally and taken off the tip of his finger. I think it affected me worse than him. Of course, my heart went through my socks! Anyway, when our lessons resumed a week later, his left hand was bandaged up while the skin was grafting. At the time, I had been working on my own arrangement of... I think it was 'Moonlight in Vermont', funnily enough. So, I played it for Johnny during the lesson. Then, he said that he had a few ideas for me to try. He sat next to me, behind the neck of the guitar. Now, you know that right-hand tapping thing that Eddie Van Halen did later on? Well, Johnny sat there and tapped my chord-melody solo with his right hand. He had only heard it that once and yet he was able to play it back to me note-for-note with the wrong hand! Oh, it was just phenomenal.

To repair the damage to Smith's injured finger, surgeon Dr. Otis 'Jack' King grafted the tip of it onto the skin on the palm of Smith's hand, leaving him unable to play for several months until the skin had transferred. As a result of the injury, his damaged finger was shortened by a quarter of an inch, which forced a considerable adjustment of his playing technique. Some of his trademark large stretches, for example, became substantially more difficult to reach. Jack King remembers carrying out the operation:

> I got a call to see a patient who had severed the end of his finger. I was told that it was a guitarist called Johnny Smith. Well, I had never heard of him. Normally, I would have put a splint along the finger, but obviously that was not going to be appropriate in this case. So, I had to stitch the finger to the palm of his hand. It was a fairly new operation, and it was the first time that it was done in Colorado. Usually, the finger would be stitched to this part of the palm of the hand [points to the flexor pollicis brevis area below the thumb], but I had to stitch it to this part, instead [points to the center of the palm]. There's less flesh there. So, I didn't know if it was going to work. Two weeks later, John called me to say that he was feeling quite a bit of pain in his finger while he was drinking a Martini. I knew then that the operation had been a success, because the blood supply was returning to the fingertip and he was regaining feeling. After that, we remained friends for life.

Bobby Greene recalls Smith telling him about his rehabilitation:

> The doctors had actually attached the finger to the palm of his hand, immobilizing the hand in that position for I forget how many weeks to get the skin graft to take. They warned him expressly not to move the finger so as not to endanger the graft. He, knowing full well the congenital weakness of fourth fingers because of sharing a tendon with the third, said he worked the finger continuously while it was stuck to his palm 'til the docs cut it loose. He told us that although the accident shortened the finger only minimally, it took some considerable wood-shedding to regain his pre-accident fingering accuracy. Gawd! Even after all these years, that still makes my skin crawl just to think of it.

Guitarist Jim Fox visited Smith at his music store in Colorado Springs almost twenty years later and inquired about the accident. He remembers the occasion vividly:

> Being still kind of young and foolish, I asked him a few personal questions. I asked him about the accident where he lost the tip of his third finger. He showed me the palm of his hand, and he showed me where they had to sew the tip of his finger to the palm of his hand to effect a skin graft. It was very painful, and it had to stay there for several weeks. What a remarkable technique they had to do that. I mean, today we have all kinds of micro-surgery and things that they didn't have then.

The royalties that Smith was receiving from the Ventures' pop cover version of his composition 'Walk, Don't Run' helped him to stay financially afloat while he was unable to accept any live engagements during this period, particularly as he was recycling the profits from his music store back into the business in order to increase the level of his stock.

A New Quartet and Reminiscing

Bobby Greene

When he returned to performing, he was reunited with Derryl Goes and Bill Bastien. Twenty-four-year-old Bobby Greene was brought in as his new pianist. He occupied the seat from December 1963 until June 1964. Greene remembers how he discovered that he was joining Smith's group:

> I actually didn't meet Johnny before I started playing with him. I went to work at the Robin's Nest (known to all as simply 'the nest') one night in November 1963 and Ray [Iverson] said, in rather off-hand fashion, something like, "Oh, by the way, you're not working here any more." As I stood there open-mouthed, he added, "You're going to work at the Bandbox (another jazz saloon in Denver) with Johnny Smith starting next week." You

> would really have to have known Iverson to fully appreciate this story. He wasn't a malicious person, just a guy who seldom passed up a chance to fuck with someone's head if the opportunity presented itself. He referred to it not as 'putting you (or whoever) on', but as 'stretching you (or whoever) out'. As I recall, when I began with Johnny, there was no rehearsal. I just went to the gig and he had chord sheets to most things he planned on doing. I really don't know the why or how particulars of my 'recruitment'. I had started at the nest towards the end of July 1962 and played there six nights per week until Ray informed me that I was going to be with Johnny, who was just then returning to playing after an accident in which he had sliced off the fleshy tip of his left ring finger while adjusting the seat of his private airplane.

For a while, the aforementioned Bandbox, which was located at 3100 East Colfax and was a major venue in Denver, provided regular work for Smith. Bobby Greene recalls the venue's management and his time with the guitarist:

> The Bandbox had previously tried to run as a Chinese restaurant, but it didn't work. They actually had to turn it back into a jazz venue to make money. The old guy who ran it was mean at the best of times. He was in his sixties, but he still went out into the parking lot to have a fight with a twenty-year-old over not paying for a drink. Anyway, he was really difficult, but John was the only guy who knew how to handle him. The only guy.
>
> It started off... We were the house-band at the Bandbox, and Johnny was the headliner six nights per week. We were backing him. After a while... Colorado Springs is about seventy miles from Denver. So, seventy miles each way, six nights per week, and being responsible for his music store... He only did it for two or three months, before he said, "Hey!" He ran into the back of a truck one night. It didn't really hurt his car, but he said, "Hey, enough is enough." So, he started just doing Thursdays, Fridays and Saturdays. On Mondays, Tuesdays and Wednesdays the trio worked with a local singer. That's generally what we did. And then the Bandbox started bringing in big names like Anita O'Day for entire week-long bookings, and I think that's when Johnny moved across to Shaner's. Some of the acts that the Bandbox brought in, like Horace Silver, brought their own musicians with them. So, the house-band wasn't always needed. John drew really well as the featured attraction for quite a while. I think we were probably billed as 'Johnny Smith and the Bobby Greene Trio'. That would be about right. You see, John is singularly unimpressed with his own virtuosity. He treated people with whom he worked with respect. He wasn't one of those 'I'm a star' kind of people. Just a regular guy.
>
> The Bandbox was the only commercial venue we worked at that time. There were some one-timers like playing for the NAJE - National Association of Jazz Educators. I remember that one because some local musician had produced a fiberglass upright bass that he wanted to pitch to the convention as a practical/indestructible public school instrument. We staged a bit where Bill Bastien not only let go of the bass, but booted it as it fell, eliciting a collective gasp from the crowd. The bass, as you can imagine, sounded like a fiberglass washtub bass, but probably didn't suffer too badly in comparison with some of the wooden Kay basses I've heard in public schools. We did a series of concerts featuring Johnny and Doc Severinson. They knew each other from New York. So, their

> relationship was relaxed and easy. Doc came early and jammed with us at the Bandbox the day before the concerts started. The Denver concerts were in conjunction with the University of Denver Stage Band and we did a more formal concert at the Air Force Academy that, besides the jazz, featured Doc doing some heavy duty trumpet repertoire with the Academy Concert Band.

In 1964, Smith recorded his *Reminiscing* album with Bobby Greene, Bill Bastien and Derryl Goes. Again, not wishing to travel the long distance to New York, it was recorded locally in the front room of Bud and Jackie Edmonds' home in Manitou Springs. At the KCMS radio station, Bud Edmonds had previously engineered the tapes that Smith had recorded in the basement of his music store for his album *The Man with the Blue Guitar*. During his New York days, Smith had habitually found himself battling against sound engineers who had tried to separate him and his musicians in the recording studio in their desire to record each instrument in clinical isolation. Smith maintained that for the musicians to interact they needed to be able to both hear and see each other. In Colorado, he now had a greater degree of control. In his own liner notes to *Reminiscing*, he remarked that the recording room had been deliberately arranged so that visual contact between the musicians was preserved. The late Derryl Goes recalled his memories of the recording during an interview in 2011:

> Well, we did one of those [albums] in a house. We set up the mics on the living room floor. John would give us his "One, two, three...", you know. We would just start playing. They were tunes that we had been playing for some time.

While it would be wrong to generally place Denver's local jazz musicians on a par with the virtuoso elite with whom Smith had worked regularly in New York, it would also be erroneous not to acknowledge the presence of some fine performers within the city's jazz community. Certainly, some of Denver's better musicians were more than capable of providing accompaniments for the cream of the visitors from New York. *Reminiscing* is evidence of the high standard of musicianship that was on the jazz scene around Denver during the 1960s. By his own admission, Bobby Greene was not in the same league as Hank Jones or Bob Pancoast, but this is largely irrelevant. Crucially, his musical style perfectly complemented Smith's sense of taste in his own musicianship. As a result, the album sits seamlessly alongside Smith's New York recordings. Derryl Goes and Bill Bastien put in equally fine performances that could easily be credited to a New York rhythm section.

As with all of his recordings for Teddy Reig's Roost label, Smith and his combo received nothing more than the standard rate for the session. This was a common practice at the time. Bobby Greene explains, "For the album that I did with Johnny, we got paid the union recording scale, which was a nice taste, but... Unless the guys in the band had an agreement, I think that happened a lot."

The pieces that were included on *Reminiscing* were largely drawn from the repertoire that the combo was regularly performing. Consequently, very little rehearsal was required. Derryl Goes recalled that Smith selected the pieces for the sessions and that most of them were successfully completed at the first attempt. There was, however, one piece that gave Greene, Goes and Bastien a torrid time. The album included a new version of the gem of a composition by Smith that he had recorded in the previous year with Art Van Damme on *A Perfect Match*. Of the compositions which came from Smith's own pen, 'Satan's Doll' has largely been overshadowed by the pop success of the Ventures' version of 'Walk, Don't Run', and until its issue on compact disc in 2002 by Mosaic Records, it had, in effect, languished in a darkened room along with much of the rest of Smith's back-catalog. As with 'Walk, Don't Run', 'Satan's Doll' was also recorded as a country-flavored interpretation by his friend Chet Atkins, who released it on his *Progressive Pickin'* album. Perhaps partly as a consequence of Atkins' continuing higher public profile, and certainly as a result of the inaccessibility of Smith's back catalog, more guitarists have associated 'Satan's Doll' with the country guitar legend than they have with its composer. Bobby Greene recalls the session in which he, Smith, Bastien and Goes recorded 'Satan's Doll':

> We really didn't do much rehearsing. We might have run over a couple of the tunes at the recording, but I really don't remember a lot of wood-shedding. What I do remember is how 'Satan's Doll' eluded Bill, Derryl and me. We took turns having brain farts during takes. I don't pretend to know why, but that tune just kicked our asses. We just could not get comfortable with it. After umpteen takes, Johnny, justifiably frustrated, told the recording engineer to just pick one as 'the' take. I guess it turned out OK, but at the time, it seemed like we were committing tune-icide, and on record, to boot! I think that was the only tune on the album that we hadn't played before the session, but I'm not sure. They say sometimes you get the bear, and sometimes the bear gets you. 'Satan's Doll' was the latter.

Smith confessed that *Reminiscing* was an album which caused him some discomfort. While he had no complaints about the performances of his musicians, the sonic mix of the recording was unsatisfactory. He attributed this to the poor playback equipment that Edmonds had employed, which did not provide an accurate representation of the finished product. Certainly, there was a surprising over-abundance of reverberation on this album.

In June 1964, the personnel of the combo changed, as Bobby Greene departed:

> I left the group on good terms. For the first two or three months, Johnny was commuting from Colorado Springs six nights per week. After a while, he decided that playing/commuting six nights plus running his music store was just too much, and he started working Thur-Sat, leaving the trio to work with local singers Mon-Wed. About June, the management [at the Bandbox] decided to return to its previous policy of bringing in name jazz acts. I don't remember whether or not they kept Johnny on as an occasional. It wasn't too long after that he started playing Shaner's in downtown Denver. I might have stayed on, but the first name in was to be Anita O'Day, and since I had only been playing professionally for two years and had little confidence in my ability to listen through her off-the-wall phrasing and keep my place, I walked away and turned it over to Neil Bridge. I had been a fan of Anita for several years and really didn't believe I had what it took to back her in the manner she deserved. I caught her several times during that engagement and, after watching Neil and bassist Paul Warburton counting 'one-two-three-four' to themselves and each other, desperately keeping track of where they were, I never regretted my decision.
>
> It was a happy time. Not only was I getting to play with someone of his stature musically, but that someone was a master musician who was never condescending to band mates not at his level of proficiency. Unlike some older or established players who,

as a rite of passage, are prone to showing you everything you don't know in about twenty minutes, he treated us with the respect he demanded for himself. He was an open, easy to work with guy who, like most of the monster players I've been privileged to meet, is seemingly unimpressed with his own virtuosity. When, for example, he had to point out the obvious that with two chord instruments you alter chords only as the chart indicates, he did it in a way that was educational, not accusatory. Johnny Smith is not, let us be thankful, Buddy Rich. As far as mementos, there might be some old newspaper clippings in a scrapbook that my mom assembled of every mention I ever got in the local papers, but the album itself is the only physical memento I have. Of course, just getting to play with him is its own enduring memento.

The Return of Neil Bridge

Bobby Greene's departure was followed by Neil Bridge's return to the fold. Bill Bastien left the combo in the mid-to-late 1960s. His place on double bass was filled for two years by the guitarist Dale Bruning, who had previously taken the guitar chair for bookings when Smith was out of town:

> When I first came to Colorado... John used to like to go deep sea fishing. He was about to go down to Baja, California, to do some fishing. I was asked to substitute for him while he was away. So, I played with his rhythm section for maybe a month or so. John only knew me as a guitarist, but I was also a bassist. This was in the mid-1960s. Sometime around 1968, John's bass player left and so he was in need of a new bassist. Someone who was familiar with the fact that I also played bass in those days said, "Why don't you call Dale? He plays bass." So, he asked me and I said, "Sure." I was very grateful, because family had come along and there were expenses. It was just a treat to play with John.
>
> I played bass with him for about two and a half years. If I recall, it started in about '68, '69, through into '70. And then I had finally begun to establish myself as a guitarist here, and John totally understood when I said that I had better leave his quartet. He said, "Dale, you can play electric bass if you want," [laughs]. I said, "Noooo John, it's not the same." He smiled. He totally understood and he was very gracious about it.

When Dale Bruning left Smith's quartet to return to his primary instrument he was succeeded by a series of bass players. Meanwhile, Neil Bridge and Derryl Goes remained constant members of the combo. In a repeat of the gesture that Smith had previously extended to Bobby Greene, his Colorado combo was rarely billed as the Johnny Smith Quartet. In an act of considerable generosity, he always tried to ensure that the group was billed as Johnny Smith and the Neil Bridge Trio.

The late Derryl Goes' recollections of his time in Smith's combo were on a par with the warmth expressed by Bobby Greene. Interviewed in 2011, the mere mention of Johnny Smith's name was enough to bring back many fond memories for the retired drummer. Neil Bridge also remembers his time in Smith's outfit with great affection, while recalling the high standard of the combo's musicianship and musical understanding:

> Oh, Jeez, every now and then, I tell my present wife about those days, and she always says that she's sorry that she missed it. They were great times. It was pretty funny. We never had a formal rehearsal. Never. He would write out the parts... At this one club that we played at in downtown Denver, we would go into the kitchen and he would put the music on the ice-cream freezer. He would play the guitar part, and we would follow it on our part, and then we would go out and play! The musicians were so good, we were so used to playing together... That was our rehearsal! If we did a concert someplace... Every now and then we would go to Kansas, Montana or different places in Colorado... Before the gig we would be in the motel room and he would say, "Well, here's the new chart." He would play on his unamplified guitar, and we would follow along.

Dale Bruning also recalls that there were no formal rehearsals. In concurring with Neil Bridge and Bobby Greene's reminiscences, Bruning's own recollections further highlight the fine local jazz scene in Denver, which was worthy of its position as a regular stop for major touring performers:

> By the time I played with him, he had written out a lot of charts. The group was well established, with piano, bass and drums, so there wasn't any rehearsal. John just handed me all the bass parts. He did most of the arranging of the songs that we played, which, obviously, in most cases featured the guitar. He put in a lot of preparation to make sure that he met his own standards on the guitar. That doesn't mean that the bass and piano parts were easy, but their purpose was to complement what was going on in the guitar parts. Sometimes, the drummer or the pianist would submit arrangements, and if he liked them he would put them in. So, not all of what we played were Johnny Smith arrangements. Derryl was a very qualified musician, so he knew what he was doing when he wrote arrangements. Neil also did some arrangements. I had also done some, but by the time that I was in the quartet there was more than enough material, for sure.
>
> Sometimes, we would have people sit in with us. Dave Grusin would come back home to Colorado from Hollywood, and he would know that we were playing at Shaner's. So, he would come and sit in. Sometimes, there were some vocalists that John had accompanied in New York when he was at NBC. They might be in town and want to visit him. So, they would come and sit in and do a couple of songs. In most of these cases there were no head charts or arrangements. He would just improvise beautifully and enjoy it. But when it was our usual quartet, he gravitated towards those arranged pieces that he had come to feel comfortable with.

Smith and his combo did not employ an agent to obtain their bookings. Their industrious diary of engagements came directly through the guitarist. Most of the venues were in Colorado and the West, although they occasionally played in the East, such as in St. Louis. It was Smith's decision not to venture far afield too often, due to his dislike of long-distance traveling. On a rare occasion when a booking was not directly arranged through the leader, a friend of Smith acquired a somewhat inappropriate gig for the quartet. Neil Bridge remembers that the engagement was not proceeding at all well until Smith took action:

> A friend of Johnny lived in Gunnison, Colorado, which is on the Western Slope. Mostly

> cowboys, ranch hands and all that. But he booked us at the Elk Club there. Well, we went in there with our jazz standards... and... oh... we were dying. Then Johnny looked at us and played 'Clarinet Polka' on the guitar, solo, and the people went ape. They just went crazy. They got up dancing, stamping their cowboy boots on the floor, and the dust came up. And after that, we had them! I'll never forget that.

Gradually, Smith allowed his diary to become more active once again. By the mid-1960s, the majority of his bookings were not at regular venues, and it is fair to conclude that by this time he had finally established himself on the Colorado jazz scene. Quite often, the quartet was performing six nights per week, with Smith and Goes both driving sixty miles to play at midway venues in Denver and not returning to their respective homes until three o'clock in the morning.

Shaner's Lounge

One particular venue in Denver is still remembered with great fondness by jazz fans in the local community. Shaner's Lounge was a regular gig for the quartet for around seven years. Neil Bridge recalls Smith's popularity at the club:

> One of the most successful gigs that we ever did was in low downtown Denver. It was called Shaner's. Man, at that place we would have people waiting in line and around the corner.

Shaner's Lounge was located on 17th Street in downtown Denver. It was a restaurant-bar with a traditional window display of hung meat advertising the quality of its food. Local resident Marc Gonzales recalls that, as the big attraction, Smith's name appeared on the marquee on the front of the building. Bobby Greene describes the area in which Shaner's was located:

> Shaner's was a place downtown. In fact, it was one of the few venues downtown that people actually went to. Back in those days, downtown, they almost rolled up the sidewalk at 5 p.m., except for the movie theaters. It was hard to get anybody down there for a nightlife type of thing. That's no longer the case, but back then you could shoot a cannon off after 6 p.m. and not hurt anybody.

With consideration of the distance in time, it is understandable that there are slight differences between the recollections of those who were present with regard to the structure of the quartet's sets, although it is also probable that the format varied over the years. According to Derryl Goes, typical nights began around nine o'clock. The combo's performances were separated into four or five sets, most of which were of around an hour's duration with fifteen-minute intervals. Neil Bridge has his own fond memories of playing at Shaner's:

> At Shaner's, we were playing for two nights a week. That went on for eight years, or something like that. We had plenty of other gigs, but generally they weren't steady. We did have a few regular ones... I can't remember where they were now. We used to get the

> members of the Denver Symphony [Orchestra]... They would do their concerts from eight 'til eleven... and then at around midnight we used to get all these musicians from the Symphony come in to hear us, saying that this was the best music in town, you know. It was great. When we played at Shaner's, we used to finish at two o'clock in the morning, but that was on Fridays and Saturdays. During the week, we usually finished by midnight.

There was a particular part of the quartet's gigs that was always treated with great reverence by all of those who were present at Shaner's. This was the point when Smith would hold the stage on his own and play a few of his solo guitar arrangements. The effect upon Colorado audiences was identical to that in New York, and Smith's fellow band members were equally hypnotized by these performances. Pianist Neil Bridge remembers:

> Now, what was so successful with Johnny, and he was a master at this, we would play usually about two sets. Then, the third set he would do about three or four solo numbers. He would do 'Black Is the Color (of My True Love's Hair)' and a standard or two, and he'd do some classical pieces. He used to play 'Pictures at an Exhibition'. He'd do 'Golden Earrings' and a Spanish classical piece. I can't remember the name of it, but the people ate that up. Now, and this would never happen nowadays, the owner was so impressed with this, that he didn't even let them sell drinks during that set. How many places would do that today? You could have heard a pin drop. It was like being in Carnegie Hall. I mean, the waitresses... No cash registers ringing... Wow, I don't think that would ever happen today. That was great.

As a guitarist, Dale Bruning was utterly spellbound by Smith's solo spots:

> One of the things that struck me about playing with John... Our home base at this time was a club called Shaner's... For a forty-five or fifty-minute set, the quartet would play for about half an hour. And then the bass, piano and drums would get off the bandstand, and John would do solo guitar for maybe ten or fifteen minutes. Now, with all due respect to Derryl, Neil and myself... Maybe I appreciate this more because I'm a guitarist, but... The highlight for me was always when we got off the bandstand [laughs] and let John do his solos. He would do beautiful arrangements of 'Shenandoah', 'Golden Earrings' and 'The Girl with the Flaxen Hair'... He did a couple of pieces by Manuel Ponce. I don't think I remember him doing any Bach, not that he couldn't. They really were the highlight for me, and I think in many ways that they were the highlight for the audience, too. He played them so beautifully.
>
> The guitar is the super-substitute instrument, because its role has been to substitute the role of other instruments. Jim Hall for example has often played in a way that has substituted for the piano. In other places it has taken the role of a horn. You get Freddie Green where it has this rhythmic, percussive role. And then, of course, you get to Johnny Smith... A solo instrument, an orchestra.

During the sets when the combo played together, Smith continued the same ethos that he had practiced in his New York days. While there were several pieces which featured different members of the group, there were no extended, self-indulgent, or overly long solos. Although the audiences came primarily to hear the guitarist, his ego stayed as modest as ever, and his sense of good taste remained as relevant to his own guitar playing as it was to his control over the rest of the group.

Kenny Vaughan remembers an occasion at Shaner's Lounge involving the legendary country guitarist Chet Atkins:

> On one of my earlier visits to Shaner's, during the latter part of the evening, my father gently motioned toward the front door. I looked over to see Chet Atkins and 'Homer and Jethro' moving to the back of the club. My father knew they were playing a show that night and figured they might show up. Jethro Burns' wife and Atkins' wife were twin sisters. It should be noted that Homer Haynes and Jethro Burns were great musicians, and that they had played sessions at King Records for Syd Nathan on quite a few hits for artists on that label. I remember Johnny introducing them with a smile, then offering his guitar as he invited Atkins to sit in. Atkins smiled and waived him off. Johnny then asked Homer Haynes up. He said, "No thanks." He then invited Jethro, who played the mandolin in the act. He accepted and took the stage and Smith's guitar. I remember the look on the faces of the Neil Bridge Trio as Burns proceeded to play some elegant jazz guitar. Smith returned for one more number and tore it up. I ran into Atkins in the 1980s at an airport, and I reminded him of that evening. We both remembered it like it was yesterday. He said that there was no way he was getting up to play the great Johnny Smith's guitar!

Guitarist Ronnie Evans also witnessed Chet Atkins expressing his utmost respect for Smith:

> I do recall when Chet did an interview while preparing for a concert in Colorado he stated that he rarely got nervous before a concert, except this one, because Johnny Smith would be in the audience. Chet remarked something to the effect that Johnny was such a good player and always played with such good taste.

Chet Atkins' nephew, Gary Atkins, shared his uncle's personal thoughts about Smith, both as a friend and as a guitarist:

> My dad [Jimmy Atkins] was a professional musician, you know. He played with Les Paul and recorded for Decca and all that. He knew Johnny in New York. They were dear friends, and he introduced Johnny to my uncle [Chet Atkins], and they became dear friends. On a personal level, when you scrape away all of the nonsense, Johnny Smith was Chet's favorite player in spite of all the things that he had to say in public about some of the other characters. Above Chet's workbench in his shop, which I helped my aunt to clean out after he died, there were some photographs. There was a picture of my father, a picture of Jerry Reed, and a picture of Johnny Smith. That's it.

By the late 1960s, Smith's style of jazz was no longer considered by many younger jazz listeners as being hip. Rock music dominated the interests of the majority of the youth generation, and even those who preferred to listen to jazz were often more likely to focus their attention upon the modal sub-genre, jazz-rock fusions, the resurgent interest in angular bebop, or the jazz revolution that had been headed by musicians such as John Coltrane. The guitarist Bill Frisell recounts how he felt as a youngster about Smith's music both in the late 1960s and now with the wisdom of maturity. His honesty in sharing his thoughts during an interview that bordered upon being a humble confessional, is nothing short of admirable:

> If I could travel back in time and do this all over again... [Sighs]... I feel like I really blew it... An incredible opportunity... Johnny Smith was playing every week at this club and I never went to see him. Just in a little club. It was the late 1960s. I was already studying with Dale [Bruning] at the time. Dale was playing bass with Johnny. It was at a time when all of these floodgates were being opened for me about jazz music in general. Dale was telling me about Charlie Parker, Monk and Miles... and I was just hearing about this stuff for the first time. And there was Jim Hall. There was just this giant wave of... kind of bebop. I just wanted to be this hipster of bebop. So, I guess what I'm trying to say is that my biggest regret, at that time, is not appreciating what Johnny Smith was. I looked at him as this older kind of guy. I mean, I totally respected him. I never went to see him play at that club. Boy! I'm just so upset with myself for not taking that opportunity. And because he was around all the time, I think I took it for granted. At the time, there were so many guitarists around who were kind of disciples of Johnny Smith, and who had copies of his chord-melody solos on paper. I wish I had saved some of that stuff.

Undoubtedly, Bill Frisell was not alone in the views that he held during the late 1960s. Fortunately, in 1970, he was able to benefit from Smith's presence when, with great appreciation, he seized the opportunity to study from the Master at the University of Northern Colorado.

Despite his less than hip status in the late 1960s, several other guitarists, both professional and amateur, retain treasured memories of witnessing some of Smith's performances on the Colorado circuit during their younger days. Many of them had been taken by their fathers to see him perform and were subsequently subjected to an almost spiritual enlightenment. Their reveries illustrate that Smith was still very much in top form and had not lowered the exceptionally high standards of his own playing. Kenny Vaughan vividly recalls his memories of seeing Smith performing at Shaner's Lounge:

> My father used to take me to see Johnny at Shaner's, a small night club in downtown Denver when I was eleven or twelve years old. He performed there most Saturday nights with the Neil Bridge Trio. I believe Charles Burrell was the bassist on at least one of those nights. Bridge played the piano and I think the drummer's name was Derryl. This would have been around '65 to '66. I had recently wanted to play guitar with my pals in a garage band and my father, being a jazz record collector, decided that watching Smith would be the thing to do. We had a copy of 'Moonlight in Vermont', as well as Tony Motolla, Kenny Burrell and Chet Atkins' records, and my father would blast all manner of cool jazz regularly. It was great to sit in the front row at Shaner's. There was a very small sound system with one Shure mic on a stand in front of the stool where Johnny sat. He played his Gibson JS through a Gibson Recording model with one JBL D-130 F. He would position the mic about 20 inches away from the guitar and would lean over

slightly to talk between songs. He was mostly soft spoken and was prone to dry humor. Between sets he would stand by the restroom and waitress station, and we would go over and chat with him. He was always pleasant.

Fred Hamilton, who is currently a Professor of Jazz Guitar at the University of North Texas, often used to see to Smith playing at Shaner's Lounge:

> I studied for six years with Jim Atkins (Chet Atkins' older brother and early Les Paul Trio rhythm guitarist) who had a job at KOA radio station in Denver. That job prevented him from 'moonlighting' or working gigs. So, he taught a lot of students. This was between 1963 and 1968. Realizing that I needed to hear live music, he told my parents when he realized I was serious that they should take me to hear Johnny Smith as often as possible. Johnny had a three or four-night gig in Denver at a club called Shaner's. When I first heard him, Dale Bruning was playing acoustic bass with him before he stopped to put all his time on the guitar. I believe Derryl Goes was playing drums and Neil Bridge was the pianist. My parents took me there at least once or twice a month for a long time. It was great! Later, when I became aware of his international fame, it struck me that a lot of people categorized him or characterized him as a rather 'commercial' chord-melody great, but not a bona fide burning jazz player. I so disagree. When I heard him live, in retrospect he played much more similar to Pat Martino and there were few if any of his solo chord arrangements. I don't think the albums truly represent what I heard live. He was smokin'! And it was always crowded when I was there.

Denver resident Dave Kintzele also has memories of Smith and his combo's appearances at Shaner's Lounge. He recalls, "I remember the great tone that Johnny got and the absolute technical brilliance. The fast runs executed with amazing precision and the complex chord melodies on the slow and fast stuff." Jock Bartley, of the rock group Firefall, was a young guitar student of Smith during the 1960s and frequently watched his Master playing in the local clubs:

> He could literally play faster than anybody else when he chose to, but he only brought that out every so often, only when it furthered the song and the music that he was playing. His precision of playing was unique and wonderful. It was never flashy and ego-centric. I don't ever think I heard Johnny show off (like so many guitarists did and do). The song, the tune, the melody was king, the only thing that mattered when soloing. Not technique, not overwhelming speed nor flash.

Another guitar student, Barry Zweig, went to considerable but worthwhile lengths to see Smith playing in Denver:

> I used to drive the seventy miles up to Denver to see him play in person. That probably was with the Neil Bridge Trio. I don't recall the name of the club but it was a pretty 'upscale' venue, not an ordinary local bar. The first time I saw him I just flipped out! All those very close voiced four-note chords connecting with each other so 'effortlessly' are even more amazing in person. He would play some voicings stretching to a six-fret

spread at times. Five-fret spans were very normal.

Gary Atkins, the late son of the aforementioned Jimmy Atkins, was a longtime close friend of Smith and regularly traveled the lengthy distance to watch him play. He recalled, “I made it for sixteen weekends in a row to see Johnny play at Shaner's.”

In reminiscing about Smith's virtuosity and his gigs around Denver, Kenny Vaughan recalls an appearance at another local club:

> I saw him sit in late one Saturday night not far from Shaner's with Gatemouth Brown. Gate didn't know who he was and lit in to 'C Jam Blues' at breakneck speed and proceeded to play everything he knew. He then told Smith to 'take it', and he did. It was the only time I ever saw him play that fast. We couldn't believe it. Neither did Gate!

Aside from Smith's work on the regular local jazz circuit with his combo, he also performed at special events with visiting musicians, many of whom were old friends from his days in New York. In September 1967, he appeared with Zoot Sims, Yank Lawson, Cutty Cutshall and Mousie Alexander at Dick Gibson's Annual Jazz Party at the Casino Vail Tavern in Vail, Colorado. A private audio tape was recorded at the Party on 15 September of Smith playing 'Just You, Just Me' and some other selections with Buck Clayton, Lou McGarity, Bob Wilber, Phil Woods, Lou Stein, Milt Hinton and Nick Fatool.

Military Band Concerts

Smith often worked around Colorado outside of the nightclub circuit. He was a significant supporter of the local military band during the 1960s and 1970s and collaborated with them on several occasions. On 20 January 1963, he performed at the Air Force Academy Band's *Concert in Modern* at the Arnold Hall Theater. One of the pieces in which he was featured was Benny Carter's arrangement of 'Turnabout', where he was accompanied by four French horns, five trombones, five trumpets and a string section. The band was promoted for the free event as an augmented dance orchestra. Three years later, on 24 April 1966, he returned to the Arnold Hall Theater to be featured as a soloist in a program of Latin-American music with the Air Force Academy Band. One of the pieces on this occasion was composed by Master Sergeant Dick Hubbard specifically for Smith to perform on his nylon-string guitar. On 15 October 1967, his quartet performed at the Cheyenne Shadows Service Club in Fort Carson, and on 15 February 1970 he returned to the Arnold Hall Theater in the Air Force Academy, this time to perform with the Falconaires. On 12 November 1972, he was a

JOHNNY SMITH WITH TWO MEMBERS OF THE FALCONAIRES

featured soloist at the Air Force Academy Band's *Homecoming Concert* at the Arnold Hall Auditorium, where he played a solo arrangement of 'There'll Be Other Times' before he was joined on stage by the Falconaires for a performance of 'Exodus', for which he wrote the band's arrangement.

The projects in which Smith engaged with military bands in Colorado should not be solely attributed to any debt that he may have felt as a result of his own post in the Army Air Corps Band during World War Two. The military bands during the 1960s and 1970s consisted of musicians of a high standard who were worthy in their own right of collaboration.

The Local Arts Scene and the Colorado Media

Colorado Springs Music Theatre
Presents
JOHNNY SMITH IN CONCERT
With the Smith Quartet
Wednesday, June 19, 1968 8:00 P.M.
FINE ARTS CENTER
Admittance $2.50 Tickets Available at
Jr. Bootery TV Specialists
Johnny Smith Music Co.

In Colorado Springs, Smith was very much involved in supporting the local community's arts scene. On several occasions he performed jazz in formal concert settings at the Fine Arts Center, such as on 19 June 1968 when he appeared with his combo under the rare title of the Johnny Smith Quartet. On 12 May 1969, he was again playing jazz at the Fine Arts Center, accompanied by the Neil Bridge Trio. Another concert took place at the same venue on 10 August 1970.

While Smith had previously suffered from the prejudices of some of the jazz critics in New York, in Colorado he endured the ignorance of the local media who were largely oblivious to his stature on the world jazz scene. The archives of the *Denver Post* and the *Rocky Mountain News* in Denver Public Library contain relatively few featured articles about Smith despite the undeniable evidence and the testimony of several local residents regarding his regular appearances around Denver for many years.

Not all of those who worked in Colorado's media were ignorant of Smith's stature within the jazz world, however. On Sunday 6 September 1975, he was the guest on a repeat-showing of the television program *Emphasis*, which focused upon the guitar, on ABC's local affiliate KRDO. On 28 December 1975, he appeared on the series again, demonstrating the different methods required for playing four types of guitar.

Former local resident Phil Leavenworth remembers another occasion on which Smith's musicianship reached out beyond jazz audiences:

I grew up in Denver. There was a club on E. Colfax (the main drag) called the Bandbox,

> and Johnny was a frequent headliner there. They advertised his appearances in the newspapers and on the neon sign out front. When I grew older I listened to a lot of classical music on Denver's KVOD radio station (very well-known station around the country), and every year on Johnny Smith's birthday they would devote one hour to his recordings, the only non-classical music they played all year. I heard it a few times and fell in love with Johnny and his playing.

While many journalists in Denver's music media were unaware of Smith's stature among the world's jazz elite, the press in Colorado Spring's were generally somewhat better informed. Dick Eliot remembers that the musicians around Colorado undoubtedly recognized his position as a world class performer:

> He had a call to go up to Denver to play at the Bandbox for Nancy Wilson, because her piano player had got snowed-in at Kansas City. He was asked to go up and help them out. He asked me if I wanted to go along. So, we drove up there in a snow storm. Of course, he read the piano book on the guitar flawlessly. He's one of the best readers of all time.

There were also certain organizers among the civic authorities who held him in high regard. Some of the engagements that he took during the 1960s and 1970s indicate that he was at the top of the list for important benefit, corporate, political and civic events. As early as 23 July 1960, he performed at the *Fetch-A-Member Fun Fest Follies* in aid of the Colorado Springs Fine Arts Center. This was a gala evening which included a dinner for one thousand people. Two months later, on 16 September 1960, he performed a thirty-minute program at the Carpenters Hall in advance of an evening of political speeches. He was accompanied on this occasion by Sammy Colon on piano, Mickey McPherson on drums, and Jim Rasmussen on bass. From 2 until 7 May 1966, he appeared at the Colorado Springs Fine Arts Center with a quartet of alto saxophone, bass and drums. The group performed the music for a Civic Players' production of sketches by the late humorist James Thurber, which was titled *A Thurber Carnival*. Smith's responsibilities included providing the music for the opening and closing 'Word Dances', which were choreographed by local ballet teachers Keith and Marjorie Willis. A review of the production in the *Colorado Springs Gazette Telegraph* declared that:

> The addition of the Johnny Smith Quartet was another mark of excellence, one of the best in the country, of course. The smooth, sophisticated sound of the quartet was a perfect match for the Thurber spirit. (Reproduced from the *Colorado Springs Gazette Telegraph*, 3 May 1966)

There are several more examples of Smith's commitment to the Colorado arts scene. On 7 December 1966, he returned to the Fine Arts Center to give a benefit concert for the Colorado Springs Opera Association. He was joined on stage by Neil Bridge, Derryl Goes, and Buddy Smith on bass. The same line-up appeared seven months later, on 2 June 1967, when they provided the music for a dance at the Valley Hi Country Club to benefit the Memorial Hospital. On 22 December 1967, Smith and his combo performed at the debutante's ball at the luxurious Broadmoor Hotel, once again generously in aid of the Colorado Springs Fine Arts Center. Eighteen months later, between 11 and 14 June 1969, Smith and the Neil Bridge Trio were hired to play at the twenty-fourth annual Colorado 4-H

Conference. Around one thousand people attended the event at the Colorado State University in Fort Collins, which ran seminars and workshops on arts and humanities, citizenship, mass media communication, as well as contests in home economics, decision-making, speech, and dairy and livestock judging. Smith and the Neil Bridge Trio took part in another benefit concert, which included jazz and classical music, at the Cheyenne Mountain High School for the School District 12 Arts and Humanities program on 3 November 1970. Dick Patterson was the bassist for Smith, Bridge and Goes on this occasion. Smith also provided the musical entertainment for three hundred and fifty guests on 26 May 1971 at a dinner in the ballroom of the University Center to mark the resignation of Dr. Darrell Holmes from his post as President of the University of Northern Colorado. He returned to Colorado Springs' Broadmoor Hotel on 29 February 1976 for a concert that was sponsored by the Broadmoor Jazz Club, Inc. and the El Paso County Heart Unit. Around forty musicians played at the event, including the Gut Bucket Seven, who were led by Phil Van Pelt at this time. Smith duetted with Ray DeWitt. In a final example of his activities on a civic level, Smith and the Doctor Jazz Group provided the musical entertainment at a fund-raising cocktail party on 27 November 1977 at the Steakery, 207 North Chelton, on behalf of El Paso's County District Attorney Robert Russel, who was running for the post of Colorado Attorney General.

Land of the Velvet Hills

In a further demonstration of his commitment to the local community, on 6 December 1966 Smith presented the first pressing of his newly composed song 'Land of the Velvet Hills' to Governor John Love at a public ceremony. Performed by Smith with Jimmy Atkins on vocals, the recording was first broadcast by Pete Smythe on KOA Radio.

Smith had been inspired to write the song while he had been hunting with Gunnison rancher Roy McCabe during the autumn of 1966. Although 'Land of the Velvet Hills' did not become the State Anthem, it was quickly adopted by parts of the Colorado community. On 2 May 1967, Palmer High School Vocal Department held it's annual Spring Concert. The evening concluded with a performance of Smith's composition by the Advanced Choir.

The Verve Recordings and the Smith Renaissance

While Smith was busy performing around Colorado, ignored by the national jazz media, Teddy Reig was making moves on his behalf back in New York. In 1965, Reig left Morris Levy's Roulette label, the company to which he had sold his Roost Records in 1957. He brokered a deal for Smith to record three new albums for Verve in 1967 and 1968. These were *Johnny Smith*, *Johnny Smith's Kaleidoscope* and *Phase II*. The first two of these albums are recognized as being among his finest works.

The recording sessions for all three albums saw Smith return to New York. For his eponymous first record for Verve, which was recorded at Capitol Studios between 28 and 30 March 1967, he was reunited with old friends Hank Jones, George Duvivier and Don Lamond. To those who had forgotten Smith since he had left New York, this album unquestionably announced that he had not been indulging in any form of retirement whatsoever. His musicianship had lost none of its virtuosity and sense of good taste. The repertoire included two of Paul McCartney's better Beatles' compositions in the form of

'Michelle' and 'Yesterday'. The latter of these two pieces was presented as a chord-melody arrangement for solo guitar. Victor Young's 'Golden Earrings' was also featured as a solo guitar piece. In this astonishingly virtuoso performance, Smith played his Gibson Johnny Smith archtop guitar unamplified. Aside from thoughtfully reinforcing the gypsy flavor of the piece, the performance also exhibited the perfect acoustic balance of his self-designed instrument. With the exception of a recording of 'Exodus', all of the material that resulted from the three sessions was released on disc. A breathtakingly beautiful new chord-melody arrangement of 'Shenandoah' did not appear on the original vinyl album, but was released as a single and ultimately on the CD version of the album which was issued in 1997. This interpretation was far more sophisticated than the arrangement that he had improvised for *The Man with the Blue Guitar* five years earlier, and it has become a favorite among jazz guitarists. The flip-side of 'Shenandoah' featured a new version of 'Land of the Velvet Hills', for which the quartet recorded a backing track in New York before Jimmy Atkins added a new vocal track in Colorado soon after.

An advertisement for the original vinyl release of the album appeared in *Down Beat* on 1 June 1967, and another promoted the record alongside a recent Verve release by Wes Montgomery, *California Dreaming*, on 29 June 1967. Nevertheless, it was not until 10 August 1967 that a review by John Hardy finally appeared in the magazine. His definition of a three-year period as "several years" once again raises questions about the authority of the critics. While Hardy could not restrain his need to question Smith's credentials as a jazz guitarist, complaining that his music lacked harmonic color, his review began positively:

> This is Smith's first recording in several years, and from an over-all musical standpoint it is one of his best. That is in some measure due to the thoughtfully chosen program as well as to a consistently interesting Hank Jones, but the high points of the album are the leader's. (Reproduced from *Down Beat*, 10 August 1967)

The *Billboard* gave the album a brief but positive review, if somewhat understated. At just forty-five years old, and merely fifteen years after the release of 'Moonlight in Vermont', the reviewer's description of Johnny Smith as a "veteran guitarist" said more about the author's own outlook than it did about Smith's actual stature within the jazz guitar world:

> Veteran guitarist Johnny Smith displays his mastery of the instrument and, at the same time, his skillful talents in improvisation. Smith scores in such numbers as 'Manha De Carnaval', 'My Favorite Things', and the Beatles' tune 'Yesterday'. A soft, but vibrant style pervades each tune – each a first-class performance. (Reproduced from the *Billboard*, 24 June 1967)

The hugely positive public reception to Smith's first Verve album no doubt encouraged his quick return to New York's Capitol Studios in November 1967 to record *Johnny Smith's Kaleidoscope*. With the same personnel, this album was a seamless continuation of its predecessor, and opened with a hot new interpretation of his own composition 'Walk, Don't Run', which he had originally recorded thirteen years earlier and released on his album *In a Sentimental Mood*. Although several of the pieces on this album began with guitar chord-melody introductions, and Smith frequently harmonized his melodies when accompanied by the combo, only a re-visited version of Claude Debussy's 'The Girl with the Flaxen Hair' was performed solo in its entirety. This time, the reviewer for *Down Beat*, Harvey

Siders, had no issues with Smith's harmonic color. The magazine's staff of jazz experts remained consistently inconsistent. Siders' review began with an acknowledgment of Smith's stature:

> The very profusion of guitarists today makes it the more imperative that geniuses such as Tal Farlow, George Van Eps, and Johnny Smith be kept in the forefront as much as possible. We always need the masters, and this album – though it has flaws – demonstrates why Smith is among that elite. (Reproduced from *Down Beat*, 27 June 1968)

Meanwhile, a reviewer for the *Billboard* was even more poetically enthusiastic about Smith's offering:

> Guitarist Johnny Smith plays 'Old Folks', 'Days of Wine and Roses' and 'I'm Old Fashioned' with all the passion and vitality of a moody voice woven into the string. Smith's long-recognized virtuosity, a beacon in the fog of electronic guitar psychedelics, continues to bear out the idea that longevity is guaranteed by talent. His depth and command of the harmonic qualities to be found in the guitar are a tribute to this fine artist. (Reproduced from the *Billboard*, 23 March 1968)

The consequence of Smith's first two albums for Verve was sizable, to say the least. His profile was temporarily raised through a renewed interest from the media. Engagements saw him venture outside of Colorado, such as on 23 November 1967 when he took a quartet to the Masonic Temple in Detroit to play opposite the Kenny Burrell Quartet, the Bola Sete Trio and the Gabor Szabo Quintet.

In November 1968, he entered Phil Ramone's A & R studios in New York to record his third album for Verve. For *Phase II*, he took Derryl Goes from his Colorado combo with him to record with Hank Jones and George Duvivier. Bob Bushnell and Joe Mack were brought in to provide electric bass on four of the pieces. This album includes some gems in the form of his interpretations of Burt Bacharach's 'This Guy's in Love with You', Antonio Carlos Jobim's 'Wave', and the theme music from Otto Preminger's film *Exodus*, which had been previously recorded and discarded from the sessions for his first album for Verve. However, in the attempts by record companies to sell more jazz discs, seemingly every jazz musician was cajoled into recording jazz interpretations of the contemporary pop repertoire. In the case of Smith's *Phase II* album, he was asked by Teddy Reig to include versions of lightweight pop songs such as 'Light My Fire' and 'Don't Sleep in the Subway', which were not to his taste at all. As was almost always the result of these marketing tactics, this disc was not as critically or commercially successful as his other two albums for Verve. Smith later commented that he felt sure that Reig had been pressured by Verve into asking him for this particular type of repertoire.

Phase II marks the last time that Smith entered a studio to record an album in his own name. It was not, however, Teddy Reig's request to record pop material that turned him away from recording again. In a revealing interview with Bob Yelin for *Guitar Player* magazine in 1982, Smith stated that he had not received any royalty payments for these three albums. Every time that he had made inquiries, he had been informed that no money would be forthcoming because Verve's parent company, MGM, had filed for bankruptcy. Sadly, it was for this reason that he stopped recording. After the 1982 interview, Bob Yelin contacted the record company and was able to have the due royalties forwarded on to Smith.

The temporary Smith renaissance which resulted from his new recordings continued. On 14

July 1968, he could be found playing at Lennie's on the Turnpike in Peadbody, Massachusetts. Lennie Sogoloff's club was a major venue on the national jazz circuit. An advertisement in the local *Boston Herald Traveler* newspaper announced that Barney Kessel, Howard Roberts and Erroll Garner were also appearing at the club during the same month. Lennie Sogoloff, who had been a longtime admirer of Smith, retains vivid memories of the guitarist's professionalism during his appearances at the club:

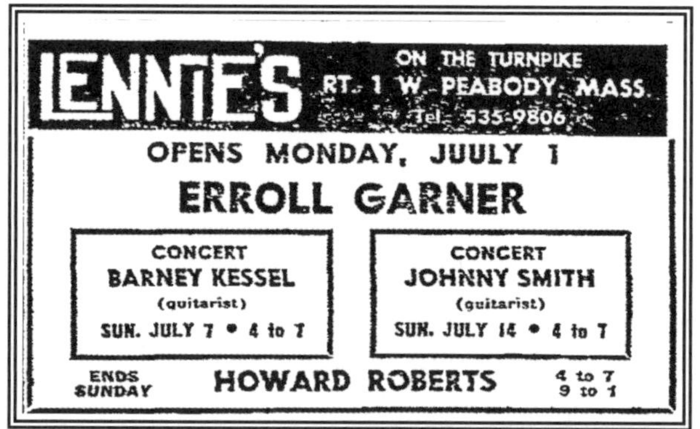

> I remember it very well. Actually, he played in a guitar workshop setting. I used to have guitar workshops and bring in those who weren't on the road as consistently as some other players. Guys like Pat Martino, Pat Metheny... Johnny Smith was one. Johnny, to me, was identified with a great recording of 'Moonlight in Vermont'. Stan Getz was on the date with him. That combination made for a delightful result. I didn't have any 'incidents' when he was here. He played his gig and that was it. I was always aware of his talent, and that he was a regular at Birdland. I had a jukebox at my my club, as well as live presentations. I had 'Moonlight in Vermont' on the jukebox. I loved that song so much. I loved Johnny's playing, and he certainly performed well at my place. I had a lot of guitarists come through my club – Wes Montgomery, Jim Hall, George Benson before he ever recorded a vocal...

In the following year, on 2 November 1969, Smith performed two more shows at Lennie's on the Turnpike, where he was followed a week later by George Benson.

Orchestral Performances and Max DiJulio

Although, the majority of Johnny Smith's public performances around Colorado were with his jazz combo, he continued to maintain his wide range of musical interests. Having worked with orchestras on several occasions in New York, including on his two albums *My Dear Little Sweetheart* and *Guitar and Strings*, he made numerous appearances with local orchestras in Colorado. His drummer, Derryl Goes, recalled that the combo performed Smith's arrangements with orchestras a few times per year from the 1960s through until the 1980s, and his bassist, Dale Bruning, remembers similarly. Smith himself recalled performing some of his arrangements from his *My Dear Little Sweetheart* and *Guitar and Strings* albums with a small orchestra at Estes Park.

He also performed some classical recitals with the local orchestras. Guitarist Kenny Vaughan attended one of his concerts with the Colorado Springs Symphony Orchestra in the mid-1970s. Significantly, he recalls that Smith played his nylon-string Ramirez guitar without a plectrum.

On 28 April 1969, Smith performed as a guest soloist with the University of North Dakota Wind

Ensemble at the convention of the North Central Division of the Music Educators National Conference. The performance was recorded and issued in a small number on vinyl, in the ensemble's name, by Century Records. Smith was featured on an arrangement of George Gershwin's 'My Man's Gone Now' and a version of Ernest Gold's 'Theme from Exodus', the latter of which he had recorded in the previous year on his *Phase II* album. It is highly likely that the arrangement that he recorded with the University of North Dakota Wind Ensemble was his own that he went on to perform with the Falconaires at the Arnold Hall Auditorium on 12 November 1972.

Considering Smith's passion for the pure-toned electric guitar, it was only natural that he should be involved in new classical-weight pieces that were composed specifically for instrument. He gave the premiere concert recitals of Max DiJulio's *Concerto for Guitar and Orchestra in One Movement* on 10 May 1968 in Englewood, Colorado, and *Littlemass: A Choral Mass for Mixed Choir and Electric Guitar* in June 1969, with the composer conducting both performances. DiJulio, who had been a member of Glenn Miller's orchestra in his younger days, was a music teacher at Loretto Heights College in Colorado and was commissioned by the President of the Board of Directors of Colorado's Community Arts Symphony, Marty Nacman, to compose the guitar concerto specifically for Smith. He deliberately created the musical work around Smith's style, including his preferred Drop-D system of tuning, and notated the guitar part at concert pitch in the grand staff system. The composer was extremely pleased with the performance, as was his longtime friend and fellow-composer Henry Mancini, to whom DiJulio sent a recording of the concert. The text of the program book of the premiere performance for the concerto offers an insight into the creation of the concerto:

JOHNNY SMITH AND MAX DIJULIO PREPARING THE CONCERTO FOR GUITAR AND ORCHESTRA IN ONE MOVEMENT

> Composed especially for Johnny Smith and the Community Arts Orchestra, this is the premiere performance of the *Concerto for Guitar and Orchestra in One Movement*.
>
> Mr. DiJulio began work on sketches for his new composition approximately a year ago. During the summer of 1967, he was able to take some of the sketches to Mr. Smith for his reactions and suggestions. To the composer's delight, Mr. Smith liked and became very enthusiastic about this new creation. Mr. DiJulio finished the work during the Christmas holidays of the same year and has since made a piano reduction of the score and in early April completed a piano reduction of the orchestration.
>
> The *Concerto in One Movement* received its title for two main reasons; first, from its ability to act as a showcase for the solo instrument, and second, from its close relationship to the sonata allegro form so typical of concerto first movements. It is American in style and idiom with some flavor of jazz. The composer had Mr. Smith in mind as he was writing, and, as a result, visualized the way he would perhaps play the

concerto. (Reproduced from the Community Arts Symphony Program Book)

Smith's daughter, Kim Stewart, retains proud memories of her father's performance of DiJulio's *Concerto*:

> You know, the proudest memory that I have of my dad playing was when he performed the premiere of Max DiJulio's *Concerto*. The audience just went crazy at the end and wanted more. Of course, they didn't have anything else to play. So, they encored the whole piece.

For the haunting *Littlemass*, which was premiered at the wedding of one of DiJulio's students in June 1969, Smith was accompanied by the Choir of the Metropolitan State College which consisted of voices of two sopranos, one alto, one tenor and one bass.

On 6 December 1970, Smith gave two further performances of the *Littlemass*, under the baton of Howard Skinner at the University of Northern Colorado's Christmas Concert. The two presentations of the free recital were held in the university's Frasier Theater where Smith also accompanied the choir in performances of 'Silent Night' and 'A la nanita nana'. The *Littlemass* was published by the University of Miami Music Publications in 1971 under the revised name of *A Sacred Service*. Inside the front cover, the composer inscribed a note to any future conductors of the work:

> *A Sacred Service* was conceived from the beginning with the exciting sound of the Electric Guitar as an integral part of the whole work, setting off, by contrast, the tone quality of the choir in any and all combinations. The guitar part is written out completely, and is meant to be played as a fully independent part, not just as an "accompaniment", whether in jazz or "straight" style. It has been edited by the famous guitarist, Johnny Smith, who played the part himself in the original performances of the music.
>
> Should a Guitar not be available, however, the part may be played on any keyboard instrument such as Piano, Harpsichord, Wind or Electronic Organ, since it appears in actual sounds at concert pitch in this edition. (Reproduced from *A Sacred Service*)

The collaboration between Smith and DiJulio proved to be so enjoyable for the two musicians, and so well received by the public in Colorado, that they intended to work together again. In 2013, a copy of DiJulio's *Toccata and Blues for Electric Guitar and Orchestra* was discovered in Smith's private collection. The manuscript, which contains the guitar part with a piano score-reduction as well as the guitar part-book in the grand staff system is dated 20 March 1970. It has not been possible to unearth any evidence that the work was publicly performed by Smith.

He did work with DiJulio again, however, on 1 August 1977 when they shared the stage at the Central City Opera House with the singer Pearle Rae. DiJulio conducted the twenty-seven-piece orchestra for the free, ninety-minute, Colorado Day pops concert.

Montreux Jazz Festival

Smith's increasingly active participation in music education around this time saw him performing with the University of Northern Colorado Big Band at Claude Nobs' fifth Montreux Jazz Festival in Switzerland on 15 June 1971. The theme in the program for this particular year was American universities' big bands. Also on the bill were Dizzy Gillespie with the University of Cincinnati Concert Jazz Band; Slide Hampton with the UMCA Big Band; Max Roach with the Bloomington University Big Band; and Gary Burton with the University of Illinois Big Band.

This was the last festival to take place at the original venue of the old Casino, before it was famously burned down six months later during a Frank Zappa concert. The venue and the events of that night were immortalized by the British rock group Deep Purple in their song 'Smoke on the Water'.

Katie Smith (1890-1974)

On 1 March 1974, Smith's mother, Katie, died at the age of 83. She was buried head-to-head from her husband in Fairview Cemetary, Colorado Springs.

Benny Goodman in Colorado

On 17 August 1974, Smith was reunited with Benny Goodman for a grand performance at Denver's stunning Red Rocks Amphitheater. In the first part of the program, the clarinetist presented a recital of classical music with the Denver Symphony Orchestra, including several works by Johann Strauss Jr., an arrangement of Gershwin's *Porgy and Bess*, and the world premiere of Malcolm Arnold's *Clarinet Concerto No.2*. As a contrast to the classical repertoire, the evening was then concluded with Goodman performing a jazz set with Smith, Derryl Goes, Hank Jones, and Slam Stewart on bass.

A preview in the *Denver Post* reflected the cultural ignorance that existed in the local media at the time, despite the city's ability to draw world-renowned jazz musicians. Writing for an apparently uninitiated readership, the author's descriptions of the performers were pitifully understated. The reference to Smith, for example, was limited to:

> Former studio musician for various radio and television networks in New York city, guitarist Smith has recorded with his own groups on several labels. (Reproduced from the *Denver Post*, 13 August 1974)

As Smith had only recorded for Roost and Verve with his "own groups", the shamefully brief and poorly researched resume of his career was not even wholly accurate. Once again, the shortcomings of the media contrasted with the respect that Smith was afforded by other musicians. Interviewed for another preview of the Red Rocks concert, in the *Rocky Mountain News*, Benny Goodman acknowledged Smith's musicianship, albeit through an inglorious attempt to take the credit for having discovered the guitarist in 1950.

Smith's memories of the quintet's line-up at Red Rocks differ slightly from the contemporary previews and reviews in the local newspapers, which reported that Hank Jones rather than Teddy Wilson took the piano stool. Nevertheless, he vividly recalled that Goodman's attitude towards money had not changed at all over the years:

> I did a thing... There's an outdoor place called Red Rocks. I did a thing with him there. So, we met with Benny at the hotel, and then went and booked into a motel. Finally, we ended up at Red Rocks. Slam Stewart was on, and Teddy Wilson. So, after all day and everything, he [Goodman] handed me a check for thirty dollars. I looked at him, and I said [sarcastically], "Benny, it's been such a pleasure, I can't take this." And the son of a bitch took it back!

Bing Crosby

By the middle of the 1970s, Smith had become very much a Colorado home-bird, continuing to play on the local jazz circuit, albeit to a much lesser degree than a decade earlier. The long residency at Shaner's Lounge had come to an end and the times were changing in Colorado. Downtown Denver had become known colloquially as Strip-City in reflection of the amount of strip bars that had begun to surface, often replacing the music venues. Advertisements for strip clubs in the local *Rocky Mountain News* and the *Denver Post* during the 1970s were abundant.

In 1976, he was contacted by the pianist Joe Bushkin and invited to join his quartet for a series of engagements in Europe and the USA accompanying Bing Crosby. Smith had been a member of Bushkin's quartet in 1953, when they played at New York's Embers club together. He had also performed with Crosby earlier in his career as a member of an accompanying network studio orchestra. Despite his reluctance to travel long distances by this stage in his life, the opportunity to work with Crosby was too tempting to refuse. The crooner was still an iconic figure for many musicians of Smith's generation.

Bushkin had assembled a new quartet for his work with Crosby in January 1976. For the first six months Herb Ellis occupied the guitar chair, with his last performance taking place at the Masonic Auditorium in San Francisco on 2 June 1976. Smith then took over the duties and remained Crosby's guitarist until the singer's death on 14th October 1977. Their first shows together were in Europe, at the celebrated London Palladium, between 21 June and 4 July 1976. Alongside Bushkin and Smith were Jake Hanna on drums and Lennie Bush on double bass. The other performers in the show included Rosemary Clooney, Crosby's family, and the Pete Moore Orchestra. The concerts on 24 and 25 June 1976 were recorded and issued as *Bing Crosby Live: London Palladium 50th Anniversary Concert*. The Bushkin quartet's contribution to the show mainly consisted of accompanying Crosby during a lengthy and prominent medley of many of his hit songs.

In an interview with Joe Bushkin for the book *Jazz Talking: Profiles, Interviews, and Other Riffs on Jazz Musicians*, author Max Jones recalled witnessing Crosby's amusement at some of the lines that the pianist or Smith had played at the Palladium shows. Bushkin responded that Crosby had wanted to keep the performances fresh, and he therefore encouraged the combo to "throw some curves" to keep him on his toes.

Smith affectionately remembered his time with Crosby in London, including the near impossibility of parking a vehicle in Britain's capital city:

> When we were over at the London Palladium, Jake Hanna, the drummer... Jake came in and said, "I found a parking place." You know what the parking is like in London. Everybody said, "You what? How did you do that?" He said, "I've bought a parked car."

When we were in London, Scotland Yard chauffeured us around everywhere we went. I got to see the Black Museum, where they've got all the murder records, Jack the Ripper, and all that stuff.

The quartet also managed to enjoy some of London's nightlife when they were not working. The trumpeter Ruby Braff happened to be playing in town. On his last night at the Pizza Express in Soho, he found himself performing to a distinguished audience of Smith, Hanna and Bushkin.

London was able to fulfill a lifelong dream for Smith. Having met Charlie Christian earlier in his life, spent time with Django Reinhardt, and become friends with Les Paul, in London he was able to meet the last of his four early and most profound influences. The classical guitar maestro Andrés Segovia was residing in the same hotel as the Crosby entourage, and Smith was proudly able to obtain his autograph.

Also while he was in London, Smith was reunited with the British jazz guitarist and educator Trefor Owen, who had spent three weeks in his company while on vacation in the USA in the previous year. Owen was grateful for the opportunity to be able to return the hospitality that he had received from his idol. Their meeting also resulted in what was, at the time, undoubtedly the most insightful interview with Smith to be published in the guitar literature. Trefor Owen recalls his reunion with Smith:

Johnny had written a letter to me, saying that he would be coming over with Bing Crosby in 1976 to do the Palladium thing with the Joe Bushkin Quartet, and he invited me down. I stayed with Ike Isaacs, who was a good friend of mine. I took Johnny around and entertained him, you know. The first night, the Monday night, we went to Ronnie Scott's, where Stan Getz was playing, coincidentally. So, he introduced me to Stan Getz. He wanted to meet Ivor Mairants. I knew Ivor very well, so I set that up.

I don't know if you're familiar with a magazine called *Guitar*. Well, it was started by a guy called George Clinton. Now, what happened was... Ike and I went and interviewed Johnny in his hotel room for the magazine. Unfortunately for Ike and myself, George never mentioned either one of us. But we knew Johnny's work very well, and so we were able to ask him the right questions. We asked about his chord-melody arrangements, his use of extended chords and all that... and that was printed in the magazine. We did that interview, not George.

When the London Palladium dates were completed, the entourage crossed the Irish Sea and took the show to the Gaiety Theatre in Dublin on 12 and 13 July. Afterward, Smith generously invited the highly respected Irish jazz guitarist Louis Stewart, and his wife, back to his hotel room where he played a repertoire of new chord-melody arrangements for them. Although he had recently recorded these pieces in private, at home in Colorado Springs, they would remain unreleased to the public until 1994 when they were issued on the *Guitar Legends: Solo Guitar Performances* album. The tour then moved on to Scotland for two performances at the Usher Hall in Edinburgh on 15 and 16 July.

Back in the US, Crosby and Bushkin's quartet re-gathered on 10 September for a performance in front of an audience of over 1,800 people at the Archdiocesan Charities Ball at the Hyatt Regency Hotel in New Orleans. Eleven days later, Crosby wrote a letter to his sister, Mary Rose, in which he recounted his thoughts of the concert and the orchestra, while also expressing his recognition and appreciation of Smith's sublime musicianship:

> We didn't have a very good band. The conductor was all right but the fellas had a little trouble with the arrangements, but Bushkin played the piano, and this fella, Johnny Smith, on the guitar is a tremendous artist. He played a lot of stuff on the electric guitar that was supposed to be for flutes and other instruments that the local musicians couldn't quite handle. (Reproduced from the *Grapevine*, September 1991)

Joe Bushkin also recognized Smith's high standard of musicianship. The pianist's daughter, Nina Bushkin-Judson, shares her father's feelings about the guitarist. She remembers, "Dad thought the world of him. He always raved about Johnny's musical ability."

Crosby then took his show to an audience of 6,000 people at the Aladdin Theater for the Performing Arts in Las Vegas on 26 November 1976, before moving on to the Uris Theater in New York from 7 to 18 December. Milt Hinton had taken over bass duties by this time, playing alongside Bushkin, Smith and Hanna.

In 1977, Crosby and the Bushkin Quartet reconvened for another year of occasional dates in the US and Europe. The first performances of the year for the *Bing Crosby and Friends* show were on stage at the Deauville Star Theater in Miami Beach from 18 until 24 February. On 26 February, the show transferred to the Center for the Performing Arts in San Jose, California, before moving on to the Ambassador College Auditorium in Pasadena, California, on 3 March. There, Crosby suffered an appalling accident when he fell twenty feet from the stage at the end of the show, which was being recorded for broadcast on television. After just a few months of recuperation, he returned to the stage on 16 August at the Pavilion in Concord, California. On this occasion Bushkin's quartet were called upon to entertain the audience for twenty minutes when a power failure silenced the theater's sound system.

Bing and Harry Crosby along with Joe Bushkin, Johnny Smith, George Duvivier and Jake Hanna then traveled to Mysen in Norway for a performance at the Momarkedet Fair on 27 August 1977. The concert was televised across most of western Europe and eventually bootlegged onto DVD. Smith remembered that there were no written arrangements when working with Crosby, as the musicians were expected to know what the singer required from them. The film footage of this concert shows that while Crosby held the front of the stage, the quartet worked from limited chord charts rather than any set arrangements. The repertoire on this show primarily consisted of another vast medley of Crosby's back-catalog. In fact, the medley was so large that the singer understandably needed to refer to his song list more than once. The weather for the outdoor concert was not favorable. It rained heavily throughout most of the evening and Crosby was suffering from the cold even before he took to the stage. Smith implemented an idea that he had picked up from the singer Rey Rodel during his days at NBC, and packed Crosby with newspaper beneath his shirt to keep him warm.

On 22 September 1977, the tour returned to Britain, beginning with a performance at the Guild Hall in Preston followed by a concert at the King's Hall in Belle Vue, Manchester, on the next night. The show then settled in for another two-week residency at the London Palladium from 26 September until 8 October, with Princess Margaret occupying the Royal Box on one night. The tour concluded at the Conference Centre in Brighton on 10 October.

Bushkin's quartet found time to record an album during the tour. Originally released on vinyl as *Joe Bushkin Celebrates 100 Years of Recorded Sound*, it was renamed for its issue on CD nearly two decades later as *The Road to Oslo*. Although this is Bushkin's album, with Crosby only making two brief appearances, the highlight for guitarists is unquestionably Smith's instrumental arrangement for nylon-string guitar and orchestra of Norwegian composer Ole Bull's song 'Sunday of the Shepherdess'. He also contributed an abridged version of his chord-melody arrangement of Paul McCartney's 'Yesterday', which had previously appeared on his eponymous first album for Verve. For the adaptation on Bushkin's album, he added parts for the accompanying Jack Parnell Orchestra, and the piece serves as an introduction to 'Ain't Been the Same Since the Beatles', which Bushkin had co-written with the British journalist Charles Hamblett.

At the end of the tour, Crosby gave each of the musicians in the quartet a personally inscribed Rolex watch to express his gratitude. Smith's late friend Gary Atkins recounted that the gift was one of the guitarist's most treasured mementos. He remembered, "He has a Rolex watch which is inscribed on the back 'To Johnny Smith, with much love, Bing Crosby'." For his part, Smith maintained a great deal of fondness and respect for Crosby, later recalling that when the singer took his family on tour, he always booked them into the first-class area of the plane, while he himself always sat in economy class with his musicians.

Later Years

By the time of Crosby's death in October 1977, the Colorado music scene had greatly declined. In an interview for the *Rocky Mountain News* in 1978, Smith admitted that he missed playing regularly in the local nightclubs, but enjoyed his occasional concert performances and his guitar seminars. He further added, "Besides, I have a heck of a good time playing for myself in the quiet of my home."

Despite his later 'forgotten man' status, knowledgeable figures in the guitar world have always been keen to acknowledge the debt that is owed to Smith. In 1979, he was inducted into the Gibson Hall of Fame in recognition and appreciation of his contributions to the world of fretted instruments.

For a rare long-distance journey in 1980, he was reunited with the accordion virtuoso Art Van Damme for three concerts at the New Zealand Accordion Association's hosting of the Coupe Mondiale competition. As guest artists in Auckland, they were accompanied by Andy Brown on bass and Frank Gibson Jr. on drums, and played to audiences of over 2,000 people in the capital city's town hall. They performed a thirty-minute set at the opening ceremony on 27 August, and again on 29 August, as well as at the closing ceremony on 30 August.

Back in Colorado Springs, Smith could be found performing occasionally at Figaro's restaurant during the early 1980s. Guitarist George Hess, who taught at Smith's music store, attended some of his performances during this period. His reliable testimony provides further evidence that, despite decreasing his activities, Smith's musicianship and virtuosity were still impeccable:

> He was one of the most graceful players I've ever seen. His hands were so fluid and his technique was just about perfect. It looked effortless to me, though I know it wasn't. By that time [1981-1986], he didn't practice much. In fact, he said he hated to practice. But what he called practice was repetition - scales, arpeggios, arrangements - learning something new wasn't practice. Still, he also complained that he didn't have much in the way of calluses, so when he had a gig coming up, he had to work on it some. Yet he never sounded rusty to my ears.

A recording of Smith performing a benefit concert for the KCME radio station on 4 October 1981 at Figaro's, which was located at 1404 South Tejon Street in Colorado Springs, corroborates George Hess' testimony that his virtuosity remained undiminished. He made further appearances at the restaurant in the company of Neil Bridge, Bill Bastien and Derryl Goes until at least July 1984. Other local venues during the 1980s included the Emerson Street East Restaurant at 900 East Colfax Avenue in Denver, which was more of a concert venue than a jazz club.

JOHNNY SMITH PERFORMING AT THE EMERSON STREET EAST RESTAURANT

In 1982, Smith joined Buddy DeFranco, George Duvivier, Urbie Green, Budd Johnson, Shelly Manne, Dave McKenna, Clark Terry, Chauncey Welsch and Phil Woods on stage for two performances at the Paramount Theatre in Denver of the annual Dick Gibson Jazz Concert. A recording was made by Feyline Video, and issued on VHS format. On 13 and 14 May 1982, he took the stage with George Duvivier, Alan Dawson, Ray Pizzi and Jack Wheaton at the Mobile Jazz Festival at the Saenger Theater in Mobile, Alabama. Later in the year, on 12 October, he sat in with Joe Bushkin, Jake Hanna and bassist Phil Flanagan for the first week of a three-week engagement for the pianist at the Café Carlyle in New York, performing two shows per night.

On 15 February 1983, Smith could be found performing at the Irons Recital Hall of the University of Texas at Arlington. For the occasion, he was accompanied by Fred Crane on piano, Kerby Stewart on bass, and Henry Okstel on drums. The printed program provided some curious instructions to the audience:

> Tonight's program will consist of various selections for the quartet as well as solo guitar. Johnny Smith will announce the selections. There will be two sets with a fifteen minute intermission. For those of you who may be attending a Jazz Concert for the first time, it is proper etiquette and highly encouraged to applaud at the end of each player's solo during the pieces. (Reproduced from *Johnny Smith: Guitarist in Concert*)

Two months later, on 13 and 14 May 1983, he performed and taught at the *Mobile Jazz Festival*, alongside George Duvivier, Alan Dawson, Ray Pizzi, Larry Lapin and Bobby Shew. Performances from the clinicians' concert, including a breathtakingly beautiful interpretation by Smith of Michel Legrand's 'What Are You Doing the Rest of Your Life?', were recorded onto video for Alabama Public Television's series *Mobile Jazz '83*. This particular highlight was posted onto the *Youtube* internet site in 2008. A separate video clip from the same broadcast, of a performance featuring George Duvivier on

'Blues for Harry Carney', was posted on the same date.

Clearly enjoying his visits to the *Mobile Jazz Festival*, Smith returned on 14 September 1985, to play alongside his old friend Mundell Lowe. Others on the stage that year included Urbie Green, Hank Jones, Ray Pizzi, Monty Budwig, Alan Dawson, Mary Wilson and the Joe Louis Trio, Roy Meriweather, Bill Berry, and Clarence 'Gatemouth' Brown. The twentieth incarnation of the festival took place at the Greater Gulf State Fairgrounds. In reviewing the day's events, the local *Mobile Register* newspaper was rightly keen to draw its readers' attention to the exposure that the festival had justifiably earned in the *New York Times* and the *New Yorker*. The concert was once again broadcast by Alabama Educational Television and syndicated through the National Public Television Network. A video recording of Smith and Lowe's stunning performance of the Charlie Christian and Benny Goodman tune 'Seven Come Eleven' was posted onto the *Youtube* internet site in 2008.

On an unidentified date around the same time, Smith made a guest appearance on a local gig in Colorado with vocalist Marguerite Juenemann. She vividly remembers that his virtuosity, taste and lack of ego were as immaculate as ever:

> We were both guests on someone's jazz gig. The experience was very full, however, since I was accepted as a band mate, not the 'chick singer' (which comes with a bunch of baggage most often which no instrumentalists appreciate although might tolerate). Mr. Smith quietly observed the arrangement of people playing, listening well to the musicianship offered and then supported everything very tastefully. He left me space to fill as I wished, without getting in the way, and musically interjected such tasteful fills that were appropriate to the lines each of us brought into our improvisations. Then, he floored everyone when he soloed. Clearly, he had been comfortable in that way for many years. It was a 'hot knife through butter' experience, albeit brief, I will always remember.

In December 1985, Smith sold his music store as he further reduced his work commitments. The following year, on 27 May 1986, he was awarded an Honorary Doctorate of Humane Letters from the University of Colorado. Although appreciative of the accolades that he had received during the 1950s and 1960s, he saw these awards as a reflection of his popularity, rather than as recognition of the quality of his work. Understandably, with consideration to his extremely humble origins, acknowledgment from academic and cultural institutions gave him a notably greater sense of pride.

Three years later, he made two increasingly rare appearances at the local Pikes Peak Jazz and Swing Society concerts. For the first of these occasions, in February 1989, he was accompanied by the Neil Bridge Trio. In October 1989, Smith and the Neil Bridge Trio were joined by saxophonist Plas Johnson. On 27 May 1989, he was reunited with Joe Bushkin for a performance at the eightieth birthday party of Dolores Hope, the wife of comedian Bob Hope. In 1992, he gave his final official public performance, at Maxi's Lounge in the Red Lion Inn, for the Ronald MacDonald House of Southern Colorado charity. Thereafter, he maintained that when he put his guitar under his bed and retired, his decision was final. This included any domestic playing. Initially, he missed performing for people and commented that having chosen to call it a day on his public performances he was not content, even at home, to play at anything but the top of his game. However, this was not entirely true and was in reality his way of politely declining requests from admirers when he was no longer playing to his own high standards. Evidence of a subsequent occasion at the North Wales Jazz Festival in 2003 when he was reluctantly cajoled into a private and informal performance in the lobby of the Holt Lodge

Hotel revealed that he did not abruptly stop playing domestically, but over a period of time the guitar remained under his bed for increasingly longer periods until ultimately on a permanent basis.

JOHNNY SMITH PLAYING HIS NYLON-STRING GUITAR ON HIS 80TH BIRTHDAY

Legends: Solo Guitar Performances

With Smith retired from public performances and recording, in 1994 the guitar world was presented with an unexpected treasure. Carl Jefferson, the President of Concord Records, had known Smith for over twenty years and had repeatedly asked him to record an album for his label. The guitarist had continually been reluctant to return to the recording studio for numerous reasons, although his previous experience at the hands of Verve was paramount. Eventually Smith called Jefferson to offer him the selection of chord-melody pieces which subsequently appeared on the *Legends: Solo Guitar Performances* album. These recordings had been kept under lock and key since they had been recorded between 23 and 25 February 1976.

Smith expressed in an interview with Jim Carlton in 2009, for his book *Conversations with Great Jazz and Studio Guitarists*, that these recordings had been intended to demonstrate the possibilities of classical music on the plectrum guitar to the students at his seminars, and were not originally intended for public release. However, Trefor Owen and Ike Isaacs had interviewed him while he was in London with Bing Crosby, for the British magazine *Guitar*, shortly after he had recorded the arrangements in 1976. It was mentioned in the introduction to the published interview that the recordings were intended for release in the ensuing twelve months.

Regardless of the intention, the performances had been recorded by Smith in a bedroom at his home in Colorado Springs on an Ampex 5000 series quarter-inch tape recorder with and an old RCA microphone. As a result, he was concerned that the sonic quality was not sufficient for public listening, but he was overjoyed with the refinements that were carried out by Jefferson's sound engineer, Phil Edwards, in California. The amount of material that he had recorded did not constitute enough for a complete album in its own right. Fortunately, Jefferson had received a similar amount of work from George Van Eps. It was therefore decided that the two guitarists should share the space on a combined CD.

The album was extremely well received for a number of reasons. Firstly, none of Smith's Roost catalog had been re-issued for several years, and until 1994 not even his recordings for Verve had been issued on CD in the USA. With the digital format having replaced vinyl some years earlier, it had become increasingly more difficult for listeners to find equipment on which to play their old records. Secondly, Smith's half of the *Legends: Solo Guitar Performances* album consisted entirely of chord-melody solo guitar arrangements, which for many guitarists constituted perhaps the most revered part of his musicianship. Unusually, all of these masterpieces were played on an unamplified archtop guitar. Furthermore, the arrangements that were presented included an eclectic range of jazz standards, his own compositions, and classical guitar pieces. His use of the plectrum throughout, particularly for the Spanish classical repertoire, was technically breathtaking. Dale Bruning recalls that classical guitarists were astounded by the plectrum technique that Smith demonstrated with their repertoire:

> While I was playing with him [in the 1960s], there was a symposium of classical guitarists that came to Denver University. They had some very high profile names. Now, that group invited Johnny Smith to go and perform with them, but he didn't play on the classical guitar. He just played his archtop jazz guitar with the plectrum. Some of the classical guitarists who were there were amazed at how effectively he could play some of that literature with a pick! Those chord-melody pieces that he played, I thought that they were real highlights.

Guitarist Louis Stewart recalls hearing Smith privately perform some of these arrangements in 1976:

> When he came to Dublin that time with Bing Crosby... We met up with him. My wife and I found ourselves in his hotel room, and he played some of those classical pieces with a pick. It was utterly unbelievable... What he could do with a pick!

As his last release of new material, he undoubtedly saved one of his finest half-hours until the end. Two original compositions were included in the form of 'Macho's Lullaby' and 'Wally's Waltz', which were named after, and dedicated to, his two Yorkshire Terriers.

Sandy and Johnny Smith with two of their Yorkshire Terriers

More Awards

On 14 June 1998, Smith was awarded the James Smithson Bicentennial Medal by the Smithsonian Institution. The certificate, which he hung proudly on the wall in his bar declared:

> His genesis of 'Walk, Don't Run', his performance of 'Moonlight in Vermont', and his manifold accomplishments as a performer, recording artist and teacher have had a profound and pervasive influence on the role of the guitar in contemporary popular culture.

The popularity of his composition 'Walk, Don't Run' as a pop hit for the Ventures in 1960, brought Smith a Citation of Achievement award in the same year from the performing rights organization Broadcast Music, Inc., and later brought him the Special Citation of Achievement from BMI for achieving over two million radio plays. As his son, David, recalls, 'Walk, Don't Run' received recognition long before the Ventures:

> Then, there was the Rock and Roll Hall of Fame. Yeah, I came back from Cleveland with this brochure, and I said to him, “It says here that you're kind of famous.” He said, “Oh shit! Do I have to give a speech?” I told him, “No, you're off the hook on that one,” [laughs]. The song ['Walk, Don't Run'] went right in there a long time before the group. The Ventures were only recently inducted.

The Ventures were inducted into the Rock and Roll Hall of Fame in 2008.

In 1998, Smith received the Lifetime Guitar Achievement Award from Duquesne's guitar camp. He was also recognized at a local level. On 14 February 1999, the Pikes Peak Jazz and Swing Society presented him with its third annual Alice Award, which was named after the late singer Alice Cardozo and was awarded to exemplary musicians who had made significant contributions to jazz in the area.

In June 1999, Smith attended a tribute concert given in his name at Hunter College's Kaye Playhouse in New York. The evening was produced by Charles Carlini for the JVC Jazz Festival. Although his friends Barney Kessel and Chet Atkins were both unable to be present due to poor health, the event was enthusiastically attended by Mundell Lowe, Sal Salvador, Jack Wilkins, Pat Martino, George Benson, Gene Bertoncini, Jimmy Bruno, Tony Mottola, Howard Alden and several other renowned guitarists upon whom Smith had been a profound influence. By way of tribute, each performer played two or three pieces, and many of them spoke emotionally of Smith's impact upon them through either his musicianship or his friendship. Jack Wilkins remembers the occasion with pride:

> June of 1999, there was a JVC jazz Festival Tribute to him at the Silvia and Danny Kaye Playhouse in New York. All the guitar greats were there. What an honor for me. I played with Carl Barry and later Jimmy Bruno. We played a few of his notable tunes like 'Moonlight in Vermont' and his own 'Walk, Don't Run'. He was there and it was super great to see him again.

The Complete Roost Johnny Smith Small Group Sessions

In 2002, another Johnny Smith treasure was released to the public. By this time, Roulette Records, who owned the Roost Records catalog, had been acquired by EMI. While two of Smith's albums for Verve had eventually been transferred to the medium of compact disc in the USA, none of his recordings for Roost had been extended the same courtesy. Many of the original tapes were thought to have been lost until EMI librarian Ian Pickavance discovered copies in the Abbey Road studios in London. Mosaic Records, who specialized in re-issuing old jazz recordings, obtained a license from EMI to release Smith's entire Roost small group recordings on an eight-CD box set as *Johnny Smith: The Complete Roost Johnny Smith Small Group Sessions*.

It is impossible to overestimate how much the prolonged unavailability of his Roost recordings had impacted upon his profile. New generations of jazz guitarists had been kept in the dark and relatively few of them had even heard of his name. Finally, however, after many decades jazz guitarists could once again enjoy what for some had been confined to distant memories. Meanwhile, the reaction of younger listeners who were new to Smith's music was described by Michael Cuscuna of Mosaic Records, who reported, "Oh my God. We're getting letters of religious-awakening proportions as players discover this guy."

The Last Bow

In 2003, Smith received the Lifetime Achievement Award from the North Wales International Jazz Guitar Festival. Mundell Lowe was an important factor in convincing Smith to make the long journey across the Atlantic Ocean:

> A few years ago [2003], we went over to Wales. I talked him into doing a guitar festival over there. I introduced him to the students, because although a lot of people had heard of Johnny Smith, a lot of people had never seen him. And I thought it would be good for them to see him and see him play a little bit. So, that's what we did.

The organizer of the event, Trefor Owen, recalls his favorite memories:

> After that experience down in London [the tour with Bing Crosby in 1976], I kept in touch with Johnny. When we brought him over for the North Wales Jazz Guitar Festival in 2003, we had Gene Bertoncini, Mundell Lowe, Jimmy Bruno and Jake Hanna, as well. That was quite a year. My favorite year of all of them. We presented him with the Lifetime Achievement Award, which was actually presented to him by the mayor of Wrexham, because that's where we used to hold it. Stefan Sonntag is a guitar maker from Germany. He made a guitar impression for the trophy. Now, Johnny would not play publicly, but he did play privately and it was video recorded. Unfortunately, the lighting was bad. It was very dark. It was done in a hotel room at about four in the morning. He wouldn't put the guitar down.

One of the memorable pieces that he played at the Holt Lodge Hotel near Wrexham was his own chord-melody arrangement of 'Send in the Clowns'. Clearly, Smith's guitar had been brought out from under his bed more than once since he had retired from performing in public in 1992.

In June 2009, another appreciative celebration was held in Smith's name when the local Pikes Peak Jazz and Swing Society gave a birthday party in his honor. In the same year, he was somewhat surprised to find himself inducted into the Maine Country Music Hall of Fame in recognition of his early hillbilly days. Hi final major award came on 21 May 2012, when he proudly received a second Honorary Doctorate of Humane Letters, from the Colorado College.

Chapter Six:
Johnny Smith Music, Inc.

One of the most important aspects of Smith's life after he relocated from New York to Colorado Springs was his music store, which kept him financially afloat during an uncertain time. On 15 March 1961, the Johnny Smith Guitar Center opened at 1727 South 8th Street in the Cheyenne Shopping Center in Colorado Springs. The premises had 800 square feet of floor space, including two soundproofed studios for teaching purposes. The purchase of the store was funded by the commission that he had received from an endorsement deal with the Gibson guitar company, which saw the production of the model that he had designed himself and which carried his name. The music shop became a vitally important part of Smith's life in Colorado Springs. It provided him with a modest degree of financial security. Even by the mid-1960s, when he was a regular feature on the Colorado music scene, his bookings were far from lucrative.

Although the shop was initially dedicated to the sale of guitars, amplifiers, basses, banjos and ukeleles, it soon became apparent that fretted-string players were too much of a niche marketplace. The remit was expanded to accommodate a more general music clientele, and a change of name was required in order to reflect the new diversity. By 1963 it had become Johnny Smith Music, Incorporated.

Sandy Smith played a significant part in the running of her husband's music store. She possessed a greater sense of business acumen and was often to be found working behind the counter. It was at her instigation that the shop broadened its services and began to offer a complete instrument repair department.

As the enterprise progressed, it became apparent that larger premises were required. Consequently, the store was relocated to the opposite side of the Cheyenne Shopping Center, at 1713 South 8th Street, before it was further expanded into the adjacent shop. As well as catering for a typical customer base over the counter, the music store also tapped into the rental market for schoolchildren.

The British guitarist and educator Trefor Owen, who spent some time helping out in Smith's shop during a vacation in 1975, remembers that it was impeccably laid out, with a good range of amplifiers, accessories and musical instruments, including a few archtop guitars. Behind the counter was Smith's immaculately organized workbench, above which were hung his own guitars in the form of his 1955 D'Angelico, his blonde Gibson Johnny Smith and a handmade classical guitar.

JOHNNY SMITH IN HIS INSTRUMENT REPAIR DEPARTMENT

Alongside his wife, Sandy, Johnny Smith was an extremely interactive shop-owner. He was not of the mind to merely sit back and let his employees carry out all of the work on his behalf. Trefor Owen recalls more details about his three weeks with Smith in his music store:

> I worked in his shop with him, setting up guitars and re-stringing guitars with him. People were traveling miles, I mean hundreds or thousands of miles, just to bring their guitars in and have them set up by Johnny Smith! He had a selection of guitars in his shop, but he didn't have any Gibson Johnny Smith guitars there, because he had a long list of people wanting them through him, and so they were sold before they had even arrived. So, he never had one in stock, but he had plenty of Gibson L-5 and L-5C guitars, and so on.

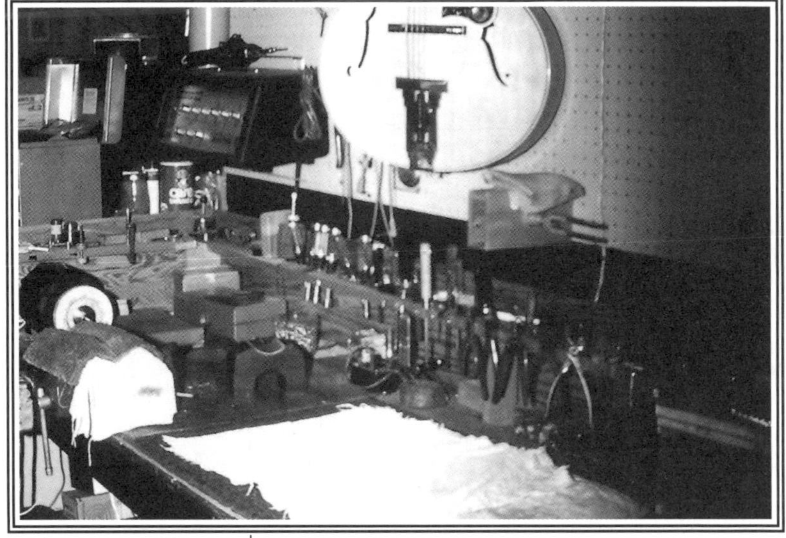

JOHNNY SMITH'S WORKBENCH IN HIS MUSIC STORE

Gordon Close, who was a student of Smith during the early 1960s and currently owns his own guitar and amplifier store in Englewood, Colorado, remembers that his former Master often used to wear a denim Gibson apron while he was repairing customers' guitars. He affectionately recalls that, with the addition of his small glasses, Smith resembled Geppetto. Fred Hamilton has a similarly fond recollection of Smith at his workbench in his store:

> I was in the Air Force with the NORAD Band stationed in Colorado Springs from 1972-1976. I remember the supply sergeant asking me what guitar I would like to play. I really don't know why, but I asked them for a Gibson Johnny Smith. They sent me to Johnny's

music store to get it from the source. I walked in and he was wearing an apron and doing a set-up on a cheap Stratocaster for a young man. He reminded me of Handyman Negri, a character on Mister Roger's television program. After he had finished, he greeted me and I told him what I wanted and he set me up. It was a beautiful instrument. I imagine when they disbanded the NORAD Band later it wound up in a warehouse like the Ark of the Covenant in *Raiders of the Lost Ark*.

Meanwhile, a journalist who visited the music store for the local *Denver Post* newspaper in 1984 described Smith as looking "like a high school math teacher or the kind of dentist you would trust." Guitarist and educator Jim Fox recalls his own pilgrimage to Smith's music store in the early 1980s, after he had graduated from the Berklee College of Music:

I had a remarkable visit to Colorado. After I got out of school and was pursuing a career... I was out on the road and I found myself in Denver. Around 1980 or 1981. I really wanted to meet Johnny Smith. So, I called up Directory Assistance for Colorado Springs. If you asked them for a 'John Smith', even then in a pretty small place... [laughs]. And then I tried 'Johnny Smith Music', 'Johnny Smith Guitars', 'Johnny Smith anything!'... And they couldn't come up with it. Nothing existed. So, I rented a car, the cheapest little rental car that I could get, and I drove from Denver to Colorado Springs. It was maybe an hour and a half's drive. Something like that. I started cruising, looking for Johnny Smith Music. So, essentially, I stalked him [laughs].

I went into his store, and I thought... Jeez... Are you familiar with the film *Sweet and Lowdown*? OK, so that moment when Sean Penn finally sees Django Reinhardt, and he faints. Well, when I saw Johnny Smith, I had to get a hold of myself. I was so excited. I went over and started leafing through the music, just giving myself time to compose myself. A lady walked in, carrying a real cheap guitar case. Johnny Smith said to her, "Hello, Ma'am. Can I help you?" And she said, "Yes, please. This is my son's guitar. It's broken." Johnny replied, "Really, Ma'am, would you like me to look at it?" She said, "Yes please." So, he picked up the box and put it onto the glass display case that he used as a counter, opened it up, looked at the guitar, and said, "Yes, Ma'am. You're right. It's broken. It has a broken string. Would you like me to fix it for you?" So, he turned around to where he stored the strings, took one out, and put in on the guitar, and

JIM FOX WITH JOHNNY SMITH IN HIS MUSIC STORE

said to her, "There you go Ma'am. That'll be thirty-seven cents." I was just about to have a stroke. I mean, Johnny Smith is fixing a $20 guitar for this lady! This is like sitting there with Segovia, or Toscanini, or Django Reinhardt, or Charlie Parker. You know, a supertalent! So, she left, and that's when I went up and introduced myself to him.

Accordionist Kenny Kotwitz experienced similar emotions regarding Smith's low-profile residency in Colorado Springs:

> I remember, one day, walking into his store. He was sitting there with his back to me. He was the only person in the store. It was in the afternoon. He had his guitar, and he was behind the counter. He was messing around with the bridge. And every time that he played it, it was more beautiful than the last. And every time that he was done, he said, "Ah, that was crap!" [laughs]. He was never satisfied with what he did, and yet everything that he did was like a work of art. Unbelievable. It struck me that here is the world's greatest guitar player, and he's living in this little town, Colorado Springs. I'm sure a lot of people thought about that. He was so unassuming.

Smith's music store was a Mecca for guitarists for nearly twenty-five years. Randy Benway was encouraged to pay a visit:

> My best friend and I toured Colorado in the Summer of 1977. I was studying jazz guitar under Bill Barker at the time (a great jazz guitarist and archtop guitar maker). He told me I should stop in Colorado Springs and meet Johnny Smith. I must admit, at twenty years old, I didn't have an appreciation for Johnny. Bill would rave about his playing, but you just didn't go down to the mall back then and buy those records. Once in town, we looked up Johnny's store and went in just after lunch. He was alone. I remember about seven or eight archtops hanging behind the register. I chatted with Johnny and found him very friendly. He turned and pulled the end archtop off the wall and handed it to me. It was his own personal Johnny Smith model! It was blonde. I remember him saying it was "more glue than wood" as he had repaired numerous cracks out on the road. It was years later that I bought my first Johnny Smith CD. I'm honored to have met Johnny, but I feel bad that I had no idea at the time of his genius.

Randy Benway was far from being the only guitarist of a younger generation who was as yet unaware of Smith's legendary guitar playing and his stature within the jazz guitar world. None of them should be criticized for their ignorance. There were other visitors, however, who did not recognize Smith, but gave him considerable mirth by requesting that he pass on their best wishes to the store's owner, claiming that they were good friends.

Several teachers of different instruments ran their practices from Smith's music store. In 2012, he recalled how his brother, Ben, came to be involved:

> We sure went through a lot of students there. We had teachers for trumpet, saxophone, trombone... Yeah, I had all different teachers there. My brother, Ben, the only one who is still alive... He lives up here in Black Forest, just north of town... Well, I had this guitar

teacher, so called. He was from Texas. He and his wife had their own music store there. They closed it and moved up here. He was teaching at my store. He had about sixty students. George Barnes was also teaching at the store. On a Friday afternoon, I was in New York... Sandy, my wife, called me and said, “What am I going to do? They just left. Just like that.” I said, “Well, get my Mel Bay Book One, and tell Ben to come in, pick up a guitar, and start teaching on Monday.” And this was Friday! He didn't play guitar, but the reason for choosing him was because he could tune the guitar. I figured that if he could tune it, then he could play it. So, sure enough, he started teaching. He taught for several years at my store.

For his own part, Ben Smith explains why his brother thought that he was a suitable candidate:

> I taught at John's store for around fifteen years. It wasn't really my thing, but he couldn't find a teacher for beginners. He said that regular guitar players couldn't go back to the very beginning. *He* couldn't! So, I took on the beginners. I couldn't play anything. He gave me a guitar and a book on Friday, and I was supposed to start with the students on Monday. They could already play, but I couldn't. That was a rough month or so!

By the second half of the 1970s, Smith had three guitar teachers working in his music store. Denisa Hanna recalls how she came to work there:

> I was always at the store while I was studying anyway, practicing... When I graduated, I started teaching there. I also taught in a small university in Pueblo, Colorado. Then, when he started touring with Bing [Crosby], that's where I met Jake [Jake]... He tells me that's why he had to sell the store, because I moved away [laughs]. I don't believe him. I helped to mind his store for him while he was away touring with Crosby.

By the early 1980s, he had around five teachers working in his basement studios. George Hess, who worked as a guitar teacher in Smith's store between 1981 and 1986, remembers how he came to work there, the family orientation of the business, and another young customer who was unaware of the legendary status of the store's proprietor:

> I got the gig based on my resume, Berklee degree and interview. I don't remember playing for him at that time, though I did later. Johnny and his wife ran the store, with an occasional assist from his daughter [Kim]. I helped out occasionally, too. Everyone else was independent, including the instrument repairman. Johnny had a picture of Chet in the store, signed, “To my good friend and great guitarist,” or something similar. Johnny told me of the time when a guy came into the store and after looking at the picture, said, “You

> must be a pretty good guitar player to know Chet Atkins." To which Johnny replied, "You don't have to be a good guitarist to be a good friend." That probably describes his personality to a tee. He was very humble and well mannered, but he also had a very dry sense of humor.

Smith's business ethos in his store was as conscientious as his famous hospitality was generous. Al Owens remains grateful for the service that he received from the store owner:

> I was searching for a used JS model. This was in the early 1980s and Gibson was having some problems. I called several archtop dealers. One of the dealers suggested I call Johnny's store. I did and he put on the phone. I don't know why, but I was not expecting to speak with the 'Burning Bush' directly. We chatted for about thirty minutes, but alas he did not have one either. Two days later, he called and told me that a customer who owned a JS model had just died and the family wanted to sell the guitar. Johnny told me he was going to fly his plane to see the family and check out the instrument. He asked if I wanted it after assuring me that if it did not measure up to his standards he would make it so, or keep looking for me. Long story short, he sold the burgundy colored JS to me for $1400. He even called me a few times to make certain I was happy with the purchase.

Smith's daughter, Kim Stewart, remembers a similar example when her father went to considerable lengths to not disappoint a customer:

> One year at the store, a woman came in and ordered one of the JS guitars as a surprise for her husband at Christmas time. The guitar was supposed to arrive in plenty of time, but Christmas Eve arrived and... no guitar. It had been delayed due to bad weather. Dad made some calls and found out that the guitar was due to arrive in Denver early that evening. He actually flew to Denver, picked up the guitar, and delivered it to their house so they would have it for Christmas.

Brandy Herbert also recalls, with fondness, Smith's generosity and sense of humor during a visit to his music store around 1983 with her Gibson Johnny Smith guitar:

> It had a rattle in the third string that I couldn't seem to get rid of. I was living in Texas at the time, but was visiting some friends in Evergreen, and had brought the guitar with me. I mentioned something to them about what a huge Johnny Smith fan I was. That's when they told me that his store was probably only ninety minutes away and we should just go down there and meet him.
>
> I walked into the store and there he was, standing behind the counter with a work-apron on and a pipe in his teeth. He had some guitar laying on the counter that he was working on. After the introductions, I told him about the rattle problem. He said, "Let's see what you've got." I pulled the '61 JS out of the case, and he looked it all over, grinned, and said, "Do you know what you've got here?" I wise-assed, "Yeah… a Johnny Smith." He grinned again and shot back, "Don't be a smart-ass." That was when he told me the details about the pre-production models having real tortoise-shell underneath

> those 6 holes in the pickup. He told me, "You hang on to this!" And of course, I said I would. And I have.
>
> He spent maybe about thirty to forty-five minutes installing several different gauges and brands of strings on it to see if one of them would eliminate the buzz. I think we must have gone through six to eight strings before we found 'the one'. It turned out that a Gibson-brand wound .20 gauge seemed to do the trick. I thanked him immensely for his time and asked him what I owed him. I figured I at least owed him for the strings he wasted in looking for the right one. He just shook his head and said, "No. Anybody that would make such a pilgrimage down here and bring that beautiful thing all the way from Texas... I wouldn't charge you."
>
> I saw him once again after I'd moved to the Denver area. That was in 1990. And I think sometime around the mid-to-late-1990s there was a guitar show at some Holiday Inn out on Tower Rd, near the airport. Their advert said that Johnny Smith would be there. So, I made a point to go to see him again. I re-introduced myself and told him the story about coming to his store and him going through a bunch of strings to find the right third for me. He remembered me and we chatted briefly. Then he signed one of the wall-poster reproductions of a Guild advert he had done years before and gave it to me. I still have that poster hanging on the wall down in my music-room.

During quiet periods in his music store, Smith pursued his own challenging musical interests. Tom Bruner recounts:

> I will never forget the time I walked into his music store one day for a lesson as he was unpacking sheet music for his store. As he opened one of the boxes, he said something like, "Oh here... I finally got the Rachmaninoff piano piece that I ordered for so-and-so..." To which he immediately picked up his guitar and began playing it at sight! His complete mastery of the guitar, technically, along with his total comfort with reading the grand staff allowed him to do what I don't believe any other guitarist could do. Including Tommy Tedesco, who a few years later I would begin to work with many times, and who was also a freak at playing anything put in front of him at sight. But when I told Tommy the story of the Rachmaninoff piece being played by Johnny, he too was very impressed.

George Hess recalls Smith meticulously working on a guitar arrangement from a full orchestral score:

> One day, I came into his store and he was sitting down with a large orchestral score of '*Iberia*' by Isaac Albéniz. He was working out an arrangement and showed me a section and said, "I can't understand why Segovia doesn't play this note. It's right here."

On 27 December 1985, when Smith was sixty-three years old, he sold his music store to Larry and Jean Rice. For a period after the sale, it was named Johnny Smith-Rice Music, while the former proprietor stayed on to help with a smooth transition for the new owners.

CHAPTER SEVEN:
THE EDUCATOR

Aside from his celebrated work as a performer, Johnny Smith was also highly respected for his innovative role as an educator during the 1960s and 1970s. He began teaching the guitar at a staggeringly early age, and by the time that he was thirteen years old he was teaching adults at pawn shops around Portland, Maine. After World War Two, when he moved to New York to take up a post working for NBC, he continued to share his superior knowledge with other guitarists. However, it was not until after his relocation to Colorado that he had his greatest impact as an educator.

TEACHING IN NEW YORK

When he arrived in 1946, Smith immediately made his mark upon the New York guitar community. Two guitar books were soon published in his name - *Guitar Interpretations Volume One* and *Volume Two* - by Charles Colin Music Publications. The full extent of the involvement of fellow guitarist Harry Volpe as the credited editor of these books is not entirely clear, but Smith was extremely displeased with the finished products. Furthermore, he did not receive any payment for them. Although the publications consisted of solo guitar pieces which often featured Smith's Drop-D tuning, the arrangements and fingerings were not in his style, and Volpe was conspicuously credited with the copyright on several selections. In 2012, Smith reluctantly shared his thoughts on his first two publications and Volpe's involvement, thereby explaining the uncharacteristic arrangements. He revealed, "Mmm, I wasn't very proud of them. Well, he [Volpe] kind of simplified them, which messed them up. I never wanted to purposely write simple. He was a little less than honest."

In New York, Smith took on a small contingent of private guitar students. Considering his huge work commitments to NBC and the other networks after his union membership application was completed in 1947, not to mention his prolific live and recording work as a jazz guitarist after the success of 'Moonlight in Vermont' in 1952, teaching was only a small part of his career while he was in New York. Nevertheless, advertisements in the music press in April and May of 1953 announced his teaching services alongside those of Charlie Parker, Sanford Gold, Bob Alexander and Eddie Safranski at the Hartnett Music Studios at 1585 Broadway in the city.

It is reflective of the reputation that Smith held as both a performer and an educator that his students were prepared to travel considerable distances to study from him. Harry Leahey, for example, commuted from New Jersey to Smith's home in Long Island for his guitar lessons. The tutor appreciated the mileage that his student was covering, and in a typical act of generosity he often flew him back to Newark airport.

Many of Smith's students, both while he was in New York and later in Colorado Springs, either became or were already renowned guitarists in their own right. Lou Mecca studied formally with Smith in New York. Sal Salvador studied informally through jamming with him during a period in which they lived under the same roof. Meanwhile, John Pisano had an interest in learning a particular aspect of Smith's technique:

> I was in the Air Force from 1951 to 1956. Johnny came into Washington D.C. where I was stationed. It was probably about 1953. Bob Pancoast was his piano player at the time, and George Roumanis was the bass player, but I don't think George had worked with him prior to that. Through some mutual friends, I talked to Johnny and he invited me to go up and see him at the hotel he was staying at. I had written some things out. He was very, very nice and spent time with me. He went through his arpeggio and scale patterns with me in all the keys. I worked with that.

Gene Bertoncini also took a few crucial lessons from him and picked up some invaluable tips:

> I studied with Johnny when I was a youngster in my late teens for a little bit. I was doing a television show for NBC called the *Children's Hour*, on Sunday mornings. Every now and then, I would go down and accompany the young kids on the show. I was only a young kid myself. I wandered into a studio next door one day, and I saw a band playing for a live mystery show. It was all live music in those days. One of the musicians was Johnny. He went over to the piano and started playing it. Then he went over to the trumpet and started playing that. He was amazing. I went up to him and asked if he could give me lessons. I had my cowboy hat on. I had no idea [laughs]. He asked me to play something for him. So, I sat down and played my little version of 'Honeysuckle Rose'. And he said, "Anytime that you're down here, if you want to drop by we can talk about the music." And he took me under his wing. It wasn't a steady thing.
>
> Later on, if he was working on a show, I would drop by and he would always spend a little time with me. I couldn't get a better start in life. I remember one time, he went home from the studio for lunch, and while his wife was feeding him, he was giving me a lesson. He's a good guy, you know. It wasn't long after that, he did that first recording with Stan Getz, 'Moonlight in Vermont'.
>
> Even though I wasn't a steady student, when I went to see him perform he always made sure I got a good seat and stuff like that. Very inspiring. He knew so much about music. He could play piano parts on the guitar. Just amazing. I learned so much from him. Techniques, sense of harmony, composition and arranging for the guitar. And that has stayed with me all my life. We worked a lot on technique, like alternate picking with

> scales, getting up speed. It was amazing, working on a couple of things, as they got faster, everything else fell into place as far as the picking went.

Mundell Lowe remembers consulting Smith briefly on some specific aspects that he wished to address:

> I remember taking a couple of lessons from him, because of his picking. He tunes his guitar differently from most other players, and I was interested in pursuing that. So, this was when he lived in Long Island, some place around there.

The alternate picking style that John Pisano, Gene Bertoncini and Mundell Lowe mention was a well-honed and much revered part of Smith's technique and a contributing factor in his ability to play smoother and faster than any other plectrum guitarist in New York. In 1956, Charles Colin published Smith's *Aids to Techniques for Guitar: Intermediate and Advanced Studies*. Unlike the dubious earlier publications, this book was certainly Smith's work. It consisted of technical exercises and scale and arpeggio patterns, and thereby provided a valuable insight into his technique, including his right-hand picking style and his left-hand fingerings for his trademark three-octave flourishes. Regrettably, however, the publication was not absolute. There were occasional misprints in the fingerings and a total absence of them in the latter part of the book. Considering Smith's meticulous attention to detail, it is possible that these shortcomings were the result of human error or cost-saving between the publisher and the printer. Nearly sixty years later, Charles Colin continues to sell Smith's *Aids to Techniques for Guitar: Intermediate and Advanced Studies*.

The encouragement of new generations of jazz musicians was undeniably an interest that was always very close to Smith's heart. In 1987, the writer Kenneth Grundy reminisced in an article for Cleveland's *Plain Dealer* about his days as a youngster in Philadelphia during the 1950s. He recalled that much of the jazz scene was inaccessible to his generation at the time, partly because it was unaffordable, but also because the minimum drinking age of twenty-one prevented many of the potential next generation of jazz audiences and performers from entering the nightclubs. However, on Friday afternoons, once per month, young jazz fans would go to the Heritage House Community Center where, musicians such as Johnny Smith, Art Blakey, Erroll Garner, Horace Silver, Ella Fitzgerald and Tony Bennett would perform free of charge for the youngsters in an intimate environment. Those in the audience who possessed sufficient courage were even allowed to join in the jam sessions.

Teaching in Colorado

When Smith moved to Colorado Springs in 1958, he increased his work in the area of education through his new teaching practice, which he based in his music store after it opened in 1961. Throughout the 1960s, although he remained busy running his store, playing on the local jazz scene, and making occasional visits to play in New York and elsewhere, he continued to teach the guitar on a private basis. By the end of the decade, he had also launched his innovative guitar seminars.

As with his teaching practice in New York during the late 1940s and the early 1950s, Smith's Colorado students were often prepared to make sizable journeys to study from him. A young Gordon Close took weekly lessons for around eighteen months in the early part of the decade:

> They were private lessons down at his store in Colorado Springs. I was in college at the time. There was no such thing as a guitar major, or anything to do with guitar in the colleges in Denver at the time. I had an opportunity to study with him. Stacey McKee lined it up for me. Stacey called him and said, "I've got a guy here that you've got to have," which was really quite nice. I had a private lesson with Johnny once per week, every week. It would take me an hour, at least an hour, to drive to him. Generally, it was supposed to be half an hour to an hour's lessons, but it always ended up at around an hour and a half. We would get really carried away with what we were doing. It was always a real thrill. Then I would drive home for an hour with all this stuff going around in my head. I couldn't wait to sit down and play it, try it, work on it. I never worked so hard in my life. It was exciting to deal with a man like that. He's a very gentle person and you learn so much in a very nice way. A very smooth way, you know. He doesn't intimidate you.

Tom Bruner explains the reasons why he, among several others, also went to great lengths to study from Johnny Smith:

> Studying with Johnny Smith was the ultimate experience for a young guitar student such as myself. I was in the US Air Force playing guitar in the Academy Band, which was located in Colorado Springs where Johnny lived. One of the main reasons I auditioned to become the very first guitarist assigned to that band was to garner the opportunity to study with Johnny. In addition to the lessons that I had with him and in which he introduced me to so many wonderful voicings and unique harmonization's of melodies, he and I became personal friends, sharing many, many dinner evenings (and Martinis!) together.

Smith was a conscientious teacher who always discouraged any parents who were inclined to excessively push their children into a musical education, maintaining that music should be a source of enjoyment. At around the same time that Gordon Close was studying from him, eight-year-old Jock Bartley also began taking lessons. Considering Bartley's young age, Smith's concern about the possible parental source of motivation was undoubtedly in his mind when he was approached by Bartley's mother. He had reservations about teaching a child of such a young age, but he gave the student the benefit of the doubt. Bartley was his youngest student at the time and he continued to study from Smith until he was fourteen years old.

The testimonies of Gordon Close and Tom Bruner that Smith was extremely generous with his teaching time is reinforced by Fred Hamilton, who is currently a Professor in Jazz Studies at the University of North Texas. Hamilton bought a Gibson Johnny Smith guitar from the man himself, and further inquired about studying from him:

> I asked Johnny for lessons shortly thereafter. His response was, "I won't give you lessons, but let's go play tunes together." Those were very meaningful times for me in that he charged me nothing and spent his time playing with me just because he loved the music. He was huge in my development as a guitarist.
>
> We would play and then he would find something that he wanted to stop and

address. He showed me substitute chord choices for 'Here's That Rainy Day' and a way to play "Round Midnight' and keep the chromatic line in the bass like Monk. We played blues and rhythm changes, I believe. He did not talk a lot about technique or guitar-related stuff, but he did talk about the music of the piece we chose to play. So, in fact he did teach, but there was nothing assigned and no expectations. We would spend around an hour before he felt he had to get back to the store. It is kind of funny, he was part of my local scene from the earliest point of music meaning something to me. I heard him play a lot and yet it took a while for it to sink in how important he was to many guitarists around the world.

Dick Eliot has similar memories from his time of studying with Smith between April 1960 and March 1962:

I was drafted into the military in '59. Out of four hundred and fifty soldiers, everybody went overseas, either to Germany or Vietnam. I was one of two blessed guys who stayed States-side. One was an engineer, and I got into a band. I wound up in Colorado Springs in the North American Air Defense Band. They were putting together a hundred-piece band with an eighteen-piece bandstand. The Colonel was looking for a guitarist, and there were none listed in the service except for me. I was a professional guitarist. So that's how I got in that band. Now, Johnny was a neighbor of mine. He was playing at a place called Eddie's in Colorado Springs, downtown. I would go and see him every night. After a couple of months, I worked up enough courage to ask if I could study with him. He said that he didn't teach anymore, but I was welcome to come out to the house. So, I did. I played for him and he took me on as a student for two years. He never charged me a dime. He wouldn't take any money! You know, that's how Johnny is. He's a man with a wonderful heart. He's so caring and very modest, as you know. He changed my life and helped me with my career. Things that I never expected to happen happened, and a lot of it I give the credit to Johnny for the time he took with me in learning my instrument.

Denisa Hanna also recalls Smith's generosity in his teaching, which included receiving his informal guidance while she was in her college years, before taking more formal lessons from him while she was at university. Her memories provide a further insight into his teaching ethos and also reflect the level of respect in which he was held by the educational institutions by the 1970s:

I grew up near Colorado. When I was a kid, I was playing the guitar in a little band, and one day I broke its neck. So, my mother took me and my broken guitar to Johnny's music store. He sent it away to get it fixed and gave me a guitar to use in the meantime. He and Sandy became very close friends. My parents opened a little music store of their own in a little town just after I graduated from college, and he helped them to get the business together and meet all the necessary people. So, I played the guitar and I showed up on Johnny's doorstep at his music store every few days or few weeks, and he would help me with my guitar.

In those days, and even when I was at college, you couldn't major in the guitar. So I majored in the French horn for a couple of years, but I continued to go up to Johnny's

> for guitar lessons. I never paid for a single lesson from Johnny. We would just sit down and play. They weren't formal lessons. We would just play and he would help me out. We were more pals than teacher and student.
>
> When I was at the University of Colorado, in Denver... Bill Fowler, he used to have the 'How To...' articles in *Down Beat* magazine, he started a guitar program there. And so I was able to study the guitar there. I asked if I could study from Johnny instead of Bill Fowler, because I couldn't understand a word he was saying [laughs]. They consented. So, I just studied from Johnny and got my degree. He and I played guitar duets for my senior recital. He was my accompanist! And then I ended up teaching for him in his music store.
>
> My pieces for my senior recital... They were all with the pick. I did Villa Lobos' 'Prelude No.1', Johnny's 'Wally's Waltz', and his arrangement of 'I'm Old Fashioned'. We did a Keith Jarrett piece - 'Spiral Dance'.
>
> He taught me... I had to learn standards. He always insisted that he wasn't a real jazz guitar player, which I never understood until I married Jake [Hanna]. But his push for me was on the use of the plectrum. Getting a good tone. His biggest thing is tone. So, I had to really work hard on the pick and moving my arm from the elbow, not clamping down with my finger on anything, keeping it fluid.
>
> He's totally against the modes. When I taught for him after college, we did the scales out of his book. You know, the three-octave scales. He's a big stickler on altered chords. He was such a stickler with me on the picking, too, like with 'Wally's Waltz', the scherzo. He taught me every pick stroke on that. My friend Howard Alden watched me do that, and said that hardly anybody does that classic picking technique. 'I'm Old Fashioned' has quite a strange picking technique, too.

Smith always ensured that his students were equipped with the correct instruments for their needs. Not knowing any better, Jock Bartley had wanted an electric guitar from the Sears catalog, but his tutor advised that he needed a 'real instrument'. Consequently, his first guitar was a three-quarter-sized student model, Gibson ES-145.

Perhaps surprisingly for a virtuoso performer who had been a high flyer on the New York jazz scene and who was accustomed to working with top class musicians, Smith was forever patient, sensitive and encouraging towards his students and not at all intimidating. In an interview with Adrian Ingram for the May 1995 issue of *Just Jazz Guitar* magazine, he discussed his approach to teaching. He explained his feeling that the development of a student's ear was a time-consuming process which started from nothing and had to be allowed to make mistakes along the way, learning which aspects to keep and which aspects to discard while gradually building a reservoir of ideas based upon a knowledge of harmony. He added that if students knew how difficult it was to play the guitar from the start of their studies, they would choose something else to do with their time. He summed up his respect for the instrument by paraphrasing the legendary violinist and guitarist Niccolo Paganini, in commenting, "Any darn fool can play the violin. Only a musician can play the guitar."

Some of Smith's ideas were unconventional, but entirely logical and extremely effective. For example, in teaching guitarists to improve their reading abilities, he advocated playing notated music that was unknown to the player. In particular, he considered harmony parts, such as second trumpet or third alto saxophone parts, to be particularly beneficial as the reading-performer was not in a position to guess the direction of the notes that lay ahead.

Importantly, he was always flexible in helping his students to study their chosen musical direction, while also guiding them in the areas in which he could see that they were most in need. His friend Gary Atkins studied from him for a period, focusing upon the technical aspects of playing while also increasing his musical vocabulary:

> We worked a lot on technique and theory. We used his Mel Bay book. Everything that's in there. And then he would enhance. You know, you learn the chord forms and then around the cycle of fourths you would play each form of a chord before moving on in the cycle to the next. He drilled that into my head. And if you look at that pattern, it's very systematic. One follows the other around the neck. And then the scales that match each chord. And for a warm up, we would play all of the scales. The majors and then the harmonic minors. And if you missed a note, you went back and started on that key all over again.

Another student during the 1960s, Barry Zweig, also appreciatively recalls his mentor directing him to focus upon these aspects:

> Johnny always stressed the importance of playing the chord-melody material as legato as possible. Part of my lessons was learning the chords and inversions on adjacent sets of strings. That was a life-changing experience. He asked me to practice my scales, arpeggios and picking techniques. He gave me finger exercises to help me build strength and finger independence. He was and still is a tremendous inspiration.

Barry Zweig's colleague in the NORAD band, the accordionist Kenny Kotwitz, studied music theory with Smith. He fondly remembers his time studying from the guitarist, as well as the most important aspect that he taught him:

> I was in the NORAD band in Colorado Springs. So, I knew John pretty well. It was in the 1960s. Barry Zweig was in that band at the same time. I talked to John, and he took me on as a student. I was his only accordion student [laughs]. He taught me theory and harmony, and the army paid for it. He had that little music store in the Springs. Barry was studying with him at the same time. We used to go up to Denver to see John play in a club with Derryl Goes. That was between '63 and '66. That's when I was there. He used to say to me [hesitantly], "Yeah, yeah, yeah, that's fine, but... it sounds contrived." He was a big stickler on the fact that it [the music] should be great, but it should sound natural.

Meanwhile, although Smith covered a small amount of improvisation with Gordon Close, he was content to focus more upon the student's desire to study chord-melody arranging:

> The first thing that he did for me was pretty exciting, and I still have his penciled copy of it. We talked about chords and we talked about arranging. He said, "Let me write you out a song that I would like you to work on and arrange for me this week. And then we'll go from there and see how you're doing and what you need to work on." So, out of his head

> he wrote out 'Prelude to a Kiss'. He wrote down the chords that he wanted me to arrange into the song, so that it would be a chord-melody type of thing. It was amazing to me, just to see the guy write it out in longhand! I wasn't real familiar with the tune, but I thought I would go home and pull out one of my Johnny Smith albums and listen to what he's doing. I was pretty good at that point at taking things off records. So, I thought I would do that. When I got home, I dug out the album that has 'Prelude to a Kiss' on it. This is the one song on the album that is all done with his piano player. Johnny only has a little part in the middle during the bridge and then it goes out again with the piano. He picked a song that I couldn't copy at all! I thought, 'Mmm, that's pretty clever!' It was a heck of an education, I can tell you. He wouldn't let me copy him off a record. Part of studying with Johnny... and he told me right off, "I'm not here to make you sound like me. I'm here to make you sound like yourself, the style that you want to have, and the type of music that you want to play. I don't want you sounding like me. I want you to be like you." That was pretty cool, you know.

This was Smith's ethos throughout the numerous aspects of guitar playing that he taught to his students. He resolutely refused to allow any of them to copy him. He saw part of his role as helping the students to be themselves. Barry Zweig concurs, "He didn't 'impose' his style on me although many of his students wanted to sound just like him." Gary Atkins explained the reasoning behind Smith's refusal to allow his students to imitate him:

> He considers music as intensely personal and creative. If you ask him a question like, 'How did you do so and so?' you won't get an answer. But if you present a problem to him in a logical manner, particularly if you write it out and say, "I've done this with this tune, and I'm not happy with this phrase," he'll spend days trying to help you to straighten it out. It gets frustrating [laughs]. He says, "Well, you could do this, or you could do this, or you could do this," and everything that he plays is better than what I thought of!

In his encouragement of his students' individuality, Smith did not instruct his pupils to adopt his favored Drop-D tuning over the standard guitar tuning. Instead, he encouraged them to use that with which they felt most comfortable. Gordon Close, for example, preferred to work mostly in the standard tuning. Barry Zweig appreciated Smith's flexibility regarding the Drop-D tuning:

> I was fortunate to have had the opportunity to study with Johnny Smith for about seven or eight months in 1965 and 1966. Unlike most of his students I wasn't interested in trying to play his solos note-for-note or re-tune the sixth string of my guitar to low D. I was a musician in the US Army, in the NORAD Band, and was based in Colorado Springs. I had a job that required me to play everyday and didn't think that I was smart enough to make the transition to that tuning. As I look back now, I think perhaps that was not a wise decision. I was a twenty-two-year-old kid when I first met Johnny. I was scared to death when I went to his music store and met him for the first time. It took me a while to get the courage to ask him if he would teach me with the conventional tuning. He said, "Sure Barry!" I had let almost a year go by. I had been playing for seven years

> when I started my studies with him. He filled in many fundamental gaps in my understanding of the fingerboard. I'll always be grateful to Johnny for his patience and guidance.

Barry Zweig is not alone in his opinion that, with hindsight, he should have made the effort to adopt Smith's Drop-D tuning. Several years after Gary Atkins had studied from Smith, he picked up a valuable piece of insight from his longtime friend and former Master:

> He told me once, about ten years ago [2001], I was working on a chord-melody piece by Schumann and I had heard him play it, of course. It's just beautiful! I was screwing around and there were a couple of chords that I just could not come up with, you know. So, he looked at me and said, "If you put the sixth string on D and leave it there, you will overcome most of those problems." Then he went on to say that in fact with Drop-D tuning, you will accomplish eighty or ninety percent of what the seven-strings guys are trying to do. So, at that point, I re-tuned to D and left it there.

While Smith always adhered to his ethos of encouraging his students to develop their own style and sound, he willingly shared his technical methodology. For example, he emphasized the importance of using guide fingers, and favoring the B-string as the strongest string for holding a melody. Gary Atkins remembered this particular and priceless piece of advice, which provides a valuable insight into Smith's guitar technique and musicianship:

> One time I was working on a tune, and he showed me how to improve... I think it was 'When I Fall in Love'. He used to say these little profound things. He said, "Never change the string you're playing the melody on, unless you're forced to." I think that was a classical thing. Not going for an easier change across the board at the expense of losing the timbre of the tone.

Gordon Close recalls that, with regard to chord-melody arranging, Smith also shared his methodology of working out the melody of a piece with a logical moving bass line before adding chords. This approach has stayed with Close fifty years later in his own chord-melody arrangements. Barry Zweig remains eternally grateful to Smith for the advice that he received during his lessons regarding not only chord-melody arranging, but also general musicianship:

> He wanted me to develop my own chord-melody solos. I learned a tremendous amount about the fingerboard from doing that. He stressed the concept of being careful to not be contrived when re-harmonizing songs.

Clearly, Smith encouraged his students to select a specific attitude towards their musicianship. As Gary Atkins recalled, the meticulous approach to every detail that Smith promoted in his students also extended to their choice of plectrum, and even their acoustic practice:

> On my first lesson, he looked at the pick I was using with disdain and said, "May I?" and then threw it in the trash! He gave me one of his and said, "Hold it like this and move

your arm like this. Never use the amplifier unless you're forced to. Never practice with the amplifier. Really." That's what he keeps telling me. Because in order to learn to truly control the instrument, you don't use an amplifier. Makes sense, doesn't it?

Gordon Close remembers his tutor stressing the importance of clean playing at all times, as well as the value of not overplaying. Again, this attention to detail has remained with Close to the present day. Along with his smooth style, it is a characteristic of his playing that he wholly attributes to Smith's impact upon his musical development:

> He was a perfectionist and everything had to be clean. To this day, I have a tendency to play very clean totally because of what Johnny put me through. A lot of players just play. They put a lot notes in there that they don't need to play. He used to tell me to think of an idea and play the idea. It doesn't have to be a lot of notes, just a nice idea. I am a very clean player because of him. It's interesting when someone like you starts asking questions, because it makes you look at yourself and your own playing. And that's when you realize your influences. I do play smoother than most other people and that's because of Johnny. I would definitely give that to him. We have a guitar quartet here. One of the guys in it also studied with Stacey McKee. So, we have a lot of similarities between us in what we play. The arrangements and so on... But there are also differences that are obvious and that's because of what Johnny brought to my playing.

As a consequence of the changes in popular youth culture, Smith's younger pupils went on to take a variety of musical paths. Some, such as Gordon Close, stayed within the realms of jazz guitar, while others were enticed into more popular forms of music. Jock Bartley was converted to rock music after hearing Eric Clapton's records with Cream, and went on to achieve commercial success with his group Firefall. Despite the different musical direction he remains indebted to Smith for shaping his musicianship:

> I have been called a very melodic lead guitarist, playing off vocal lines and other instrumentalists in an instinctive and non-thinking manner. I trust absolutely my melodic sense. Looking back, I don't think Johnny ever said the words to me, "Taste is not what you play. It's what you don't play." He never said that to me, but it was the greatest lesson I ever learned from him. Leaving spaces in improvisation speaks oftentimes much louder than anything you could play. Letting melodic phrases stand on their own, like sentences in a narrative. Only using speed or gimmicks in your playing to enhance the music. All of those things I learned from him by watching and listening.
>
> The single biggest thing I learned from him, he showed me by example. He didn't have to tell me. Oh, he would tell me plenty when I was playing sloppy, or not holding my notes out long enough, or playing with too heavy a hand on something needing delicate treatment, but he never told me the most important lessons he was imparting. I thank my lucky stars still today that I was in the right place at the right time and became one of his first students when he was a guitar instructor in his little music store in Colorado Springs. Johnny Smith was the best thing that ever happened to me.
>
> The magic and foundation he gave me was priceless, life-changing, and I am

forever in his debt. I have gold and platinum records on the wall because of Johnny Smith. He put me in position to become a great guitarist. Years later, I started experiencing the wondrous and other-worldly ability to transcend all your technique, limitations and boundaries, and soar, playing in the moment without much rational left-brained thought. Just reacting in the 'now' to where you are, to what the song calls out for, without caring what you just played, without knowing what your next note is going to be before you play it. It is that timeless and holy place that is perfect. The music you are adding at that moment is the best and most spontaneous it could be. Of course, those moments on stage or in the studio are rare and fleeting, but when a player can tap into those other-worldly, non-thought places and transcend into other realms... Wow! I attribute that ability of mine to Johnny Smith. Everything flows back to the superb training I received as a child. I am forever and humbly in his debt.

Smith's interest in the development of his students did not switch off at the end of each lesson. He obtained a scholarship for Jock Bartley to attend the guitar camp at Stan Kenton's music clinic in Estes Park, Colorado, in 1964, at which he was teaching.

Johnny Smith with his guitar students at the 1964 Kenton Clinic in Estes Park, Colorado. Jock Bartley is featured in the inset.

Smith was extremely dedicated in his commitment to music education across Colorado. Aside from his direct tutelage of young students, he also performed concerts with and for them. He was the featured guest artist at the Greeley Central High School auditorium on 7 December 1964, on which occasion he was accompanied by the nineteen-piece Greeley Jazz Lab Band. Later, on 26 October 1971, he gave a concert with the Neil Bridge Trio at the Cheyenne Mountain High School, sponsored by the Cheyenne Mountain Enrichment Program.

Sometimes, Smith's involvement in the education circles of Colorado took him in unexpected directions. In 1974, he found himself composing and playing the soundtrack for Sharon Betz's fifteen-minute wildlife film *Pawnee Pronghorn*, which was produced at Colorado State University and approved for international release. Sharon Betz, now Sharon Rushton, recalls Smith's participation in the production of her film:

I produced *Pawnee Pronghorn* as my Master's thesis at Colorado State University. It was

> used by the Natural Resource Ecology Laboratory and the Wildlife Department under the College of Natural Resources. The film won a Golden Eagle Award from The Council on International Non-theatrical Events (CINE), which was fairly prestigious recognition at the time.
>
> My major professor, Fred Shook, suggested the single guitar and recommended Johnny. The first and last time that I met Johnny was in the studio. He instantly amazed me with his talent. I don't think he even viewed the film before we went into the studio. He brought his guitar, which was the only instrument that we requested. As we played the film, he just composed as he watched it. Truly astonishing! He far exceeded my expectations. We had a small budget and he was kind enough to work within the meager amount that we had available.

Sharon Rushton has kindly provided a copy of *Pawnee Pronghorn*. Smith's sympathetic soundtrack greatly contributed to her already fine documentary. The music seamlessly merges with the images without falling into the trap of mimicking the action.

To return to his private teaching practice, Smith passionately encouraged his students to perform in public. On 8 May 1966, he presented two groups of students at a recital concert sponsored by his music store at the Cheyenne Canon Grade School. Two years later, on 15 December 1968, Johnny Smith Music Studios presented another guitar recital at Canon Grade School. Of the many students who performed, Bobby Montoya played a duet with the Master. Allen Daley, Smith, and his brother Ben were the teachers who were represented by their students on this occasion. On 18 May 1969, more guitar students from Smith's music store gave a recital at Canon Grade School. The tutees were presented by their relevant teachers, who once again consisted of Allen Daley, Ben and Johnny Smith, as well as John DiMatteis. Smith's students played a repertoire which included 'Sunny' and 'Light My Fire', both of which had been featured on his recent *Phase II* album. On 23 May 1971, another crop of guitar students from the music store were presented at a recital at the Canon Grade School by the Smith brothers and Allen Daley.

In a further example of his dedication to his students, Smith paid for a contingent from his teaching practice at his music store to view a film about the classical guitarist John Williams, for whom he had a great deal of respect. Unfortunately, the film's producers had chosen to promote the beauty of the classical instrument by degrading the worth of its electric relation, clumsily using distortion as justification for their assault. Smith was so aggrieved that he wrote an open letter to Williams, expressing his opinion that amplification was perfectly valid. He subsequently received a reply from somebody purporting to represent Williams in Britain, stating that the classical guitarist did not care about his opinions. It must be noted that it is highly unlikely that the liberally-minded Williams was involved in the caustic reply. The supreme irony is that he went on to use an amplified guitar with the experimental rock group Sky during the 1970s.

In his role as an educator, Smith felt frustrated at the refusal of record companies to re-release old jazz recordings. This, it must be pointed out, had nothing whatsoever to do with an attempt to increase royalty payments for the re-issue of his own back-catalog. As has already been mentioned, he was paid the standard union rate per session and did not receive any sales-attached royalties for his recordings for Roost. Rather, his contention was that new generations of musicians were unable to hear important players from the past, which thereby restricted their own musical development. He also felt that a new generation of jazz musicians was emerging without a marketplace, and lamented the demise of the traditional small intimate nightclubs, citing the economics that had attracted performers into large concert halls and encouraged them to overprice themselves to the point that clubs had to pass on the costs to customers, which in turn rendered access to jazz unaffordable for many people.

In his dedication towards his students, Smith had no qualms about terminating a student's lessons when it was clearly time to do so, and continuation would have been pointless. Gary Atkins recounted:

> I studied with him for a couple of years when I was in my twenties, and I was going through a divorce. So, I wasn't a very good student. One day, I finished playing an accompaniment part that he had written for 'Prelude to a Kiss' by Duke Ellington. He said, "Well, congratulations!" He stood up and shook my hand and said, "You now have all the tools and know all the rules. Now go make it your music. Goodbye." And I thought [sighs], 'Oh well' [laughs]. I wish I had done it four or five years later when I would have been a little more mature and through the stupid divorce and all that.

Although Smith found in due course that his music store demanded his increasing attention as it became busier, causing him to wind down his private teaching practice, he also became gradually less committed to teaching. Many tutors suffer frustration over prolonged periods of teaching students who could take their studies rather more seriously. By the late 1970s, he had three teachers conducting lessons in his store, including Denisa Hanna. By the early 1980s, Smith had five tutors working in his basement studios beneath his music shop. George Hess was one of those teachers. Currently Associate Professor of Music Technology at Yong Siew Toh Conservatory in Singapore, he retains an eternal debt to Smith for his musical development:

> I was never a formal student of Johnny, although I learned a great deal from him when I taught guitar in his store in Colorado Springs for about five years. By the time I was there, from about 1981 to 1986, he no longer took private students. He would answer my questions, show me things he was working on and was my friend and mentor. I went through his books while I was there and he would show me things about them too. All in all, the things I learned from him were probably the most important to my development as a guitarist and musician.
>
> One day, I was working on a tune, I can't recall which one, and I asked Johnny how he approached reharmonization of the tune. He just looked at me with a puzzled expression and asked, "Reharmonization?" We went around a few times until I finally said the right thing and he said, "Oh you mean change the chords." Of course, he knew what I had meant all along, but that one exchange completely changed my way of thinking.

Teaching Further Afield

Smith's activities as an educator extended well beyond his own private practice at his music store. As early as 1959, he had begun teaching at Stan Kenton's National Stage Band Camps. Between 5 and 11 August 1962, he taught at the Stan Kenton Music Clinic at Michigan State University. For the 1964 season, he was joined in Kenton's unit of clinicians by Neal Hefti, Woody Herman, Charlie Mariano and John LaPorta. A camp was also conducted between 19 and 25 July 1964 at Phillips University in Enid, Oklahoma, before moving on to the University of Connecticut where it ran from 26 July until 1 August. Two years later, on 13 and 14 May 1966, Smith worked at the Stage Band Festival at Olympic College in Bremerton, Washington. On 23 August 1966, the *Deseret News* reported that he was working at a National Stage Band Clinic at the University of Utah. He also taught guitar classes at Colorado Springs' District Eleven Summer School program in 1968. The *Billboard* announced on 3 May 1969 that he would be appearing as a judge alongside Clark Terry, Oliver Nelson, Paul Horn and Dr. M. E. Hall at the national finals of the Intercollegiate Music Festival in St. Louis. On the evening of 27 July 1970, he gave a concert performance at the ninth annual Colorado State University Music Camp, where his old friend and former member of his New York combo Ed Shaughnessy was also a clinician. Jack Petersen recalls a reverie from when he and Smith were teaching at a Stan Kenton summer camp in the early 1960s:

> There was a young guitar player who came to the summer camp. I remember he was from Philadelphia, but I can't remember his name. In the first class that we were doing, Johnny was talking, and this kid started playing a lot of Johnny Smith solos note-for-note, without an amplifier. It started bothering Johnny. Finally, he picked up a guitar and played the same solo all in double-stops, you know. This kid's mouth almost dropped to the floor.

By the end of the 1960s, Smith had become even more far-reaching in his teaching. Initially, this was achieved through the national guitar press. From April 1969 until June 1971 he contributed a bi-monthly column called 'Try It This Way!' to *Guitar Player* magazine. In each issue, he presented the melody and chords of a song and offered an alternative and more colorful set of chord changes. These charts were not intended to provide an explanation of his approach to his chord-melody arrangements. Rather, they encouraged readers to experiment with their own reharmonizations instead of adhering to those that were presented in typical sheet music. The featured pieces consisted of 'Once in a While' (April 1969); 'I'm in the Mood for Love' (June 1969); 'Don't Blame Me' (August 1969); 'Blue Moon' (October 1969); 'Have Yourself a Merry Little Christmas' (December 1969); 'Laura' (February 1970); 'Greenleaves of Summer' (April 1970); 'Over the Rainbow' (June 1970); 'Time on My Hands' (August 1970); 'For All We Know' (October 1970); 'Taking a Chance on Love' (December 1970); 'Try a Little Tenderness' (April 1971); and 'Whispering' (June 1971).

Although most of his teaching remained on a private, one-to-one basis during the 1960s, changes in the educational environment towards the end of the decade began to offer new opportunities. A decision by institutions to include jazz music in their programs had been in no small way influenced by the tireless work of Stan Kenton through his music clinics. As a result of the new policy, Smith became involved in jazz education programs at universities across the USA, as well as those in Colorado.

In 1970, he taught at both the University of Colorado in Boulder, and the University of Northern Colorado in Greeley. In an article in April 1971, the *Greeley Tribune* reported that he was working for one day per week as a guitar instructor at the University of Northern Colorado, and had thirty-five students under his instruction. He had begun the engagement in the autumn of 1970, and he coincided the trips with his commitments to the University of Colorado on the same days. However, at a distance of some one hundred and twenty-five miles, he soon found that it was too far to travel, even by airplane, and had to relinquish the post. Guitarist Bill Frisell was one of Smith's students at the University of Northern Colorado. He recalls his cherished memories of his lessons:

> I only studied with Johnny for a very short time. Maybe one or two semesters in 1970. I think it was close to when I left Colorado for Boston. I was majoring in clarinet at the school. They didn't even have a guitar program at the time. So, it was kind of a special thing that he taught there. At the time he was going around different schools in the area, but I don't think he taught for long at my university. He mainly taught at his music store in Colorado Springs, but that was like a three-hour drive from where I was living. I was doing gigs at the time, but it was more a kind of rock band thing. I was playing in the jazz big band at school. Derryl Goes was the director of the jazz band that I played in. He was head of the jazz department at the university, and he was responsible for bringing in Johnny.
>
> I was at the university just outside of Denver and Johnny came to teach a guitar class. So, I took the class and there were only about five guys. It was just a few. But what was really amazing... It's terrible... It's sad when I think about it.... I really took it seriously, but the other people in the class, they had no idea who he was. As the weeks went by, they dropped away, and it ended up with just me and Johnny Smith. So, that way I got to study privately with him.
>
> You know, most of what we talked about was very technical, like scales, fingerings and basic technique for the guitar, chord inversions... I can't remember playing an actual song with him. It was more arpeggios and fingerings, and the physical way of playing the guitar. He didn't impose his Drop-D tuning on me. I was just a kid and he was so nice. One thing that I still cannot do, but he was really hard on me about... He would bar things with his little finger. Every week he would be on me. And I still can't do it! But, and I'm incredibly grateful for this, he was so encouraging to me. This was a time when I wanted to play, but I wasn't sure if I had it in me. At the end of the whole thing, he took me aside and said, "You really got something here. You've got to keep going." It was one of those really, really, super-important moments in my life. Giving me the confidence to go on.
>
> It was quite a few years later that my appreciation for Johnny Smith really ballooned up into what it is now. Oh... [sighs] I'm just so annoyed with myself for what was right in front of me. There are things that I've come to figure out on my own in the forty years since those lessons, but he was doing all those things before. The way that he would approach folk music like 'Shenandoah' or 'Black Is the Color (of My True Love's Hair)', and his attention to the harmony. Already back then, he planted these seeds in my brain, although I didn't even know it at the time. He was looking at the guitar like a piano. He would insist that we read... You know... He would write things out in two staffs and then he would write the notes where they actually sounded. The detail that's in the inner workings, the harmonies, of all of the arrangements that he does, the reharmonizations, he's really thinking of it like an orchestra.
>
> Oh my, this is like a huge confessional! I mean, now, I've just come to love his music so much! It's just... The sound and the beauty of it. And when I think of the things

> that I could have asked him, you know. Stories about when he was in New York...
>
> There's a bass player called Buddy Catlett, in Seattle. He played with Louis Armstrong. He lived in Colorado for a while and played with Johnny. I met him. It was very strange. I was playing in a jazz club in Seattle, maybe five years ago [2006]. He came to my gig and that was the first time that I had met him. He came backstage and he said, "You know, I was looking at your hands, and... Have you ever heard of a guitar player named Johnny Smith?" I said, "What?" [laughs]. And I realized that there must be something in the manner that I play the guitar or hold the pick, or something. He said that he had never seen anybody play who reminded him of Johnny.

Fred Hamilton also recalls Smith's visits to the University of Northern Colorado:

> When I went to college at the University of Northern Colorado where Bill Frisell first went to school, there was no guitar teacher. So, occasionally Johnny would fly his small airplane from Colorado Springs where he lived and had his music store, to Greeley and do a workshop for a small number of guitar students and then to Ft. Collins at Colorado State University and do the same.

Guitarist and bassist John Thornburg remembers that Smith carried out some teaching commitments at the University of Colorado in Denver during the late 1970s:

> I attended UCD from 1975-1979 and William Fowler was the guitar professor there. He put together a few impromptu visits from Johnny. These were heavily attended and very informal. The topics covered varied from performance advice, technique, guitar sight-reading tips and more. 'Doc' Fowler made sure everyone was aware of Smith's importance. He shared an immense amount of these insights with us.

In addition to his own private teaching practice in Colorado Springs and his attachments to universities, Smith's passion for education began to reach an even greater number of guitarists through his guitar seminars. In a review titled 'Johnny Smith Seminar... Huge Success!', the October 1969 issue of *Guitar Player* magazine reported that fifty-six students had attended the first Johnny Smith Guitar Seminar, which began on 21 July 1969 in Colorado Springs. This was an innovative concept in guitar instruction. The magazine reported that many of the students had traveled lengthy distances from points across the USA, including Florida, Nebraska and Oregon, to study for five days with the Master in the first seminar of its kind. As with his private teaching practice in Colorado Springs, this gesture reflected the great regard in which Smith was still held by many guitarists despite having left the limelight of New York City over a decade earlier. The magazine article went on to report that if it had not been for the limited accommodation in the area, which restricted the number who were able to attend, even more students would have been present. The local *Rocky Mountain News Festival* also reviewed the seminar on the front page of its issue on 27 July 1969. In an interview for the newspaper, Smith stated that the only publicity prior to the event, which was held at the Holiday Inn hotel, had been a brief editorial in *Guitar Player* magazine. He had been overwhelmed by the response, to the point that several inquirers had been turned down, and he was hoping to discontinue his commitments to Stan Kenton's National Stage Band Camps so that he could focus upon reaching more guitarists through his seminars. Clearly, there was a demand for the instruction that Smith was offering, and which was undoubtedly partly inspired by the masterclasses that were common within the classical music genre, particularly those that were presented by the classical guitarist Andrés Segovia.

The daily timetable for the inaugural seminar began at 9 a.m., running through until lunch at noon. The class then resumed at 1:30 p.m. and finished at 5 p.m., with breaks provided every hour because smoking was not permitted during the class. Even these break periods were educationally productive as Smith made himself available to help individuals with their particular problems. He focused the course upon basic chord forms, the tasteful use of inversions, the correct notation of chord symbols, and scales. Howard Roberts appeared as a guest clinician and directed his presentation onto the subject of rhythm playing within small combo groups as well as discussing the obstacles that a studio musician was likely to encounter. Roberts and Smith also performed together with the latter playing bass. Dr. William Fowler from the University of Utah was reported in the *Guitar Player* magazine article as having presented a humorous and highly educational presentation about the career opportunities for guitarists. The *Rocky Mountain News Festival* observed that he also discussed the legitimacy of jazz guitar in the college curriculum. Composer Max DiJulio, who had recently written his *Concerto in One Movement for Guitar and Orchestra* for Smith was also present alongside classical guitarist Joe Flava from the Wayne State University.

Smith's friend and former student Gary Atkins, who had his own music store in Denver at the time, was one of those who attended. Atkins commented in an interview for the *Guitar Player* review that Smith had been able to casually drop small but absolutely priceless pieces of information that would open up successive doors to his students. Another of Smith's longtime friends, Mundell Lowe, remembers the same habit several years later:

> You know, he has little titbits of information that are invaluable. For instance, when we were in Wales [in 2003], he was talking to students about the art of picking. He showed them how if he slanted the pick a little bit on the attack that he would get a softer more melodic sound. They didn't know that. I didn't know that! So, I learned something, too!

Tim May, now a highly respected studio guitarist in Los Angeles, was only fifteen years old when he also attended Smith's first guitar seminar. With a father who was a jazz bass player, May was brought up listening to Smith's records before he even picked up a guitar:

> I attended the very first Johnny Smith Guitar Seminar in July 1969, in Colorado Springs. In 1968, my dad took me to the NAMM Show where we met Bruce Bolen from Gibson. He suggested that I go to Johnny's seminar in the following year. I was only fifteen years old at the time, but... Wow... It was such a wonderful experience.
>
> When I got there, my luggage had been lost in transportation. So, I was a bit uptight. Johnny was great. He was really sympathetic and approachable both as a teacher and as a human being. I remember that Howard Roberts was his guest clinician and Johnny played bass for him. The course was really well structured. I learned so much during that week. It was incredible.
>
> The alternate picking thing opened up a whole new world for me. That was just so important. I can't tell you how much. But also, his attention to the tone of his playing... That was a real influence on me, too. He gets such a beautiful sound out of the

instrument, that tone, and plays with incredible taste. I used to listen and try to emulate his playing. His perfectness was just ridiculous.

Just as Smith's recordings and performances on the New York jazz scene in the 1950s had appealed to musicians and audiences outside of the jazz genre, in the 1960s his musicianship attracted more than jazz purists to his classes. Rick Gustafson, who was another attendee of the first seminar, recalls, "I was a kid of twenty-one and simply in awe of Johnny Smith. I was mostly a rock player at that time but really liked jazz guitar, especially Johnny Smith."

The *Rocky Mountain News Festival* painted a vivid picture of the diverse range of backgrounds of those rock and jazz musicians and teachers who had assembled not only from across the USA, but also from Canada, describing the attendees as a room full of "long-haired bearded types," "balding tourist types," "hip Las Vegas types in casual couture," and an "Oregon priest in Bermuda shorts and sandals." The priest in question was Father Don Walster, who was rector of St. Mary Episcopal Church in Eugene. He was attending Smith's seminar to learn how to incorporate jazz into liturgical services. Another student, Jim Miller from Florida, had been recommended to attend by his tutor Chet Atkins, in order to learn how to apply Smith's technique to his Nashville sound. Also present in the predominantly male class were a professional guitarist from Stan Kenton's band, a piano tuner from Philadelphia who merely played the guitar as a hobby, and several rock guitarists.

Interviewed by the local newspaper, the *Colorado Springs Gazette Telegraph*, Smith drew attention to the main issue that he wished to address during his seminar, describing the guitar as the instrument that is the easiest to play badly, and the most difficult to play efficiently.

In hindsight, some of the facilities at the Holiday Inn venue in Colorado Springs fell short of expectations, but he received several letters inquiring about the possibility of further seminars. He conducted another one in Boston shortly after and was recruited as a visiting guest instructor for three days in December 1970 at the University of Utah, which had begun to offer a degree program in jazz music.

Relocating to a new venue, almost fifty students attended Smith's second annual Guitar Seminar in the Colorado Room of the Garden Valley Motel in July 1970. The guest clinicians on this occasion were guitarist Herb Ellis, composer Max DiJulio, and Dr. William Fowler. From 18 July through to 23 July 1971, Smith conducted a seminar at the Alpine Musicamp, Snowmass-At-Aspen, Colorado.

JOHNNY SMITH GUITAR SEMINAR
DAILY SCHEDULE

Day	Date	Time	Activity
Monday	July 21	9:00 - 12:00	Class
		Lunch	
		1:30 - 5:00	Class
		7:00 - 9:00	Individual Problem Session. (Last names beginning with A thru M)
Tuesday	July 22	9:00 - 12:00	Class
		Lunch	
		1:30 - 5:00	Class
		7:00 - 9:00	Guest Clinician Howard Roberts with the Neil Bridge Trio
Wednesday	July 23	9:00 - 12:00	Class
		Lunch	
		1:30 - 5:00	Class
		7:00 - 9:00	Dr. William Fowler, University of Utah, and the National Stage Band Camps
Thursday	July 24	9:00 - 12:00	Class
		Lunch	
		1:30 - 5:00	Class
		7:00 - 9:00	Individual Problem Session. (Last names beginning with N thru Z)
Friday	July 25	9:00 - 12:00	Class
		Lunch	
		1:30 - 5:00	Class
		7:00 - 9:00	Drinks and Dinner Courtesy of MERSON MUSICAL PRODUCTS CORPORAT

PLEASE WEAR YOUR IDENT BADGES TO ALL SESSIONS

THE DAILY SCHEDULE FOR THE FIRST JOHNNY SMITH GUITAR SEMINAR

It was described in *Guitar Player* as "a comprehensive study of the guitar for both the novice and the professional player." The course cost $125 per student and places were once again limited. It is a reflection of the respect within the education system for Smith as a teacher, that many colleges and universities across the USA awarded credit to students who attended.

In 1970, Smith decided to compile the course materials that he was employing in his seminars into published method book for advanced guitarists. He set to work on it while on a two-week fishing trip. The idea of a sizable publication that was specifically aimed at this particular level of guitarist was almost unheard of at the time. Previously, publishers had generally focused upon the much more lucrative beginner's marketplace. In 1971, the two resulting volumes, *Mel Bay Presents the Johnny Smith Approach to Guitar: Part One* and *Part Two*, were published. The books offered invaluable information concerning his harmonic and melodic approach to music on the guitar. They included chord shapes and updated scale and arpeggio patterns which differed from those that he had presented in his *Aids to Techniques for Guitar: Intermediate and Advanced Studies*. Unlike this earlier publication, there were no shortcomings in presentation. The meticulous attention to detail, particularly with regard to the scale and arpeggio fingerings, resulted in these two volumes being far more worthy additions to any jazz guitarist's library. However, while he did not employ his favored grand stave system in the two volumes of his method book, he did notate at concert pitch using frequent changes between the treble and bass clefs. He later conceded that this may have restricted the number of sales. In fairness, his system of notation probably had only a minor impact upon the sales figures. Jazz guitar had very much been replaced by rock guitar in youth culture. Furthermore, the marketplace for advanced material will always be smaller than that at the other end of the spectrum.

In 1980, Mel Bay unified and republished the two volumes into a single book titled *Mel Bay's Complete Johnny Smith Approach to Guitar*. To serious jazz guitar students, Smith's combined method book still remains essential study material. Mundell Lowe explains its importance:

> He was very interested in students and passing on his knowledge of the guitar. That guitar method that he wrote for Mel Bay is like the Bible. I mean, there's not a better method book on the market than that book. The students that I had in the past... I've demanded that they go out and get that book so that we can work from it. There's invaluable information in that book that young students need to know. Listen to the Master and try to duplicate what he's getting across. Yeah, Johnny Smith, he's special.

Despite his bi-monthly magazine articles, his book of technical exercises and his guitar method, many plectrum jazz guitarists have understandably felt frustrated that Smith never published any transcriptions of his chord-melody arrangements. There are a few unpublished autograph copies in existence, such as the single-line 'Wally's Waltz', which was transcribed for private teaching purposes. However, Smith always disliked, with a passion, the time-consuming chore of putting pen to paper. This is ultimately the underlying reason why he did not transcribe many of his chord-melody arrangements. Some unpublished copies of handwritten transcriptions by Stacy McKee have been in circulation for several years. These are written in an unconventional form of notation which often includes fingerboard boxes. Regrettably, they are not entirely accurate. The same criticism is also true of many attempts by other guitarists which have surfaced in recent years. Although there has yet to be a published and accurately transcribed collection of Smith's chord-melody arrangements, Steve Silverman succeeded in excellently transcribing around fifty of Smith's single-line solos. Twenty-one of these were published by Hal Leonard in *Johnny Smith: Guitar Solos*.

To return to the classroom, Smith served as a judge and clinician alongside Urbie Green, Richard Payne, Dr. William Fowler, Captain Ken Green, Ira Swingle and Cathy Preston at the All American High School Stage Band Festival in Mobile, Alabama, between 8 and 10 June 1972. The event, which included evening performances at the Municipal Theater, was sponsored by the Mobile Jazz Festival. On the second day, Smith and most of the other clinicians joined some of the high school students, as well as the US Air Force's Airmen of Note, for a jam session in the Ascension Hall at Spring Hill College. Mundell Lowe, who was an active supporter of the festival, also made an appearance at the jam session.

JOHNNY SMITH DEMONSTRATING AT A GUITAR SEMINAR

The fourth annual Johnny Smith Guitar Seminar took place at Denver's Ramada Inn between 16 and 23 July 1972. An article in the *Colorado Springs Gazette Telegraph* described the purpose of the seminar as:

> To equip the individual with the basic knowledge and understanding of the instrument so that the player can better, more accurately and more quickly reach the point of being able to help himself. (Reproduced from the *Colorado Springs Gazette Telegraph*, 12 July 1972)

As well as teaching master classes each day, Smith also performed each night. For this week-long seminar, he recruited his dear friend Chet Atkins as the guest clinician. Smith and Atkins jammed an impromptu version of 'Lover Come Back to Me'. The completion of the entire course qualified the students for two hours of credit through the University of Utah.

Guitarist Pete Kennedy shares his vivid memories of attending one of Smith's courses, and the impact that the tutor had upon him:

> The year was around 1974. I saw a very small advert in *Guitar Player* for 'The Johnny Smith Guitar Seminar'. I had discovered the 'black album' on Verve in a record store, and bought it solely for the lovely photo of a Gibson archtop, knowing nothing about the music on the disc. As soon as I heard the guitar tone, touch and taste, so different from the flamboyant rockers of the day, I felt that this was a real voice, like a singer, rather than a series of riffs. As great singers can do, it spoke directly to me. I had been looking for an avenue to take me away from imitating Cream and Eric Clapton, since everyone else was already covering that ground, and Johnny's sound and phrasing were the signpost. This almost seemed like a secret club with the members not knowing each other, because I knew literally no one else who had ever heard of Johnny Smith until I

answered the ad for the seminar and made my way to River Edge, New Jersey, a suburb of New York.

Johnny took over a music store in River Edge for five consecutive weekdays. Tables were set up in a classroom style with a copy of his guitar method, published by Mel Bay, at each place. Each day he would progress through the book. His clear explanations and constant demonstrations on the guitar created a sort of mental template for me that totally opened up the neck. His concept of learning chromatic scales, followed by major scales, and then finding triads for every chord on every set of three strings freed me from imitating the licks of other players and enabled me to play as a pure musician, hearing internal melodies and then simply playing them on the guitar just as a pianist/composer does on their own instrument. This was a gift and it was completely different from the then-current, and unfortunately still-current, notion of teaching guitar by having the student memorize songs by rote, which gives them a small repertoire of tunes that they can barely play and teaches them nothing about music itself. Johnny's approach was the same as if we were studying violin at a conservatory - learn music, learn where the component elements are on your instrument, and then play. It's astonishing that that's still a rare approach to teaching guitar, and part of the downside is that guitar students are typically very resistant to learning theory on the basis that it will 'ruin their playing', a quote they read from (insert rock star's name here) in a magazine. Anyway, no one at the Johnny Smith seminar was resistant. We were enthralled by his clear, generous teaching method that opened up the instrument, but the best part came at the end of every day.

Johnny had brought with him a lovely blonde Gibson JS model with a highly figured art-deco pickguard. It had a great acoustic sound. So, he never had a need to plug it in. At the end of each session, he would play a mini concert of solo tunes. His early album *The Man with the Blue Guitar* was long out of print and his later album *Masters* with George Van Eps didn't come out until the 1990s. So, Johnny playing solo rather than with a combo was yet another revelation. He combined jazz standards with contemporary classical harmonies and played with his trademark touch and taste. As a ballad player, I think he stands alone among guitarists and while there are better specialists in bebop (Joe Pass), swing (Kessel, Ellis), Johnny is the only guitarist in a class with Bill Evans when it comes to playing a ballad in that unique style that sounds like Debussy improvising.

I clearly remember him playing ''Round Midnight', 'Golden Earrings', 'I'm Old Fashioned', and 'Norteno', and when he played Debussy's 'The Girl with the Flaxen Hair', I resolved that if I could ever play that on the guitar, with it's deceptively simple pentatonic theme that skips seamlessly though several keys, I would consider that my major life accomplishment on the instrument. I've been playing professionally for forty years in every possible situation, but I still consider learning Johnny's arrangement of the little piano prelude to be the most satisfying thing I've done on the guitar and I play it every day.

Meanwhile, another guitarist and educator, Mike Ellis, recounts his memories of attending one of Smith's single-day seminars in the early 1970s and the impact that it had upon his musicianship:

> The seminar was an eight-hour visit with Johnny Smith in a meeting room at McCord Music Company in downtown Dallas. I had been taken under the wing of Terrill Gardner, who was teaching me how to teach. I had been working with Terrill for about a year when another employee of McCord's told us about the seminar. I'll call him Jim since I can't remember his name.
>
> It was an eight-hour seminar on a Saturday and cost $80 way back then. I gladly paid and went. My strongest recollections are that Johnny spent most of the time talking about pick control - How to hold the pick, how to attack the string with the leading edge rather than the back edge, using what I now call the rest-stroke, etc. I remember thinking how I kind of wasted my money, but as time passed I found more and more how really important that information was.
>
> I had been playing rock for eleven years, sloppily, and when Terrill took me through sight-reading from 'Mary Had a Little Lamb' all the way through *Modern Method for Guitar Books I, II, and III* from Berklee College in Boston, all that Johnny Smith had taught me became strikingly obvious and necessary.
>
> At the end of the seminar, 'Jim' and Johnny sat with guitars and Johnny told another McCord's employee to write jazz chords on a blackboard as fast as he could. As he was writing the chords, 'Jim' and Johnny started playing leads, sometimes in harmony, sometimes widely diverting, then coming back and passing each other. It was one of the most amazing things I ever saw at the time. I was really impressed and it topped-off the day for me.

While on vacation in the USA, the British guitarist and educator Trefor Owen accompanied Smith to a jazz guitar clinic that he was presenting in Denver in 1975. On this occasion, Smith explained his approach to improvisation and performed some of his self-composed solo arrangements. Although he used the material that he had compiled into his method book for the week-long seminars, it is clear from the testimony of those who attended his clinics that he selected different areas of study for each of his shorter presentations.

Denver's *Rocky Mountain News* reported on 3 August 1978 that Smith was to run a five-day clinic at the local Loretto Heights college from 7 August. Over fifty guitarists were expected to attend the course, which was to be closed with a concert given by the teacher and his combo of Neil Bridge, Bill Bastien and Derryl Goes.

Some of Smith's guitar clinics during the 1970s were sponsored by the Gibson guitar company. For example, on 22 October 1974, he ran a clinic and gave a concert at Critchett's music store in Omaha, Nebraska. Ticket prices were just $2 for the two and a half-hour session. Another Gibson-sponsored event took place at a music store in Tucson, Arizona, in 1978. Larry Grinnell remembers that particular clinic, including its format:

> I think it was just sheer luck that I found a small listing in a local musician's newspaper that mentioned that Johnny Smith would be doing a clinic at a local Tucson-area music store (the name now escapes me). It was scheduled for a Saturday morning. I brought my camera with the hopes of getting some good shots of Johnny. The clinic was held in the winter or early spring of 1978, just a few months after Johnny made his last tour, with Bing Crosby.

I got to the music store a little early. There were maybe twenty to twenty-five people there. Not a large crowd by any means. Johnny arrived and, with the assistance of the music store staff, set up and pulled out his Gibson Johnny Smith model guitar which by that time had the unusual Oettinger tailpiece that appeared on all the later Gibson Johnny Smith models, as well as the later LeGrande models (made after Johnny withdrew his endorsement). I don't recall if there was an amp problem or if he just preferred to play acoustically. He was there for an hour to maybe ninety minutes if memory serves. Mostly, he didn't have anything planned, and just ran a very free-form Q&A. He played fragments of tunes to illustrate answers to questions. Then, after all the questions were answered, he played solo for fifteen to thirty minutes. After the show was over, Johnny stayed around for almost another hour to talk to the folks.

The *Billboard* announced on 14 December 1974 that Smith had been booked to conduct a seminar at the second annual National Association of Jazz Educators' convention, which took place at the luxurious Pick/Congress Hotel in Chicago from 15 to 18 December 1974. With an educational environment that was now favorable towards jazz, he began to accept more part-time posts at universities. An advertisement appeared in the *Billboard* on 13 September 1975 for a B.Sc. in Music and Media course at the University of Colorado at Denver, at which Smith was listed as one of the visiting faculty. The other listed musicians, to be selected as scheduling allowed, included Hal Blaine, Billy Byers, George Duke, Paul Horn, Tom Malone, Oliver Nelson, Howard Roberts, Tom Scott, Clark Terry and Phil Wilson.

If he became disheartened with private teaching over the years, Smith thoroughly enjoyed teaching the guitar in more formal environments, and he only ended his university and college engagements when the institutions faced budget limitations and were unable to continue funding them. He began to wind down his own guitar seminars in the late 1970s, partly because of the increasing trade at his music store which left him with insufficient time, and partly because of his desire to take life at a slower pace. Furthermore, Colorado was awash with tourists during the summer season and it had become increasingly difficult for him to find accommodation for the students and even a venue for the seminars themselves.

JOHNNY SMITH TEACHING AT UTAH STATE UNIVERSITY

His activities in music education continued, albeit on a more intermittent basis, throughout the 1980s. On 13 and 14 May 1982, he joined Alan Dawson, George Duvivier, Ray Pizzi and Jack Wheaton in a teaching role at the eleventh annual *Mobile Jazz Festival*. The proceedings included a concert performance by the clinicians on the first night. A year later, on 13 and 14 May 1983, Smith returned to the festival to work alongside Duvivier, Dawson, Pizzi, and new clinicians Bobby Shew and Larry Lapin. As late as 18 April 1989, he conducted a workshop in the Eccles Conference Center at the Utah State University. This was followed by a concert with his Colorado combo of Neil Bridge, Adolphe Mares and Derryl Goes. Tickets for the workshop were sold at a single dollar each, while tickets for the concert were available for six dollars, or four dollars for students.

Smith was still happy to contribute to the education of new generations of jazz guitarists well into his retirement. In 1996, he appeared at the National Association of Music Merchants (NAMM) Show in Nashville, where he presided over the international guitar competition.

The wisdom that he passed on to others over the years occasionally delved beyond the teaching of the guitar and music theory. George Hess recalls some precious knowledge that he acquired from Smith while working in his music store:

> He passed a couple of gigs with the Colorado Springs Symphony on to me. I had to play banjo on one, which I didn't play at all. Johnny told me that studio players usually just tuned it like the top 4 strings of a guitar. That trick has helped me with quite a few gigs.

Naturally, Smith's recorded output has been employed by highly respected teachers to educate and enlighten new generations of jazz guitarists. Jack Petersen shares his thoughts on which aspects of Smith's tasteful playing style caught not only his own ear, but also those of his students:

> The sound, primarily, and his legato kind of playing. He was so smooth and clean. He was impeccable. He was amazing with that. Both single-line and chords. He would fool you. Sometimes he used three notes, but it sounded like four.
>
> I taught at the University of North Texas for about ten years. I would always make sure that my students heard the great guitar players. And I played all these guys, but every time I put on a recording of Johnny Smith, they would all react to it more than the others. He would catch their ear immediately with how fluent he was. He surprises everybody. He's just such an amazing player.

Aside from through his own direct teaching and his recordings, there was an additional channel through which Smith had a profound impact upon jazz guitar education. The importance of the Berklee College of Music in Boston, Massachusetts, upon the education of several generations of jazz musicians cannot be overestimated, and the importance of William Leavitt as chairman of the college's guitar department is of equal significance to the inner circle of jazz guitarists. Leavitt, along with Jack Petersen, created the jazz guitar degree program at Berklee. He also authored a series of invaluable books that reached far beyond the campus to developing jazz guitarists around the world. Guitarist and educator Jim Fox, himself a former student at Berklee and a former private student of Leavitt, recognizes the crucial influence of Smith upon his tutor:

> I studied privately for two and a half years with Bill Leavitt at Berklee, and he drew upon Johnny Smith's work. Bill wrote an incredible three-volume *Modern Method for Guitar*. I consider it to be the Bible if you're studying pick-style guitar. In those books, he primarily drew upon his own material. He was his own man with his own ideas. However, he also drew upon Segovia, particularly for his two and three-octave fingerings. And he drew upon George Van Eps, particularly for his triads and four-part

chords across the fingerboard. Van Eps had written a method in the 1930s. The most obvious thing that Leavitt drew from Johnny Smith, and I think this is very important, is that guitar students at the time that I was there were required to play for their jury each semester, which is twice per year... They were required to play a classical piece with a pick.

Now, as you know, Leavitt has a book called *Classical Pieces for Pick-Style Guitar.* But, as you also know, Johnny Smith had recorded a number of classical pieces with a pick. In particular Ravel and Debussy. At that time Berklee was the only place where you could get a degree in pick-style guitar. Everywhere else was classical. All the universities, colleges and conservatoires when I went, which is early to mid-1970s... So, Bill said, "You can't study guitar with me until you've been through all of my books and the program." That took something like two or three years. And you had to play classical pieces with a pick. So, he was saying that we were going to take plectrum guitar seriously. And I think he got a bit of that spirit from Johnny Smith, because of Johnny's recordings of classical pieces. And then when I studied with Leavitt privately for the last two and a half years of school out of the four, he referred to Johnny Smith quite a bit, personally. I don't think you'll find it in his books, but I think the three – Segovia, Van Eps and Smith – were three very important elements of his program.

There are a lot of really good guitarists who came through Berklee, like Mike Stern, and they all had to do that. Playing classical pieces with a pick. And I think that's all because of Johnny Smith and the impact that he had upon William Leavitt.

The other thing that the students had to do was to arrange a piece of music for solo guitar, and it had to be completely written out and performed. You had to hand your sheet music to the panel. There were maybe three or four professors. We were advised to listen to a lot of guys, such as Barney Kessel, Jimmy Raney, Wes Montgomery, Chuck Wayne... But Johnny Smith was high up on the list regarding the chord-melody concept.

Chapter Eight:
Musical Equipment

Aside from his revered work as a performer and educator, Johnny Smith was also a crucial figure in the development of archtop guitar construction. He began to experiment with the design features of the instrument early in his professional career in New York. The knowledge that he came to accumulate over the ensuing years ultimately resulted in the Gibson Johnny Smith model, which stood head and shoulders above the other archtop guitars that were available at the time and for many years afterward. Meanwhile, the electric jazz guitar community is further indebted to him not only for his role in the development of amplifiers which were specifically designed for electric guitars in the pre-rock music era, but also for his determination to realize a unit that would provide jazz guitarists with a faithful reproduction of the archtop instrument. His attention to detail in both guitar and amplifier construction was a contributing factor to the immaculately clean and well-balanced tone that was always present in his music and which was such an attraction to listeners. Dale Bruning shares his own observations about Smith's musicianship:

> The thing that I noticed, as soon as I started to play bass with him, was how meticulous John was about everything. As a musician, he was just so careful about everything. About his music, about his equipment, even right down to the pick and so on.

Guitars

Smith was associated with a handful of guitars, most notably those made by the luthier John D'Angelico and his own Gibson Johnny Smith model. Naturally, there were guitars within his private collection which were not employed on his recordings or in his public performances. For example, in a letter to the luthier Bob Benedetto on 5 August 1977, he mentioned a 1936 Gibson Super 400 that was in his possession at the time. There is no documented evidence of this instrument appearing on any recordings or live dates. The Super 400 was later bought by the jazz editor of *Guitar Player* magazine, Bob Yelin.

It is not practicable to attempt to reconstruct an inventory of every instrument that formed a part of his private collection throughout his lifetime. Instead, this chapter is intended to identify and focus upon the instruments with which Smith was publicly associated during his career, either as a performer, endorser, or designer.

Gibson Kalamazoo and Martin D-28

Although Smith began playing the guitar when he was a very young child, he did not actually have an instrument of his own until 1937 when he was fifteen years old. By this time he was teaching students in pawn shops and had been permitted to practice on the stores' guitars in return for keeping them in tune. The first guitar that he could call his own was a small, budget-ranged Gibson Kalamazoo flat-top acoustic model, which was given to him by one of his adult students, Bill Glovsky, who had bought himself a Gibson L-7 guitar.

The relatively lucrative earnings that Smith made as a youngster playing with hillbilly groups around Maine enabled him to upgrade to a Martin D-28 flat-top guitar. He later recalled, “I remember I had a Martin guitar. There was this fan oscillating... That was the only 'air conditioning' up in the roof. One night, I took my guitar off and stuck the end of it right in the fan.”

As his musical preferences began to develop, he soon found that the Martin guitar was unsuitable for the music that he was beginning to play on it.

Gibson L-5

His next instrument was a Gibson L-5 archtop non-cutaway model, for which he paid in installments. This was in the closing years of the 1930s, before the invention of the easily available electric guitar. Consequently, the instrument was not fitted with a pickup. Smith had to position himself close to the microphone when playing his solos. The stylistic suitability of the Gibson guitar over the Martin instrument is testimony of his changing musical direction. In the hands of popular performers, such as Maybelle Carter, the Gibson L-5 archtop guitar had been a familiar instrument in country music circles. However, its use by jazz guitarists, such as Eddie Lang, had brought it new affiliations. The flat-top Martin guitar became more typical in hillbilly music, while the Gibson L-5 archtop guitar developed a stronger association with jazz. Indeed, it was the jazz dance bands which influenced Smith's conversion to the *f*-hole archtop guitar. He found that the Gibson instrument was more accommodating for playing chords, melodies and virtuoso solo pieces across the entire fingerboard. It also had better projection, hence its use in orchestral dance bands.

By the early 1940s, Smith was less focused upon playing hillbilly music, and had begun to play more jazz. While he was working with the variety trio the Airport Boys, he fitted a DeArmond pickup to his Gibson L-5 and played it through an Epiphone amplifier. It was a common practice among guitarists at this time to fit aftermarket pickups themselves. The most popular model was the floating DeArmond Rhythm Chief, which could be attached to the side of a guitar's neck via a bracket, while the volume control was mounted onto the guitar's tailpiece. Smith kept and used his Gibson L-5 throughout the war years and returned to Maine after his discharge from the Army Air Corps with it still in hand. In 1946, only a week before he was due to move to New York to take up a position with NBC, it was stolen from a hotel where he was performing in Portland. The thief had told the checkroom staff that Smith had sent him along to pick it up on his behalf. He saw the guitar again several years later, after receiving a telephone call from the police in Texas. It was still fitted with the same strings with the same plectrum wedged between them.

GRETSCH SYNCHROMATIC 400F

FRETTED INSTRUMENT
News
An Independent Bi-Monthly Devoted to the Advancement and Culture of the Romantic Instruments
NOVEMBER-DECEMBER 1942
Vol. 11, No. 4 —ENTERED AS SECOND CLASS MAIL MATTER MAY 25, 1939, AT PROVIDENCE, R. I.

HARRY VOLPE
America's most popular artist of the Plectrum Guitar

RESTORE BANJO TO UNCLE SAM'S KNEE
NEWS OF THE AMERICAN GUILD OF B. M. & G.
DEPARTMENTS OF FRETS
MUSIC: "TWO BAGATTELLES"; TREMOLO STUDY

As a consequence of the theft of his Gibson L-5, Smith arrived in New York without a guitar. While he waited for his necessary union membership application to be processed, fellow guitarist Harry Volpe took him to the Gretsch guitar company to obtain a new instrument. Volpe was a Gretsch endorser himself. The result of their visit to the guitar manufacturer was that Smith came away with a Gretsch Synchromatic model.

Gretsch's prewar line of their Synchromatic archtop range had already been distinguishable for its characteristic 'cats-eye' sound-holes in place of the conventional violin type *f*-holes. Although the archtop side of the Synchromatic range maintained its feline associations in its postwar revival, the new flat-top line, which were purely acoustic instruments, came with a triangular-shaped sound-hole.

Smith later recalled that this was his own design feature, which increased the aperture without disturbing the bass bars of the instrument's bracing system. However, Volpe had earlier appeared on the cover of the November-December 1942 issue of *Fretted Instrument News* holding a Gretsch guitar with a triangular sound-hole. It is possible that his memory confused this distinctive sound-hole feature with an equally unconventional one that he introduced to an Epiphone model soon afterward. Smith was photographed for advertising purposes holding a top-of-the-range, eighteen-inch, flat-top, natural finish, Gretsch 400F Synchromatic with a DeArmond floating pickup. Considering his undoubted preference for the archtop style of guitar, it is curious that he was seen holding a flat-top instrument, particularly as he did not have an archtop guitar in his possession at this time. Of further interest, the guitar in this picture was fitted with an archtop's tailpiece, which accommodated the attachment of the DeArmond pickup's volume control.

Clearly, this was an attempt at a hybrid of the two types of guitar. The Gretsch model that was featured in this advertisement was not a mass-produced instrument. The guitars that Gretsch actually sold in their Synchromatic flat-top range were fitted with a somewhat larger, height-adjustable, rosewood bridge, which did not allow for the attachment of a volume control for any aftermarket pickup. Another photograph of Harry Volpe for a Gretsch advertisement shows him with a similar hybrid instrument. It is possible, therefore, that this model was intended for nothing more than eye-catching publicity purposes, and it should not necessarily be assumed that this was the specific guitar that Smith himself took from the factory.

Unfortunately, the neck on Smith's Gretsch guitar warped badly within a few weeks as a result of the company's impatient policy of kiln-drying their wood instead of allowing it to dry out naturally over a longer period of time. Although this practice reduced the moisture content to the optimum seven percent, the wood did not shrink in the process. It was consequently liable to reabsorb moisture and warp. Understandably, Smith lost faith in the company and discarded the guitar.

Epiphone Deluxe, Emperor and Emperor Concert

Finding himself once again without a guitar in his possession, he then approached the Epiphone guitar company, who were willing to furnish him immediately with two instruments in the form of their Deluxe and Emperor models, both of which were non-cutaway guitars. Smith used the reliable Emperor archtop as his main instrument from 1947 until 1950, including for his infamous live performance and recording of Schönberg's *Serenade* in 1949. Again, he fitted a floating pick-up to the guitar himself, although for his appearance on the *Serenade* he played unamplified.

Johnny Smith with his Epiphone Emperor guitar (c. 1949)

In 1950, he became the victim of yet another thieving magpie when this guitar was stolen from the NBC studios during a break in broadcasting a five-nights-per-week show with the pop singer Mindy Carson. Having enjoyed a short break with the other musicians at Hurley's bar before the show, Smith returned to the studio to find that his guitar had disappeared. It was not uncommon for guitars and even far less portable musical instruments to disappear from the NBC studios around this time. Guitarist Mundell Lowe recalls that theft could occur on a grand scale:

> I was doing Tallulah Bankhead's show with Meredith Willson. We [the musicians] had a break. So, we went downstairs to Hurley's near NBC, on the corner. We had a sandwich, came back, and the piano was missing! Jesus... In the meantime, two guys in overalls with Steinway written on the back had come in, taken the piano down the elevator onto the street, put it in the truck, and taken it away. Never did find it! And that was in the days when everything was live, you know. There was a lot of scuffling around to get another piano in there quickly.

Smith had an arrangement with Epiphone, but not a binding contract. During his association with the company, he designed the Emperor Concert model for them. In the 1940s, Epiphone were renowned for building loud archtop guitars that were especially popular with orchestral rhythm guitarists. The Emperor Concert model was in line with this ethos, but it also had an additional capability. Smith's new design elevated it from a role as merely a rhythm instrument, by greatly improving its ability as a guitar that was capable of projecting melodies.

While this guitar was a purely acoustic instrument, it was most distinguishable for its trapezoidal sound-hole. This may have been inspired by the design feature on the Gretsch Synchromatic 400F, upon which the traditionally round sound-hole was replaced by a triangular version that did not interfere with the bracing system. However, Mario Maccaferri's guitar designs for the Selmer company in the 1930s had employed an unconventional oval sound-hole and a D-shaped sound-hole. Both of these instruments had been associated with the legendary gypsy guitarist Django Reinhardt in the 1930s and 1940s. Although Smith had spent a brief period as Reinhardt's chaperone around the time of the start of his involvement with Epiphone in 1946, the gypsy had famously arrived in America without his guitar, assuming that one would be presented to him. If there was a Maccaferri influence in Smith's design, it may stem from his younger days when he was an avid admirer of the gypsy guitarist.

EPIPHONE EMPEROR CONCERT

Unlike his brief association with Gretsch, this time Smith was able to remain closely involved in the guitar's construction while he was staying in a hotel near to Epiphone's factory on 14th Street in New York. As well as the unconventional sound-hole, he also introduced two other new aspects to the existing Emperor design. The spruce top was carved to reduce in thickness around the sound-hole, and the parallel bracing within the eighteen-and-a-half-inch lower bout was widened. The more customary features of this particular model included maple sides and back. The neck was constructed from seven-ply, with an adjustable steel truss rod. Meanwhile, at the other end of the instrument, the tailpiece was a gold-plated Frequensator.

Although Smith felt that the Emperor Concert model was a good guitar, he was a little disappointed by the results of his first experiment and found its large body to be too cumbersome. The standard Frequensator tailpiece was also an irritation as it required longer bass strings that could only be obtained from Epiphone. He resorted to using the longer treble-string reaches from two Frequensators, so that he could use other brands of strings. At some point in time, the neck on this guitar was damaged and subsequently replaced by the revered luthier John D'Angelico. Eventually, Smith passed the instrument on to a friend. Completed in 1950, he later recalled that it was Epiphone's intention to mass produce the model, but to his knowledge it turned out to be a unique item.

Although Smith employed his Emperor Concert for a limited amount of acoustic work at NBC, he predominantly used his standard Epiphone Emperor guitar. As well as the live performance and subsequent recording of Arnold Schönberg's *Serenade* and his recording of Jacques Ibert's *Entr'acte* with the flautist Julius Baker, the two sides that he recorded with Mary Lou Williams in 1947, 'Kool' and 'Mary Lou', were made with this guitar. It is doubtful, however, that his first appearances with Benny Goodman on the television show *Star Time*, from 5 September 1950, were also carried out on the Epiphone Emperor. The guitar was stolen in 1950, and it is implied in interviews given by Smith that he ordered a replacement instrument from luthier John D'Angelico as a result of its disappearance, rather than as an upgrade prior to the theft. Smith's first bespoke D'Angelico guitar was ready for collection on 27 November 1950, and would have taken a considerable amount of time to build. The Epiphone guitar is therefore likely to have disappeared several weeks or months earlier, before his first dates with Goodman. Paul William Schmidt, the author of *Acquired of the Angels: The Lives and Works of Master Guitar Makers John D'Angelico and James L. D'Aquisto*, has stressed that the luthier's ledger is not always precise with regard to the dates therein. Therefore, it is possible that the D'Angelico guitar was ready for collection a few days earlier than appears in the ledger, and that it was available for use on the final television appearances with Goodman. However, it is more probable that an interim instrument was used while the D'Angelico guitar was still under construction.

D'Angelico Small New Yorker and Johnny Smith

The master luthier John D'Angelico was well known to guitarists in New York, including Smith, for his particular focus upon the acoustic quality of his instruments, although he also fitted pickups when requested by his customers.

Smith's first D'Angelico guitar was a blonde-colored instrument with the ornamentation of the New Yorker model on a body that had been reduced from the standard eighteen inches to seventeen inches. These smaller dimensions corresponded with those of D'Angelico's Excel model. In helping to assemble a full account of Smith's musical equipment, Paul William Schmidt has kindly referred to his private and complete copies of D'Angelico's ledger. Smith's first D'Angelico guitar is listed therein as the first item in the second ledger book and is described as a small New Yorker with a cutaway. It is recorded in the ledger as completed on 27 November 1950, with the serial number 1850.

The ornamentation of D'Angelico's New Yorker model that Smith wanted to retain on an Excel-sized body were stunning Art Deco features. The pickguard had more steps than the Excel, and the headstock inlay, which many guitarists erroneously believe to be a representation of the famous Chrysler Building in Manhattan, was in fact an image of its contemporary, the New Yorker Hotel.

After the discomfort of the oversized bodies of his Gretsch and Epiphone instruments, Smith had clearly decided to downsize. He was delighted with his new D'Angelico guitar. As beautiful as it was, however, his sole reservation was that he could not get used to the twenty-two frets on the fingerboard, which placed the floating pickup into the area where he preferred to pick the strings and reduced the warmth of the tone.

Sadly, this guitar was lost under tragic circumstances. While Smith was out dining with the guitarist Mary Osborne and her husband one Sunday night, the house that he was renting on Long Island was burned to the ground. The D'Angelico guitar was lost in the fire, along with his beloved dog. The following night, he was scheduled to work with Benny Goodman and Fletcher Henderson. The sympathetic Osborne kindly lent him an unidentified small Gibson guitar for the performance. It is understandable that, by his own admission, he did not play well on that particular night.

Smith's brother, Ben, recalls that the purchase of a guitar from D'Angelico was not a straight forward transaction:

> John D'Angelico would not make a guitar for someone until he had met them. When he had built his first guitar for John, he wouldn't give it to him straight away. They went

across the street first and had coffee. When they went back, he made John play it before he would let him have it. That was the guitar that he lost in the fire on Long Island.

Smith's appointment with Benny Goodman and Fletcher Henderson was none other than the famous Goodman concert for the Fletcher Henderson Fund, which took place on 1 April 1951. The date of the concert places Smith's house-fire, and therefore the demise of his first D'Angelico guitar, at the end of March 1951.

Smith's friend John Collins, who was Nat 'King' Cole's guitarist, then lent him a 1930s D'Angelico guitar with a notably wider neck, which he used until his next D'Angelico was eventually completed in 1955. His recording dates with Goodman in April, June and September of 1951, as well as his performance under the baton of Dimitri Mitropoulos of Alban Berg's *Wozzeck* in April 1951 at Carnegie Hall, occurred during the period when he was using Collins' D'Angelico guitar. His early recordings with his own combo, beginning with 'Moonlight in Vermont' through to the album *In a Sentimental Mood*, also span the period when he was using Collins' guitar. The instrument was a twenty-fret model, which he found to be preferable. Although he initially considered the wider neck to be awkward, over the ensuing few years he came to connect with this particular instrument so much that he was reluctant to return it to Collins. When commissioning a replacement guitar from John D'Angelico, he submitted an additional order for a new instrument for Collins. The 1930s D'Angelico guitar remained Smith's primary instrument until his next bespoke model was completed in 1955.

JOHNNY SMITH WITH JOHN COLLINS' 1930s D'ANGELICO GUITAR

Smith fondly remembered John D'Angelico as being an incredible craftsman and perfectionist who could contour the underside of a guitar bridge by hand, in a single showing, to fit the curve of an archtop. Mundell Lowe recalls that on the handful of occasions when he bought guitars from D'Angelico, the luthier always insisted that he played the new instruments for him and allow him to make adjustments before he would release them from his workshop. Meanwhile, he would also ply Lowe with substantial amounts of red wine. By the time that the luthier was satisfied that a guitar was fit to leave, Lowe was most certainly not, and D'Angelico habitually had to put him into a cab, pay the driver, and provide him with a delivery address.

Although Smith had an empirical knowledge of guitar construction and music technology prior to meeting John D'Angelico, he learned a great deal more from the master luthier and his apprentice, Jimmy D'Aquisto, in their New York workshop. Smith visited D'Angelico as often as he could and the luthier was extremely open with him about his craft.

As there was no humidity control in D'Angelico's workshop, there were days when, to his mind, the weather was not conducive to the artistry of shaping wood. This no doubt contributed, albeit in a small way, to the prolonged period that it took him to finish building Smith's replacement guitar. There was also another significant factor, however. Smith had once again requested a guitar that was not a standard piece of work. While he had asked the luthier to build another scaled-down, Excel-sized New Yorker, in addition he had requested a fingerboard with a shorter, twenty-five-inch scale-length, as he felt that his hands were small and would benefit from more comfortable stretches in his trademark closed-voice chord inversions. It should be pointed out that Smith's hands were actually of an average size. The unconventionally shorter string-length was one of several features that would later be repeated on the Gibson guitar which Smith designed. Indeed, the Gibson model which later bore his name was largely based upon the design requirements that he had presented to D'Angelico and which included the continuation of the neck underneath the full length of the twenty-fret fingerboard up to the cross bracing, in order to increase the sustain of the notes in the higher register. It was the first time that D'Angelico had carried out these particular requests, but in due course he began to receive similar orders from several other high-profile guitarists who knew Smith, including Mundell Lowe.

JOHN D'ANGELICO IN HIS WORKSHOP AT 40 KENMARE STREET, NEW YORK

D'Angelico obtained his timber from surprising sources. Much of it was well aged and came from the demolition sites of Brownstone houses around New York. Furthermore, he had his own unique method of assessing his instruments upon their completion. He would fit and pluck a solitary, heavy-gauge B-string to check that it responded well. If he was satisfied, he would fetch a bottle of wine and drink a toast to the instrument.

Smith's sunburst guitar was entered into his ledger on 5 January 1955 as an Excel 1000 Cutaway model, serial number 1963. There are several entries listed in the ledger as Small New Yorker, Excel 1000, New Yorker Special 1000, New Yorker Special, Excel Johnnie [*sic*] Smith and Excel New Yorker, all of which were synonymous with Smith's popular design.

JOHNNY SMITH WITH HIS 1955 D'ANGELICO GUITAR

When he collected the guitar, Smith was taken aback by the quality of the sound that emanated from his new D'Angelico instrument. He was so eager to play it on a booking that he had on that particular night at the Embers in April 1955, opposite George Shearing, that he didn't wait for the luthier to fit a pickup. Instead, he played the guitar into the microphone throughout his set. Shearing's guitarist, Toots Thielemans, was so impressed by its tone that he set aside his own electric guitar and borrowed the D'Angelico, also playing it into the microphone. A floating pickup was, however, fitted in due course. Such was Smith's satisfaction with his new guitar, that he parted company with the old 1930s model shortly afterward.

When he relocated to Colorado Springs in February 1958, his sunburst 1955 D'Angelico accompanied him. For a while, it continued to be his primary instrument. In 1960, he used it for his *Guitar and Strings* album, the cover of which unexpectedly featured a photograph of a blonde-topped D'Angelico guitar lying with Smith's string score. Gordon Close recalls the accident that had befallen the instrument while its owner was playing at the Bandbox club in Denver:

> One evening, Johnny got sick. He had the flu, but he was playing the gig. He began to feel nauseous. So, he unhooked his guitar, handed it down to the nearest bartender and asked him to take it. He turned around and headed down the steps into the restroom. Well, the bartender dropped the guitar. The top of the guitar fell against one of the beer spigots, and it cracked the top of the D'Angelico. So, Johnny sent it back to John D'Angelico to have a whole new top put on it. D'Angelico said that it would take something like two months to get it fixed. Well, Johnny had a job to do over at Birdland in New York within that two-month period. So, he called D'Angelico and asked if he could use it for the Birdland gig, and then take it back to him so that he could finish it. The top had been formed and glued onto the guitar, but it was still in its natural state. The rest of the instrument was sunburst. D'Angelico put a light coat of laquer on the top and put the bridge and strings back on it. Johnny took it on the gig and didn't take it back to have it finished. So that's why Johnny's D'Angelico had a blonde top and a sunburst back and sides.

JOHN D'ANGELICO, JOHNNY SMITH AND JIMMY D'AQUISTO

The guitar remained unique among D'Angelico archtops for a brief period with its blonde top and sunburst back and sides. It was, however, eventually returned to its full sunburst glory.

Smith commented that all of his recordings for Roost Records were carried out on D'Angelico guitars. If this recollection was accurate, he used his 1955 D'Angelico guitar through to his *Reminiscing* album in 1964. Even though he acquired his Gibson Johnny Smith guitar in early 1961, and his endorsement contract stipulated that he should use only this instrument in all public engagements, he appears to have enjoyed interchanging between the two guitars for a period of time. It is also possible, however, that this final Roost album was recorded with the Gibson model. Smith came to feel that with the existence of a self-designed, first-class Gibson Johnny Smith model, he perhaps should not have been playing another maker's guitar. He reluctantly sold his 1955 D'Angelico to Phil Marin, the owner of a bar and restaurant in Denver, on the condition that he should have first refusal to buy it back if Marin ever decided to sell it. After John D'Angelico died on 1 September 1964, Smith felt uncomfortable about having sold the guitar. Fortunately, on 21 November 1970, Marin sold it back to him for $1,000 and a Gibson ES175D guitar. Gordon Close often jammed at Marin's bar. He seized the opportunity to play the D'Angelico guitar whenever possible. In his opinion, to this day it remains the best guitar that he has ever played. During the 1970s, the guitar was displayed above Smith's workbench alongside his blonde Gibson Johnny Smith model in his music store. On 13 August 1988, he sold it to the collector Hank Risan for $20,000.

Guild Johnny Smith Award

Although Smith's D'Angelico guitar had been completed in April 1955, on 20 September 1955 he entered into an initial two-year agreement with Al Dronge's Guild guitar company for the production of a signature model. Smith had an extremely high profile at this time, and his endorsement was therefore something of a coup for the manufacturer. He had been voted by the readers of *Down Beat* magazine as their favorite guitarist at the end of the previous year and would achieve the same accolade at the end of 1955. He had also won the corresponding polls in *Metronome* magazine in 1953 and 1954, and would triumph again at the end of 1955.

Considering his elation with his recently acquired D'Angelico guitar, it is questionable that this Guild model was an instrument that he intended to play himself, and it is possible that financial motives were at work. Regardless, Smith drew up his design while he was staying at the Wolverine Hotel in Detroit during an engagement in the summer of 1955. When he returned to New York, he made sure that he was able to stay involved in the construction process by making regular visits from his home at 9-22 College Place in College Point to Guild's factory in Hoboken, New Jersey. The bottom line that he presented to the company was that the guitar should either equal or surpass the quality of his D'Angelico instrument.

JOHNNY SMITH AND AL DRONGE BACKSTAGE AT BIRDLAND

The Guild Johnny Smith Award began production in 1956, with Smith receiving a five per cent commission on the sale price to retailers. After previously requesting a scale-length of twenty-five inches on his 1955 D'Angelico guitar, Smith's design for the Guild model was even shorter, at twenty-four and three-quarter inches. This was experimental, as he continued to search for an equilibrium in a length of string that would facilitate his large stretches without an unacceptable loss of tone. The company accommodated almost all of his design requirements, including the cross bracing and the solid neck as far as the top fret, which provided an even sustain across the full length of the twenty-fret fingerboard. The model came with Smith's favored seventeen-inch wide body, as well as a slightly crude stepped pickguard, in imitation of D'Angelico's Art Deco design. A DeArmond 1000 floating pickup was also fitted.

Despite several photographs for press releases, Smith did not own one of these guitars himself. His contract with Guild stipulated:

> I further agree to use a Guild Johnny Smith model guitar in my professional appearances if and when Guild Guitars, Inc. is able to furnish me with a guitar equal to the instrument I am presently using.

However, the workshop foreman had refused to carve the top and back before removing the cutaway as the guitarist had requested. Worse still, Al Dronge, the owner of Guild, did not stand by his valuable endorser. At the time, Smith felt that this method of carving was a traditional approach, which gave the guitar a more even tone across the entire range of the fingerboard. This appears to be information that he had gathered from his visits to John D'Angelico's workshop. Jimmy D'Aquisto, D'Angelico's understudy, later stated that his master had carved the tops and backs of his guitars before removing the cutaways only because he was reluctant to make another template. This prompted Smith to graciously correct himself, admitting that the quality of sound was not dependent upon whether the top was carved before or after the cutaway was shaped, although he still felt aggrieved about the foreman's lack of flexibility. With hindsight, he admitted that the Guild Johnny Smith Award was an excellent guitar, but the psychological damage of his disagreement with the factory's foreman and the lack of intervention by its proprietor had caused him to feel uncomfortable with the instrument. In fairness to Guild, it is possible that Smith's experimental reduction of the string length had not resulted as he had hoped.

Understandably, Guild were eager to publicize their partnership with Smith. Several advertisements were placed in the press, proclaiming him as America's number one jazz guitarist. With a degree of irony, considering the dispute regarding the carving of the top, one particular Guild advertisement declared that the Johnny Smith model had been built to the guitarist's precise specifications:

> An inspiring experience when you hear Johnny Smith play his Guild guitar. He is an unusual type of musician, completely at home in any of the musical forms either as conductor, composer, arranger or performer. Johnny Smith has appeared with the greatest names in jazz. Goodman, Kenton and Krupa are but a few. Johnny led his own group at NBC and conducted the music for the *Fireside Theater*, the *Dave Garroway Show* and many other radio and television programs. Many of Johnny's records will someday become collectors' items.
>
> Johnny Smith plays a Guild guitar because he knows that he can always count on Guild to give him exactly what he wants. Highly skilled craftsmanship and consistent top

quality has made Guild the first choice of Stars everywhere.

Smith's contract with Guild contained an option to continue for a further two-year period if both parties were in agreement. This was duly fulfilled. In 1961, when Smith terminated the contract, Guild continued to produce the guitar under the new name of the Artist Award. Gradual but significant changes were made which increasingly distanced the model from Smith's original design. These included an increase in the instrument's scale-length and the introduction of an eighteen-inch body. In 1973, the company ceased production of its entire archtop range with the exception of the prestigious Artist Award.

Gibson Johnny Smith

During the period when Smith had been contractually obliged to Guild, Ted McCarty had been pursuing him to move across to the Gibson Guitar Corporation. McCarty had joined Gibson as General Manager in 1948 and then became President shortly afterward. In 1960, he began to recruit prominent jazz guitarists in his drive to increase the company's share of the archtop market. As well Smith, McCarty also brought Barney Kessel and Tal Farlow on board. McCarty's own musical preferences were well rooted in the mellow sounds of jazz, and Smith was his favorite guitarist. His smooth playing and warm tone were the benchmark for all others as far as Gibson's President was concerned.

In 1960, Smith contacted McCarty and asked him if he would be willing to build an instrument to his exact specifications. McCarty took his measuring tools to Smith's house in Colorado Springs, where the two men dissected the guitarist's design over the kitchen table. Smith had a few guitars at hand, but work was carried out mainly from his D'Angelico and a Gibson L-5, taking every measurement of both of these instruments. McCarty noted the specific details that Smith wanted to be included on his model, as well as the reasons behind them. Whereas Tal Farlow and Barney Kessel had limited inputs on their signature guitars, McCarty empowered Smith with complete control of the entire design of the Gibson Johnny Smith model, including the bracing, the carving of the top, the dimensions and the binding. In return, Smith permitted Gibson to make a few cosmetic adjustments, as this aspect was of no importance to him.

Smith was very particular about his requirements. Returning to his design for his 1955 D'Angelico, he wanted the neck of the guitar to continue along the entire length of the fingerboard. This not only improved the sustain of the notes above the fourteenth fret, but also meant that there was no need for the neck to curve in this area. In addition, he requested that the neck continued up to the cross bracing, which further contributed to improving the sustain of the higher frets. This was particularly true with regard to the balance between the first and second strings. On most archtop guitars, prior to Smith's design, the second string often overpowered the first string in both volume and sustain. For Gibson's range, Smith was resurrecting the cross bracing system, which had been a feature on their guitars back in the 1930s. Although a parallel bracing system increased the volume of a guitar, and was therefore preferable for a rhythm instrument, the cross bracing system provided a more balanced tone and sustain across a wide range. He insisted upon the omission of any tone control on his Gibson model, as he preferred to command this aspect manually through varying the position of his right hand when picking and adjusting the angle of the plectrum, thereby transferring the technique that classical guitarists employed with their fingernails across to the plectrum instrument. Most of Gibson's archtop guitars in 1960 had a body depth of three and a half inches. Smith requested that his model be reduced to three and one-eighth inches. This made the guitar more comfortable to hold and also reduced any rumble in the bass range. The body width was set at his preferred seventeen inches and included a rounded Venetian cutaway, both of which matched his D'Angelico. At one and three-quarter inches wide, the fingerboard was an eighth of an inch larger than the standard Gibson L-5 neck. This was inspired by the 1930s D'Angelico guitar that had been lent to him by John Collins. After his experiment with Guild, he returned to a scale-length of twenty-five inches. The tailpiece was borrowed from the Gibson L-5 model, with Smith's name added to the wooden inset feature.

A floating pickup, which Smith insisted upon, was attached to the neck of the guitar, and the volume control was fitted to the pickguard. By this time it was standard practice for guitar manufacturers, including Gibson, to cut both the pickup and any volume or tone controls into the vibrating top, which disrupted the bracing system and diminished the acoustic quality of the instrument. Crucially, Smith's old-fashioned demand for a floating pickup and a volume control on the pickguard preserved the acoustic properties of the guitar by allowing the important sound-producing top to vibrate unhindered.

Contrary to popular belief, the Johnny Smith model was not the first Gibson guitar to be factory-fitted with a floating pickup. One of Ted McCarty's first actions after joining the company in 1948 was to design a pickup that avoided cutting into the tops of their guitars. The result was a unit that was incorporated into the pickguard. However, it proved to be unpopular with guitarists, because it was prone to excessive movement.

In 1955, Seth Lover had developed the humbucking pickup for Gibson's solid-bodied electric guitars. He subsequently evolved a smaller mini-humbucker for the company's Epiphone subsidiary. The floating version of this unit was code-named the PU-120. The Gibson Johnny Smith model was the first guitar to use this particular floating pickup.

After the disagreement with Guild, Smith was determined that Gibson should follow his instructions to the letter. He had spent many years objectively observing the acoustic consequences of variations in the design of guitars. He also has strong opinions about the perception of the archtop guitar by other instrumentalists. Gary Atkins recalled:

> He gave me a big lecture about a twenty-fret neck [laughs]. He said that the jazz guitar will never be recognized by legitimate musicians, the term he used, unless it is standardized. Unless it is standardized, it will always be considered a folk instrument. Therefore, it needs to be built thus, with a twenty-fret neck that's joined solidly to the body, a seventeen-inch bout, and very little variation. The neck, above all, has to be standardized. I'll never forget that.

Jock Bartley was studying from Smith in 1960 when Gibson was completing the prototypes. He remembers a visit to his teacher's store by representatives from the guitar manufacturer:

> I was nine or ten years old. Mom dropped me off, and I walked into his store for my Saturday morning lesson. He was there with two official guys in lab coats. He said, "Go on back and warm up. We'll start in a few minutes." So, I went out back and warmed up. When asked, he told me after the lesson that those were the technicians from Gibson, out from Kalamazoo, to finish the final design for his Johnny Smith model that would soon

become a reality and go into manufacture. He had been 'arguing' with them over where to drill the hole for the volume knob. Johnny was adamant about not drilling into the wood (other than the *f*-holes). Between them, they came up with putting the volume knob on the pickguard, which I think had never been done before.

JOHNNY SMITH WITH HIS GIBSON GUITAR

Gibson built two prototypes of the Johnny Smith model, which were registered in their factory records on 29 December 1960 as numbers A35621 and A35622. One of these was sent to Smith at the Dyckman Hotel in Minneapolis in February 1961. His only bone of contention was that the workshop had put twenty-two frets on the fingerboard, rather than the twenty that he had specified. Ted McCarty had found that there was, to his mind, enough space for the extra two frets, hence their inclusion. However, in repeating the problem with Smith's first D'Angelico guitar, this pushed the pickup into the area where he preferred to pick the strings and reduced the warmth of the instrument's tone. He telephoned McCarty and asked him to remove the extra two frets on the prototype that was still in the workshop. This was carried out, and the second guitar was then shipped to him. He was ecstatic with the results.

With his requirements met by Gibson, Smith terminated his endorsement with Guild in a letter to Al Dronge on 1 February 1961. A fortnight later, on 15 February 1961, he signed a five-year contract with Gibson which would earn him five per cent of the price of each instrument to retailers, with an advance of $1,000 against these royalties. Shortly afterward, the Gibson Johnny Smith model was put into commercial production in the Custom Department on the third floor of the revamped Kalamazoo factory, alongside the Barney Kessel and Tal Farlow models, which were Gibson's other high-end Artist Series guitars. The company's 1961 catalog declared the new Johnny Smith model to be “the most perfect combination of acoustic response and electronic amplification ever produced.” It came with a carved spruce top; an ebony bridge and slanted saddles; bound *f*-holes with a matching maple rim, neck and carved back; pearl inlays on an ebony fingerboard; a twenty-five-inch scale length; an adjustable truss rod through a curly maple neck; gold-plated hardware, including Sealfast machine heads; and a humbucking neck-mounted pickup with the volume control sited on the celluloid pickguard. Complete with a hard case, the blonde version retailed at $810, while the sunburst model was priced at $795. Although this was the most expensive of the three Artist Series guitars, it was only temporarily Gibson's most expensive model. The re-priced Super 400 soon retailed at $850 for the blonde version and $825 for the sunburst model, with an additional cost for a hard case.

The endorsement provided Smith with the financial means to start his own business in Colorado. McCarty sent him $1,000 as per the contract, which he used to open his music store.

Smith later admitted that the Gibson deal caused him to feel some considerable embarrassment towards John D'Angelico. The luthier reassured him that there was no reason to feel uncomfortable, and that he was actually benefiting guitarists as he, D'Angelico, could only produce a very limited amount of instruments himself.

Although Smith loved his 1955 D'Angelico guitar, he preferred his Gibson model. the D'Angelico instrument had a warm tone, but he felt that the Gibson guitar gave a better response and sustain in the higher register. There were a few changes made to the Gibson Johnny Smith model during its production between 1961 and 1989. Gibson introduced a double pickup version in 1963, which increasingly displeased Smith, as it made no sense to him whatsoever. A substantially larger pickguard was necessary in order to accommodate the five volume, tone and switch controls that Gibson included with the extra pickup. In his store, over the ensuing years, Smith frequently found himself removing the rear pickup and the excessive controls from these guitars at the request of his customers.

The other notable change to his design was positive, however. In 1978, Ray Matty presented Smith with a new type of tailpiece. With distinctive protruding 'fingers', it allowed for the individual adjustment of the downward pressure of each string onto the top of the guitar and also reduced the vibration of any string causing resonance in the others. Smith was so impressed by Matty's conception that he brought it to the attention of Bruce Bolen at Gibson. Bolen was equally impressed with the new tailpiece and struck a deal with Matty to use them on Gibson's guitars, including the Johnny Smith model. It should be noted that Matty's tailpiece was not actually a wholly new invention. Many banjos and mandolins had already been fitted with a similar feature, known as an Oettinger tailpiece, for decades. Indeed, Matty was a luthier who made mandolins in a style that was heavily influenced by John D'Angelico's designs.

The Gibson Johnny Smith model was undeniably the cream of archtop guitars. With a price that reflected its position at the top end of Gibson's range, a substantial amount of these instruments were bought by collectors and rarely used. Consequently, many of the guitars which appear for sale today are in fine condition and carry weighty prices. Dedicated guitarists, however, appreciate the craftsmanship of its design and construction, and cherish the playability and tone of the instrument. Brandy Herbert has owned a 1961 Gibson Johnny Smith for several years. She explains why the instrument is precious to her:

> For the last six and a half years before I retired in January, I was on the road with long-term assignments in places like Santa Fe, Little Rock, Boise, Detroit, and so on. I always took a couple of guitars and amps to find local gigs and participate in whatever jazz-scenes I could find. I always left my Johnny Smith guitar at home in Colorado, because I didn't want to take the chance on it being stolen or damaged. So, I picked up a couple of other archtops. I also have a custom Epiphone Emperor model and an Eastman John Pisano model. They are fine instruments, and they did the job well. But I remember when I finally retired in January and came home to Colorado and started gearing up to work in the jazz clubs again, I spent a couple of weeks doing nothing but practicing and working my chops back into shape and getting back up to speed. After a couple of days of working with the Epiphone and finding it somewhat stiff to play (even though it had been my 'go-to guitar' for jazz), I finally pulled the Johnny Smith out and started working with it. I remember sending my friend in Santa Fe an email saying, "I've fallen in love with the Johnny Smith all over again." The feel of it, the ease of the action, the distinctive sound of it through the amp, and so on. It was like rediscovering an old friend.

Smith used the sunburst prototype guitar from 1961 until 1975, including on his three albums for Verve in 1967 and 1968. At the end of this period, he sent it to Gibson for restoration work, as it had become the worse for wear over the years. Unfortunately, it was subsequently lost or stolen. Gibson replaced it with a blonde version which had not originally been intended to be a Johnny Smith model, as Gary Atkins recalled:

> The replacement was to be a Gibson Citation. The very top of the line archtop they ever built. When the JS was discovered missing, they intercepted the Citation and made the minor changes needed for it to become a JS, which they gave to the Master.

British guitarist Trefor Owen remembers this particular guitar hanging above Smith's workbench in his music store in 1975, and guitarist Randy Benway recalls that he was offered the opportunity to play the instrument when he visited Smith's store in 1977. Smith used this guitar on his tours with Bing Crosby in 1976 and 1977, and it can be seen on the video recording of the European-wide television broadcast *Bing in Norway*. Denisa Hanna remembers it as a rather well-used and well-traveled instrument. She recalls, "Well, that blonde Gibson was pretty beat up. It had popsicle sticks holding it together on the inside!"

Sometime shortly before an interview with Bob Yelin for *Guitar Player* magazine in 1982, this second Gibson guitar was all but destroyed by airline baggage handlers. The neck was broken in several places and the top was caved in, requiring its return to Gibson for extensive repair work. This reckless incident was made all the more sickening because Smith had always found airline travel with his guitar and amplifier to be a traumatic experience. Consequently, whenever possible, he flew his own small plane on short journeys to universities and colleges for the teaching of masterclasses. In October 2011, he donated this instrument to the Smithsonian Institution in Washington D.C..

DAVID SMITH AND KIM STEWART WITH THEIR FATHER'S GIBSON JOHNNY SMITH GUITAR AT THE SMITHSONIAN INSTITUTION IN MAY 2013

Smith felt that his Gibson model was a well-built instrument, but during the course of his endorsement arrangement he became aware that the factory was not tooling-up correctly for all of their work, and therefore the guitars were not consistent. Each neck was different, which he found to be a frustration and a criticism that he had to endure for several years. He expressed that he could have done better himself with a jack knife. The circumference of each neck varied by as much as a quarter of an inch. He eventually complained to Gibson in no uncertain terms, asking them to terminate the contract if they were not prepared to build the guitars to his specifications. In response, the company sent Wilbur Marker to remeasure the neck of Smith's own guitar.

BENEDETTO CREMONA

In 1977, Smith received an exquisite Benedetto Cremona guitar from its maker, Bob Benedetto. Unfortunately, he was only able to play it privately. Randy Benway remembers a conversation that he had with Smith in the latter's music store:

> He talked about a great guitar maker down in Florida that had just sent him a guitar. He opened the case and pulled out a Benedetto. He said that it was a wonderful guitar, but he couldn't play it out in public due to his contract with Gibson. I told this story to Bob and Cindy Benedetto a few years ago when I was in Savannah. Bob said he remembers getting that first order from Johnny in '77. It was a huge order. Before Johnny, the biggest name he had built for was Bucky Pizzarelli.

Although the guitar came with twenty-one frets, luthier Bob Benedetto was well aware of Smith's preferences in an archtop guitar. The Cremona model had a scale length of twenty-five inches, a one and three-quarter-inch nut, a seventeen-inch bout, a body depth of three inches, a Venetian cutaway, cross bracing, and a floating pickup.

Benedetto's name has since become hugely celebrated within the jazz guitar community for his craftsmanship. In his own words, he explains the profound influence that Smith had upon him:

> During my early years of guitar making I was constantly drawn to the players, their styles and sounds. I couldn't begin to list them all, but certainly Johnny stood out. He epitomized the voice of mainstream jazz guitar, with his perfectly balanced and quality tone. Early on, I learned that the player has all to do with the voice of the instrument. A great player can make even a substandard instrument sound like a masterpiece. Conversely, a perfectly made guitar can sound terrible in the wrong hands. That being said, I always believed the ideal is a marriage between the consummate player and his instrument. It felt right. That's how the best music would be created.
>
> I have been fortunate to have had many wonderful influences in my early years learning how to make the archtop. There were no schools, books or any other learning media. Guitar makers of the day learned by doing, and the few in the field only occasionally shared information. What we all had in common was a bond with the player. It was the player that kept us focused on the task at hand, which was to make a better guitar.
>
> The Gibson Johnny Smith model was, in my opinion, the most refined model in Gibson's line-up of archtop jazz guitars. The one and three-quarter-inch wide nut, twenty-five-inch scale, three-inch body depth, refined graduating of top and back, X bracing and floating pickup collectively contributed to the warm, well-balanced voice and playability of the jazz guitar.
>
> I made a guitar for Johnny in 1977. It was my ninth guitar, a Cremona model, serial number 0977, and it was far from being refined. For the next few years we communicated once in a while about the appointments of the guitar and what Johnny felt would work better, including neck specs, bracing, etc. Also within these few years, I had many opportunities to repair and play many of the top brands of the day: D'Angelico,

Gibson and New York Epiphone. From all, I learned a lot about guitar making. One repair that I recall was a rare Guild Johnny Smith Award. It was unlike any Guild I had ever seen or played. I also did repairs on Gibson Johnny Smith models. It was very easy to make a connection with the appointments of that model and Johnny's playing. It was perfection across the board.

In 1988, I made Johnny a second guitar. It also was a Cremona model (serial number 14388), but a much more refined instrument than the 0977. At this point in time, I felt confident that I was making a pretty good guitar, but realized years later how much more I had to learn. Johnny's input had a profound influence on my guitar making career.

Although Bob Benedetto has, with hindsight, reservations about the quality of the guitar that he sent to Smith in 1977, Randy Benway's memories of his visit to the guitarist's music store concur with a letter of appreciation that Smith wrote to the luthier at the time:

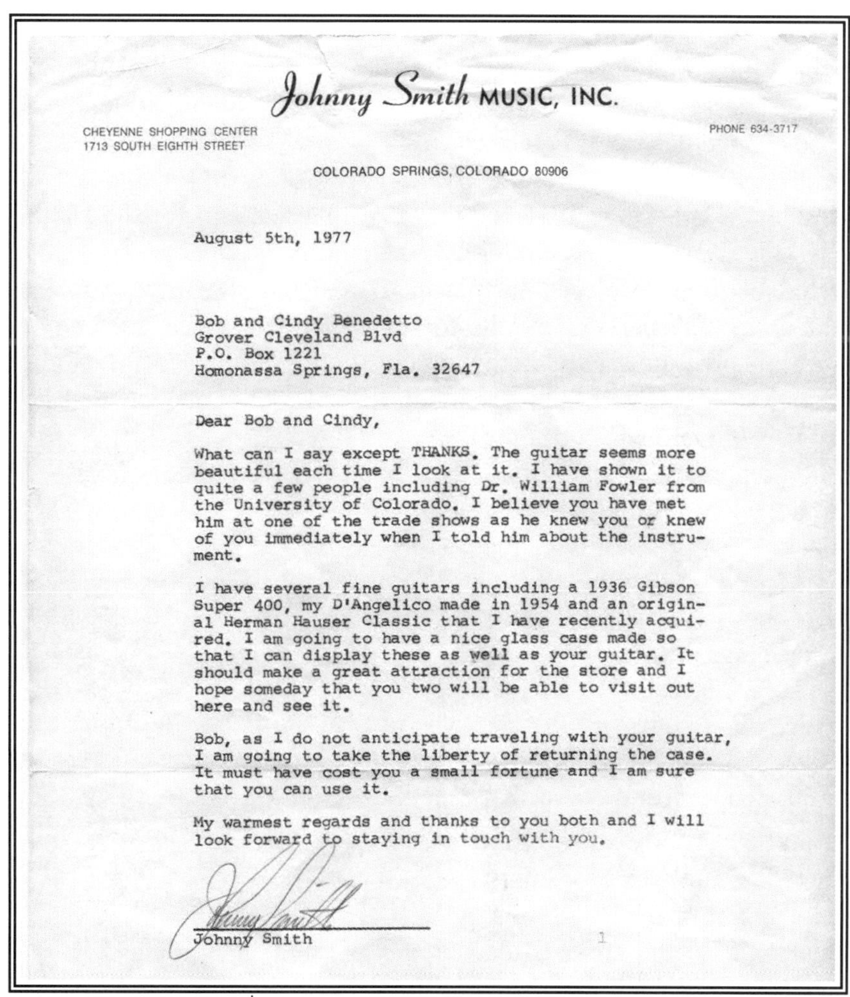

Johnny Smith MUSIC, INC.

CHEYENNE SHOPPING CENTER
1713 SOUTH EIGHTH STREET

PHONE 634-3717

COLORADO SPRINGS, COLORADO 80906

August 5th, 1977

Bob and Cindy Benedetto
Grover Cleveland Blvd
P.O. Box 1221
Homonassa Springs, Fla. 32647

Dear Bob and Cindy,

What can I say except THANKS. The guitar seems more beautiful each time I look at it. I have shown it to quite a few people including Dr. William Fowler from the University of Colorado. I believe you have met him at one of the trade shows as he knew you or knew of you immediately when I told him about the instrument.

I have several fine guitars including a 1936 Gibson Super 400, my D'Angelico made in 1954 and an original Herman Hauser Classic that I have recently acquired. I am going to have a nice glass case made so that I can display these as well as your guitar. It should make a great attraction for the store and I hope someday that you two will be able to visit out here and see it.

Bob, as I do not anticipate traveling with your guitar, I am going to take the liberty of returning the case. It must have cost you a small fortune and I am sure that you can use it.

My warmest regards and thanks to you both and I will look forward to staying in touch with you.

Johnny Smith

1

Johnny Smith's letter of appreciation to Bob and Cindy Benedetto on receipt of his 1977 Cremona

Heritage Johnny Smith Rose

When Gibson moved their factory from Kalamazoo to Nashville in 1984, Smith continued with his endorsement deal. However, the company left behind a significant percentage of their workforce who set up their own Heritage enterprise. On 5 January 1989, Smith terminated his Gibson endorsement and entered into an agreement with Heritage. His frustration with the Gibson model's variance in neck shape may have been resolved, but correspondence between Smith and Gibson indicates that the manufacturer had fallen some considerable way behind with royalty payments.

The Johnny Smith model had been Gibson's longest running signature guitar. They continued to produce it, albeit renamed as the Le Grand. Smith felt that the guitar that Heritage subsequently built in his name was an excellent and consistently built instrument that he was proud enough to own himself. In fact, he possessed two of them. The cross-braced Heritage Johnny Smith Rose model came with all of the expected features of a guitar that bore Smith's name, including a floating pickup; the micro-adjusting tailpiece design that had been introduced on the late Gibson models; a twenty-five-inch scale-length; a one-and-three-quarter-inch fingerboard width; and a seventeen-inch bout. Each guitar's internal label was personally signed by Smith. He also gave the model its 'Rose' title, and chose to have the hardware in a black finish, rather than the typical gold-plating which habitually tarnishes quickly on well-used guitars. He had reservations about the aesthetic design of the headstock, but he could not persuade Heritage to change it.

On 26 March 1990, Smith received a royalty check of $500 for the sale of the first ten guitars. In an accompanying letter, Bill Paige at Heritage stated that demand for the Johnny Smith Rose model had greatly exceeded the company's expectations, particularly in Japan.

Over a period of time, however, he began to feel that Heritage was losing some of its key people. Some of the company's carvers and the foreman had been replaced. The new personnel brought their preferred working practices with them, which altered Smith's original design. Although these changes did not reduce the quality of the instrument, they were not aspects that he wanted to see on his signature model. On 30 October 2001, he wrote to the Heritage company, advising that he had been approached by Bill Schultz at Fender, and that he was moving his endorsement to their Guild subsidiary.

Gary Atkins receiving Johnny Smith's personal Heritage guitar

With typical generosity, Smith gave one of his Heritage guitars to his dear friend Gary Atkins:

> He gave me his Heritage. It's a most beautiful instrument. It's my prized possession, and everybody knows that I have it. It's an extraordinary instrument. He inscribed a note saying, "Dear Gary, to be appreciated is the greatest reward in life. Please accept this token of my appreciation for your appreciation. Your friend,

Johnny Smith." I had it copied, and reduced in size, and then put inside the guitar by the maker's label.

Guild Johnny Smith Award (Revisited)

Schultz wanted Smith to endorse a re-vamped Guild Artist Award, the model which had previously carried his name. As Bob Benedetto was to be placed in control of the operation, Smith agreed. It is not an exaggeration to say that the endorsement would not have happened without the trusted luthier's involvement. Bob Benedetto recalls:

> From 1999-2006, I had a licensing agreement with FMIC (Fender Musical Instruments Corporation). One of my responsibilities was to redesign the Guild Artist Award. After brief discussions with Bill Schultz, then CEO of Fender (Fender owns Guild), Johnny agreed to once again endorse Guild. The Artist Award model was then renamed the Johnny Smith Award model, as it originally was in the 1950s. I was thrilled to be part of the project, and of course I loved working with Johnny.

Fender clearly took their decision to revitalize the Guild brand seriously. Producing an average of eight guitars per month, only four luthiers were chosen to work on the Johnny Smith model in Guild's workshop. Meanwhile, Bob Benedetto not only trained each one of them, but also spent one week in every month overseeing their work and inspecting the quality of their instruments. This ensured that the guitars met his own high standards and were worthy of carrying Johnny Smith's name. For the model's launch on 18 August 2004, Smith was accompanied by Benedetto to Guild's headquarters in Corona, California, where he personally signed the first eighteen guitars in gold paint. He also signed copies of Mosaic Records' box set of his Roost recordings, which were to accompany the guitars. These first eighteen instruments were dispatched to retailers in 2004 with a recommended retail price of $11,000.

Johnny Smith signing a Guild Artist Award watched by Bob Benedetto

Bob Benedetto introduced some changes to the design of the original 1956 Guild Johnny Smith Award. For example, the scale-length was now set at a longer twenty-five and nine-sixteenth inches. Nevertheless, Smith was most agreeable regarding the alterations. When Benedetto's contract with Fender ended in 2006, Smith closed his Guild endorsement.

Amplifiers

The guitarist Les Paul is often cited as a great pioneer in sound technology. Although this is an accurate assessment, it is often overlooked that his attention focused upon multi-track recording techniques and the search for new sounds from the electric solid-bodied guitar. Johnny Smith's quest was markedly different. He sought to create the perfect archtop instrument and then to amplify it faithfully. His particular area of knowledge in sound technology made him unique among New York's guitar community during the 1940s and 1950s.

Aside from his pioneering contribution to the improvement of archtop guitar design, he was also an active participant in the development of amplification that was specifically intended for use with electric guitars. Until the mid-1950s, there was in reality very little to distinguish guitar amplifiers from those which were used in conjunction with microphones. In his younger days, Smith tried an array of amplifiers, but they were so woefully inappropriate for direct guitar usage that they frequently burned out. On these occasions, he was forced to complete his gigs by playing into the microphone. His first recognizable guitar amplifier was an Epiphone model which he used with a DeArmond floating pickup on his Gibson L-5 guitar while he was a member of the Airport Boys in the early 1940s.

As amplifiers for electric guitars became increasingly commonplace, Smith realized that most of the mass-produced units were being equipped with insufficient mid-range boost. This not only provided an unsatisfactory tone, but also contributed to the presence of feedback. In referring to the nylon-string classical guitar, he observed that the ideal instrument was one with an equal, or flat, frequency response. The component harmonic series of each note not only determined the tone but also the projection of the instrument. He felt that by overlooking this aspect of sound technology, amplifier designers were missing the point and were unnecessarily increasing the power output of their units in order to render the electric guitar audible within ensembles. For this reason, he was reluctant to use inappropriate, mass-produced amplifiers. He campaigned for the production of units which could amplify the archtop guitar faithfully with sonic quality rather than amplitude in mind. At one point, he even submitted an article to a guitar magazine, which criticized the Fender company for the excessive bass boost on their amplifiers. The magazine, somewhat understandably, refused to publish it on the grounds that it would have been commercial suicide for it to criticize one of its most frequent and popular advertisers.

During the late 1940s and early 1950s, Gibson amplifiers were generally the most popular with electric jazz guitarists. However, they were cumbersome and prone to emitting excessive noise, which was particularly unacceptable in the environment of a recording studio. Smith recalled the problems that he had endured with amplifiers during his early days in New York:

> Well, when I first went to NBC in 1946, the amplifiers were very unreliable. In the middle of a broadcast they would start frying eggs. Once, I was working in the recording studio and it started picking up local radio stations, so I had to leave the amplifier off until the music started. The two main companies who were making amplifiers, that I knew about, were Gibson and Epiphone. I used Altec Lansing, which was more reliable. I used that for quite a while. Then, I used an Ampeg. It was pretty good. At least it was reliable.

The Altec-Lansing was not a dedicated guitar amplifier, but as far as Smith was concerned it was the lesser of the available evils at the time. Meanwhile, the Ampeg amplifiers that he began to use were better than merely reliable. Many of his recordings featured these units, and they should be acknowledged as significant elements in his tone production.

Ampeg Johnny Smith and Fountain of Sound

In Everett Hull, the proprietor of Ampeg, Smith found someone who was both willing and able to help him in his quest for a dedicated, reliable and correctly designed amplifier for the archtop guitar. The Ampeg Bassamp Company had been created, as its full name suggests, to focus upon providing amplification for double bass players. Gradually, the enterprise expanded into the production of units for guitarists and accordionists, as well. As something of a jazz musician himself, Hull was fond of the jazz scene, but he also had some degree of business acumen. He was a regular presence at the jazz musicians' hangouts, particularly the studios and the clubs. He actively encouraged professional performers to test his products in their workplace and then provide him with their observations, opinions and criticisms. As a staff musician at NBC, Smith became one of these test pilots. As a consequence of his input alongside those of others, a pair of respectable and dedicated guitar amplifiers was finally introduced to the market in 1950 in the form of the 500 Guitaramp and the 700 Guitaramp.

In the ensuing years, Smith and Hull worked together on the development of a new amplifier, which was to be based upon the guitarist's quest for a unit with the Holy Grail of a flat frequency response. The first Ampeg Johnny Smith model was a top-of-the-range unit. The company's August 1955 price list details this amplifier as having thirty watts of power with a fifteen-inch Altec 602A speaker, later to be replaced with a JBL D-130, and was valued at $350.

Never one to rest on his laurels, Smith continued to strive for improvements. His next request to Ampeg produced perhaps the most unlikely looking amplifier to grace a jazz club or a recording studio. In 1956, Ampeg's new engineer, Jess Oliver, began to design the Fountain of Sound model to Smith's instructions. The most striking visual feature of this amplifier was the speaker located in the top of the cabinet facing upwards, while the cabinet itself stood on four legs and resembled a coffee table. The purpose of this unusual design was to provide everybody present, both fellow band members and audiences, with the same volume and tone. If required, it could also be stood conventionally with its speaker facing the audience. The spectacularly titled Johnny Smith Fountain of Sound was available in 20w and 30w models, both of which were fitted with a

fifteen-inch JBL speaker, an OC3 voltage regulator and a 6SJ7 pentode preamp unit.

The JS-20 and JS-30 models were manufactured from 1957 to 1958. Guitarist Pat Martino remembers seeing Smith using the Fountain of Sound amplifier at a performance at the Red Hill Inn in Cherry Hill, New Jersey, in 1956. It is quite plausible that he was using the unit before it entered production for the public market. The January 1958 Ampeg price list shows the JS-30 version to be their most expensive model at $435, while the JS-20 was their third most costly model at $395. The Johnny Smith Fountain of Sound was a popular amplifier among professional jazz guitarists for many years after production finished.

JOHNNY SMITH AT A GIG IN COLORADO ALONGSIDE PIANIST DAVE GRUSIN AND DRUMMER MICKEY MCPHERSON. THE AMPEG FOUNTAIN OF SOUND CAN BE SEEN IN THE BOTTOM RIGHT-HAND CORNER WITH ITS UPWARD-FACING SPEAKER.

Gordon Close remembers that although Smith brought his Fountain of Sound amplifier with him when relocated to Colorado in 1958, Gibson tried to encourage him to use their amplifiers when his guitar endorsement took effect three years later. At the time, however, Gibson did not make an amplifier that satisfied his requirements. Consequently, there was an issue that Smith had to be overcome:

> When he started playing Gibson guitars, they said that he should also have a Gibson amplifier, but he didn't like them at all. So, he gutted a Gibson amp and put the electronics of the Ampeg into it. Then it looked like he was endorsing Gibson's amps.

Bobby Greene recalls that Smith used a Fender amplifier at the time that he was in his combo:

> I remember Johnny's amp as an old Fender Twin, which he always asked one of us to carry for him because of its weight. I, being the youngest at twenty-four and still overflowing with testosterone, generally obliged. I don't know what that sucker weighed, but the sumbitch was seriously heavy. It really should have been on wheels.

The Fender amplifier that Smith was using during this period was a temporary measure while Gibson had possession of his Ampeg unit for analysis. He was as uncomfortable with Fender's range of amplification as he was with that which was being produced by Gibson. None of their units provided him with the flat frequency response that he sought.

Gibson GA-75L Recording

Gibson eventually agreed to build Smith an appropriate amplifier. As with the Gibson Johnny Smith guitar, he insisted that the manufacturer build according to his specifications. To this end, the company analyzed and worked from the circuitry of his Ampeg amplifier. The resulting unit was awarded a revived model number from one of the company's discontinued combo amplifiers. The original Gibson GA-75 amplifiers had been produced between 1950 and 1955 and were intended for use with both guitars and basses.

The two new Smith-designed Gibson GA-75 Recording and GA-75L Recording combo models were built between 1964 and 1967. From 1964 to 1965 they were furnished with a brown cover, which was then replaced by a black alligator cover for the models that were produced between 1966 and 1967. The 'L' version came with Smith's favored fifteen-inch JBL speaker, instead of a pair of ten-inch speakers. These models were part of the last series of amplifiers to be built by Gibson in their Kalamazoo factory. Both the GA-75 and GA-75L came with two inputs, two tone controls (treble and bass) and one volume control for each of the two channels. They also had a monitor jack, a standby switch, a polarity switch, three diodes and six tubes. These were two 6EU7, one 6CG7, two 6L6 and one 6C4, which gave an estimated power rating of 25w.

Gibson GA-75L Recording amplifier

Demand for these amplifiers was not great. Gibson produced only thirteen of the GA-75L in 1964 and another twenty five, sixteen and twenty in the three ensuing years respectively. While total production for this model reached only seventy-four units, the GA-75 version fared better. One hundred and eighty-one units were produced over the four-year period. Although the GA-75L was an excellent amplifier with the flat frequency response that was ideal for archtop jazz guitars, it was produced at a time when rock music with its distorted, multi-control amplifiers and solid-bodied guitars was dominating popular music. The minimalist control panel and clean sound of these Gibson units were never going to appeal to the bigger rock music marketplace, and its days were always numbered. Smith summed up the problem succinctly when he recalled, "Gibson built me an amplifier that was called the Recording amplifier, which wasn't very popular because it only had three knobs."

Guitarist Kenny Vaughan recalls that Smith used his Gibson GA-75L Recording amplifier on his gigs at Shaner's Lounge in Denver around 1965 and 1966. Towards the end of the decade, he sold it to his friend Gary Atkins, who remembered the unit fondly:

> It was the Gibson GA-75L. It was a wonderful amp. Essentially, I traded it so that I could afford the EMRAD, which wasn't bad, but I liked the 75L better, personally. It had a rounder, smoother tone.

Gary Atkins' appraisal of the Gibson GA-75L was well founded. Smith used this model on his three albums for Verve – *Johnny Smith*, *Johnny Smith's Kaleidoscope*, and *Phase II*. The immaculate sonic quality and warmth of the amplifier is clear for all to hear.

Derryl Goes remembered that Smith always had his amplifier tilted back when they were performing together, thereby partly replicating the Ampeg Fountain of Sound's most obvious design feature. Meanwhile, he positioned the amplifier on the neck-side of the guitar. Smith explained, "I found that the placement of the amp on the neck side of the instrument, at the neck point, would give me less feedback."

EMRAD Johnny Smith

Other than the aforementioned Ampeg and Gibson amplifiers, the only other unit with which Smith ever felt comfortable was made by a local electrical engineer in Littleton, Colorado, trading under the name of the Electro Mechanical Research and Development (EMRAD) Corporation. Smith approached R.E. 'Ev' Evans with a request to build a transistor version of his Gibson tube amplifier. Working from Smith's Gibson GA-75L unit, Evans designed and built the EMRAD Johnny Smith amplifier with a flat frequency response and the guitarist's favored fifteen-inch JBL speaker. After building the initial bespoke model, Evans inquired if he could commercially produce it. Smith consented, but unfortunately the venture only lasted for a few years due to the same cultural climate which had also curtailed the days of the Gibson GA-75L.

An advertisement for the EMRAD amplifier appeared in the February 1971 issue of *Guitar Player*, showing Smith with one of the combo units. The advertisement advised that the amplifiers were available exclusively through Smith's own music store.

Ev Evans and the EMRAD Johnny Smith amplifier have become the subject of legend among the guitarist's admirers. Little has been known about the electrical engineer. The handmade amplifiers that he constructed in his workshop were few in number compared to the big corporate manufacturers. Kenny Vaughan recalls that Smith began using the EMRAD amplifier around 1968. Gary Atkins agreed with this approximate date. Sound engineer Lee Brenkman remembers Ev Evans and his amplifiers:

> As an aspiring sound man and roadie, I was a complete gear head and took a Fender Bandmaster amp to his shop for service. He was friendly and very patient in answering some of my dumb questions in the months to come, since his shop was not far from where I lived. This would have been in the early 1970s. The mailing and business address was in the 2500 block of Main Street in downtown Littleton, Colorado, but the actual entrance to the shop was around the corner on Curtice Street.
>
> He was a trained and licensed professional engineer, which required a State of Colorado examination of some sort. He had previously worked at one of the sub-contractors for Martin Marietta, the aerospace firm that built bits for the Atlas missiles in the 1960s. I believe he also was a partner in a firm that developed an electronic device for automobile wheel alignment. When that partnership either failed or dissolved, he got into the amplifier repair business.
>
> His main business was repairs at first. There was a receiving counter in the front, and the shop behind. It was at first a one man business, but eventually he took on a

couple of helpers. Amp manufacture was just something he slid into after Johnny Smith commissioned that signature amp after being impressed with the quality of Ev's repair work. The woodwork for the amps was farmed out to a nearby cabinet making shop. Ev certainly spoke fondly of Johnny Smith. He said that they talked as much about airplanes as they did about amps and music.

The amp was based on a 100w circuit straight out of the RCA semiconductor 'cookbook'. The preamp circuit Ev designed himself at Johnny Smith's request for an elimination of the built in 'smiley face' low and high frequency boost equalization that most other contemporary guitar amps included. The tone controls on the EMRAD Johnny Smith were very subtle in their effect. The logo was on all of the Johnny Smith model 1x15" combos that I ever saw.

Initially there was only the Johnny Smith model, but later there were bass amps, both combos and separate head and cabinet sets. The bass amps and all subsequent guitar amps were all based on the same 100w transistor output circuit. EMRAD and the nearby Bruce amplifier company were early adopters of the powered speaker cabinet. The idea was that you started with the combo guitar amp which had a preamp output and as you played bigger gigs you would add additional 1x15", 2x12" or in the case of bass 1x15" or 2x15" speaker cabs with a built in 100w amp.

At the request of the rock players, the tone controls were altered to be a bit more aggressive, but on order you could specify whether you wanted the 'jazz' or 'rock' version. The amps he built for Sugarloaf had black speaker grilles instead of the silver mesh ones and their band logo in the corner of each cabinet's speaker grille. They had over a dozen assorted combo's amp tops and powered speaker cabinets. All other EMRAD amps just had the generic 'EMRAD' badge on the grille.

I returned to the West Coast in 1973 and visited Colorado a year later. Ev had lost the lease on his Littleton location and moved to a former auto repair shop on South Broadway in Englewood. He had by that time pretty much reverted to repair work only. I think that manufacturing had exceeded his capability and capital, and the business had just not taken off. By my next visit in 1976, there was no shop. I have no idea what became of him. The rock bands that were buying walls of amps by that time just wanted Marshall, Fender, or if they wanted solid state, Acoustic.

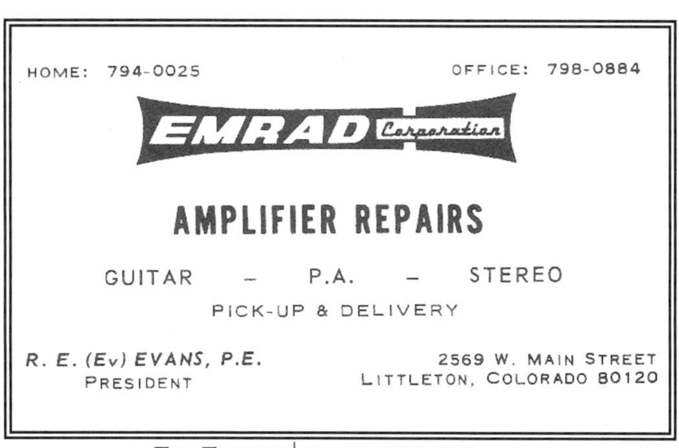

Ev Evans' business card

As with the Gibson GA-75L Recording amplifier, the EMRAD Johnny Smith model was quite uncluttered in comparison to most of the contemporary guitar amplifiers. This undeniably contributed, once again, to its limited appeal. The control panel on the Johnny Smith version had merely a power on-off switch; a bright switch; volume, bass and treble controls; and high and low impedance input sockets. The rear of the unit had two output jack sockets for connection to a powered slave unit.

For a series of performing dates with Bing Crosby in 1976 and 1977, Smith had the amplifier section removed from the cabinet of his EMRAD combo and placed inside a smaller, speaker-less one. This was more practical for touring purposes, where he would be furnished with a speaker by each venue. He kept the separated EMRAD unit that he used with Crosby until his death in June 2013. Gary Atkins recalled that Smith had more than one EMRAD amplifier:

THE EMRAD HEAD UNIT WHICH ACCOMPANIED SMITH ON HIS TOURS WITH BING CROSBY IN 1976 AND 1977

> Another one of them, he had broken into a separate head and speaker case, and he sent pieces of it, if not the whole thing, to my cousin in Atlanta, Jimmy Lowell Atkins, who is another Smith fanatic in the Atkins family.

Strings and Plectrums

Smith's meticulous attention to detail in his musical equipment extended further than his choice of guitars and amplification. His focus continued through to his selection of strings and plectrums as well as his methods for tuning and setting the intonation of his guitars. During the early part of his career he favored round-wound strings over flat-wound strings, the latter of which often suffered from severe inaccuracies in intonation. However, the round-wound strings came with their own problems. They were prone to causing excessive finger noise, particularly when they were fresh, which was unacceptable in the recording studio. To overcome this hurdle, Smith ritually raised the height of newly fitted strings by placing a pencil between them and the fingerboard at the first fret, before rubbing the side of a glass along the strings in order to remove the roughness.

During his endorsement deal with Gibson, the manufacturer produced a set of Johnny Smith electric guitar strings with wound third to sixth strings. The gauges for the JS-40 set were: .012, .014, .023, .031, .042, .058. Smith did not use these strings himself. It was merely a financial arrangement. The oversized sixth string accommodated his preference of the Drop-D tuning, but the strings were ultimately not of a high quality. Kenny Vaughan once asked him about the Gibson strings that carried his name. He remembers that Smith gently guided the conversation onto another subject.

In the early 1960s, Smith began to use Black Diamond #100 burnished strings with a standard gauge of .012 to .052. To accommodate his use of the Drop-D tuning system, he replaced the .052 gauge of the sixth string with a heavier .056 string, thereby maintaining the balance with the other strings in tone, intonation and volume. When Black Diamond strings ceased production, he bought up the entire remaining stock. Guitarist Trefor Owen remembers that in 1975 Smith's own Gibson archtop guitar was fitted with heavy gauge La Bella flat-wound strings.

With regard to plectrums, Smith favored Ernie Ball Stubbies, which were small and heavy gauged at one millimeter thick. When these ceased production he stockpiled all that he could obtain. These plectrums had a tapered point so that the leading edge on one side and the diagonally opposed leading edge on the other side met the strings with flat surfaces. Bob Yelin recalls, "They were small, in a round and pointed shape. But in order to get a blues or sad feel for single-note playing, he filed the point of the pick to make it thinner."

Intonation and Tuning

Guitar intonation was another aspect of equipment to which Smith applied meticulous attention. As the late Gary Atkins observed, "The way he had that thing intonated and perfectly tuned, and the amplifier's response curve... You'll swear that there's a third note in there that's not played."

The accurate intonation of a guitar is essential if all of the notes across the fingerboard are to be in tune. The standard method for checking the intonation of a guitar is to compare the harmonics on each string at the midway point of the twelfth fret against the corresponding fretted note at the same location. Any discrepancies are subsequently removed either through the adjustment of the height of the strings from the fingerboard, or by adjusting the string-lengths through repositioning the location of the bridge. This remained Smith's favored approach when setting up archtop guitars.

While the use of harmonics is an established practice in setting the correct intonation of a guitar, their frequent employment for tuning the instrument is more contentious. A perfectly tuned guitar is impossible to attain. The laws of physics cause discrepancies across the fingerboard, such that the guitarist must settle for an acceptable compromise. Smith was aware of the insufficiency of harmonics for tuning the instrument without reference to fretted notes. The act of playing fretted notes on the guitar causes a string to be stretched to varying degrees as it is moved onto the fingerboard. A guitar that is tuned purely through the use of harmonics provides no provision for actual playing and will therefore be out of tune when the guitarist is performing. Consequently, Smith's superior system of tuning compared fretted notes against harmonics.

According to his method, after ensuring that the first string of the guitar is tuned to concert pitch, the fretted E at the fifth fret of the second string should then be brought to the same pitch. The relationship between these two strings should then be checked by comparing the harmonic at the twelfth fret of the second string with the fretted B at the seventh fret of the first string. It is important to note that these pitches are an octave apart, although the following combinations all target unison pairs of notes. The fretted E of the third string should then be adjusted against the open first string. The relationship between these two strings should then be checked by comparing the harmonic at the twelfth fret of the third string against the fretted G on the top string. The fretted B on the fourth string should next be compared to the open second string. Continuing this methodology, checking can then be carried out by comparing the harmonic at the twelfth fret of the fourth string against the fretted D of the second string. The fretted G on the fifth string should be adjusted to correspond with the open third string. Again, refinement can be achieved by comparing the harmonic at the twelfth fret of the fifth string against the fretted A on the third string. Finally, in standard tuning, the fretted D of the sixth string should be adjusted to correspond with the open fourth string, and checked by the comparison of the harmonic at the twelfth fret of the sixth string against the fretted E on the fourth string.

Chapter Nine:
The Private Man

Despite his workaholic lifestyle, particularly during his time in New York in the 1950s, Smith never sought or reveled in the limelight. He always maintained interests outside of the music spectrum. Not least of these was his passion for playing chess. The walls of the bar in his house in Colorado Springs were decorated with some of his awards, such as his honorary doctorates, but these took second place to the more treasured mementos of flying and fishing. His bar was far from being a music temple. Visitors to his house were required to donate and sign a single dollar bill, which entitled them to drink free of charge on a lifelong basis. The dollar bill was subsequently glued to the ceiling in the bar alongside those that had been presented by previous visitors, many of whom were world-renowned musicians.

George Hess recalls an afternoon at the Smith residence:

> He invited my wife and me to his home one afternoon. We each had to pay one dollar for our first drink at his bar, which we signed and then he posted them on the ceiling. There were hundreds of dollars there with the names of a lot of very well-known musicians. I was never in better company. Anyway, he told me that a friend of his was coming over that afternoon. A little while later, there was a knock on the door and he came back and said, "I would like you to meet Barney Kessel." They spent the afternoon trading stories and licks. I do wish he had warned me, so I could have prepared some more intelligent questions for him, though. I was, of course, in awe and was more than a little dumbstruck. There were many other well-known musicians who came through the store that I got to meet. George Duvivier, Roy Clark, Stan Getz...

Smith remembered frequent visits to his Colorado Springs home by trumpeter Doc Severinson. He also recalled, with a touch of mischief, unwinding after-hours with country guitarist Roy Clark:

> I used to cook Italian food. I learned in New York from the best chef. Every time Doc Severinson came around, I would fix him clam sauce à la diablo. I would pick him up, bring him to the house, and cook him clam sauce. He would eat two heaping bowl-fulls. I don't know where he put it! Jack Tardy, a very fine trumpet player, he lives in town here... He used to invite Doc out to the academy here. Another friend of mine, Roy Clark... I was playing this thing in Monterey, California, with Bing. When we finished, the restaurants were closed. I started to get on the elevator... Roy Clark came up. He was one of the guests at the Bing Crosby National Pro-Amateur golf tournament. He invited me up to his room and ordered sandwiches. I played some guitar for him. We ended up

finishing at four o'clock in the morning, I think. They couldn't wake him up to go to the golf tournament. He didn't show up. Nothing [laughs]. Roy used to come here when he was in town. We would end up at the kitchen table, playing guitars. He didn't know any of the jazz things, so we would play and he would keep time by tapping on the top of his guitar.

Smith's hospitality was infamous, and his modest house in Colorado Springs was often packed with guests. His son, John, recalls, "He and Sandy used to have all kinds of parties. They loved to have people over, and they did all that entertaining in that little house."

Sometimes, Smith found himself providing hospitality on a grand scale. On one particular occasion, Teddy Reig decided to throw a party at Smith's house:

JOHNNY SMITH IN HIS KITCHEN IN COLORADO SPRINGS

> Well, it was a quiet Sunday afternoon. This Greyhound bus backfired down the street, turned around, and the whole Count Basie orchestra plus some other people got off. Teddy Reig was here, and he had invited them to come over. He was going to cook hamburgers for everybody. In fact, he ended up setting fire to the patio. Anyway, they were very quiet and very well behaved in the backyard. I had some neighbors in the back who weren't too fond of black people. They made quite a fuss. They were bigots. Well, a week later Harry Belafonte's group came [laughs], and that did it! They moved out of town. Good riddance.

Former student Tom Bruner recalls sharing a precious drink, or three, with Smith:

> I informally learned as much from him with drinking one of his 'potent' Martinis as I did in formal lessons. His true nature of humility and humbleness made his one of my most trusted and long-lived friendships.

Aside from music, chess, transparent vodka-Martinis and cooking, the other great passions in his life included flying. Taking to the skies was a comparatively primitive and novel experience when Smith became enamored by it while living in Maine during the 1930s. He was a frequent pilot by the 1950s and went on to become a member of Ye Ancient and Secret Order of Quiet Birdmen.

While living the not-so-quieter life in Colorado Springs, he enjoyed working as a flying instructor, and gave flying lessons at Peterson Field for many years. By the time that he retired, he had earned an Airline Transport Pilot's License and was a certified flight instructor in single and multi-engine aircraft. He flew multi-engined Cessna 310 and Piper Seneca airplanes, and partly owned two Beechcraft Bonanza V35 aircraft. He also partly owned a Beechcraft Bonanza A36 plane that he flew to various colleges on the west coast of America when he was conducting his seminars. His eldest son, John, reflects upon his father's passion for flying:

JOHNNY SMITH WITH HIS FATHER AND HIS SECOND WIFE, ANN, DURING THE 1950S

> You know, my dad was a licensed instructor for small planes. This lady... She was well into her eighties, and she wanted to learn how to fly. So, Dad says, "OK." They went out to the airport, because she just wanted to go up for a flight at first to make sure that this was what she wanted to do. They got into the plane and taxied off to the end of the runway. Now, with these small, single-engined planes they do what they call a run-up. They hold the brakes down and they power-up the engine to make sure that everything is running alright. He explained it to her. He said, "Ma'am, I'm going to power-up the plane." She nodded, so he started. Well, these little planes vibrate when you power them up, sometimes rather violently. He looked over, and this lady had fainted! [laughs]. But, bless her heart, she went on to learn to fly. She soloed and got her license. I think she was eighty-three or eighty-four. But on her first flight, she just passed out.
>
> He was a very accomplished pilot. He used to fly a twin-engined Beechcraft Baron with some of his fishing buddies all the way from the Springs down almost to the tip of Baja. He did that many, many times. He loved to fly. He really did. He used to come up to Maine on occasions, when we were kids, and pick us up. Rather than take the train, he would fly us back. Flying was a true passion for him, but I also think it was a release from all the high pressure stuff that he was doing. You know, the long hours, the traveling, the long sets and everything.

JOHNNY SMITH THE PILOT

Smith's daughter, Kim Stewart, remembers the instigation for the aforementioned elderly student's desire to fly:

> I remember that the little lady he taught to fly wanted to learn because her husband was a pilot, but he wasn't in the best of health. She wanted to know how to land the plane if she had to. She was such a little tiny thing. Dad just grinned from ear to ear after she soloed.

Buddy Greene also recalls Smith's pride when the student passed her flying exams:

> I remember his pride when he got a grandmother to fly solo and the story made the Colorado Springs paper. He showed me the headline at one of our regular Monday meetings. You would have thought he had written a symphony.

Smith's other great passions away from music included his hobby of deep sea fishing, in which he regularly indulged while living in New York, as his eldest son, John Smith III, recalls:

> He used to take me bluefishing off the coast of New Jersey. Bluefish is a game fish. He would work all night, come home and grab me at five o'clock in the morning. He hadn't even been to bed. We would drive to a place called Freeport in Long Island, and then we would fish all day. He would do that without any sleep. That's where I first met Teddy Reig.

JOHNNY SMITH (FIFTH FROM LEFT) ON A FISHING TRIP WITH HIS ELDEST SON, JOHN (SECOND FROM LEFT) AND TEDDY REIG (THIRD FROM LEFT)

After his move to Colorado, friends such as Gordon Close often accompanied him on fishing trips off the coast of Mexico. John Smith III further recalls:

> We used to fish together a lot at Baja. A lot of his friends would come fishing with him. We would sit around the bar after a day of fishing, and I would listen to them telling all these stories. Oh man... It was pretty interesting, to say the least!

Smith's hospitality stretched much further than that of merely hosting parties. Jazz guitarist Sal Salvador remained eternally grateful to him for his generosity. When Salvador moved to New York in the late 1940s, Smith paid for three weeks of hotel rent on his behalf. A short while later, he was again on hand when Salvador returned penniless after working out of town. After Salvador's car died on Smith's driveway, he was invited to move in, as he was in no position to go anywhere else. Salvador lived with Smith for several weeks while Smith took him around the studios and introduced him to the people that he needed to know on the music scene in New York. Mundell Lowe is also grateful for Smith's help at an important time in his career:

> I met Johnny during the early 1950s when he was on the staff at NBC in New York. When he left there, he was instrumental in getting me the job that he vacated. We've been friends ever since.

Others within the jazz guitar community who have enjoyed his generosity include the British guitarist and educator Trefor Owen, who took a vacation to the USA in 1975 with a visit to Smith top of his agenda:

> I went over to the States in 1975 on holiday [vacation]. One of the things that I wanted to do was to meet Johnny Smith. I had written him a letter, but I didn't get a reply. When I got to Chicago, doing the tourist thing, I called him up. He said, "Oh, I got your letter. Come on over. When you get to the airport in Colorado Springs, call me and I'll send the wife to pick you up." So, I did just that. And instead of spending a couple of days with him, I spent about three weeks with him. Instead of touring the rest of the States, as I had planned to, I just spent the time with him, and stayed in a motel nearby. He lent me his Johnny Smith guitar while I was there, so that I could practice in the motel room. I hung out with him for a while in his music store in Colorado Springs. He took me flying. We had dinner parties... Mel Bay came over. He bought Johnny's cottage in the mountains. Johnny is very keen on fishing and that sort of thing, and so was Mel Bay. So, that's how I met him. I could have been anybody off the street, you know. But he was great.

Bob Yelin found himself living in Denver in 1982, and in his capacity as the jazz editor of *Guitar Player* magazine he interviewed Smith shortly after his arrival:

JOHNNY SMITH WITH BOLA TIE AND GOATEE BEARD IN 1982

> The first time I drove to his store, I must have driven at a new world speed record! When I arrived, I entered the store and asked if Johnny was there. He replied, "I'm Johnny Smith." I was so embarrassed. He wore an American Indian bola tie and had a white goatee. He told me to go downstairs for the interview. He sat on a piano bench, just by his piano. I fully taped four cassette tapes, front and back. He couldn't have been any nicer.

Jim Fox remembers Smith's kindness in gesture when he also visited him at his music store in the early 1980s:

> Johnny played his D'Angelico for me when I was in his store, while he was still wearing his denim apron. I told him that I had studied and transcribed some of his music. I asked him if he would be kind enough to play something for me. He played his arrangement of 'Golden Earrings'. Then, he handed me his guitar and asked if I would play something for him. He said that it was only fair. And I thought, 'Well, that's pointless!' [laughs]. But that just shows you his kind spirit, that he would ask a young guitarist to play for him. I can't think that there was anything in it for him when I was playing, but it was an incredibly kind thing to do.

Kenny Kotwitz studied music theory with Smith during the mid-1960s. By coincidence, he happened to meet his tutor in Las Vegas while on the road with the NORAD band:

> One time, the NORAD band was in Las Vegas. I ran into John, and he asked if I wanted to fly back with him. I told him that I would love to, but I asked him when would he be leaving. He said the following day. I told him that the band was going back on that very day. He said, "Oh, don't worry about it. I'll call the Colonel." So, he called Colonel for me. Of course, the Colonel would do anything that he asked, you know. So, John and I flew back in his plane. It was terrific. What a wonderful guy.

Jack Wilkins was also moved by Smith's kindness:

> I was fortunate to meet him when I did a festival in Denver, near where he lives. I called him, and me and my friend, Tom LaVenia, went to see him. I was so knocked out with his charm and graciousness. His persona was as beautiful as his playing. Lots of times, great players are not as nice their music. Johnny is the total package. It seems anyone who has met him says the same thing.

Dale Bruning feels that Smith's personality is clear to hear through his music:

> In my experiences as a musician, I can't separate the personality of the musician from the music. I don't think I've ever found an exception to this. Perhaps the closest to an enigma was Miles Davis, but just about everybody else... You get to know the person by the way they play. For example, Jim Hall, who I've done duets with and know very well, he gets a sound that's as warm as toast. And that's exactly how Jim is! I once asked a friend of mine, Gus Johnson, who was a drummer with Basie and Ellington... He spent quite some time hanging out with Oscar Peterson on tours... I asked him what Peterson was like. He said, "Dale, you've heard him play. Oscar Peterson does not like to lose at tiddly winks! You can hear that in his playing." So, you can see what I'm trying to say. We can't separate ourselves from the way that we play, and I think that's exactly the case with Johnny Smith. A perfect gentleman and a very caring person who puts a lot of thought into everything he does, with high standards.

> If someone were to ask me to describe Johnny Smith, not musically, but as a person, I would describe him as a perfect gentleman. That's how he was with me. Totally. Everything from a business standpoint was done so professionally. His regard, not only for other musicians, but other people was... Just the perfect gentleman.

Jack Petersen concurs and describes Smith's personality succinctly:

> You know, a good word to describe John... People talk about him being a gentleman. Well, he's also a really gentle man.

As an appreciative customer in Smith's music store, Al Owens shares this perception of Smith. He also recalls one of the Master's self-deprecating one-liners:

> Johnny is an old school gentleman. From my conversations with him (twenty years ago), I truly believe he does not understand what the big fuss is about. Why so many people want to know about him. During my first conversation with him I asked if he would sign a photo for me. He did so after telling me that he kept his publicity photos in the basement to scare the roaches and other undesirable varmints away.

Smith was always reluctant to embrace typical celebrity characteristics. Rick Gustafson, who attended the first Johnny Smith Guitar Seminar in Colorado Springs, recalls, “He told us that his wife, Sandy, signed many of his autograph requests.” He was also renowned for his dry sense of humor. Bobby Greene remembers his wit onstage:

> One night [at the Bandbox] we had a full house of enthusiastic listeners except for a drunk at the bar, seated directly in front of Johnny, who kept imploring him to play 'Theme From 'A Summer Place" between tunes. Johnny ignored him for as long as he could. He finally leaned over into the mic and said, “Ya know buddy, you remind me of a guy who goes into a Chinese restaurant and orders spaghetti.” The crowd erupted into laughter and applause, but this dude was so trashed he was totally oblivious to the fact that he had just been cut off at the knees.

Dale Bruning has his own memories of Smith's humor:

> I did a recording with him, here in Denver, and the recording engineer was a heavy-set individual who smoked a pipe like a steam engine. I think he was a little intimidated by the fact that Johnny Smith was there in the recording studio. When we were listening to the playback, he mishandled the tape machine, and the tape ended up going all over the place. He was frantically puffing his pipe. John went up to him and jokingly said, “I knew I should have done this in New York.” Well, we all just fell about laughing. On this occasion, it was the regular quartet plus a trumpet player, who I think had been in Ellington's band. It was some music for Lear Jets, I think. For some promotional thing they were doing. Johnny had been asked to provide some music. I guess it was because the poor guy knew John's reputation for being so meticulous. He was trying to put his

best foot forward, but... [laughs].

The first time that I played bass with him was during the warm weather months. It was outside, but it was windy. So, you couldn't really have any [sheet] music because it would blow away. John just called some standard tunes that we all knew. But there were a couple of tunes that I hadn't played in a long time. Being a guitarist, I was watching his left hand, so that I could follow him. Sometimes, I would play these wrong notes, but I couldn't figure out why they were wrong. John just looked across at me... What I had forgotten was that he tuned his bottom E string down to D [laughs]. We finished our set, and he couldn't stop laughing. So, in future, instead of looking at his left hand, I used my ears. That was a lot more effective.

The late Gary Atkins also fondly remembered Smith's wit:

> Johnny has been like a kindly uncle to me. Somebody asked him if his kids played music. He said, "No, they're normal." He has always had a really dry sense of humor. He and my uncle [Chet Atkins] were so similar. They were born under the same star, and I've always wondered about that. Their sense of humor, demeanor, mannerisms... They could have been brothers.

Chapter Ten:
Coda

On 11 June 2013, Johnny Smith died of natural causes at his home in Colorado Springs, in the company of his sons, John and David, and his daughter, Kim. He was two weeks short of his ninety-first birthday. He had suffered a fall two years earlier, which had badly damaged his hip and left him in considerable pain thereafter, but ultimately, although his mind and memory remained sharp until the end, his aged body was too tired to continue any further. Despite the frailties of his old age, he was determined to remain at home until the end. With a significant amount of help from his family, he was able to fulfill his wish. A memorial service was held in his honor at Shove Chapel on the campus of Colorado College on 22 August 2013. His ashes were interned along with those of his third wife, Sandy, in a mausoleum at Fairview Cemetery in Colorado Springs, just a few feet from the graves of his parents.

The mausoleum which houses Johnny and Sandy Smith's ashes at Fairview Cemetery in Colorado Springs

From a desperately impoverished childhood, he became a world-class musician. Although he grew up in a musical environment, his folk roots were far removed from the sophistication of the art music in which he excelled. As his brother, Ben, recounts, he was the only member of the family to find a career in music:

> The oldest one was George. He was a very fine electrician. He designed some motor winding things that the company patented. He didn't get anything for it. Tom was in charge of a bronze forge for years. I have a few things that he gave me. I know it was in Massachusetts. Here, we call it a brass factory, which is the same thing as a bronze forge. He was there for years and years. Eventually, they put him in charge of the place. Herman died of diphtheria in 1925. His grave is in Birmingham, Alabama. Then, there was John. I did a little bit of everything. I was a letter carrier, I worked in construction... A little bit of everything. Then, Emmett was a salesman.

Despite some undoubtedly tragic events during his life, such as the untimely death of his second wife in childbirth and the loss of his dog in a house fire, which would have made lesser men bitter, Smith still considered himself to have been fortunate:

> I have to tell you, you'll never look at a more fortunate and blessed person than I am. Every dream that I ever had when I was young came true. First, I always dreamed of being able to play with the best musicians in the world, you know. That came true. The second one... I dreamed of flying. That came true. The third one was to be able to catch big fish on my own little boat. I had a sixteen-foot boat, and we'd be fishing thirty or forty miles out in the Pacific Ocean. Just Sandy and I on the boat, catching big fish. The fourth dream was to be able to hunt for big game. Elk and deer... That came true. I also dreamed that one day I would be able to get the hell out of New York City. The best view of New York City that I ever had was in the rear-view mirror when I was leaving. So, I'm one of the most fortunate and blessed people that you'll ever look at.

John Smith III is just one of many who find this appreciation of his life to be admirable:

> Anyone who can sit and look you right in the eye and say, "I'm the luckiest man in the world. I've accomplished everything that I wanted to do in this life." I don't think I've ever heard anybody say that before.

Meanwhile, David Smith puts his father's achievements succinctly:

> The man has had a great life and will leave a lasting impact on music. From a very humble beginning to a world-class musician with limited schooling, he has had an amazing run.

The Recordings

Almost all of Johnny Smith's prolific recorded output in his own name between 1952 and 1964 was released by the small Roost Records label. The sole exception was the album *Jeri Southern Meets Johnny Smith*, which was issued on the Roulette label shortly after it had acquired Roost. Even though Teddy Reig sold Roost to Morris Levy's bigger Roulette company in the late 1950s, the change in the musical tastes of the record-buying public soon distracted Levy's attention away from jazz towards the more lucrative rock 'n' roll music. As a result, Smith's back-catalog, along with those of many other jazz musicians, was neglected for decades. By the time that the giant EMI bought Roulette in 1989, jazz music had long been considered as a small market that was not worth a great deal of attention, let alone investment. Smith's Roost recordings largely continued to languish beyond the reach of many jazz guitarists who came after him. This lack of access to his recordings was undoubtedly a contributing factor towards his regrettably low profile since the late 1960s. Two of his three albums for Verve in 1967 and 1968 were made available in the USA on the contemporary medium of compact disc in the mid-1990s. Since then, there have been sporadic CD releases of some of his Roost albums in Japan and Spain, which have been available via the world wide web. In 2002, Mosaic Records released Smith's Roost small group sessions under license in a limited edition, eight-CD, box set. It is lamentable that this precious collection was restricted by license to a fixed number of pressings, and it remains to be seen if his Roost catalog will be available on a more secure basis in the future.

In documenting Smith's commercially released recordings, it was decided to provide full details where possible, such as track listings, recording dates and personnel. To avoid unnecessary repetition, only those compilation albums which are considered to be noteworthy have been included. Similarly, important EPs have been included, but singles in Smith's own name have not. On albums where he appeared as a sideman, only the individual pieces on which he played are identified, unless otherwise stated.

Key to Instrumentation:

Guitar (g); piano (p); organ (org); bass (b); Fender bass (fb); drums/percussion (d); vibraphone (vb); accordion (acc); orchestra (orch); arranger (arr); conductor (cond); saxophone (sax); alto saxophone (as); tenor saxophone (ts); baritone saxophone (btn); trumpet (tpt); trombone (tbn); tuba (tub); flugel horn (flh); French horn (frh); violin (vln); viola (vla); cello (cel); mandolin (mand); clarinet (cl); bass clarinet (bcl); flute (flt); oboe (ob); bassoon (bsn); vocal (voc).

Johnny Smith: Guitar Interludes for Low Level Background

c.1947, Lang-Worth 16" Vinyl LP YTNY 8389. New York: Lang-Worth Feature Programs #1325. Copy held in the Library of Congress. Call Number: NCPC 13957.

Song Of India; *Rhythm*; *Oh, Bury Me Not*; *Oh, Susanna*; *The Little Shanty*; *Home Sweet Home*; *Carry Me Back to Old Virginny*; *Auld Lang Syne*

Mary Lou Williams: Mary Lou/Kool

1947, Asch Recordings 78rpm 5033.
1999, Classics CD 1050 *The Chronological Mary Lou Williams 1945-1947*.
Recorded 1947, New York. Personnel: Mary Lou Williams (p); Kenny Dorham (tpt); Johnny Smith (g); Grachan Moncur (b).

Arnold Schönberg: Serenade Opus 24. Dimitri Mitropoulos and the New York Philharmonic

1949, Counterpoint/Esoteric Vinyl LP 5501. Recorded December 1949, New York. Personnel: Dimitri Mitropoulos (cond); Clark Brody (cl); Eric Simon (bcl); Sal Picardi (mand); Johnny Smith (g); Louis Krasner (vln); Ralph Hersch (vla); Seymour Barab (cel); Warren Galjour (voc).

March; *Menuet*; *Variations*; *Sonnet by Petrarca (For Baritone)*; *Dance Scene*; *Song (Without Words)*; *Finale*

Ibert: Concerto For Flute and Orchestra; Entr'acte for Flute and Guitar; Trio-Sonate in C-Moll for Flute, Oboe and Piano; Trio-Sonate in E-Moll for Flute, Oboe and Piano

c. 1950, Oxford Recording Company Vinyl LP OR 104. Personnel: Julius Baker (flt), Johnny Smith (g).

Entr'acte

Benny Goodman and His Sextet: Oh Babe

1950, Columbia 78rpm 44431.
2003, Ocium CD DL B-32640-2003 *Benny Goodman: New Sextet Sessions*.
2007, Classics CD 1436 *The Chronological Benny Goodman and His Orchestra 1949-1951*.
Recorded 10 October 1950, New York. Personnel: Benny Goodman (cl); Terry Gibbs (vb); Teddy Wilson (p); Johnny Smith (g); Bob Carter (b); Terry Snyder (d); Jimmy 'Rickey' Ricks, Nancy Reed (voc).

Benny Goodman and His Sextet: You're Gonna Lose Your Gal

1950, Columbia 78rpm 44432.
2003, Ocium CD DL B-32640-2003 *Benny Goodman: New Sextet Sessions.*
2007, Classics CD 1436 *The Chronological Benny Goodman and His Orchestra 1949-1951.*
Recorded 10 October 1950, New York. Personnel: Benny Goodman (cl); Terry Gibbs (vb); Teddy Wilson (p); Johnny Smith (g); Bob Carter (b); Terry Snyder (d); Jimmy 'Rickey' Ricks (voc).

Benny Goodman and His Sextet: Walkin' with the Blues

1950, Columbia 78rpm 44433
2003, Ocium CD DL B-32640-2003 *Benny Goodman: New Sextet Sessions.*
2007, Classics CD 1436 *The Chronological Benny Goodman and His Orchestra 1949-1951.*
Recorded 10 October 1950, New York. Personnel: Benny Goodman (cl); Terry Gibbs (vb); Teddy Wilson (p); Johnny Smith (g); Bob Carter (b); Terry Snyder (d); Jimmy 'Rickey' Ricks (voc).

Benny Goodman and His Sextet: Lullaby of the Leaves

1950, Columbia 78rpm 44674
1987, CBS CD 450411 2.
2003, Ocium CD DL B-32640-2003 *Benny Goodman: New Sextet Sessions.*
2007, Classics CD 1436 *The Chronological Benny Goodman and His Orchestra 1949-1951.*
Recorded 24 November 1950, New York. Personnel: Benny Goodman (cl); Terry Gibbs (vb); Teddy Wilson (p); Johnny Smith (g); Bob Carter (b); Charlie Smith (d).

Benny Goodman and His Sextet: Then You've Never Been Blue

1950, Columbia 78rpm 44675.
2003, Ocium CD DL B-32640-2003.
2007, Classics CD 1436 *The Chronological Benny Goodman and His Orchestra 1949-1951.*
Recorded 24 November 1950, New York. Personnel: Benny Goodman (cl); Terry Gibbs (vb); Teddy Wilson (p); Johnny Smith (g); Bob Carter (b); Charlie Smith (d); Nancy Reed, The Pastels (voc).

Benny Goodman and His Sextet: Walkin'

1950, Columbia 78rpm 44676.
2003, Ocium CD DL B-32640-2003.
2007, Classics CD 1436 *The Chronological Benny Goodman and His Orchestra 1949-1951.*
Recorded 24 November 1950, New York. Personnel: Benny Goodman (cl); Terry Gibbs (vb); Teddy Wilson (p); Johnny Smith (g); Bob Carter (b); Charlie Smith (d); The Pastels (voc).

Benny Goodman and His Sextet: Temptation Rag

1950, Columbia 78rpm 44677.
1987, CBS CD 450411 2.
2003, Ocium CD DL B-32640-2003 *Benny Goodman: New Sextet Sessions*.
2007, Classics CD 1436 *The Chronological Benny Goodman and His Orchestra 1949-1951*.
Recorded 24 November 1950, New York. Personnel: Benny Goodman (cl); Terry Gibbs (vb); Teddy Wilson (p); Johnny Smith (g); Bob Carter (b); Charlie Smith (d).

The Benny Goodman Trio Plays for the Fletcher Henderson Fund

1951, Columbia Vinyl LP CL516.
2007, Classics CD 1436 *The Chronological Benny Goodman and His Orchestra 1949-1951*.
Recorded 1 April 1951, New York. Personnel: Benny Goodman (cl); Teddy Wilson (p); Gene Krupa (d); Lou McGarity (tbn); Buck Clayton (tpt); Johnny Smith (g); Eddie Safranski (b).

After You've Gone; *Basin Street Blues*; *Honeysuckle Rose*; *One O'Clock Jump*

Alban Berg: Wozzeck. Dimitri Mitropoulos and the New York Philharmonic

1951, Columbia Masterworks Double Vinyl LP SL-118.
1997, Sony Double CD MH2K 62759.
Recorded 12 April 1951, New York. Personnel: Dimitri Mitropoulos (cond); Philharmonic-Symphony Orchestra of New York (orch).

Benny Goodman and His Orchestra: Down South Camp Meetin'

1951, Columbia 78rpm 45670.
2007, Classics CD 1450 *The Chronological Benny Goodman and His Orchestra 1951-1952*.
Recorded 26 April 1951, New York. Personnel: Jimmy Maxwell, Billy Butterfield, Chris Griffin, Al Stewart (tpt); Lou McGarity, Cutty Cutshall, Will Bradley (tbn); Benny Goodman (cl); Hymie Schertzer, Al Klink (as); Peanuts Hucko, Boomie Richman (ts); Art Drellinger (btn); Stan Freeman (p); Johnny Smith (g); Bob Haggart (b); Terry Snyder (d).

Benny Goodman Orchestra: Mean to Me

1951, Columbia 78rpm 45671.
2007, Classics CD 1450 *The Chronological Benny Goodman and His Orchestra 1951-1952*.
Recorded 26 April 1951, New York. Personnel: Jimmy Maxwell, Billy Butterfield, Chris Griffin, Al Stewart (tpt); Lou McGarity, Cutty Cutshall, Will Bradley (tbn); Benny Goodman (cl); Hymie

Schertzer, Al Klink (as); Peanuts Hucko, Boomie Richman (ts); Art Drellinger (btn); Stan Freeman (p); Johnny Smith (g); Bob Haggart (b); Terry Snyder (d).

Benny Goodman Orchestra: South of the Border

1951, Columbia 78rpm 45672.
2007, Classics CD 1450 *The Chronological Benny Goodman and His Orchestra 1951-1952.*
Recorded 26 April 1951, New York. Personnel: Jimmy Maxwell, Billy Butterfield, Chris Griffin, Al Stewart (tpt); Lou McGarity, Cutty Cutshall, Will Bradley (tbn); Benny Goodman (cl); Hymie Schertzer, Al Klink (as); Peanuts Hucko, Boomie Richman (ts); Art Drellinger (btn); Stan Freeman (p); Johnny Smith (g); Bob Haggart (b); Terry Snyder (d).

Benny Goodman Orchestra: Muskrat Ramble

1951, Columbia 78rpm 45673.
2007, Classics CD 1450 *The Chronological Benny Goodman and His Orchestra 1951-1952.*
Recorded 26 April 1951, New York. Personnel: Jimmy Maxwell, Billy Butterfield, Chris Griffin, Al Stewart (tpt); Lou McGarity, Cutty Cutshall, Will Bradley (tbn); Benny Goodman (cl); Hymie Schertzer, Al Klink (as); Peanuts Hucko, Boomie Richman (ts); Art Drellinger (btn); Stan Freeman (p); Johnny Smith (g); Bob Haggart (b); Terry Snyder (d).

Benny Goodman and His Orchestra: Lulu's Back in Town

1951, Columbia 78rpm 45674.
2007, Classics CD 1450 *The Chronological Benny Goodman and His Orchestra 1951-1952.*
Recorded 29 April 1951, New York. Personnel: Jimmy Maxwell, Billy Butterfield, Chris Griffin, Al Stewart (tpt); Lou McGarity, Cutty Cutshall, Will Bradley (tbn); Benny Goodman (cl); Hymie Schertzer, Al Klink (as); Peanuts Hucko, Boomie Richman (ts); Art Drellinger (btn); Stan Freeman (p); Johnny Smith (g); Bob Haggart (b); Terry Snyder (d).

Benny Goodman and His Orchestra: Stardust

1951, Columbia 78rpm 45675.
2007, Classics CD 1450 *The Chronological Benny Goodman and His Orchestra 1951-1952.*
Recorded 29 April 1951, New York. Personnel: Jimmy Maxwell, Billy Butterfield, Chris Griffin, Al Stewart (tpt); Lou McGarity, Cutty Cutshall, Will Bradley (tbn); Benny Goodman (cl); Hymie Schertzer, Al Klink (as); Peanuts Hucko, Boomie Richman (ts); Art Drellinger (btn); Stan Freeman (p); Johnny Smith (g); Bob Haggart (b); Terry Snyder (d).

Benny Goodman and His Orchestra: Wrappin' It Up

1951, Columbia 78rpm 45676.
2007, Classics CD 1450 *The Chronological Benny Goodman and His Orchestra 1951-1952*.
Recorded 29 April 1951, New York. Personnel: Jimmy Maxwell, Billy Butterfield, Chris Griffin, Al Stewart (tpt); Lou McGarity, Cutty Cutshall, Will Bradley (tbn); Benny Goodman (cl); Hymie Schertzer, Al Klink (as); Peanuts Hucko, Boomie Richman (ts); Art Drellinger (btn); Stan Freeman (p); Johnny Smith (g); Bob Haggart (b); Terry Snyder (d).

Benny Goodman and His Orchestra: King Porter Stomp

1951, Columbia 78rpm 45677.
2007, Classics CD 1450 *The Chronological Benny Goodman and His Orchestra 1951-1952*.
Recorded 29 April 1951, New York. Personnel: Jimmy Maxwell, Billy Butterfield, Chris Griffin, Al Stewart (tpt); Lou McGarity, Cutty Cutshall, Will Bradley (tbn); Benny Goodman (cl); Hymie Schertzer, Al Klink (as); Peanuts Hucko, Boomie Richman (ts); Art Drellinger (btn); Stan Freeman (p); Johnny Smith (g); Bob Haggart (b); Terry Snyder (d).

Benny Goodman and His Sextet: Farewell Blues

1951, Columbia 78rpm 45842.
1987, CBS CD 450411 2.
2003, Ocium CD DL B-32640-2003 *Benny Goodman: New Sextet Sessions*.
2007, Classics CD 1450 *The Chronological Benny Goodman and His Orchestra 1951-1952*.
Recorded 13 June 1951, New York. Personnel: Benny Goodman (cl); Terry Gibbs (vb); Paul Smith (p); Johnny Smith (g); Eddie Safranski (b); Sid Bulkin (d).

Benny Goodman and His Sextet: Toodle-Lee-Yoo-Doo

1951, Columbia 78rpm 45843.
2003, Ocium CD DL B-32640-2003.
2007, Classics CD 1450 *The Chronological Benny Goodman and His Orchestra 1951-1952*.
Recorded 13 June 1951, New York. Personnel: Benny Goodman (cl); Terry Gibbs (vb); Paul Smith (p); Johnny Smith (g); Eddie Safranski (b); Sid Bulkin (d); Nancy Reed (voc).

Benny Goodman and His Orchestra: When Buddha Smiles

1951, Columbia 78rpm 47080.
2007, Classics CD 1450 *The Chronological Benny Goodman and His Orchestra 1951-1952*.
Recorded 26 September 1951, New York. Personnel: Bernie Privin, Billy Butterfield, Chris Griffin, Al

Stewart, Carl Poole (tpt); Lou McGarity, Cutty Cutshall, Will Bradley (tbn); Benny Goodman (cl); Hymie Schertzer, Al Klink (as); Peanuts Hucko, Boomie Richman (ts); Art Drellinger (btn); Stan Freeman (p); Johnny Smith (g); Bob Haggart (b); Terry Snyder (d).

Benny Goodman and His Orchestra: Sunrise Serenade

1951, Columbia 78rpm 47081.
2007, Classics CD 1450 *The Chronological Benny Goodman and His Orchestra 1951-1952.*
Recorded 26 September 1951, New York. Personnel: Bernie Privin, Chris Griffin, Al Stewart, Carl Poole (tpt); Lou McGarity, Cutty Cutshall, Will Bradley (tbn); Benny Goodman (cl); Hymie Schertzer, Al Klink (as); Peanuts Hucko, Boomie Richman (ts); Art Drellinger (btn); Stan Freeman (p); Johnny Smith (g); Bob Haggart (b); Terry Snyder (d).

Bob Houston-Sanford Gold Orchestra: It's Christmas Every Day (When You're In Love)/This Is the Real Thing Now

1952, Wheeler Records Vinyl Single P-100/1.

Gene Krupa and His Orchestra: Bolero, Part 1/Bolero, Part 2

1952, Clef MGC 607 (Unreleased)
1952, Verve MGV 4016 (Unreleased)
Recorded 9-10 December 1952, New York. Personnel: Bernie Glow, Chris Griffin, Steve Lipkins, Charlie Shavers (tpt); Bobby Byrne, Chuck Evans, Jack Satterfield, Kai Winding (tbn); Lewis Simon (tub); Stan Ferguson, Lenny Hambro, Al Howard, Stewart McKay, Toots Mondello, Ben Ross (sax); Johnny Smith (g); Doc Goldberg, George Yorke (b); Gene Krupa (d); George Williams (arr, cond); unidentified strings.

Johnny Smith Quintet: Jazz at NBC

1952, Roost Vinyl EP 303.
1953, Roost Vinyl LP 410 *Jazz at NBC.*
2002, Mosaic CD MD8-216 *The Complete Roost Johnny Smith Small Group Sessions.*
Recorded 11 March 1952, April 1952*, New York. Personnel: Johnny Smith (g); Stan Getz, Zoot Sims* (ts); Sanford Gold (p); Eddie Safranski (b); Don Lamond (d).

Moonlight in Vermont; *Tabu*; *A Ghost of a Chance**; *Where or When*

Johnny Smith Quintet: Jazz at NBC

1952, Roost Vinyl EP 305.
1953, Roost Vinyl LP 410 *Jazz at NBC*.
2002, Mosaic CD MD8-216 *The Complete Roost Johnny Smith Small Group Sessions*.
Recorded 11 March 1952*, April 1952**, November 1952***, New York. Personnel: * Johnny Smith (g); Stan Getz (ts); Sanford Gold (p); Eddie Safranski (b); Don Lamond (d). ** Johnny Smith (g); Zoot Sims (ts); Sanford Gold (p); Eddie Safranski (b); Don Lamond (d). *** Johnny Smith (g); Stan Getz (ts); Sanford Gold (p); Bob Carter (b); Morey Feld (d).

*Tenderly****; *Jaguar**; *My Funny Valentine***; *Vilia***

Johnny Smith Quintet: Jazz at NBC

1953, Roost Vinyl LP 410. Compilation of EP 303 and EP 305.
1989, Fresh Sound CD FSR-CD-37 (Omitting: My Funny Valentine).
2002, Mosaic CD MD8-216 *The Complete Roost Johnny Smith Small Group Sessions*.
Recorded 11 March 1952, April 1952, November 1952, New York. Personnel: Johnny Smith (g); Stan Getz, Zoot Sims (ts); Sanford Gold (p); Eddie Safranski, Bob Carter (b); Don Lamond, Morey Feld (d).

Moonlight in Vermont; *Tabu*; *A Ghost of a Chance*; *Where or When*; *Tenderly*; *Jaguar*; *My Funny Valentine*; *Vilia*

Johnny Smith Quintet Featuring Stan Getz

1953, Roost Vinyl EP 310.
1954, Roost Vinyl LP 413 *Johnny Smith Quintet Featuring Stan Getz*.
2002, Mosaic CD MD8-216 *The Complete Roost Johnny Smith Small Group Sessions*.
Recorded November 1952*, August 1953, New York. Personnel: Johnny Smith (g); Stan Getz*, Paul Quinichette (ts); Sanford Gold (p); Arnold Fishkin, Bob Carter* (b); Don Lamond, Morey Feld* (d).

Yesterdays; *Sometimes I'm Happy**; *I'll Be Around*; *Nice Work If You Can Get It**

Johnny Smith Quintet Featuring Stan Getz

1953, Roost Vinyl EP 311.
1954, Roost Vinyl LP 413 *Johnny Smith Quintet Featuring Stan Getz*.
2002, Mosaic CD MD8-216 *The Complete Roost Johnny Smith Small Group Sessions*.
Recorded November 1952*, 5 June 1953**, August 1953***, New York. Personnel: * Johnny Smith (g); Stan Getz (ts); Sanford Gold (p); Bob Carter, Arnold Fishkin (b); Morey Feld (d). ** Johnny Smith (g); Joe Mooney (org); Eddie Safranski (b); Don Lamond (d). *** Johnny Smith (g); Paul Quinichette

(ts); Sanford Gold (p); Arnold Fishkin (b); Don Lamond (d).

*Stars Fell on Alabama**; *Cherokee****; *Terry's Theme from Limelight***; *Cavu****

Johnny Smith Quintet Featuring Stan Getz

1954, Roost Vinyl LP 413. Compilation of EP 310 and EP 311.
2002, Mosaic CD MD8-216 *The Complete Roost Johnny Smith Small Group Sessions*.
Recorded November 1952, 5 June 1953, August 1953, New York. Personnel: Johnny Smith (g); Stan Getz, Paul Quinichette (ts); Sanford Gold (p); Joe Mooney (org); Eddie Safranski, Bob Carter, Arnold Fishkin (b); Don Lamond, Morey Feld (d).

Stars Fell on Alabama; *Sometimes I'm Happy*; *Terry's Theme from Limelight*; *Nice Work If You Can Get It*; *I'll Be Around*; *Cavu*; *Yesterdays*; *Cherokee*

Jazz Studio 1

1954, Decca Vinyl LP DL-8058.
2004, Lone Hill Jazz CD LHJ10145.
Recorded 10 October 1953, New York. Personnel: Johnny Smith [as Sir Jonathan Gasser] (g); Paul Quinichette, Frank Foster (ts); Benny Green (tbn); Joe Newman (tpt); Hank Jones (p); Eddie Jones (b); Kenny Clarke (d).

Tenderly; *Let's Split*

Johnny Smith: In a Mellow Mood

1954, Roost Vinyl LP 421.
2002, Mosaic CD MD8-216 *The Complete Roost Johnny Smith Small Group Sessions*.
Recorded 9 May and 10 September 1954, New York. Personnel: Johnny Smith, Perry Lopez (g); Arnold Fishkin (b); Don Lamond (d).

What's New; *I'll Remember April*; *Sophisticated Lady*; *Easy to Love*; *S' Wonderful*; *Stranger in Paradise*; *Our Love Is Here to Stay*; *Lover Man*

Johnny Smith: In a Sentimental Mood

1954, Roost Vinyl LP 424.
2002, Mosaic CD MD8-216 *The Complete Roost Johnny Smith Small Group Sessions*.
Recorded 1954 and 1955*, New York. Personnel: Johnny Smith, Perry Lopez (g); Bob Pancoast* (p);

Arnold Fishkin, George Roumanis* (b); Don Lamond, Jerry Segal* (d).

In a Sentimental Mood; *Walk, Don't Run*; *Autumn in New York*; *How About You*; *Someone to Watch Over Me*; *Dancing on the Ceiling**; *Blues for Birdland**; *Have You Met Miss Jones**

Johnny Richards: Annotations of the Muses

1955, Legende Vinyl LP 1401.
2005, Mosaic CD MS-017 *Mosaic Select – Johnny Richards*.
Recorded 22 February 1955, New York. Personnel: Joe Wilder (tpt); John Barrows (Fr horn); Vincent Abato (cl); Julius Baker (fl); Bob Bloom (ob); Harold Goltzer (bsn); Johnny Smith (g); Jack Lesberg (b); Sol Gubin (d).

Annotations of the Muses (Part One); *Annotations of the Muses (Part Two)*; *Annotations of the Muses (Part Three)*

Johnny Smith Plays Jimmy Van Heusen

1955, Roost Vinyl LP 2201.
1963, Roost Vinyl LP 2250 *Johnny Smith Plays the Songbook of Jimmy Van Heusen*.
2002, Mosaic CD MD8-216 *The Complete Roost Johnny Smith Small Group Sessions*.
Recorded 1955, New York. Personnel: Johnny Smith (g); Bob Pancoast (p); George Roumanis (b); Jerry Segal (d).

But Beautiful; *Swinging on a Star*; *I Could Have Told You*; *It Could Happen to You*; *Oh You Crazy Moon*; *I Thought About You*; *Deep in a Dream*; *So Help Me*; *Nancy (with the Laughing Face)*; *Polka Dots and Moonbeams*; *Darn That Dream; Imagination*

The Johnny Smith Quartet

1955, Roost Vinyl LP 2203.
2002, Mosaic CD MD8-216 *The Complete Roost Johnny Smith Small Group Sessions*.
Recorded 1955, New York. Personnel: Johnny Smith (g); Bob Pancoast (p); George Roumanis (b); Mousie Alexander (d).

Django; *Wait 'Til You See Her*; *0500 Blues*; *More Bass*; *Un Poco Loco*; *Easy Living*; *Old Girl*; *Little Girl Blue*; *Tired Blood*; *Spring Is Here*

Beverly Kenney Sings for Johnny Smith

1956, Roost Vinyl LP 2206.
1989, Fresh Sound CD FSR-CD79.
2008, Toshiba-EMI CD TOCJ-5384.
Recorded 1955, New York.Personnel: Beverly Kenney (voc); Johnny Smith (g); Bob Pancoast (p); Knobby Totah (b); Mousie Alexander (d).

Surrey with the Fringe on Top; *Tis' Autumn*; *Looking for a Boy*; *I'll Know My Love (Greensleeves)*; *Destination Moon*; *Ball and Chain (Sweet Lorraine)*; *Almost Like Being in Love*; *Stairway to the Stars*; *There Will Never Be Another You*; *This Little Town Is Paris*; *Moe's Blues*; *Snuggled on Your Shoulder*

Tito Puente and His Orchestra: Moritat

1956, RCA Vinyl Single 47-6417.
1993, BMG CD 74321-16445-2 *Mucho Puente*.
Recorded 9 January 1956, New York. Also known as 'Mack the Knife'.

Hank Jones: Urbanity

1956, Clef Vinyl LP MGC 707.
1997, Verve CD 314 537 749-2.
Recorded 4 September 1953, New York. Personnel: Hank Jones (p); Johnny Smith (g); Ray Brown (b).

Thad's Pad; *Thing's Are So Pretty in the Spring*; *Little Girl Blue*; *Odd Number*

Moonlight in Vermont: With Johnny Smith Featuring Stan Getz

1956, Roost LP 2211. Compilation of previous releases.
1963, Roost LP 2251.
1991, Roulette CD CDP 7977472.
2002, Mosaic CD MD8-216 *The Complete Roost Johnny Smith Small Group Sessions*.
Personnel: Johnny Smith (g); Stan Getz, Zoot Sims, Paul Quinichette (ts); Sanford Gold (p); Eddie Safranski, Bob Carter, Arnold Fishkin (b); Don Lamond, Morey Feld (d).

Moonlight in Vermont; *Tabu*; *Tenderly*; *Cavu*; *A Ghost of a Chance*; *Jaguar*; *Stars Fell on Alabama*; *Where or When*; *I'll Be Around*; *Cherokee*; *Yesterdays*; *Vilia*

The 1991 Roulette CD issue further includes: *Jaguar* (Alt. Take); *My Funny Valentine*; *Sometimes I'm Happy*; *Nice Work If You Can Get It*; *What's New*; *I'll Remember April*; *Lullaby of Birdland*

Johnny Smith: Moods

1956, Roost Vinyl LP 2215. Compilation of previous releases.
2002, Toshiba-EMI CD TOCJ-66157.
2002, Mosaic CD MD8-216 *The Complete Roost Johnny Smith Small Group Sessions*.
Personnel: Johnny Smith (g); Perry Lopez (g); Bob Pancoast (p); Arnold Fishkin, George Roumanis (b); Don Lamond, Jerry Segal (d).

What's New; *I'll Remember April*; *Sophisticated Lady*; *Easy to Love*; *Autumn in New York*; *Walk, Don't Run*; *Lover Man*; *Dancing on the Ceiling*; *Blues for Birdland*; *Have You Met Miss Jones*; *Someone to Watch Over Me*; *How About You*

The New Johnny Smith Quartet

1957, Roost Vinyl LP 2216.
1989, Fresh Sound CD FSR-CD80.
2002, Mosaic CD MD8-216 *The Complete Roost Johnny Smith Small Group Sessions*.
Recorded 24 October 1956, New York. Personnel: Johnny Smith (g); Johnny Rae (vb); George Roumanis (b); John Lee (d).

It Never Entered My Mind; *Samba*; *Black Is the Color (of My True Love's Hair)*; *Pawn Ticket*; *S' Wonderful*; *You'd Be So Nice to Come Home to*; *Blue Lights*; *Montage*; *Bags' Groove*; *'Round Midnight*

Tito Puente and His Orchestra: Mucho Puente

1957, RCA Vinyl LP 1479.
1993, BMG CD 74321-16445-2.
Recorded 6 and 7 May 1957, New York. It is not known which selections featured Smith.

La Ola Marina; *Ecstasy*; *What a Difference a Day Makes*; *Son De La Loma*; *Un Poquito De Tu Amor*; *Tea for Two*; *Almendra*; *Tito's Guajira*

The 1993 BMG CD issue further includes: Moritat (Recorded 9 January 1956, New York).

Ruth Price Sings with the Johnny Smith Quartet

1957, Roost Vinyl LP 2217.
1989, Fresh Sound CD FSR-CD 36.
Recorded 1956, New York. Personnel: Ruth Price (voc); Johnny Smith (g); John Rae (vb); Clyde Lombardy (b); John Lee (d).

I'm Nobody's Baby; *It Never Entered My Mind*; *Wonderful Guy*; *Until the Real Thing Comes Along*; *This Heart of Mine*; *When You Wish Upon a Star*; *Time after Time*; *Goodbye*; *Back in Your Own Back Yard*; *I'll Be Seeing You*; *Run Little Rain Drop Run*; *Sleeping Bee*

Richard Wess and His Orchestra: Music She Digs The Most

1957, MGM Vinyl LP E3491. It is not known which selections featured Smith.

Autumn Leaves; *I Didn't Know What Time It Was*; *Hey Now*; *I Got It Bad*; *Why Shouldn't It*; *Somewhere*; *Give Me the Simple Life*; *Cabin in the Sky*; *You'd Be So Nice to Come Home to*; *Lover Man*; *Honest Abe*; *Blues for Someone*

The Johnny Smith Foursome

1957, Roost Vinyl EP 313.
1957, Roost Vinyl LP 2223. *The Johnny Smith Foursome.*
2002, Mosaic CD MD8-216 *The Complete Roost Johnny Smith Small Group Sessions.*
Recorded 18 March 1957, New York. Personnel: Johnny Smith (g); Bob Pancoast (p); Knobby Totah (b); Jerry Segal (d).

Hello Young Lovers; *Love Letters*; *Love for Sale*; *Good-Bye*

The Johnny Smith Foursome

1957, Roost Vinyl LP 2223. Includes EP 313.
2002, Mosaic CD MD8-216 *The Complete Roost Johnny Smith Small Group Sessions.*
Recorded 18 March 1957, New York. Personnel: Johnny Smith (g); Bob Pancoast (p); Knobby Totah (b); Jerry Segal (d).

Hello Young Lovers; *Love for Sale*; *The Maid with the Flaxen Hair*; *Love Letters*; *Tickletoe*; *Good-Bye*; *Body and Soul*; *Lover*; *The Boy Next Door*; *Potter's Luck*; *Autumn Nocturne*; *Band Aid*

The Johnny Smith Foursome Volume II

1957, Roost Vinyl LP 2228.
2002, Mosaic CD MD8-216 *The Complete Roost Johnny Smith Small Group Sessions.*
Recorded September 1957, New York. Personnel: Johnny Smith (g); Bob Pancoast (p); George Roumanis (b); Mousie Alexander (d).

Angel Eyes; *Deep Night*; *These Foolish Things*; *East of the Sun*; *There's a Small Hotel*; *Laura*; *Tea for*

Two; *You Go to My Head*; *I'm Getting Sentimental over You*; *Zing Went the Strings*

The Johnny Smith Quartet: Flower Drum Song

1958, Roost Vinyl LP 2231.
2002, Mosaic CD MD8-216 *The Complete Roost Johnny Smith Small Group Sessions*.
Recorded 1958, New York. Personnel: Johnny Smith (g); George Roumanis (b); Mousie Alexander (d); Charles McCracken (cel).

You Are Beautiful; *I Enjoy Being a Girl*; *Sunday*; *A Hundred Million Miracles*; *Grant Avenue*; *Love Look Away*; *Like a God*; *Finale*

Jeri Southern Meets Johnny Smith

1958, Roulette Vinyl LP SR-52016.
1989, Fresh Sound CD FSR CD-28.
2003, Toshiba-EMI CD TOCJ-9492.
Recorded 19 and 22 May 1958, New York. Personnel: Jeri Southern (voc); Johnny Smith (g); Bob Pancoast (p); George Roumanis (b); Mousie Alexander (d).

Music, Maestro, Please; *Robins and Roses*; *Without a Word of Warning*; *Ungrateful Heart*; *The Things I Love*; *Where or When*; *Until the Real Thing Comes Along*; *Shake Down the Stars*; *Have You Forgotten So Soon*; *When the Sun Comes Out*; *Isn't It Romantic*; *Two Sleepy People*

Johnny Smith Trio: Easy Listening

1959, Roost Vinyl LP 2233.
2002, Mosaic CD MD8-216 *The Complete Roost Johnny Smith Small Group Sessions*.
2005, Toshiba-EMI CD TOCJ-9649.
Recorded 19 November 1958, New York. Personnel: Johnny Smith (g); George Roumanis (b); Charlie Mastropaola (d).

When I Fall in Love; *It Might as Well Be Spring*; *I Didn't Know What Time It Was*; *Black Is the Color (of My True Love's Hair)*; *Like Someone in Love*; *You Don't Know What Love Is*; *Isn't It Romantic*; *I Remember the Corn Fields*; *A Foggy Day*; *Scarlet Ribbons*; *People Will Say We're in Love*; *The Nearness of You*

The Johnny Smith Trio: Johnny Smith Favorites

1959, Roost Vinyl LP 2237.
2002, Mosaic CD MD8-216 *The Complete Roost Johnny Smith Small Group Sessions*.
Recorded 20 May 1959, New York. Personnel: Johnny Smith (g); George Roumanis (b); Mousie Alexander (d).

Moonlight in Vermont; *My Funny Valentine*; *Little Girl Blue*; *My One and Only Love*; *Darn That Dream/Polka Dots and Moonbeams*; *Satin Doll*; *Blues Back Stage*; *Everything Happens to Me*; *Pavane*; *Willow Weep for Me*

Johnny Smith Trio: Designed for You

1959, Roost Vinyl LP 2238.
2002, Mosaic CD MD8-216 *The Complete Roost Johnny Smith Small Group Sessions*.
Recorded 20 May 1959, New York. Personnel: Johnny Smith (g); George Roumanis (b); Mousie Alexander (d).

Fools Rush In; *I'll Remember Clifford*; *The Lady Is a Tramp*; *There Will Never Be Another You*; *Autumn Leaves*; *Mood Indigo*; *Sentimental Journey*; *Three Little Words*; *My Romance*; *Sometimes I'm Happy*; *I'll Take Romance*

The Johnny Smith Guitar: My Dear Little Sweetheart

1960, Roost Vinyl SLP 2239.
2004, Toshiba-EMI CD TOCJ-9602.
Recorded 1960, New York. Personnel: Johnny Smith (g); Irwin Kostal (cond); Gene Orloff (vln).

My Dear Little Sweetheart; *Indian Summer*; *Softly, as in a Morning Sunrise*; *All the Things You Are*; *It's So Peaceful in the Country*; *Once in a While*; *Flamingo*; *Spring Is Here*; *Violets For Her Furs*; *It Never Entered My Mind*

Johnny Smith: Guitar and Strings

1960, Roost Vinyl LP 2242.
Recorded May 1960, New York. Personnel: Johnny Smith, Barry Galbraith (g); George Duvivier (b); Don Lamond, Sol Gubin (d); Gene Orloff, Arnold Eidus, Leo Kruczek, George Ockner, Avram Weiss, Harry Katzman, Paul Winter, Hinda Barnett, Maurice Wilk, Al Brown, Felix Giglio, Jules Brandt, Max Cahn, Dave Nadien, Morris Lefkowitz, Sam Shamper, Earl Hummel (vln); Ralph Hersch, Al Brown, Izadore Zir, George Brown (vla); Charles McCracken, Maurice Bialken, Harvey Shapiro, Morris Stonzek (cel).

The Things We Did Last Summer; *The Inch Worm; Yesterdays*; *What Is There to Say*; *Stormy Weather*; *Where or When*; *Have You Forgotten So Soon*; *Golden Earrings*; *Deep Purple*

Johnny Smith Plus the Trio

1960, Roost Vinyl LP 2243.
2001, Roulette CD 7243 5 31792 2 9, *The Sound of the Johnny Smith Guitar – Includes Johnny Smith Plus the Trio*.
2002, Mosaic CD MD8-216 *The Complete Roost Johnny Smith Small Group Sessions*.
Recorded 1960, New York. Personnel: Johnny Smith (g); Bob Pancoast (p); George Roumanis (b); Mousie Alexander (d).

I Got It Bad (and That Ain't Good); *Let's Fall in Love*; *I Can't Get Started*; *Some of These Days*; *You Took Advantage of Me*; *Over the Rainbow*; *Out Of Nowhere*; *Prelude to a Kiss*; *Un Poco Loco*; *"Hippo" the Sentimental "Hippy"*; *It's You or No One*

The Sound of the Johnny Smith Guitar

1961, Roost Vinyl LP 2246.
2001, Roulette CD 7243 5 31792 2 9, *The Sound of the Johnny Smith Guitar – Includes Johnny Smith Plus the Trio*.
2002, Mosaic CD MD8-216 *The Complete Roost Johnny Smith Small Group Sessions*.
Recorded 1961, New York. Personnel: Johnny Smith (g); Hank Jones (p); George Duvivier (b); Ed Shaughnessy (d).

Come Rain or Come Shine; *Gypsy in My Soul*; *Embraceable You*; *Misty*; *As Long as There's Music*; *'Round Midnight*; *This Can't Be Love*; *Blues Chorale*; *Prelude*

Don Gibson: Girls, Guitars and Gibson

1961, RCA Victor Vinyl LP LSP-2361.
1999, Eagle Records CD EAMCD090.
Recorded 1 and 2 May 1961, Nashville. Personnel: Don Gibson (voc); Johnny Smith (g); Hank Garland (g); Harold Bradley (g); Anita Kerr Singers (voc); Floyd Cramer (p); Bob Moore (b); Buddy Harman (d); Anita Kerr (arr).

Lonesome Road; *Born To Lose*; *White Silver Sands*; *No One Will Ever Know*; *Fireball Mail*; *Above and Beyond*; *Driftwood on the River*; *Camptown Races*; *Beautiful Dreamer*; *Cute Little Girls*; *The Last Letter*

Don Gibson: Some Favorites of Mine

1962, RCA Victor Vinyl LP LSP-2448.
Recorded 12 and 13 March 1962, Nashville. Personnel: Don Gibson (voc); Johnny Smith (g); Joe Tanner (g); Grady Martin (g); Harold Bradley (g); Velma Smith (g); Jordanaires (voc); Floyd Cramer (p); Bob Moore (b); Buddy Harman (d).

It Makes No Difference; *Settin' the Woods on Fire*; *Baby, We're Really in Love*; *We Live in Two Different Worlds* (Unreleased); *Blue Dream* (Unreleased); *Where Is Your Heart Tonight?* (Unreleased); *This Cold War with You* (Unreleased); *I'm Sorry for You, My Friend* (Unreleased); *I Love You So Much It Hurts* (Unreleased); *It's a Sin* (Unreleased); *How's the World Treating You?* (Unreleased); *May You Never Be Alone* (Unreleased)

Johnny Smith: The Man with the Blue Guitar

1962, Roost Vinyl LP 2248.
2002, Mosaic CD MD8-216 *The Complete Roost Johnny Smith Small Group Sessions*.
Recorded 1962, Colorado Springs. Personnel: Johnny Smith (g).

My Romance; *Little Girl Blue*; *Pavane*; *Prelude*; *Black Is the Color*; *Wait 'Til You See Her*; *The Maid with the Flaxen Hair*; *Shenandoah*; *Green Leaves of Summer*; *My Funny Valentine*; *Dancing in the Dark*; *Old Folks*; *I Loves You Porgy*

Don Gibson: I Wrote a Song

1963, RCA Victor Vinyl LP LSP-2702.
Recorded 11 and 12 February 1963, Nashville. Personnel: Don Gibson (voc); Johnny Smith (g); Joe Tanner (g); Harold Bradley (g); Jordanaires (voc); Floyd Cramer (p); Hargus Robbins (p); Junior Huskey (b); Buddy Harman (d); Anita Kerr (arr).

I Can't Stop Loving You; *Don't Tell Me Your Troubles*; *(I'd Be) a Legend in My Time*; *Blue, Blue Day*; *Oh, Such a Stranger*; *Love Has Come My Way*; *Oh, Lonesome Me*; *Lonesome Number One*; *Just One Time*; *After the Heartache*; *Give Myself a Party*; *Anything New Gets Old (Except My Love for You)*

The Art Van Damme Quintet with Johnny Smith on Guitar: A Perfect Match

1963, Columbia Vinyl LP CS 8813.
2000, Sony Collectables CD COL-CD-6633.
Recorded 1963, Chicago. Personnel: Art Van Damme (acc); Johnny Smith (g); Bob Wessberg (vb); Herb Knapp (b); Marty Clausen (d).

Bye Bye Blackbird; *In the Wee Small Hours of the Morning*; *Tickle-Toe*; *Gone with the Wind*; *Valse Hot*; *The Best Thing for You*; *Satan's Doll*; *Bluesy*; *Spring Is Here*; *Tangee*; *Poinciana Nicolette Avenue Breakdown*

The Guitar World of Johnny Smith

1963, Roost Vinyl LP 2254. Compilation of previous releases.
2002, Mosaic CD MD8-216 *The Complete Roost Johnny Smith Small Group Sessions*.

I'll Remember Clifford; *Black Is the Color*; *I Could Have Told You So*; *It Never Entered My Mind*; *The Maid with the Flaxen Hair*; *Prelude*; *Walk, Don't Run*; *Shenandoah*; *Pavanne*; *My Dear Little Sweetheart*; *Someone to Watch Over Me*; *Moonlight in Vermont*

Johnny Smith: Reminiscing

1964, Roost Vinyl LP 2259.
2002, Mosaic CD MD8-216 *The Complete Roost Johnny Smith Small Group Sessions*.
Recorded 1964, Manitou Springs. Personnel: Johnny Smith (g); Bob Greene (p); Bill Bastien (b); Derryl Goes (d).

Soon; *There'll Be Other Times*; *Satan's Doll*; *I'm Old Fashioned*; *I Remember You*; *Fitz*; *'Lil Darlin'*; *Time After Time*; *You Are Too Beautiful*; *Sweet and Lovely*

Johnny Smith

1967, Verve Vinyl LP V-8692.
1997, Verve CD 314 537 752-2.
Recorded 28-30 March 1967, New York. Personnel: Johnny Smith (g); Hank Jones (p); George Duvivier (b); Don Lamond (d).

Memories of You; *Manha De Carnaval (Morning of the Carnival)*; *Here's That Rainy Day*; *Yesterday*; *Spring Can Really Hang You Up the Most*; *The Shadow of Your Smile*; *Michelle*; *My Favorite Things*; *Golden Earrings*; *On a Clear Day You Can See Forever*; *The Girl from Ipanema*

The CD issue also includes previously released vinyl single: *Shenandoah*; *Land of the Velvet Hills*

1967, Verve Vinyl Single VK 10528.
1997, Verve CD 314 537 752-2 *Johnny Smith*.
Recorded 31 March 1967, New York. Personnel: Johnny Smith (g); Hank Jones (p); George Duvivier (b); Don Lamond (d); Jimmy Atkins (voc).

The CD issue also includes previously unreleased: *Shenandoah* (Breakdown); *Land of the Velvet Hills* (Instrumental Only)

The University of North Dakota Wind Ensemble

1967, Century Records vinyl LP 26893.
Recorded 1967. Personnel: Michael Polovitz (cond.). Guest Soloists: Johnny Smith (g); Larry Wiehe (tbn).

Exodus; *My Man's Gone Now*

Johnny Smith's Kaleidoscope

1968, Verve Vinyl LP V6-8737.
1994, Verve CD POCJ-2595.
Recorded 27-30 November 1967, New York. Personnel: Johnny Smith (g); Hank Jones (p); George Duvivier (b); Don Lamond (d).

Walk, Don't Run; *Old Folks*; *Days of Wine and Roses*; *The Girl with the Flaxen Hair*; *My Foolish Heart*; *By Myself*; *I'm Old Fashioned*; *Sweet Lorraine*; *Choro da Saudade*; *Dreamsville*

Johnny Smith: Phase II

1968, Verve Vinyl LP V6-8767.
Recorded 11-14 November 1968, New York. Personnel: Johnny Smith (g); Hank Jones (p); George Duvivier (b), Bob Bushnell, Joe Mack (fb); Derryl Goes (d).

Can't Take My Eyes Off of You; *Don't Sleep in the Subway*; *Shiny Stockings*; *Emily*; *This Guy's in Love With You*; *Light My Fire*; *Sunny*; *By the Time I Get to Phoenix*; *Exodus*; *Maybe September*; *Wave*

Bing Crosby: Bing Crosby Live, London Palladium 50th Anniversary Concert

1976, United Artists Records Double Vinyl LP 5C 138-98550/1.

Recorded 1976, London. Personnel: Bing Crosby (voc); Joe Bushkin (p); Johnny Smith (g); Lennie Bush (b); Jake Hanna (d).

Now You Has Jazz; Medley: *The Man That Got Away*; *Hallelujah*; The Crosby Medley: *I Surrender Dear*; *Swinging on a Star*; *Wrap Your Troubles in Dreams (and Dream Your Troubles Away)*; *True Love*; *Don't Fence Me In*; *Pennies from Heaven*; *Blue Hawaii*; *Sweet Leilani*; *Too-Ra-Loo-Ra-Loo-Ral*

That's an Irish Lullaby; *Just One More Chance*; *Them There Eyes*; *Moonlight Becomes You*; *You Are My Sunshine*; *I'll Be Seeing You*; *The White Cliffs of Dover*; *When the Lights Go on Again*; *Ac-cent-tchu-ate the Positive*; *Please*; *Baby Face*; *South of the Border*; *Galway Bay*; *Dinah*; *San Fernando Valley*; *I Found a Million Dollar Baby*; *San Antonio Rose*; *I'm an Old Cowhand from the Rio Grande*; *In a Little Spanish Town*; *Wait Till the Sun Shines*; *Nellie*; *It's Easy to Remember*; *Blue Skies*; *It's Been a Long, Long Time*; *Mississippi Mud*; *Ol' Man River*; *That's What Life Is All About*

Joe Bushkin: Joe Bushkin Celebrates 100 Years of Recorded Sound

1977, United Artists Vinyl LP UAG30142.
1995, Joe Bushkin CD DRG 8490 *The Road To Oslo*.
Recorded 1977, London and Oslo. Personnel: Joe Bushkin (p,voc, flh); Bing Crosby (voc); Johnny Smith (g); Milt Hinton (b); Jake Hanna (d); Jack Parnell (orch).

Now You Has Jazz; *Hallelujah*; *Bess, You Is My Woman/How Long Has This Been Going On/The Man I Love*; *Yesterday/Ain't Been the Same Since The Beatles*; *(There'll Be a) Hot Time in the Town of Berlin*; *Oh, Look at Me Now/I Love Piano*; *Phone Call to the Past*; *I've Grown Accustomed to Her Face*; *Someday You'll Be Sorry*; *Sunday of the Shepherdess*; *Sail Away From Norway*

Lee Konitz: From Newport To Nice

1992, Philology CD W65-2.
Recorded 1955 *The Tonight Show* New York. Personnel: Lee Konitz (as); Johnny Smith (g); Frank Carroll (b); Don Lamond (d).

My Melancholy Baby

Johnny Smith/George Van Eps: Legends: Solo Guitar Performances

1994, Concord Jazz CD CCD-4616.
Recorded 23-25 February 1976, Colorado Springs. Personnel: Johnny Smith (g).

This CD contains individual solo performances by Johnny Smith and George Van Eps. Only those by the former are listed below.

I'm Old Fashioned; *Macho's Lullaby*; *'Round Midnight*; *Wally's Waltz*; *Black, Black, Black*; *Golden Earrings*; *Romance De Los Pinos*; *Norteña*; *Maid with the Flaxen Hair*; *Waltz*; *The Old Castle*; *Sevilla*

Johnny Smith: The Complete Roost Johnny Smith Small Group Sessions

2002, Mosaic CD MD8-216.
This box set of eight CDs contains the following Roost vinyl LP issues listed above:

LP 410 *Johnny Smith Quintet: Jazz at NBC*; LP 413 *Johnny Smith Quintet Featuring Stan Getz*; LP 421 *In a Mellow Mood*; LP 424 *In a Sentimental Mood*; LP 2201 *Johnny Smith Plays Jimmy Van Heusen*; LP 2203 *The Johnny Smith Quartet*; LP 2211 *Moonlight in Vermont*; LP 2215 *Moods*; LP 2216 *The New Johnny Smith Quartet*; LP 2223 *The Johnny Smith Foursome*; LP 2228 *The Johnny Smith Foursome Volume II*; LP 2231 *Flower Drum Song*; LP 2233 *Easy Listening*; LP 2238 *Designed for You*; LP 2243 *Johnny Smith Plus the Trio*; LP 2246 *The Sound of the Johnny Smith Guitar*; LP 2248 *The Man with the Blue Guitar*; LP 2259 *Reminiscing*

The following recordings in this collection were not previously issued on vinyl:

Swinging Shepherd Blues/These Foolish Things
Recorded 1958. Personnel: Johnny Smith (g); Bob Pancoast (p); George Roumanis (b); Mousie Alexander (d).

Song for Jimmy Atkins (mx 60075-5)/**Vilia** (mx 60059-10)
Recorded 1959. Personnel: Johnny Smith (g); George Roumanis (b); Mousie Alexander (d).

Bibliography and Resources

Ademy, J. 1964. 'Whole Notes and Half Notes' in *The Greensboro Record*. pA-10. 11 June. (North Carolina).

Alkyer, F. 2004a. 'Johnny Comes Home' in *Down Beat*. p24. November.

_____ 2004b. 'Guild Relaunches Johnny Smith Model' in *Music INC.* p26. October.

Ardoin, J. (ed.). 1999. *The Philadelphia Orchestra: A Century of Music*. (Philadelphia: Temple University Press).

Baker, M. 1955. *Mickey Baker's Complete Course in Jazz Guitar: A Modern Method in How-to-Play Jazz and Hot Guitar – Book 1*. (Carlstadt: Lewis Music Publishing).

_____ 1959. *Mickey Baker's Complete Course in Jazz Guitar: A Modern Method in How-to-Play Jazz and Hot Guitar – Book 2*. (Carlstadt: Lewis Music Publishing).

Balliett, W. 1986. 'Jazz' in *The New Yorker.* p75. 13 January. (New York).

Barrett, M. 1970. 'Tribute to Widely Known Area Composer Set' in *The Rocky Mountain News*. p57. 19 January. (Colorado).

Barron, M. 1950. 'Says Musicians at Best Playing for Live Audience' in *The Springfield Sunday Republican*. p4D. 19 November. (Massachusetts).

_____ 1974. 'A Long Way from 'Dime a Dance' Days' in *The Rocky Mountain News*. pp153-54. 17 August. (Colorado).

Bassoir, J. 2005. *Space Patrol: Missions of Daring in the Name of Early Television*. (Jefferson: McFarland and Company).

Bell, T. 1999. 'Alice Award' in *The Colorado Springs Gazette Telegraph*. p-unknown. 19 February. (Colorado).

Benson, E. 1995. 'Q&A: Carl Jefferson, President of Concord Records' in *Just Jazz Guitar.* pp60-61. May.

Berenson, S. 1954. 'Sparkling Shows for Blinstrubs and Latin Quarter' in *The Boston Daily Record*. p45. 10 May. (Massachusetts).

Berger, E. 1993. *Bassically Speaking: An Oral History of George Duvivier.* (London: Scarecrow Press).

Boukas, R. 1999. 'Johnny Smith Tribute Concert: A Player's Account' in *Just Jazz Guitar.* pp8-11. August.

Buchanan, B. 1961a. 'A Candid Report' in *The Boston Daily Record*. p42. 14 July. (Massachusetts).

_____ 1961b. 'Gleason in One-Man-Show' in *The Boston Daily Record*. p45. 3 February. (Massachusetts).

Brooks, E. 1954. 'Kenton Concert Acoustics Fail – Sounds Bounced Around in Huge Field House' in *The Times – Picayune*. p24. 21 November. (Louisiana).

Campbell, B. 2001. 'Guitar Legend Johnny Smith: Alive and Well in Colorado Springs' in *Colorado Springs Independent*. 15 March.

Campbell, R. 1976. *The Golden Years of Broadcasting: A Celebration of the First 50 Years of Radio and TV on NBC*. (New York: Charles Scribner's Sons).

Carlton, J. 2009. *Conversations with Great Jazz and Studio Guitarists*. (Pacific: Mel Bay Publications).

Chapman, C. 2001. 'Johnny Smith – (September 1996)' in *Interviews with the Jazz Greats... and more*. pp61-63 (Pacific: Mel Bay).

_____ 2002. 'Johnny Smith Goes Full Circle' in *Just Jazz Guitar.* May.

Clarke, G. 1955. 'Around Boston – Les Paul, Mary Ford Set for Ed Sullivan TV Show' in *The Boston Daily Record*. p24. 2 February. (Massachusetts).

Clayton, B. 1986. *Buck Clayton's Jazz World*. (Oxford: Bayou Press).

Cochran, B. and S. Van Hecke. 2003. *Three Steps to Heaven: The Eddie Cochran Story*. (Milwaukee: Hal Leonard).

Cook. H. 1958. 'Distributor News' in *The Billboard*. p12. 13 October.

Corwin, A. 2010. *Circling Round Time*. (Bloomington: Xlibris Corporation).

Crosby, J. 1950. 'NBC Scores With "Big Show" Proving Radio Isn't Dead' in *The Oakland Tribune*. 10 November. (California).

Crow, B. 1992. *From Birdland to Broadway: Scenes from a Jazz Life*. (Oxford: Oxford University Press).

Crozier. N. 1972a. 'Stage Band Festival Rocks to Heavy Beat' in *The Mobile Register*. p6-A. 9 June. (Alabama).

_____ 1972b. 'Houston Band Chosen as Best in Country' in *The Mobile Register*. p4-C. 11 June. (Alabama).

Dance, S. 1967. 'George Benson: Guitar in the Ascendency' in *Down Beat*. pp20-22. 29 June.

Dannen, F. 1990. *Hit Men: Power Brokers and Fast Money inside the Music Business*. (New York: Times Books).

Demuth, D. 2004. 'Guitarist Johnny Smith talks of Illustrious Career' in *Colorado Correspondent*. pp9-11. Winter.

Dietsche, R. 2005. *Jumptown: The Golden Years of Portland Jazz, 1942-1957*. (Oregon: Oregon State University Press).

DiJulio, M. 1971. *A Sacred Mass for Mixed Voices (S.S.A.T.B.) and Electric Guitar (or Piano)*. Music Score. (Miami: University of Miami Music Publications).

Doll, M. 1972. 'Di Julio Enjoys 'Putting it Together'' in *The Denver Post*. p16. 28 May. (Colorado).

Duchossoir. A. 1994. *Gibson Electrics: The Classics Years – An Illustrated History from the Mid-'30s to the Mid-'60s*. (Milwaukee: Hal Leonard).

Eastman, L. 1967. 'Johnny Smith' in *Guitar Player*. pp12 and 34-35. October.

Feather, L. & I. Gitler. 1999. *The Biographical Encyclopedia of Jazz*. (Oxford: Oxford University Press).

Fini, F. and L. Rigazio. 1992. *The Oscar Peterson Discography*. (Imola: Fini Editions).

Finucane, B. 1947. 'Along the Streets of Chester' in *The Chester (P.A.) Times*. p10. 3 September. (Pennsylvania).

Fisch, J. and L. Fred. 1996. *Epiphone: The House of Stathopoulo*. (New York: Amsco Publications).

Fishel, J. 1974. 'Campus: Jazz Profs At Chicago Convention' in *The Billboard*. p20. 14 December.

Forster, P. 2004. 'Impressions of the London Palladium Concerts - 1977' in *Bing Magazine*. p41. No.138.

Giffin, G. 1974. 'Red Rocks Concert: Premiere Right for Goodman' in *The Denver Post*. p18. 19 August. (Colorado).

Goldblatt, B. 1977. *Newport Jazz Festival: The Illustrated History*. (New York: Dial Press).

Grace, R. 2003. ''Day in Court', 'Winchell-Mahoney Time,' Du Mont Shows: Not to Be Seen Again' in *Metropolitan News-Enterprise*. p15. 29 May.

Grudens, R. 1999. *Jukebox Saturday Night: More Memories of the Big Band Era and Beyond*. (South Dakota: Pine Hill Press).

Gruhn, G. and W. Carter. 2008. 'Classic Instruments: Gibson Johnny Smith' in *Vintage Guitar Magazine*. January.

Grundy, K. 1987. 'Heights Does Jazz Proud' in *The Plain Dealer*. p5-B. 2 April. (Ohio).

Hancock, H. 1965. 'Herbie Hancock: Watermelon Man' in *Down Beat*. 21 October.

Hanna, P. 1969. 'Guitarists Flock to Learn from Johnny Smith: Modest Man is a Jazz Master' in *The Rocky Mountain News Festival*. pp1 and 3. 27 July. (Colorado).

Hardy, J. 1967. Record Review in *Down Beat*. p32. 10 August.

Harris, S. 2003. *The Kenton Kronicles: A Biography of Modern America's Man of Music, Stan Kenton*. (Pasadena: Dynaflow Publications).

Hartley, J. and J. Wölfer. 1999. *Johnny Richards: The Definitive Bio-Discography*. (Lake Geneva: Balboa

Books).
Hausch, M. 1970. 'Johnny Smith in the City with Guitar' in *The Colorado Springs Gazette Telegraph*. p21-D. 25 July. (Colorado).
Hembree, G. 2007. *Gibson Guitars: Ted McCarty's Golden Era 1948-1966*. (Milwaukee: Hal Leonard).
Hevesi, D. 2012. 'Mort Lindsey, 89, Pianist and Versatile Bandleader' in *The New York Times*. p-unknown. 11 May. (New York).
Hopkins, G. and B. Moore. 1999. *Ampeg: The Story behind the Sound*. (Milwaukee: Hal Leonard).
Ingram, A. 1995. 'Where are they now? - Lou Mecca' in *Just Jazz Guitar*. pp51-2. May.
_____ and E. Benson. 1995a. 'A Conversation with Johnny Smith' in *Just Jazz Guitar*. pp13-15. May.
_____ 1995b. 'Where are they now? - Sal Salvador' in *Just Jazz Guitar*. pp53-55. May.
Iwamoto, S. Unknown. *Hank Jones: A Discography*. (Tokyo: Published privately).
Johnston, R. and J. Gress (eds.). 2001. *How to Play Guitar: The Basics & Beyond: Chords, Scales, Tunes & Tips*. (San Francisco: Backbeat Books).
Jones, M. 2000. *Jazz Talking: Profiles, Interviews, and Other Riffs on Jazz Musicians*. (Cambridge: Da Capo Press).
Jordan, S. 1981. 'Wet Days, Lean Years Led to Job Filling Hungry Huskers' in *The Sunday World Herald*. p7-B. 19 July. (Nebraska).
Kanes, C. 2010. 'Maine History Online: South Portland's Wartime Shipbuilding'. Accessed online 7 February 2010.
<http://www.mainememory.net/sitebuilder/site/856/page/1266/display?use_mmn=>.
Keillor, G. 1984. 'A Reporter at Large: Country Golf' in *The New Yorker*. p38. 30 July. (New York).
Kelly, B. and R. Jain. 1959. 'A Man with a Guitar: Meet Johnny Smith, a Jazz Recording Artist of the New School; a Happy Father; and a Man who has Decided to Live in Colorado' in the *The Denver Post Empire*. pp10-11. 12 July. (Colorado).
Kernodle, T. 2004. *Soul on Soul: The Life and Music of Mary Lou Williams*. (Boston: Northeastern University Press).
Kienzle, R. 2003. *Southwest Shuffle: Pioneers of Honky-Tonk, Western Swing and Country Jazz*. (New York: Routledge).
Kilday, M. 1982a. 'Mobile Jazz Festival' in *The Mobile Register*. p1-D. 7 May. (Alabama).
_____ 1982b. 'Saenger Comes Alive with Best Red-Hot Jazz' in *The Mobile Register*. p6-C. 14 May. (Alabama).
_____ 1982c. 'Mobile Jazz Festival – A Most Note-Worthy Hit' in *The Mobile Register*. p2-B. 15 May. (Alabama).
_____ 1983a. 'Jazz Fest Smoooooth' in *The Mobile Register*. p1-B. 14 May. (Alabama).
_____ 1983b. 'Saturday Night 'Live' at Jazz Festival Finale' in *The Mobile Register*. p8-A. 15 May. (Alabama).
Kilgallen, D. 1956a. 'The Voice of Broadway: Miss Midnight's Notebook' in *The Greensboro Record*. pA-14. 1 February. (North Carolina).
_____ 1956b. Untitled in *The Palm Beach Daily News*. p4. 26 February. (California).
_____ 1960. 'The Voice of Broadway' in *The Greensboro Record*. pA-12. 24 May. (North Carolina).
Kinigstein, S. 2012. 'The Big Cat Turns 90: A Retrospective of the Career of Mundell Lowe' in *Just Jazz Guitar*. pp95-100. November.
Larson, H. 1954. 'Grand Larsony' in *The Oregonian*. p6-M. 21 September. (Oregon).
Leavitt, W. 1966. *A Modern Method for Guitar: Volume One*. (Boston: Berklee Press).
_____ 1968a. *A Modern Method for Guitar: Volume Two*. (Boston: Berklee Press).
_____ 1968b. *Classical Studies for Pick-Style Guitar*. (Boston: Berklee Press).
_____ 1971. *A Modern Method for Guitar: Volume Three*. (Boston: Berklee Press).
Leonard, W. 1955. 'On the Town' in *The Chicago Daily Tribune*. pJ4. (Illinois).
_____ 1956. 'On the Town' in *The Chicago Daily Tribune*. pE8. (Illinois).
Lester, J. 1994. *Too Marvelous for Words: The Life and Genius of Art Tatum*. (New York: Oxford University

Press).
Levinson, P. 2001. *September in the Rain: The Life of Nelson Riddle*. (New York: Billboard Books).
Lewis, D. 2008. 'Birmingham Iron and Steel Companies'. Accessed online 9 September 2011. <http://www.encyclopediaofalabama.org/face/Article.jsp?id=h-1597>.
Local 802 American Federation of Musicians. 1947. *Directory*. (New York: Self-published).
_____ 1948. *Directory*. (New York: Self-published).
_____ 1949. *Directory*. (New York: Self-published).
_____ 1950. *Directory*. (New York: Self-published).
_____ 1952. *Directory*. (New York: Self-published).
_____ 1957. *Directory*. (New York: Self-published).
Loeb Cone. T. 1954. 'Kenton Heads Jazz Stars in Oakland Arena Concert' in *The Oakland Tribune*. pE-13. 20 September. (California).
Lord, T. 1999a. *The Jazz Discography: Volume 21*. (Redwood: Cadence Jazz Books).
_____ 1999b. *The Jazz Discography: Volume 23*. (Redwood: Cadence Jazz Books).
Lundstrom, H. 1966. 'Our Man from the Tonight Show' in *The Deseret News*. pA15. 23 August. (Utah).
MacCluskey, T. 1972. 'Top Musicians Sparkle at Broadmoor: Sonic Waves Vibrate from Jazz Party' in *The Rocky Mountain News*. p66. 5 September. (Colorado).
MacFarlane, M. 2001. *Bing Crosby: Day by Day*. (Lanham: Scarecrow Press).
Mack, J. 1955. 'Off the Records' in *The Boston Herald*. 2 February. p25. (Massachusetts).
Magee, J. 2005. *The Uncrowned King of Swing: Fletcher Henderson and Big Band Jazz*. (New York: Oxford University Press).
Maher, J. 1962. 'Suddenly It's Summer Jazz Time' in *The Billboard*. p5. 2 June.
Martino, P. and B. Milkowski. 2011. *Here and Now! The Autobiography of Pat Martino*. (Milwaukee: Backbeat Books).
Marx, W. 2009. *Gibson Amplifiers 1933-2008: 75 Years of the Gold Tone*. (Minneapolis: Blue Book Publications).
McClellan, J. and D. Bratic. 2004a. *Chet Atkins in Three Dimensions: 50 Years of Legendary Guitar – Volume One*. (Pacific: Mel Bay Publications).
_____ 2004b. *Chet Atkins in Three Dimensions: 50 Years of Legendary Guitar – Volume Two*. (Pacific: Mel Bay Publications).
Mecca, L. 1995a. 'An Encounter with John D'Angelico' in *Just Jazz Guitar*. p56. May.
_____ 1995b. 'Who's Johnny Smith?' in *Just Jazz Guitar*. p19. May.
Mercer, C. 1958. 'Godfred [*sic*] Hopes to Rescue Jazz, from 'Eggheads'' in *The State Times*. p14-A. 25 February. (Louisiana).
Moore, D. 1969. 'Guitarists Have Their Day at Johnny's Class' in *The Colorado Springs Gazette Telegraph*. p1-B. 22 July.
Morrison, B. 1977. 'Pearle of a Home-Town Singer will Perform in Central City' in *The Denver Post Roundup*. p8. 24 July. (Colorado).
Moust, H. 1995. *The Guild Guitar Book: The Company and the Instruments 1952-1977*. (Milwaukee: Hal Leonard).
Murphy, C. 2008. *New England Country & Western Music: Self-Reliance, Community Expression, and Regional Resistance on the New England Frontier*. Unpublished PhD dissertation. (Rhode Island: Brown University).
Owen, T. 1995. 'The Visit' in *Just Jazz Guitar*. p20. May.
_____ and I. Isaacs. 1976a. 'Johnny Smith: King of Good Taste' in *Guitar*. p21. August.
_____ 1976b. 'Johnny Smith: King of Good Taste – Part 2' in *Guitar*. pp12-13. September.
Piburn, B. 2001. 'There's No Substitution' in *Fingerstyle Guitar*. pp22-26. November-December.
Polic, E. 1989. *The Glenn Miller Army Air Force Band: Sustineo Alas/I Sustain the Wings: Volume One*. (Metuchen: Scarecrow Press).

Porter, L. 2000. *John Coltrane: His Life and Music*. (Michigan: University of Michigan Press).
Ratliff, B. 1999. 'Jazz Review; Paying Homage to a Guitar Idol Who Sees No Cause' in *The New York Times*. 17 June.
Reed, B. 2003. 'The Forgotten Master: Jazz Guitarist Johnny Smith Passed up the Spotlight' in *The Gazette* (Colorado Springs). 12 January.
Reig, T. and E. Berger. 1990. *Reminiscing in Tempo: The Life and Times of a Jazz Hustler*. (Lanham: Scarecrow Press).
Rohde, A. 2006. 'Portsmouth's Rock Roots' in *The Wire*. 18 January.
Rolontz, B. 1954. '1-Nighter Packages Find Road's Rocky' in *The Billboard*. p16. 13 November.
_____ 1958a. 'Music As Written' in *The Billboard*. p11. 20 October.
_____ 1958b. 'Music As Written' in *The Billboard*. p8. 22 December.
_____ 1959. 'Devine [*sic*] Sarah Sparkles at Birdland' in *The Billboard*. p11. 18 May.
Ruggere, S. 1980. 'Two Orchestral Works for Electric Guitar' in *Guitar Player*. p50-58. September.
Russell, T. 2004. *Country Music Records: A Discography, 1921-1942*. (New York: Oxford University Press).
Russell Connor, D. 1988. *Benny Goodman: Listen to his Legacy*. (Metuchen: Scarecrow Press).
_____ and W. Wickes. 1969. *Benny Goodman on the Record: A Bio-discography of Benny Goodman*. (New Rochelle: Arlington House).
Sampson, P. 1956. 'Basie's Jazz Rhythms Rock National' in *The Washington Post*. p11. 27 February. (District of Columbia).
Sargent, W. 1956. 'Popular Records: Swing High, Swing Low' in *The New Yorker*. pp84-85. 28 April. (New York).
Saunders, W. 1978. ''Moonlight in Vermont' Just One More Time?' in *The Rocky Mountain News*. p66. 3 August. (Colorado).
Schmidt, P. 1998. *Acquired of the Angels: The Lives and Works of Master Guitar Makers John D'Angelico and James L. D'Aquisto*. (Lanham: Scarecrow Press).
Schönberg, A. 1924. *Serenade* Op. 24. Music Score. (Copenhagen: Wilhelm Hansen).
Schonberg, H. 1955. 'Music: Jazz Comes of Age in Newport' in *The New York Times*. p17. 18 July 1955. (New York).
Schroeter, J. 2001. 'Raising the Bar' in *Fingerstyle Guitar*. p24. November-December.
Scott, J. 1992. *The Guitars of the Fred Gretsch Company*. (Fullerton: Centerstream Publishing).
Shearer, J. 2002. *Jazz Basics: A Brief Overview with Historical Documents and Recordings*. (Dubuque: Kendall/Hunt Publishing).
Shere, C. 1977. 'Bing Still Sings Nice, Easy' in *The Oakland Tribune*. p33. 17 August. (California).
Siders, H. 1968. Record Review in *Down Beat*. pp29-30. 27 June.
Silverman, S. 1998. *Johnny Smith: Guitar Solos*. (Milwaukee: Hal Leonard).
Singular, S. 1984. Untitled in *The Denver Post Magazine*. pp20-22. 19 February. (Colorado).
Smith, J. 1946a. *Guitar Interpretations: Volume 1*. ed. by H. Volpe. (New York: Charles Colin).
_____ 1946b. *Guitar Interpretations: Volume 2*. ed. by H. Volpe. (New York: Charles Colin).
_____ 1956. *Johnny Smith: Aids to Technique for Guitar*. (New York: Charles Colin).
_____ 1969a. 'Try It This Way!: Once in a While' in *Guitar Player*. pp30-31. April.
_____ 1969b. 'Try It This Way!: I'm in the Mood for Love' in *Guitar Player*. pp32-33. June.
_____ 1969c. 'Try It This Way!: Don't Blame Me' in *Guitar Player*. pp28-29. August.
_____ 1969d. 'Try It This Way!: Blue Moon' in *Guitar Player*. pp32-33. October.
_____ 1969e. 'Try It This Way!: Have Yourself a Merry Little Christmas' in *Guitar Player*. pp32-33. December.
_____ 1970a. 'Try It This Way!: Laura' in *Guitar Player*. pp26-7. February.
_____ 1970b. 'Try It This Way!: Don't Blame Me' in *Guitar Player*. pp30-31. April.
_____ 1970c. 'Try It This Way!: Over the Rainbow' in *Guitar Player*. pp28-29. June.
_____ 1970d. 'Try It This Way!: Time on my Hands' in *Guitar Player*. pp26-27. August.

_____ 1970e. 'Try It This Way!: For All We Know' in *Guitar Player*. pp34-35. October.
_____ 1970f. 'Try It This Way!: Taking a Chance on Love' in *Guitar Player*. pp32-33. December.
_____ 1971a. 'Try It This Way!: Try A Little Tenderness' in *Guitar Player*. p31. April.
_____ 1971b. 'Try It This Way!: Whispering' in *Guitar Player*. p31. June.
_____ 1971c. *Mel Bay Presents the Johnny Smith Approach to Guitar: Part One*. (Pacific: Mel Bay Publications).
_____ 1971d. *Mel Bay Presents the Johnny Smith Approach to Guitar: Part* Two. (Pacific: Mel Bay Publications).
_____ 1980. *Mel Bay's Complete Johnny Smith Approach to Guitar*. (Pacific: Mel Bay Publications).
_____ 1984. 'The Art of String & Tuning' in *Guitar Player*. pp14-26. July.
_____ 2001. 'Stringing & Tuning' in *How to Play Guitar: The Basics & Beyond*. R. Johnston and J. Gress (eds.). pp7-12. Originally published in *Guitar Player* July 1984. pp14-26. (San Francisco: Backbeat Books).
Snitzler, L. 1984. 'Johnny Smith plays Schönberg' in *Guitar Review*. No.57, pp24-29. Spring.
Sparke, M. 2010. *Stan Kenton: This is an Orchestra!*. (Denton: University of North Texas Press).
Stewart, J. 1983. 'Invitational to Feature Jazz Greats' in *The Colorado Sun*. p5-A. 20 September. (Colorado).
Talbot, B. 2004. *Tom Talbert - His Life and Times: Voices from a Vanished World of Jazz*. (Lanham: Scarecrow Press).
Tatum, G. 1985. 'Jazz Festival Goes Outdoors and All Day' in *The Mobile Register*. p2-G. 18 August. (Alabama).
Taubman, H. 1954a. 'Newport Rocked By Jazz Festival' in *The New York Times*. 19 July. (New York).
_____ 1954b. 'Newport Festival: Jazz Goes Respectable In Resort Town' in *The New York Times*. 25 July. (New York).
Vacca, R. 2012. *The Boston Jazz Chronicles: Faces, Places, and Nightlife 1937-1962*. (Belmont: Troy Street Publishing).
Vail, K. 1996a. *Bird's Diary: The Life of Charlie Parker 1945-1955*. (Chessington: Castle Communications).
______ 1996b. *Lady Day's Diary: The Life of Billie Holiday 1937-1959*. (Chessington: Castle Communications).
Watrous, P. 1998. 'Dick Gibson, Jazz Producer And Fan, 72' in *The New York Times*. 20 June. (New York).
Watt, D. 1954. 'Tables for Two: A Little Night Music' in *The New Yorker*. pp90-91. 6 February. (New York).
Wein, G. and N. Chinen. 2004. *Myself Among Others: A Life in Music*. (Cambridge: Da Capo Press).
Wolters, L. 1954. 'Where to Dial Today' in *The Chicago Tribune*. pA-10. 21 October. (Illinois).
Yelin. R. 1982a. 'Johnny Smith: A Rare Interview with a Jazz Legend' in *Guitar Player*. pp36-50. January.
_____ 1982b. 'Gibson's Johnny Smith Guitar' in *Guitar Player*. p38. January.
_____ 1995. 'My Story' in *Just Jazz Guitar*. pp70-74. May.

Anonymous Newspaper and Magazine Articles

The Atchison Daily Globe. 16 September 1954. (Kansas).
The Augusta Chronicle. 10 November 1954. (Georgia).
The Barrier Miner. 19 July 1946. (New South Wales, Australia).
The Billboard. 14 March 1942, 4 April 1942, 25 April 1942, 14 April 1951, 22 March 1952, 22 November 1952, 26 September 1953, 21 November 1953, 5 June 1954, 24 July 1954, 31 July 1954, 21 August 1954, 28 August 1954, 11 September 1954, 9 October 1954, 30 October 1954, 30 October 1954, 8 January 1955, 19 February 1955, 23 April 1955, 3 September 1955, 31 December 1955, 28 January 1956, 4 February 1956, 18 February 1956, 25 February 1956, 15 September 1956, 6 April 1957, 27 April 1957, 8 December 1958, 4 May 1959, 31 August 1959, 7 December 1959, 7 March 1960, 21 March 1960, 29 August 1960, 23 January 1961, 17 April 1961, 8 May 1961, 18 December 1961, 1 September 1962, 25 May 1963, 24 June 1967, 25 November 1967, 23 March 1968, 3 May 1969, 17 April 1971, 3 July 1971, 13 September 1975.

The Boston Daily Record. 27 June 1955, 30 January 1956. (Massachusetts).

The Boston Herald Traveler. 28 June 1968. (Massachusetts).

The Boston Sunday Herald Traveler. 2 November 1969. (Massachusetts).

The Boston Traveler. 6 October 1954. (Massachusetts).

The Brooklyn Eagle. 24 October 1954. (New York).

The Charleston Daily Mail. 5 February 1956. (South Carolina).

The Cheyenne Edition. 20 July 1984. (Colorado).

The Chicago Daily Tribune. 5 February 1956. (Illinois).

The Cleveland Plain Dealer. 9 June 1955, 12 June 1955, 20 June 1955, 22 June 1955, 23 June 1955, 24 June 1955, 25 June 1955, 16 October 1955, 23 October 1955, 19 February 1956, 22 February 1956, 15 May 1956, 19 May 1956, 3 July 1957, 7 July 1957. (Ohio).

The Colorado Springs Gazette Telegraph. 17 July 1960, 11 September 1960, 16 September 1960, 22 November 1960, 14 March 1961, 29 March 1961, 3 October 1962, 16 January 1963, 19 January 1963, 20 September 1963, 16 April 1966, 30 April 1966, 3 May 1966, 8 May 1966, 20 September 1966, 20 November 1966, 3 December 1966, 10 December 1966, 29 April 1967, 23 May 1967, 9 October 1967, 14 October 1967, 14 November 1967, 17 June 1968, 25 May 1968, 11 December 1968, 3 May 1969, 10 May 1969, 13 May 1969, 15 February 1970, 2 August 1970, 24 October 1970, 31 October 1970, 16 May 1971, 16 September 1971, 2 October 1971, 12 July 1972, 5 November 1972, 6 September 1975, 27 December 1975, 22 February 1976, 27 November 1977. (Colorado).

The Coshocton, Ohio, Tribune. 11 February 1956. (Ohio).

The Corona Daily Independent. 4 March 1977. (California).

The Dallas Morning News. 19 September 1959, 6 February 1983. (Texas).

The Denver Post. 13 August 1974. (Colorado).

The Deseret News. 16 April 1989.

Down Beat. 31 December 1952, 26 August 1953, 30 December 1953, 1 June 1967, 29 June 1967.

The Fitchburg Sentinel. 21, 22 and 23 October 1941. (Massachusetts).

Fretted Instrument News. November- December 1942.

The Gazette, Montreal. 3 November 1954. (Montreal, Canada).

The Grapevine – A Bing Crosby Newsletter. September 1991.

The Greeley Tribune. 1 December 1964, 22 May 1969, 28 July 1970, 2 December 1970, 4 December 1970, 27 May 1971, 20 April 1971, 11 November 1974, 16 July 1977. (Colorado).

Guitar Player. October 1969, March 1970, September 1970, February 1971, June 1971, August 1971.

The Hartford Courant. 19 September 1954. (Connecticut).

The Long Island Star-Journal. 27 January 1959. (New York).

Metronome. February 1947, February 1952, February 1953, April 1953, May 1953, June 1953, August 1953, February 1954, February 1955, January 1956, January 1957, June 1958.

The Mobile Register. 6 June 1972, 10 June 1972, 3 July 1983, 14 September 1985. (Alabama).

The Morning Herald, Uniontown. 28 September 1954. (Pennsylvania).

The Morning Star. 5 August 1962. (Michigan).

The New Yorker. 10 November 1951, 24 November 1951, 8 December 1951, 22 December 1951, 5 January 1952, 25 April 1953, 2 May 1953, 9 May 1953, 16 May 1953, 5 September 1953, 12 September 1953, 19 September 1953, 26 September 1953, 3 October 1953, 5 December 1953, 12 December 1953, 19 December 1953, 26 December 1953, 2 January 1954, 9 January 1954, 16 January 1954, 23 January 1954, 30 January 1954, 6 February 1954, 13 February 1954, 20 February 1954, 20 March 1954, 27 March 1954, 3 April 1954, 10 April 1954, 31 July 1954, 7 August 1954, 14 August 1954, 21 August 1954, 28 August 1954, 27 November 1954, 4 December 1954, 11 December 1954, 18 December 1954, 25 December 1954, 1 January 1955, 8 January 1955, 15 January 1955, 22 January 1955, 29 January 1955, 26 March 1955, 2 April 1955, 16 April 1955, 23 April 1955, 9 July 1955, 16 July 1955, 23 July 1955, 13 August 1955, 20 August 1955, 27

August 1955, 5 November 1955, 12 November 1955, 19 November 1955, 26 November 1955, 3 December 1955, 10 December 1955, 17 December 1955, 24 December 1955, 31 December 1955, 7 January 1956, 14 January 1956, 21 January 1956, 28 January 1956, 28 January 1956, 4 February 1956, 24 March 1956, 31 March 1956, 7 April 1956, 14 April 1956, 26 May 1956, 16 June 1956, 23 June 1956, 23 June 1956, 30 June 1956, 30 June 1956, 7 July 1956, 7 July 1956, 14 July 1956, 21 July 1956, 8 September 1956, 15 September 1956, 22 September 1956, 27 October 1956, 19 January 1957, 26 January 1957, 2 February 1957, 9 February 1957, 2 March 1957, 16 March 1957, 23 March 1957, 30 March 1957, 27 July 1957, 3 August 1957, 10 August 1957, 21 September 1957, 28 September 1957, 5 October 1957, 12 October 1957, 16 November 1957, 23 November 1957, 30 November 1957, 25 January 1958, 1 February 1958, 8 February 1958, 17 May 1958, 24 May 1958, 31 May 1958, 7 June 1958, 19 July 1958, 30 August 1958, 8 November 1958, 15 November 1958, 24 January 1959, 25 April 1959, 2 May 1959, 9 May 1959, 16 May 1959, 24 October 1959, 31 October 1959, 7 November 1959, 14 November 1959, 7 May 1960, 14 May 1960, 21 May 1960, 28 May 1960, 11 October 1982, 14 June 1999. (New York).

The New York Times. 24 April 1953, 11 October 1954, 5 February 1956. (New York).

The Oakland Tribune. 15 September 1954, 23 February 1977. (California).

The Omaha World Herald. 21 October 1974. (Nebraska).

Palm Beach Daily News. 26 February 1956. (California).

Park City Daily News. 10 October 1954. (Kentucky).

Playback: Monthly Newspaper of KOA & KOAA TV. December 1966. (Colorado).

The Portsmouth New Hampshire Herald. 22, 23, 24 and 25 October 1941. (New Hampshire).

The Post-Standard. 1 November 1954. (New York).

The Racine Journal-Times. 14 July 1954. (Wisconsin).

Reading Eagle. 16 December 1959. (Pennsylvania).

Register-Republic. 17 February 1956. (Wisconsin).

The Register Star News. 7 February 1956. (Ohio).

The Richmond Times-Dispatch. 31 October 1954. (Virginia).

The Rockford Morning Star. 29 January 1956. (Illinois).

The Rocky Mount Evening Telegram. 7 November 1954. (North Carolina).

The San Diego Union. 17 September 1954, 3 June 1956. (California).

The Seattle Daily Times. 23 September 1954. (Washington).

The Seattle Times. 6 May 1966. (Washington).

The Springfield Daily Republican. 4 December 1941. (Massachusetts).

The Springfield Union. 16 May 1958. (Massachusetts).

The Sunday World-Herald. 26 September 1954. (Nebraska).

The Syracuse Post Standard. 22 January 1956. (New York).

The Times-Picayune. 7 November 1954, 20 November 1954. (Louisiana).

The Trenton Evening Times. 12 October 1954. (New Jersey).

The Trenton Sunday Times-Advertiser. 10 July 1955. (New Jersey).

The Wichita Eagle and Beacon Magazine. 15 December 1968. (Kansas).

The World-Herald. 19 September 1954. (Nebraska).

CONCERT AND TOUR PROGRAMS

1980 Coupe Mondiale World Accordion Championships and International Orchestra Festival: August 27th - 30th 1980, Auckland Town Hall and Hotel Intercontinental New Zealand. New Zealand Accordion Association.

Birdland Stars of '56. 1956.

Community Arts Symphony, Englewood, Colorado. 10 May 1968.
Denver Symphony Orchestra Program Books in the Colorado Symphony Library.
Mobile Jazz Festival. 1982, 1983 and 1984.
Newport Jazz Festival. 1954 and 1955.
Stan Kenton Presents a Festival of Modern American Jazz. 1954.
Johnny Smith, Guitarist in Concert. 1983. University of Texas at Arlington.

Library Collections and Resources

California State University Los Angeles. *Stan Kenton Collection*.
Colorado Symphony. *Denver Symphony Orchestra Program Books*.
Denver Public Library. Western History Department. *Denver Post*; *Rocky Mountain News*.
Institute of Jazz Studies at the State University of New Jersey. Rutgers Libraries. *George and Ismay Duvivier Collection*; *Leonard Feather Papers*; *Festival Program and Related Papers*; *Newport Jazz Festival Records*; *Teddy Reig Collection*; *Johnny Smith File*; *Tommy Talbert Collection*; *George Wein Scrapbooks*; *Mary Lou Williams Collection*.
Library of Congress. Recorded Sound Reference Center. *The NBC Index Cards*; *The NBC Master Books*; *The Voice of America Music Library Collection*.
University of Arizona. *Nelson Riddle Collection*.
University of Iowa. *Keith/Albee Vaudeville Theater Collection*.
University of North Texas. *Stan Kenton Collection*.
Wisconsin Historical Society. *Ernest Kinoy Papers*; *Mass Communications History Collection*.

Extra Discography

Airport Boys, The. 1940. 'You Are My Sunshine'. Bluebird 78rpm B-10939.
_____ 1941a. 'Worried Mind'. Bluebird unreleased.
_____ 1941b. 'It Ain't Gonna Rain No Mo'. Bluebird 78rpm B-11290-A.
_____ 1941c. 'You Can Depend on Me'. Bluebird unreleased.
_____ 1941d. 'Pay Me No Mind'. Bluebird unreleased.
_____ 1941e. 'You're My Inspiration'. Bluebird unreleased.
_____ 1941f. 'You Belong to Me'. Bluebird 78rpm B-11290-B.
Atkins, Chet. 1957. *Hi-Fi in Focus*. RCA Victor vinyl LP 1577.
_____ 1964. *Progressive Pickin'*. RCA Victor LP 2908.
Deep Purple. 1972. *Machine Head*. EMI vinyl LP TPSA 7504.
Gillespie, Dizzy. 1956. *Concert in Paris*. Roost vinyl LP 2214.
Montgomery, Wes. 1966. *California Dreaming*. Verve vinyl LP V6-8672.
Parker, Charlie. 1956. *All-Star Sextet*. Roost vinyl LP 2210.
Peterson, Oscar. Unknown. *Canadian Keys*. Alto vinyl LP AL718.
Segovia, Andrés. 1956. *Andrés Segovia with Strings of the Quintetto Chigiano*. Decca vinyl LP DL 9832.
Vaughan, Sarah. 1961. *After Hours*. Roulette vinyl LP SR-52070.
Ventures, The. 1960. 'Walk, Don't Run'. Blue Horizon vinyl single 101.

PRIVATE RECORDINGS

DiJulio, Max. 1968. *Concerto for Guitar and Orchestra in One Movement* (Soloist: Johnny Smith). Reel-to-reel tape.

_____ 1969. *Littlemass: A Choral Mass for Mixed Choir and Electric Guitar* (Soloist: Johnny Smith). Reel-to-reel tape.

Kenton, Stan. 1954. *The Second Festival of Modern American Jazz Tour.* Recorded on 21 September 1954 in Portland, Oregon. Reel-to-reel tape held in the Stan Kenton Collection in the library of the California State University.

Smith, Johnny. 1981. *Live at Figaro's*. Recorded in Colorado Springs. 4 October.

_____ 1982. *Live In Greeley.* Recorded in Greeley, Colorado.

FILMOGRAPHY

Allen, W. 1999. *Sweet and Lowdown*. Sweetland Films.

Anon. 1975a. *Emphasis*. Television broadcast on ABC affiliate KRDO. 7 September. (Colorado).

_____ 1975b. *Emphasis*. Television broadcast on ABC affiliate KRDO. 28 December. (Colorado).

_____ 1983a. 'Johnny Smith – What Are You Doing For The Rest Of Your Life'. Accessed online 1 October 2008. <http://www.youtube.com/watch?v=mQHRPC81DDg>.

_____ 1983b. 'Blues For Harry Carney (1984)'. Accessed online 1 October 2008. <http://www.youtube.com/watch?v=mE6I4lpYF9Y>.

_____ 1985. 'Mundell Lowe & Johnny Smith – Seven Come Eleven 1985'. Accessed online 1 October 2008. <http://www.youtube.com/watch?v=0jlDZ4OqMtI>.

Bacon, L. 1950. *The Fuller Brush Girl*. Columbia.

Bergh, J. 1977. *Bing in Norway.* Live television broadcast across mainland western Europe on 27 August from Mysen. Bootlegged onto DVD.

Betz, S. 1974. *Pawnee Pronghorn*.

Darley, D. 1950-1955. *Space Patrol*. ABC Television.

Davies, V. 1956. *The Benny Goodman Story*. Universal.

Doyle, B. 2004. *Body and Soul: A Portrait of Master Guitarmaker Robert Benedetto*. DVD. (Pacific: Mel Bay).

Robbins, J. and R. Wise. 1961. *West Side Story*. Mirisch Company/United Artists.

Ryan, D. 1982. *Gibson Jazz Concert*. Feyline Video.

Smithsonian National Museum of American History. 2011. *Johnny Smith Interview – Jazz Oral History Program*. DVD NMAH Archives Center Collection #808, October 17-18, 2011.

Spielberg, S. 1981. *Raiders of the Lost Ark*. Lucasfilm Ltd.

Star Time DuMont Television Network. 21 November 1950. UCLA Call Number unavailable.

_____ DuMont Television Network. 28 November 1950. UCLA Call Number T41522.

Wise, R. 1965. *The Sound of Music*. 20th Century Fox.

Interviewees

Atkins, Gary.
Atkinson, Marjorie.
Baker, Ruth.
Bartley, Jock.
Benedetto, Bob.
Benway, Randy.
Bertoncini, Gene.
Brenkman, Lee.
Bridge, Neil.
Bruner, Tom.
Bruning, Dale.
Bushkin-Judson, Nina.
Carlton, Jim.
Close, Gordon.
Coryell, Larry.
DiJulio-Nielsen, Adele.
Eliot, Dick.
Ellis, Mike.
Evans, Ronnie.
Fox, Jim.
Frisell, Bill.
Goes, Derryl.
Gonzales, Marc.
Greene, Bobby.
Greene, Buddy.
Grinnell, Larry.
Gustafson, Rick.
Hamilton, Fred.
Hanna, Denisa.
Herbert, Brandy.
Hess, George.
Hibler, Jude.
Hulsey, Laura.
Ingram, Adrian.
Juenemann, Marguerite.
Kennedy, Pete.
Kerr, Anita.
King, Jack.
Kintzele, Dave.
Kotwitz, Kenny.
Leavenworth, Phil.
Lowe, Mundell.
Lynn, Dame Vera.
Martino, Pat.
May, Tim.
Owen, Trefor.
Owens, Al.
Petersen, Jack.
Pisano, John.
Price, Ruth.
Roumanis, George.
Rushton, Sharon.
Schmidt, Paul William.
Silverman, Steve.
Smith, Ben.
Smith, David.
Smith III, John.
Smith, Johnny.
Sogoloff, Lennie.
Stewart, Kim.
Stewart, Louis.
Thornburg, John.
Uscinski, Ron.
Van Damme-Mummert, Sandra.
Vaughan, Kenny.
Wessberg, Bob.
Wilkins, Jack.
Yelin, Bob.
Zweig, Barry.

Photograph Credits

Cover Photograph:

Chapter One

Page 4, *Smith Family*, Photograph courtesy of the Johnny Smith Estate.
Page 6, *Kiana Hawaiians*, Photograph courtesy of the Johnny Smith Estate.
Page 7, *Uncle Lem and His Mountain Boys*, Photograph courtesy of the Johnny Smith Estate.
Page 8, *Uncle Lem and His Mountain Boys*, Photograph courtesy of the Johnny Smith Estate.
Page 9, *Django Reinhardt*, Photograph courtesy of the William P. Gottlieb/Ira and Leonore S. Gershwin Fund Collection, Music Division, Library of Congress.
Page 9, *Les Paul Trio*, Photograph courtesy of Fred Waring's America, Pennsylvania State University Archives.
Page 11, *Airport Boys*, Photograph courtesy of the Johnny Smith Estate.

Page 12, *Army Air Corps Band*, Photograph courtesy of the Johnny Smith Estate.
Page 14, *Public Relations Office Orchestra*, Photograph courtesy of the Johnny Smith Estate.

Chapter Two

Page 15, *Wally Harwood Orchestra*, Photograph courtesy of the Johnny Smith Estate.
Page 16, *Letter from Roy Shield*, Photograph courtesy of the Johnny Smith Estate.
Page 17, *Art Tatum*, Photograph courtesy of the William P. Gottlieb/Ira and Leonore S. Gershwin Fund Collection, Music Division, Library of Congress.
Page 21, *Mary Lou Williams*, Photograph courtesy of the William P. Gottlieb/Ira and Leonore S. Gershwin Fund Collection, Music Division, Library of Congress.
Page 22, *Schönberg program*, Photograph courtesy of the Arnold Schönberg Center.

Chapter Three

Page 25, *Johnny Smith in television studio*, Photograph courtesy of the Johnny Smith Estate.
Page 26, *Chauncey Morehouse with Johnny Smith*, Photograph courtesy of the Johnny Smith Estate.
Page 31, *Benny Goodman*, Photograph courtesy of the William P. Gottlieb/Ira and Leonore S. Gershwin Fund Collection, Music Division, Library of Congress.

Chapter Four

Page 40, *Invitation to the Albert club*, Photograph courtesy of the Cy Walter Estate, www.cywalter.com
Page 40, *Cy Walter*, Photograph courtesy of the Cy Walter Estate, www.cywalter.com
Page 41, *Zoot Sims*, Photograph by William "*PoPsie*" Randolph.
Page 41, *Sanford Gold*, Photograph courtesy of the William P. Gottlieb/Ira and Leonore S. Gershwin Fund Collection, Music Division, Library of Congress.
Page 41, *Eddie Safranski*, Photograph courtesy of the William P. Gottlieb/Ira and Leonore S. Gershwin Fund Collection, Music Division, Library of Congress.
Page 41, *Don Lamond*, Photograph by William "*PoPsie*" Randolph.
Page 42, *Stan Getz with Miles Davis*, Photograph by William "*PoPsie*" Randolph.
Page 43, *Teddy Reig*, Photograph courtesy of the William P. Gottlieb/Ira and Leonore S. Gershwin Fund Collection, Music Division, Library of Congress.
Page 44, *Morey Feld*, Photograph courtesy of the William P. Gottlieb/Ira and Leonore S. Gershwin Fund Collection, Music Division, Library of Congress.
Page 47, *Johnny Smith and Ann Westerstrom on wedding day*, Photograph courtesy of Kim Stewart..
Page 47, *Johnny Smith and Ann Westerstrom with daughter Kim*, Photograph courtesy of Kim Stewart.
Page 47, *Joe Mooney*, Photograph courtesy of the William P. Gottlieb/Ira and Leonore S. Gershwin Fund Collection, Music Division, Library of Congress.
Page 48, *Hank Jones*, Photograph by William "*PoPsie*" Randolph.
Page 49, *Cozy Cole*, Photograph courtesy of the William P. Gottlieb/Ira and Leonore S. Gershwin Fund Collection, Music Division, Library of Congress.
Page 50, *Clyde Lombardi*, Photograph courtesy of the William P. Gottlieb/Ira and Leonore S. Gershwin Fund Collection, Music Division, Library of Congress.

Page 51, *Entrance to Birdland*, Photograph by William "*PoPsie*" Randolph.
Page 53, *Oscar Peterson*, Photograph by William "*PoPsie*" Randolph.
Page 56, *Stan Kenton*, Photograph courtesy of the William P. Gottlieb/Ira and Leonore S. Gershwin Fund Collection, Music Division, Library of Congress.
Page 61, *Morris Levy*, Photograph by William "*PoPsie*" Randolph.
Page 66, *Johnny Richards*, Photograph courtesy of the William P. Gottlieb/Ira and Leonore S. Gershwin Fund Collection, Music Division, Library of Congress.
Page 67, *Johnny Smith at a jam session*, Photograph courtesy of the Johnny Smith Estate.
Page 68, *Newport Jazz Festival advertisement*, Courtesy of the Boston Daily Record.
Page 72, *Johnny Smith Quartet at Birdland*, Photograph courtesy of the Johnny Smith Estate.
Page 75, *Johnny Smith with the Count Basie Orchestra*, Photograph by William "*PoPsie*" Randolph.
Page 78, *Johnny Smith and Johnny Rae*, Photograph courtesy of the Johnny Smith Estate.

Chapter Five

Page 84, *Arthur Godfrey and Johnny Smith*, Photograph courtesy of the Johnny Smith Estate.
Page 85, *Johnny Smith with his Afghan Hound*, Photograph courtesy of Kim Stewart.
Page 90, *Johnny and Sandy Smith on their wedding day*, Photograph courtesy of Kim Stewart.
Page 91, *Kim Stewart*, Photograph courtesy of Kim Stewart.
Page 96, *Johnny Smith with his Gibson guitar*, Photograph courtesy of the Johnny Smith Estate.
Page 101, *Bobby Greene*, Photograph courtesy of Bobby Greene.
Page 112, *Johnny Smith with the Falconaires*, Photograph courtesy of the Johnny Smith Estate.
Page 119, *Johnny Smith and Max DiJulio*, Photograph courtesy of Getty Images.
Page 126, *Johnny Smith at the Emerson St. East*, Photograph by Fred Steckman.
Page 128, *Johnny Smith on his 80th birthday*, Photograph by Ron Uscinski.
Page 129, *Johnny and Sandy Smith with their two terriers*, Photograph courtesy of the Johnny Smith Estate.

Chapter Six

Page 133, *Johnny Smith in his instrument repair department*, Photograph courtesy of the Johnny Smith Estate.
Page 133, *Johnny Smith's workbench*, Photograph by Trefor Owen.
Page 134, *Jim Fox and Johnny Smith*, Photograph courtesy of Jim Fox.

Chapter Seven

Page 149, *Kenton Clinic*, Photograph courtesy of Jock Bartley.
Page 156, *Johnny Smith Guitar Seminar timetable*, Photograph by Rick Gustafson.
Page 158, *Johnny Smith at guitar seminar*, Photograph courtesy of the Johnny Smith Estate.
Page 161, *Johnny Smith at Utah State University*, Photograph courtesy of the Johnny Smith Estate.

Chapter Eight

Page 167, *Johnny Smith with Epiphone Guitar*, Photograph courtesy of the Johnny Smith Estate.

Chapter Nine

Chapter 10

About the Author

Lin Flanagan MA(Mus) BA(Hons) FVCM(Hons) FLCM LGSM LLCM(TD) DipABRSM is a guitarist and educator living in Britain. During a music career that has spanned almost three decades, he has performed a broad range of genres including classical, jazz and folk music, and spent two years with the Mantovani Orchestra in the UK. He was a regular columnist for *Acoustic* magazine and has frequently contributed to *Just Jazz Guitar* magazine in the USA. He is a former guitar examiner and has lectured at the London College of Music. For over a decade, he has been a course director at Guitar Weekends.

More Great Guitar Books from Centerstream...

SCALES & MODES IN THE BEGINNING

INCLUDES TAB

by Ron Middlebrook

The most comprehensive and complete scale book written especially for the guitar. Chapers include: Fretboard Visualization • Scale Terminology • Scales and Modes • and a Scale to Chord Guide.

00000010 .... $11.95

CELTIC CITTERN

by Doc Rossi

Although the cittern has a history spanning 500 years and several countries, like its cousin the Irish bouzouki, it is a relative newcomer to contemporary traditional music. Doc Rossi, a wellknown citternist in both traditional and early music, has created this book for intermediate to advanced players who want to improve their technique, develop ideas and learn new repertoire. Guitarists can play all of the tunes in this book on the guitar by tuning C F C G C F, low to high, and putting a capo at the second fret. The lowest line in the tablature then corresponds to the fifth string. The CD features all the tunes played at a medium tempo.

00001460 Book/CD Pack $19.99

KILLER PENTATONICS FOR GUITAR

by Dave Celentano

Covers innovative and diverse ways of playing pentatonic scales in blues, rock and heavy metal. The licks and ideas in this book will give you a fresh approach to playing the pentatonic scale, hopefully inspiring you to reach for higher levels in your playing. The 37-minute companion CD features recorded examples.

00000285 Book/CD Pack $19.95

MELODY CHORDS FOR GUITAR

INCLUDES TAB

by Allan Holdsworth

Influential fusion player Allan Holdsworth provides guitarists with a simplified method of learning chords, in diagram form, for playing accompaniments and for playing popular melodies in "chord-solo" style. Covers: major, minor, altered, dominant and diminished scale notes in chord form, with lots of helpful reference tables and diagrams.

00000222 .... $24.95

GUITAR CHORDS PLUS

INCLUDES TAB

by Ron Middlebrook

A comprehensive study of normal and extended chords, tuning, keys, transposing, capo use, and more. Includes over 500 helpful photos and diagrams, a key to guitar symbols, and a glossary of guitar terms.

00000011 .... $11.95

THE CHORD SCALE GUIDE

by Greg Cooper

The Chord Scale Guide will open up new voicings for chords and heighten your awareness of linear harmonization. This will benefit jazz ensemble players, rock guitarists and songwriters looking to create new and unique original music, and understand the harmony behind chords.

00000324 .... $15.95

IRISH YOU A MERRY CHRISTMAS

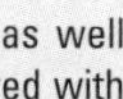

by Doug Esmond

This book includes Christmas melodies as well as lesserknown tunes from Scotland paired with seasonal titles. All the songs can be played solo or with other instruments. A CD is included with recordings of the author playing using both steel and nylon string guitars.

00001360 Book/CD Pack $15.99

MUTING THE GUITAR

by David Brewster

This book/CD pack teaches guitarists how to effectively mute anything! Author David Brewster covers three types of muting in detail: frethand, pickhand, and both hands. He provides 65 examples in the book, and 70 tracks on the accompanying CD.

00001199 Book/CD Pack $19.99

P.O. Box 17878 - Anaheim Hills, CA 92817

(714) 779-9390 www.centerstream-usa.com

More Great Guitar Books from Centerstream...

ASAP POWER PICKING

For Electric and Acoustic Guitars

by David Brewster This book will help beginning guitarists "find" the strings of the guitar through a series of basic (yet melodic) picking exercises. As you become more comfortable striking the strings of the guitar with a pick using the exercises and examples here, you should eventually create your own variations and picking exercises.

00001330 Book/CD Pack $15.99

LATIN STYLES FOR GUITAR

by Brian Chambouleyron

A dozen intermediate to advanced originals in notes & tab display various Latin American styles. For each, the CD features the lead part as well as an accompaniment-only rhythm track for play along.

00001123 Book/CD Pack $19.95

GUITAR TUNING FOR THE COMPLETE MUSICAL IDIOT

by Ron Middlebrook

There's nothing more distracting than hearing a musician play out of tune. This user-friendly book/DVD pack teaches various methods for tuning guitars – even 12-strings! – and basses, including a section on using electronic tuning devices. Also covers intonation, picks, changing strings, and much more!

00000002 Book/DVD Pack..$16.95

00001198 DVD $10.00

ASAP CLASSICAL GUITAR

Learn How to Play the Classical Way

by James Douglas Esmond

Teacher-friendly or for self-study, this book/CD pack for beginning to intermediate guitarists features classical pieces and exercises presented progressively in notes and tab, with each explained thoroughly and performed on the accompanying CD. A great way to learn to play ASAP!

00001202 Book/CD Pack $15.95

THE COUNTRY GUITAR STYLE OF CHARLIE MONROE

Based on the 1936-1938 Bluebird Recordings by The Monroe Brothers

by Joseph Weidlich

This great overview of Charlie Monroe's unique guitar performance style (he used just his thumb and index finger) presents 52 songs, with an in-depth look at the backup patterns & techniques from each chord family (G, F, D, C, E, A), plus special note sequences, common substitutions and stock backup phrases. Includes the bluegrass classics "Roll in My Sweet Baby's Arms," "My Long Journey Home" and "Roll On, Buddy," plus a discography and complete Bluebird recording session info.

00001305 ....$19.99

ASAP GUITARIST GUIDE TO STRING BENDING & VIBRATO

Learn How to Bend the Correct Way

by Dave Brewster

String bending and vibrato are two of the most popular guitar techniques used in all musical styles, yet for most beginning and intermediate players, gaining control of them might seem overwhelming. This book outlines some of the most common bending and vibrato techniques and licks, teaching them in an easy-to-digest manner to help you see and hear how to use them with confidence in a musical context. Contains more than 150 helpful examples!

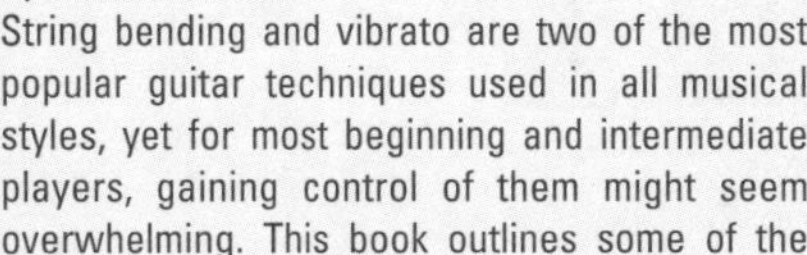

00001347 Book/CD Pack $19.99

HYMNS AND SPIRITUALS FOR FINGERSTYLE GUITAR

by James Douglas Esmond

Originating in the South during the antebellum days on the old plantations, at religious revivals and at camp meetings, hymns and spirituals are the native folk songs of our own America. This collection features 13 songs, some with two arrangements – one easy, the second more difficult. Songs include: Were You There? • Steal Away • Amazing Grace • Every Time I Feel the Spirit • Wade in the Water • and more.

00001183 Book/CD Pack $19.95

P.O. Box 17878 - Anaheim Hills, CA 92817

(714) 779-9390 www.centerstream-usa.com